THE PILGRIM ARCHIVES • BOOK ONE

A PROMISE OF SIRENS

V.L. BARYCZ

A PROMISE OF SIRENS:
THE PILGRIM ARCHIVES BOOK ONE

Published by Outland Entertainment LLC
3119 Gillham Road
Kansas City, MO 64109

Publisher: Jeremy D. Mohler
Creative Director: Cullen Bunn
Editor-in-Chief: Alana Joli Abbott
Games Director: Anton Kromoff

Paperback ISBN: 978-1-964735-17-7
Ebook ISBN: 978-1-964735-18-4
Worldwide Rights
Created in the United States of America

Editor: Alana Joli Abbott
Copy Editor: Scott Colby
Cover Illustration: Ann Marie Cochran
Cover Design: Jeremy D. Mohler
Interior Layout: Jeremy D. Mohler

Printed and bound in the United States of America.

Visit outlandentertainment.com to see more, or follow us on our Facebook Page facebook.com/outlandentertainment/

DEDICATION

Thaddeus,
I would burn worlds for you. I would tear and bite and wound. How beautiful that you asked me to rest and build a garden with you instead.

ACKNOWLEDGEMENTS

My fellow queers, I see you. I love you. A life of found family and simple joy is the greatest middle finger to those who would snuff you out.

My husband Thaddeus, to be seen and loved by you is a true miracle. You believed in Detroit, Brigitte, and me when I couldn't.

My editor Alana for her genius. Without your brilliance, Brigitte would never have found her voice.

“Speramus Meliora; resuget cineribus.” – Motto of Detroit

(We hope for better things; it will rise from the ashes.)

•••

CHAPTER 1

In my line of work, you got slammed face first into a lot of things. We're talkin' into tables after breaking up illegal sprite wrestling competitions, into the meaty fist of a Hibagon[1], and as the grey morning started, into the slick and filthy alley wall by the Nain Rouge[2]. While meeting force with force had its merits, I preferred to quote Jake Gyllenhaal.

"This is a goddamn bitch of an unsatisfactory situation."

The Nain snarled, red claws snagging into my curls like a worn brush, but it was the bright laughter of my partner, from his spot in the alley, that made me hiss.

"Jack Twist, *Brokeback Mountain,*" Graceland called before he sipped his coffee.

Mashed into brick, I should probably have been more concerned about the state of my mortality, but the only thing I could think was that my last dollar was going to him for that lucky guess. Unless—

"We can argue about mind reading later," Graceland said mildly, pulling thin fingers through his black hair. "We're on the job."

"*Now* you care about the job," I muttered against the brick.

"Guys, are we fighting or talking?" the Nain asked.

"Shut up, Carl," we said in unison.

He just shrugged and smashed my cheek further into the wall while Graceland took another sip of coffee.

"Care about the job? Nah," he said, "but you humans do. Plus, I have plans tonight, so move it along."

"You move it along," I snapped and jabbed a sharp elbow into the Nain's ribs. "What if I have plans?"

"You gonna mope in your bathtub again?"

---

1 The Japanese equivalent of the American Bigfoot. Often seen around Mt. Hiba. Wicked temper but excellent at backgammon.

2 An impish creature of chaos that causes misfortune to those who cross him or if he just feels like it. Took the name Carl because he thought it was distinguished.

It was a cheap shot, meant to rile me, and I let it. As soon as my elbow connected, I pressed my free palm to my fist. Instantly, the magic of my mother—tendrils of Vodou—curled up my bare forearm in scrawling glyphs. The language of La, lines and dots, blood and pain, pulsed a bright purple against my brown skin.

"Last chance, Carl," I said mildly, watching the Nain's eyes widen.

"That's cheating," he snarled, but he began to shrink until he was only about the height of my belt.

"So is pretending to be someone's child. Did you really think the Johnsons would buy the whole bonnet in the crib thing? You have a beard."

"It's a goatee," he huffed, rubbing at the black fuzz on his red face, "and it was funny."

It was, in fact, hysterical, so much so that Graceland and I could only cackle in the Uber to the Johnsons' mansion, but business was business.

"Give me the jewelry and I'll tell them I sent you back to the bowels of Cass Corridor. You go on your way alive and live to be ugly another day."

"The nymphs down on Third[3] told me the goatee is distinguished."

"How much did you pay them?" I asked. "Because—"

The smell always came first, but I stopped and looked around anyway, eyes searching the grime as the taste of blood flooded my mouth. Both the Nain and Graceland straightened, but I only waved my ringless left hand in their direction.

"Carl, give Graceland the jewelry and get out of here."

"I—"

"Now, or I'll invoke, and it will be a lot more painful."

"Goddamn Pilgrims," he muttered, but backed up.

My body swayed slightly, eyes beginning to cloud, the scent of blood, that horrible tang of metal, pulling me deeper into the alley. It was a gift my mother would have liked to see pass her only child over, but death was an old friend to both the Laveau and the Fitzpatrick

---

3 Third Avenue in Cass Corridor was part of an unofficial red-light district before the "rebirth" of Detroit. Now home to the Nain Rouge Brewery. Carl personally enjoys 15% stake in the company for the use of his likeness.

families. Pain radiated in the bricks under my feet; the history of the roads of Midtown held violence and screams, but I passed by the piles of garbage. I wasn't here for old wounds. Finally, near the end of the alley, I was pulled against my will to my knees.

The body was tossed, hidden by the alley trash, which meant she hadn't been killed here. She was young, face done up to look older, but most of it had been washed away by last night's winter sleet. The thick trails of mascara streaked down like the trenches of claws to the wound on her throat.

"Oh, honey," I said quietly, trying to think of a proper prayer, then straightened, my face like stone. "I don't have time for a murder, Graceland."

"Is that an 'I don't have time so get rid of the body,' or you just being contrary?"

I dipped down to touch my fingers to the blood, ignoring the gag of disgust coming from Graceland. It was congealed, too far gone for use.

"I didn't realize this was an ingredients trip as well," he snarked. "Third one of these in the last two weeks."

"Everything's a multitool if you're creative enough," I countered, voice mild. "Third one?"

When no answer came, I dragged my gaze from the body to him, curious. He watched the mouth of the alley, his frigid blue eyes unblinking and mouth tight enough that his bottom lip was almost nonexistent. I'd known him long enough to know it was the careful polite mask he wore for wrong breakfast orders at McDonald's—and trouble.

I eased up from my crouch and reached for his elbow gently. "Focus Graceland. Do you think—"

"Shush."

Anyone else I would have gleefully broken in half, but I only flicked my hand down to the pouch at my waist and mumbled a soft prayer to Maman and Baron Samedi[4]. The seconds were marked by the taps of my fingertips on the soft leather, but finally Graceland relaxed. I'd known him my entire life, but when his blue eyes shone

4 Maman Brigitte and Baron Samedi, head of the Ghede family of loa. Maman Brigitte is also the ancestor of the Laveau family, having been very invested in the free love movement before it was a movement.

along with his sharp grin, there were infinite lifetimes of secrets in his ageless face.

"False alarm," he said cheerfully and took another sip from his coffee, offering me the one in his other hand. "You need this, but I want what I'm owed for getting that human reference right."

Unconvinced, I passed him the dollar and took a slug, shivering at the rush of warmth in the cold. "But there was something?"

"Oh yeah, Horace inbound, less than thirty seconds," he said.

If it would have accomplished anything, like getting me out of the alley in time to avoid a lecture, I would've beaten him to death right there. Instead, I pulled at my shirt—a rumpled Henley I'd found in the semi-clean pile on my floor—and wished for a cigarette.

"You promised your mother you'd quit," Graceland pointed out.

Exhaling through my nose, I snatched the dollar from in between his fingers, smiling at his squawk of surprise. Horace was going to worry about my rumpled-looking ass no matter what I did, so I eased back down to examine the body.

I pried open the rigid lid of the corpse's right eye as I listened to the approaching footsteps. Milky white pupil, a fine slit in a field of black. A siren. Leaning closer, I ignored the creaking in my knees as I scrutinized the face, more specifically the smudge on her neck. Even before I rubbed my thumb through the greasy foundation, I could see the faint tattoo, probably a brand from whoever owned her. A grim concept, but not a new one, not in a town as old as Detroit. At the very least it gave me a starting point—and an excuse to break some asshole's hand.

"He's here."

The "he" was a hulking shadow that moved remarkably well for someone his size. The sound of his footsteps resembled a quick tap routine, even though he walked a straight line. Three beat cops trailed behind him but stopped at the mouth of the alley, eyes on me, hands rested on the weapons at their hips. My mouth twitched as I watched them fan out to cover the entrance from curious eyes. If Horace hadn't come, it would have been another Devil's Night incident, and I would've ended up owing Graceland more than the dollar I'd snatched back.

Horace J. Glen had been chief for about eight years, the first magical creature to earn the position. Standing at seven feet tall, he was small for a troll—the byproduct of a fairy mother, as was the sharp mischievousness of his face. That mother, who'd raised him by herself from the time of his conception, was the proud owner of Gomorrah, a strip club on the West Riverend.

I knew him from the Wednesdays and Fridays he'd been my babysitter growing up.

For that fact alone, I gave an apologetic smile when his eyes drifted to the blood on my hand. With said fingers, I pointed to the mouth of the alley.

"Watch the street, Graceland."

"You watch the street," he shot back as he sauntered away.

He hadn't been this mouthy with my father, but if I was honest, I didn't really mind. The biting banter often kept me from wallowing in the tub he teased about. But it wasn't sarcasm that came to mind as I looked back to the body. Gently, because I knew it wouldn't be knocked away, I touched a hand to Horace's back and kept my tone light.

"What do you think, Bukowski?"

My small joke about his poetry habits never failed to make the angles of his face spread out into a smile, but his eyes were grim as he stared at the body.

"Third one in two weeks," he said, voice lilted, another product of his fairy blood.

"Told you," Graceland called.

I ignored both as the bitter taste of blood hit me again. She was younger than me, closer to twenty than thirty, with brown hair—someone had taken a lock with them, judging by the jagged tendrils. But they'd crossed her delicate hands over her naked chest, an illusion of modesty. The gash on her neck resembled an elaborate ruby choker, sparkling in the grime of the alley.

"Is she one of your mother's?" I asked, voice pitched so only the two of us could hear. "Were the others?"

"No," Horace said.

I kept my hand on his back, even though his voice was flat. He'd always been a gentle touch, and every scene affected him in a way that I wouldn't allow but envied. He was at least fifteen years my senior but would live three of my lifetimes. Maybe that was why I was the one who'd gotten harder.

"I'll clear my case schedule for this."

His snort was amused. "The way I hear it, that shouldn't be a problem."

My hand dropped and I brought up the other, the one with my father's silver insignia ring on it, and flashed a middle finger. I'd inherited the ring along with all the problems of Senior Pilgrim when he stepped down.

"Hey, I worked my dick off the last couple months so next week goes smoothly," I said with a shrug, "You'd think spearheading an entire organization that loved my father would be easy. Turns out, while they loved him, they tolerate me."

I hoped for at least a sympathetic smile, but Horace only laughed.

"Well, you do give them ammunition whenever you open your mouth."

I rolled my eyes and instantly felt ten again. "Ugh, you sound like Graceland."

"I can handle this. You got the treaty coming up. I know you're nervous."

He would be the one to see it, since he'd been my shadow since childhood. I should have been amused, but I only felt prickling irritation at the softness in his eyes. Gods, I hated being handled. He wouldn't see it that way after the last year, but the time for that was done as well.

"Is that why I wasn't told when it was one murder," I asked calmly, "or two?"

"Brig, the treaty—"

"Did you do this for my father? Keep him in the dark on investigations because it eased his way?" I asked and watched his head dip. "Then you won't for me. Send me the files, and I'll take care of it. Graceland, let's go."

"Wait," Horace called.

The seriousness of his voice forced me to turn, but I only raised a brow as he stared back.

"Asim and Moira are in Black Bottom—robbery at Tomes & Bones. Might be worth taking a peek at."

"Thanks."

"How are you?"

The words were simple, but the meaning, the worry in them, chewed on me the way my teeth had my inner cheek.

"Tell your mother I said hi," I offered and pulled at Graceland. "Let's go."

I tucked my chin into my beaten leather jacket as the bitterness of January snapped at me. Detroit was awake, shuddering with the gusts of wind, pushing the urban tumbleweeds of BBQ chip bags past us. Sometimes that was all I could see: the grime, the never-ending beating of my head against a wall. But now, as the sun crept across the brick and people hustled down Cass Avenue, I felt the heartbeat of the city, a survivor.

As I shrugged deeper into my jacket, I wondered for the millionth time if Mother Eorthe[5] would feel the growth or only the turmoil, only the chaos. How could she be blamed when there was the body of one of her lost children laying on the cold concrete, her blood coating my fingers? In return, what would the Allfather[6] think of my willingness to set aside everything to handle something solely magic? Balance, the thin lines like cracks in the sidewalk that I avoided as a child, was now my only job.

Hadn't Gran pulled magic out of hiding in the forties? Then Dad stabilized it in the eighties? In three days, it would officially be in my hands. My gnawed-nailed hands.

"You still have blood on your fingers; don't you dare put them in your mouth," Graceland said as he trailed behind. "Your father would have given her last rites."

"She was fay," I corrected, "and past the point of collection."

"Cold."

It was a favorite game of his, to bait me into a discussion, one I normally would engage in with fervor. But the exhaustion of the last

---

5 The Creator of the Fay. Mother Nature.

6 The Creator of Man. God.

year was still in my bones, like thick, heavy liquid lead, and in the end, I agreed with him. It was cold—being a Pilgrim often was, had been, would be. Margot was that lesson.

"It's not fun when you don't bite back."

My snort was short as I led the way down the street, hands tucked into pockets, expertly weaving through the hustle of the morning commuters. They'd spent the most money here, in these few square blocks, to bring Detroit back to something the world could look at without seeing splatters of blood and the husks of houses.

I wasn't particularly worried about what the world thought, being more concerned with the fact that the fringes of the city, the most loyal of citizens, the true survivors of Detroit, were passed over in the name of progress. History repeating itself. Sometimes that was all life felt like: get out of bed, potentially shower, dress, fill out paperwork, repeat.

"All right, I've given you enough moping time, and I bought you a coffee," Graceland announced, jostling me. "Speak."

As we rounded the corner, the sun finally broke free, its weak rays playing across the icy sidewalk. Tilting my head, I smiled.

"I swear, if I didn't know better, I'd think *you* were the only child."

His own smile dimmed, like his internal power might have faltered for a half a second, before he shrugged. "Being the youngest of dozens is just as lonely."

"Now who's moping?" I teased back but gave his arm a pat. "We have work to do. And Graceland?"

"Yeah?"

"I tasted the shot of luck in that latte."

"I plead the fifth."

CHAPTER 2

There was a time when Black Bottom, now Lafayette Park, had been flashes of color, jazz and blues birthed and blasting from the frame homes of the Bottom and the clubs of Paradise Valley, hosting the greats like Holiday and Fitzgerald. A Black community of culture, where luxuries often denied because of segregation were up for possession. It was a place of loud voices, laughing children, and bright futures.

Now the majority was cold steel and glass, a product of modern design and gentrification, considered an architect's dream. But the true marvels were the tiny pockets of the past. While most of the shops had been in Paradise Valley, Tomes & Bones was tucked back and in between the silver skyscrapers of what used to be Black Bottom. It still had its soft, lead-lined windows and the barber pole from the old neighborhood shop. Anton and Chantelle Young inherited the house, endured the wrath of so-called progress, and kept their mother's house of wooden slats and pointed roof character. How furious the city still was, that such a piece of the past stood out among the soulless beams and geometric shapes.

The siblings opened Tomes & Bones long after their mother had passed, but they liked to believe she would have appreciated a place where pieces of magic and history came together along with the people of the city. While neither of them was adept with magic, the fay they employed were, and that combined with their love of history to make T&B profitable. Even if it hadn't been, the siblings would have kept at it, determined to never let anyone forget, not even the wealthy, that Detroit had been built on the backs of the people they tried to bury.

I could see my Junior Pilgrims, Moira Mana and Asim Badem, through the broken glass of the front door. Both were formidable, built from thick muscles and strong shoulders that couldn't be hidden by their winter jackets. As was her way, Moira was in front, dark hair pulled back, one braid roped behind her ear, exposing the tribal tattoo that curled from her lower shoulder up to her neck. Her tawny fingers touched it as she tilted her head to listen to the pixie sitting on the counter. Asim was back a step, trying and failing as he always did, to make himself look smaller, less threatening. His softness wasn't in the angles of his bronze face but in the vibrant green of his eyes, the way he worried his lip and nodded at something the pixie said.

"Why does Asim always look like he's about to cry?" Graceland asked as we walked up the cobble path to the shop.

"Same reason Moira always looks like she's gonna crush you with her fist," I said. "That's why I send them together. I don't see Anton or Chantelle."

Moira noticed us first, body tensing before her head snapped up. She nudged Asim, who startled, his notebook jumping from his hand to hit the floor. I stayed outside the shattered door but nodded at both.

"Boss," Moira said. "Slow day?"

Her polite way of asking why I was there made me bite down on my smile. Moira had a good ten years on me, had been my father's right hand and watched me grow up. It was hard to hold it against her when I knew she'd lived through my goth phase.

"Never is," I said easily. "Horace mentioned you got a robbery?"

As her jaw tightened, Asim scrambled to get his notebook and gave me a bright smile. I gave him a small nod and he motioned to the pixie sitting.

"Ruby Vale called it in this morning. Someone really did a number, tossed the building."

"Ms. Chantelle is gonna be so sad," the pixie said, her tiny hands worrying over each other. "They shredded our original Bane tome—we have copies, but the original was a gift from the Darkchild Pack."

"Just damage?" I asked, finally easing the door open.

Moira shook her head, feather earrings swinging. "They destroyed the tome and took a box of arrowheads from the back stock."

"Weapon heads," the pixie corrected. "Arrow-, spear-, maybe even dagger tips. We got a shipment in from Caja Scabbath in exchange for sending her brother some bones. We were planning on going through it and cataloguing once Ms. Chantelle got back from vacation."

"Who would steal a box of junk?" Asim asked.

The pixie's wings fluttered at that, and she rose from the counter to jab a finger at him. "Junk! Typical human. If you can't use it to destroy something, then it must be garbage! If—"

"Ms. Vale," I interrupted, voice soft, "the Youngs aren't going to blame you."

The pixie whipped around to glare at me, then hung her head. Fluttering back down to the counter, she wiped at the tiny tears on her cheeks.

"I set the alarm, Pilgrim; I know I did, but the cameras don't show anything."

Asim opened his mouth, but both Moira and I shook our heads at him. I reached out a hand for Ruby, and Moira moved toward the back of the shop to grab the tapes.

"Is anyone else coming in today, or would you like us to help you clean up?"

Her tiny hand gripped my pinky like a lifeline. "Mr. Anton is already on his way back from Mackinaw. Ms. Chantelle will be back in a few days. They want me to board the door and go home."

"Then you listen to them," I said gently. "I promise we'll find something. You tell the Youngs they can call me directly, any time, day or night."

Her nod was sharp even as her eyes watered again. "Safe travels, Senior Pilgrim."

"To you as well, Ms. Vale."

The four of us continued down the path to Moira's car, Asim flipping through his notebook as he muttered to himself. Even as Graceland nudged past me, I felt eyes on me, and I wanted to wave at Moira, tell her to get on with it.

"Should you have made that promise?" Moira asked.

There it was. I let Graceland's deep sigh speak for me as we approached the car.

"Brigitte."

My name prickled across my skin, feeling too much like a lecture from a parent.

"The Youngs are not only friends of the Darkchilds, but of my mother," I reminded her.

"Senior Pilgrims don't show bias. And when you become Divine Arbiter—"

The whistle of air that passed through Graceland's teeth made her glance to him, which gave me the time I needed to unclench my jaw.

"What? It's the truth," she said

"So is the fact that you have terrible taste in men," Graceland informed her, brushing at his jacket, "but that doesn't mean I need to remind you every time I set eyes on you."

"I don't—"

"Maurice?" Graceland interrupted. "Phillip."

"Chancellor," Asim added.

"No one asked you!" she said, whipping around.

"Exactly the point," I said flatly as they all turned to me. "While I appreciate input and feedback, I don't need another parent, so if that's going to be an issue, I can have a transfer approved for after the treaty."

The silence between the four of us was as cool as the wind, the sweat dripping between my shoulder blades icy as I held my temper. Finally, she shook her head.

"I'm sorry. You don't need another Bronson right now."

"Or ever," Graceland offered.

I let my smile crack but poked a finger in his direction. "He's my blood. Only I get to talk bad about him."

"I just want you to know we can do our job," Moira said. "Your father never checked on me."

"I'm not my father," I said, wondering when that will become obvious. "But I wasn't. Horace sent me here because of the *Bane Tome*. Vlkodlak[7], vamps, cursed shit."

"You really think someone from Deep Europe came all the way for a box of junk and to destroy an old tome?" Asim asked.

"No, I think destroying the tome is a bit like pissin' on someone's shoes," I said, "and the Scabbath family never sends junk."

"So, who did it?"

---

7 Wolf-skin. A Slavic term for werewolves that reside in Deep Europe.

"I suppose that's up to me to find out," I said, "because you two need to be at the Whitney to make sure the other Junior Pilgrims are prepped to take your routes this week."

"We're ready," he said. "I lost the coin toss, so Moira gets to choose the music today."

"And not a single *Now That's What I Call Music* will be played," Moira said happily and nodded to me. "Safe travels."

"Safe travels."

I didn't wait or watch them leave, knowing Moira was already stewing for a fight. Instead, I turned in the direction of Jefferson and started walking. When I'd taken over as Senior Pilgrim of the North American Chapter, I studied all the profiles of the juniors, having been given the freedom to pick my left and right hands. I scoured hundreds of profiles of humans who had been given magic's favor but couldn't pass through the divine gate to Arcadia or Eden. As much as Moira pissed me off, she was one of the best.

"We are really gonna have to work on getting that stick out of her ass, huh?" Graceland said.

"If I somehow managed that, she'd just beat me to death with it," I said blandly. "Would be nice for one of you fuckers to just take my word for it, just once."

"Hey, that's not fair. Asim always takes your word for it," Graceland said, then shrugged. "Of course, he is the dumb one."

My laughter was an ugly snort as I made way to the busted bus stop on the corner of Rivard and Jefferson. It was old, a bench with broken legs, devoid of the flimsy plastic sheltering.

"She'll get there. When you get the Creator's stamp of approval this week, that will go a long way—with a lot of humans and fay."

"If," I corrected. "Sit"

"Modesty doesn't become you," he scoffed but plopped next to me on the bench. "We both know you have the magic, the talent, and—despite your best efforts—the support."

I pushed my tongue against my teeth. "Graceland."

"Brigitte."

He was what I always imagined having a younger brother would be like: annoying and funny and utterly punchable. I just never imagined he would be immortal. Tapping my knuckles against the collapsed leg of the bench, my father's signet ring clanged.

"Hang on, I won't come back for you this time," I reminded him.

"It was one ti—"

Before he can finish his sentence, the world twisted, the bench flipping forward. We should've crashed into the half-busted concrete of the street, but instead we went straight through it. I didn't even get a second breath in, and we were right side up. Around us, Corktown was shaking off sleep, only the barbershop and brunch shops lit up on Trumbull.

"I hate traveling like that."

"Then agree to pay for an Uber," I told him for the millionth time. "You got the money."

"Or you could work a driver into the budget."

"Cheapskate," I teased, nodding to up the street. "I have my final call with Constantin Dragos today."

"At least you can't smell him through the phone."

I rolled my eyes. "Brood Dragos has given me their word."

"Oh, well, then by all means, if they gave their word."

"What would you have me do? Sit on my hands?"

At the sharp bite of my words, his head jerked up. "That wasn't a slight at you. As long as you don't self-sabotage, and Deep Europe doesn't stab you in the back, you'll pull something off even I've never done."

My steps faltered at that, and I gave him a confused look. "What?"

"You'll have the Allfather's approval."

There was so much pain in that sentence, even though his tone was light, with layers of betrayal and shame that coated each fragment. Around us, I smelled burning feathers, and the taste of ozone trickled down my throat.

"Oh, gross, it was a joke," Graceland said to the air, waving his hand like it would clear the ambient magic. "Don't look at me like that."

"Graceland."

"Nope," he said and motioned ahead. "Your boyfriend is outside today."

Swallowing against the need to comfort him, I glanced in the direction of the Bearded Folly, my favorite pub that doubled as my humble abode. Against the wall, Thaddeus Stevens leaned, a curl of smoke coming from his mouth before he tapped the ash out of his cigarette. It was common knowledge that I'd engaged in a mild flirtation with the owner of the Bearded Folly and landlord of my apartment exactly *one* time. In my defense, I'd lost a significant amount of blood, and his large hands had been surprisingly delicate when he stitched me up. Rubbing at the scar on my hip, I glared as Graceland strode forward. Trailing behind, I gave Thaddeus a nod while Graceland motioned for the cigarette.

"Graceland," I said in exasperation.

"I'm getting it this time."

With an amused look, Thaddeus held out the cigarette, and Graceland reached for it with the precision of a surgeon. As soon as his fingers made contact, it crumbled to dust, as did Thaddeus's hand. We all stared at the swirling matter as it spiraled back up to form a hand again.

"This is bullshit."

"I don't make the rules," Thaddeus said. "Take it up with your wife."

"She changed the rules just to make my life difficult," he lamented. "I could have made any ghost do a jig before."

"When you ruled the world, Grandpa," I said, grabbing his arm. "We have work. Nice seeing you, Thad."

He nodded. "Left a glass on your desk."

"Go raibh maith agat.[8]"

He smiled at that, and I forced Graceland through the doorway. Immediately, the heavy smell of yeasted dough warmed me, and I inhaled as we moved through the dark wood booths to the creaky back steps.

"You know, I could probably talk Penny into giving you one night with ghost boy."

I grinned despite myself but wouldn't give him the satisfaction of turning around. Instead, I walked the hall to the door at the end.

---

8 Expression of gratitude. "Goodness is in you." Or "You have goodness." Gaelic.

Living above the Bearded Folly had a lot of perks, but the main was the thick glass of Guinness I always found on my desk when I came home. It never failed to make me smile and miss Dad all at once.

"She likes you more than me anyway," Graceland said and dropped, a tangle of limbs, into a chair I'd found in a fake vampire's lair. Lazily, he unwound his scarf and tucked it like a pillow behind his head.

"You aren't supposed to tell blatant lies," I reminded him. "Sometimes I think I'm the one who got cursed by being stuck with you, not the other way around."

"Isn't it a little early to be partaking? And she doth protest—"

"I'm part Irish. There is never a time not good. And shut it," I shot back. "So three in two weeks. Why didn't you say anything when it was two?"

He sighed dramatically and let his head drop so it hung off the back of the chair.

"Sirens' lifespans are notoriously short, Brig. Am I supposed to just stand outside the police station and demand an update by the hour?" He paled. "No. No, ignore that."

"That's exactly what you're going to do."

"This isn't my job. I'm not a messenger."

"No, that's your brother, Hermes," I conceded and took a slow sip. "But it's your job today."

The groan that left him was a single drawn out note of despair, one that made me laugh a little too manically as I threw a notebook at him.

"You did this to yourself."

"What if I say no?"

My fingers gripped the glass a little tighter, but I kept my tone flat. "Then I remind you that you owe me; you owe my father."

Grumbling, Graceland stood and jerked his scarf from the chair "There's no reason to be so fatalistic about it. But I'm only staying there until dinner."

"Are you cooking?"

Most of the time his face was a myriad of amusement. But in times like this, when he was serious, it was cut from icy stone. "I have a date."

"Graceland," I warned, "you know the rules."

"It isn't serious—he's—he works at the Fisher Theatre; he's letting me backstage tonight."

The laughter shot from me, the lecture about gods procreating with humans leaving with the beer in my mouth to splatter across the haggard wood floor. In typical dramatic form, Graceland jumped back and stared, as he often did, like I was insane.

"I don't see what's so funny," he said, eyes narrowing.

With deliberate care I set the beer down and cleared my throat. "Replay the words you said."

"What? He's letting me backstage tonight for the—oh, sweet Zeus, really. Are you twelve?" he demanded as he wrapped his scarf around his narrow throat. "I'll be here early tomorrow with the police gossip."

I couldn't quite wipe the smirk off my face as I waved and dropped into my own chair. It creaked and slid, gouging the well-worn grooves in the floor a bit deeper. As soon as the old glass door rattled shut, I exhaled, and it felt like my shoulders crashed down from around my ears for the first time in hours.

Horace hadn't been kidding—my load was light. The scarred desk that had once served as a barrier between Dad and a horde of undead was empty. With the help of a severe number of caffeine pills and lo-fi beats, I'd made a mad dash to close out everything else so I could focus on the treaty. The swell of pride, when the last folder was sent off to be filed, was quickly killed by the panic. Now there was no choice but to become the Divine Arbiter.

The last year had been a slow-moving wave, eroding the honor of being chosen to temporarily fill Dad's position, to be given first crack at the treaty over the rest of the Fitzpatrick clan. I'd been so sure, in the first couple months, that he'd realize retirement was boring and knock me back down to the streets.

But nothing came, and I learned that even though I'd avoided this position like the plague my whole life, my ship ran as tightly as the indominable Rory Fitzpatrick's. Dad deserved that. Gran deserved that.

The stink of failure had briefly evaporated by the pure delight of pulling on Gran's leather jacket, sent from Ireland when I became Senior Pilgrim. The leather was well loved, with its creaking lines in the elbows and the starburst of burnt magic on the left shoulder from when Gran stared down her first sphinx, waiting to see if her answer fit the riddle she'd been given. It was a story I'd grown up with, and I could only hope some wisdom had seeped into the silk lining. It certainly hadn't given me Dad's diplomacy, something the overseers never failed to remind me in their daily missives.

I could go over them, I thought, but my hand reached for the top right drawer. Tapping my fingers across the handle, I jerked it open and grabbed the small flask within. Another gift, Dad's battered copper, filled with Mama's hot pepper rum. It never failed to make me hiss, letting the heat burn my throat as I stared down at the only other thing in the drawer. The picture was no bigger than a palm: my arms wrapped around Margot, chin tucked on her shoulder. Margot always smiled with every single tooth; it didn't matter if we were breaking up goblin slavers or tangled up in bed together. Swallowing hard against the alcohol and pain, I stroked a thumb over the picture, as if even now Margot would pass some of her warmth onto me.

The hard knock of knuckles, heavy ugly slams, made me jump, but I didn't bother fixing my clothes as I stood. I knew who waited, so I paused an extra second to open the door, just because I knew it would frustrate him.

"Bronson."

My cousin watched me like he always had, from down his pasty nose. It was an aristocratic beak, which probably accounted for his weak chin. His eyes were anything but, their sharp biting green like broken beer glass. In his hands were two boxes.

"How is it, Madam Brigitte," he asked snidely, using the wrong precursor to Mama's roots as he always did to try to get a rise from me, "that I'm stuck running errands for the Senior Pilgrim like I'm a secretary and not an equal?"

Self-righteous shit. Instead of taking the boxes from him, I held the door open wider and gave him a smile. "Put them on my desk." I waited a beat until he was almost there to speak again. "And it's because we're not. Equals, that is, Bronson. Not anymore. I'm assuming the reports on the sirens are among those."

It was always amusing to see him outraged, because his pale skin blatantly displayed his anger in two pink patches across his cheeks. Out of all my cousins, only he took after the fairness of our original homeland and looked like his last name would be Fitzpatrick. I always considered myself lucky to have gotten some of the richness of my mother's skin, the beautiful curl of her hair, as well as the same splash of Irish freckles that dotted my father's face.

His glare was probably supposed to be intimidating, but I'd lived a good chunk of my life being shorter than most people. Mostly their glares just made them look cross-eyed.

He paused as if suddenly struck by a thought. "Is this an acceptable use of time for the future Divine Arbiter? Procrastinating your speeches won't win you any favors with the Creators."

As if I didn't know that. As if I hadn't spent the last couple months scouring documents and legislation to make sure every side was represented. I'd made myself sick over decisions, knowing the consequences and not knowing how my own family would react when I told them.

Wouldn't Bronson, and Cousin Bernard for that matter, love it if I failed? The other cousins would watch me with sad eyes and give comfort, but the two of them would clamber over each other's backs to take my spot.

"You said it yourself, Bron: future Arbiter. Right now, I'm still the head of this chapter. My people, my problems."

"I think—"

I really didn't care, so I raised a hand. "Sit down."

"Excuse me?"

"I didn't stutter, Bronson," I said, slipping into my own seat. "You want to see what peace I've been sowing?"

He sat, perched on the edge of chair, as I tapped the conference speaker in front of me. It lit up, and I leaned back, crossing my arms.

"Starlight Switchboards, speakin' to Madria, whatcha need?"

"Hey, Madria, Senior Pilgrim Fitzpatrick," I said easily, eyes on Bronson. "I need a secure line from 313."

Bronson's eyebrows shot up, nearly collapsing his forehead, but I just smiled when Madria popped her gum.

"Oh, big fancy meeting, Brigitte," she said. "Or is this a personal call?"

"Unfortunately, it's just a boring old meeting, but if you want to talk it up, make it sound salacious to the other pixies running the switches, knock yourself out."

Her laughter drowned out Bronson's scoff, and then there was the clicking of machines, the crackle of cords. I leaned close and tapped in the numerical code I knew by heart now.

"Fitzpatrick."

Head of Brood Dragos, Constantin Dragos had a voice of gravel with an accent so thick I had to lean forward toward the speaker to hear his words properly.

"Constantin, I have my second, Bronson Fitzpatrick, sitting in. How are you?"

There was a pause, then a sigh crackled through the speaker.

"It's the beginning of a Judas moon cycle, Pilgrim, so I suppose I can only say it is unsettling. House Stoja send their regards. You've received the finalized contracts?"

I saw Bronson shift, his eyes narrowing as he studied my face.

"Notarized and everything," I assured. "Within a week I'll be calling on you with congratulations, Constantin."

"Many will not see it that way," he warned. "House Acheron is already whispering."

"I've kept your and House Stoja's confidence, Pilgrim's promise. You have my word as soon as the council accepts the vlkodlak and vampires into the fold, protection will follow immediately. I've handpicked them myself. This is momentous, for both the vlkodlaks' future and for peace."

"Ah, a concept neither the Houses nor the Broods of Deep Europe have a word for. If you are successful, I think I look forward to creating one," he said. "If you are not, then, well, I've lived centuries steeped in blood before."

"A delight as always," I said and listened to his crackling laugh. "We start Monday, and you'll be my first call *when* I succeed."

"I look forward to it, Pilgrim. What is it your kind says? 'Travel lightly?'"

"Safe travels," I corrected.

"Safe travels," he repeated, and the call clicked off.

I leaned back into my seat, pushing the toes of my boots into the grooves my chair had made over the years. Bronson, seemingly muted, was turning several different shades of red, none of which were attractive.

"Not tryin' to pat myself on the back," I said and watched the vein in his neck throb, "but I think I'm gonna crush this treaty."

"You—that—"

"This is when you say 'Brigitte, I am so impressed with your ability to get two of the oldest and most respected broods and houses in Deep Europe to submit themselves for inclusion,'" I offered.

"You've lost your mind."

I squinted as I moved a hand back and forth in a so-so motion. "As you've told me multiple times, over many years, mostly when I'm about to do something you wish you weren't afraid to."

"This isn't a game," he snapped. "Does Bernard know?"

"Were you not listening? No one knows besides Graceland and Beafore Darkchild. I gave them my word—if the other Broods or, Gods forbid, the Houses knew, they would see it as weakness and would crush them. By the time anyone knows, Pilgrims will already be there, the others will fall in line, or we do what we have to."

"Pilgrims are already there; our cousin is there!"

That had me up, biting my lip as I crafted words instead of spitting out venom.

"Bronson, you and I both know that Bernard hasn't even pretended that he has dominion over them. At least when his mother was alive there was attempt, that even though they hadn't submitted, they still toed a line. I won't look the other way, not when I know what's going on there."

"It's the same as what goes on here."

The sting of the words curled my fingers into my palm, and I tried. I really did. But the words came. "Do you just let Bernard spoon feed you bullshit now?! Blood sacrifices and unrestricted hunting aren't even the worst of the reports I've found, and if you think I let those go unpunished on my own streets, then fuck you."

The word vomit has exactly the reaction I didn't want, but I saw the second Bronson straightened.

"You said reports—that go back how long?"

Rolling my shoulders back, I nodded. "Through my father and yours."

"So, you're trying to fix things, cover them up with a neat little patch."

There was so much anger in the clipped words, for the past and for a future he felt I'd taken from him.

"I know Bernard promised you Deep Europe, Bronson," I said softly, "if you got me to step down."

That surprised him; the way he wrapped his arms around himself told me so, and I nodded again.

"We've let Deep Europe feast on itself since our ancestors fractured. You know they aren't satiated by themselves anymore. Look around—the blood banks I've set up, the bone breaking rooms for vlkodlak who haven't been trained. If we don't do something, how long before we can't extend a hand and have to use a fist?"

"Betrayer to betrayer, reaching out to help one of your own instead of strengthening ties with *our* people."

A tired line that still felt like a barb.

"I can't change my lineage any more than you can stop trying to prove you aren't your father. Don't you have any of your own thoughts anymore?"

He circled the room slowly, weighing his words, and despite my irritation I only shook my head. We were too alike. Couldn't be helped, given my parents raised us both—or tried to, in Bronson's case. When his eyes cast upward, to the ceiling where my protection ward was eroded, I felt my throat clench even before he spoke.

"I have plenty of my own thoughts, little cousin. Like how prepared you are to lead us when you can't even keep yourself safe. If all it takes is a single death to destroy you, then I don't expect you're the right type for this job."

Oh, there was pain, deep in the crevices of my bones, but I turned my smile up a notch, then softened my voice and drenched it in honey. It was a trick of Mama's, to let that little bit of Louisiana catch them off guard before you eviscerated them. And I was going to do maximum damage.

"I share your concern," I granted. "Fortunate that I've already completed all the necessary forms and sent them ahead with Asim and Moira. They'll be filed this afternoon."

That stopped his feet, the smugness melting away. "Asim is just out of training. He barely passed his rites," he said slowly, shaking his head like he was trying to dispel the words. "This is too much. You would destroy everything out of some misguided—"

"Enough!" I interrupted, voice hard as stone. A delicious surge of pleasure washed over me when Bronson took a step back. "*I* am the daughter of Rory Fitzpatrick, original descendent of Patrick himself and Odette Laveau, favorite of Marie the Vodou queen, named for *Maman* Brigitte. That alone should strike you mute, but let me add one more title, one I know you won't dismiss. I am Senior Pilgrim, soon to be Divine Arbiter of the Creators. My decisions *are* yours. I'll lead negotiations, but *they* will be with me as advisors. You, Bronson, will *never* again be my second, and you certainly will never hold North America, much less Deep Europe. You will be going west. There's a nest of something destroying outposts in the Dakotas."

The silence was thick, normal for us, except I could see it was panic, not anger, that made his eyes bulge.

"You would take me off this? You have no one else—no other Seniors for the North!"

"And you'll miss it," I assured him. "I'm sorry that you think you should be in my shoes, and after the last couple months, if it were up to me, I'd let you have it. But I can't, and so your ass will be freezing out west—now get out of my office."

He did, backing up like he was afraid to take his eyes off me. "I'll take this to the overseers; they'll have to do something. I should be handling these talks. I should be running North America."

For nearly a year this had been brewing when they agreed to let me have the position until the treaty. He'd gone from slightly unbearable older cousin to full-on pain in the ass. Bernard was easier, being far across the ocean handling Deep Europe, but I wasn't a fool; I knew where Bronson got his ideas.

"We both know if I fail, Bernard will get his chance, and you'll be his second," I told him. "But we both know I won't."

"This is my legacy."

"Muscle Shoals, Alabama, ended your dreams of legacy."

His face lost the two red patches until he resembled a corpse, fingers clenching the frame of the door. "That was sealed; I was young. You shouldn't know about that."

"You were old enough," I said simply. "When I became Senior Pilgrim, I got everything. I need to know who my agents are, so if you think the council will overturn my decision, then go ahead."

Instead of answering, he pulled his jacket tighter around himself and stalked down the hall. I watched him go, let the door shut softly, and leaned on it. I hadn't wanted to push that pain, but there was no other way. I needed to send a letter, let the overseers know so they weren't blindsided if he pressed. I'd do it, I promised myself, as soon as I could find the energy to peel myself off the wall.

The clattering of my phone vibrating on my desk made the decision for me. I dropped into my chair as I accepted the video call.

"Mama," I said, more a breath of relief than anything else.

Even if I were able to see her every day, I would still declare her the most beautiful woman in the world. Smooth skin, the color of the obsidian she used in many of her healing rituals, matched the thick swath of braids she roped over her left shoulder. Her face was often curled up in a delighted smile, but her eyes, bright like a pale moon, were what drew people to her. The idea that even though she was blind, she saw you.

Odette Laveau had lost her sight three days after her thirteenth birthday, when her grandmother Marie Laveau III passed. Mama took absolute darkness the same as she took everything: with a sense of adventure. It only took a week for the power of her grandmother to transfer to her, much to the dismay of her sisters and her mother.

"My baby!" she squealed, holding the camera just a bit too high so all I could see was the softness of her forehead.

"Down a bit, Mama," I said, voice soft. "Why are we video calling anyway?"

Undeterred, she blew me a kiss as she lowered the camera.

"Because technology is incredible! And once your father is done buildin' my new pen outside, he'll want a look at you. Make sure you don't look tired. You soundin' tired, baby."

It's because I am, I wanted to say. "I'm all right, it's just the treaty coming that has me a little beat up. What's the new pen for? More chickens?"

Growing up, we practically owned a zoo. Odette Laveau never met an animal she didn't like, and they all adored her. Her favorite was Jelly Roll, a particularly obese skunk who'd died two months ago, and I'd been forced to fly down to New Orleans for a proper jazz funeral. Mama wore black, face hidden, as Dad led us to the family plot.

"I've got a gator!"

There were few times in my life that I found myself with nothing to say. It was a trait that had caused my teachers and parents untold grief. But here I was, silent and staring at my beaming mother and wondering how Dad had ok'd this one.

"An—an alligator?"

"Crisco! Just a baby now—only about fifty-five pounds," she affirmed.

"Mama, fifty pounds is not a baby. That's a medium-sized dog!"

"Soundin' like your father," she scoffed. "He's gonna be my seein' eye gator. Already begun trainin', which would go faster if your father would let him sleep in the house."

"Yes, Gods forbid Dad would want the wild alligator to live outside."

"Brigitte Marie."

"Sorry, Mama," I said automatically.

"He's a good boy. He tries, bless his heart, to snuggle your father's legs. Shocks him every time, nearly pitches over. I'm going to train him to tend the markets with me."

And wouldn't that shock both the customers and my aunties. Grinning, I imagined Mama and Crisco in matching aprons, dishing out advice and potions for various ills.

"Your Daddy is gonna build him a condo with a pool."

Of course, he was. Rory Fitzpatrick would have built a tower to heaven and damned his soul to hell for Odette Laveau. Over the years, people insinuated he already had, simply by marrying her. It'd been the shock of the family, that one of the Allfather's most devout chose a woman who was often found among the bones of the animals she loved or whispering soft prayers of betrayer magic to the peppers in her garden.

I'd spent a lifetime watching Dad gaze at Mama. Despite the rumors, their love wasn't something done for Baron Samedi to get more power or for Mother Eorthe to watch over her old protégé. It was because the scars that lived inside them, the pain of the past, softened around each other. Mama called it quiet, and I hadn't understood until Margot was gone and everything was deafening.

"I'm gonna let this condo go for a while," she chattered on, "but what if I need help when your father's not home? Crisco needs to be a house gator."

"The first of his kind—" I agreed, then paused for a second. "Wait, Mama, you've already snuck him into the house, haven't you?"

"Shhh!" she demanded, flapping her hand at the screen. "He was tired and it's so hot here. He needed to cool off. He's in the tub."

I cast my eyes to the ceiling, praying to both parents' gods for patience. Before Mama could speak more nonsense, the screen door behind her opened and Dad came into view. Rory Fitzpatrick was impressive, even over a thousand miles away. Built like a golem with forearms of sheer muscle covered in red hair, he had been a brawler in his youth. His eyes were a jeweled green that held a hint of mischievousness, and after retiring, he'd finally grown the thick red beard that Mama was fond of. It was a hefty mass of curls that hid a jaw that could, and had, withstood the beating of a troll. Waving, he moved toward the hall, and I watched in amusement as Mama trailed after him.

"Rory, where are you goin'? Our baby is on the line," she said as she shook the phone.

At her motion, the screen blurred a bit, but I grinned when Dad spoke.

"Dette, I'm just going to the bathroom. I can wash my hands before I talk to our daughter."

"Why are you goin' to our bedroom? Use the kitchen or the side bathroom," Mama demanded, her voice panicked even through the tinny speaker.

"Because I like the soap you bought the other day, why do you—Odette, you didn't."

It was telling that Dad's voice was more resigned than angry. He was closer to giving in than Mama thought.

"Oh, oh Rory, mon cher,[9] he was hot. He was pantin'!"

My snort stopped their argument cold, and I was met with twin glares. I hid my smile as I gave a wave and disconnected the call.

It was what I needed—Mama would have seen it—the love to balance out the next hours filled with death. She would also have my hide for doing zero prep, no protection wards laid across the floor or ceiling. I ignored that small pull of guilt and slid the lid off the closest box. Files, neatly packed and sorted, were all in bland beige folders, but I smelled the wisps of magic. What had started as ancestral, the gift or curse, grew more powerful when I completed my pilgrimage to Arcadia[10] and received Mother Eorthe's blessing.

The tang of earth, metallic and sharp, filled the room, making my tongue curl against my cheek as I plunged my hands wrist deep into the files. I closed my eyes against the tug of a thousand strings, like the sting of hooks in my skin, slowly peeling away from bone. As a child, it had been overwhelming to the point of fear, but I'd long stopped being afraid of my own power.

Flashes of mangled bodies treated as trash that people absently discarded. Fear and a fur coat soaked in perfume, the taste of blood permeating. Lifting one hand out of the files, I held it out to the empty office as if to ward off a blow, and I felt the slice of claws through my palm. The pain stuttered, the body trying to reject it before it flowed, never ebbing, like breath hissing out. Blindly, I stared upward—or she did, I couldn't be sure—as our throat was slit.

Hands free from the files, I grabbed at my neck, feet unsteady, gurgling. Stumbling, the smell of sweat and anise flooded my nose,

---

9 My cherished.

10 The original homeland of the Mother Eorthe and the Fay. A wild, everchanging landscape that many humans would find hedonistic and strange.

and I opened my mouth. Irritated, I spat and watched the thick blood splatter against the worn wood. It never stopped being intrusive, always took a little piece of me to feel what the victims felt. *That wasn't a human,* I reminded myself as tears welled up against my will. *No human makes that mark. Some sort of beast.*

My fingers were frigid against the heat of my throat, and I rubbed at the intact skin, mumbling a prayer of protection. The shakes would come later, as would the nightmares, but I slipped back down into my chair and began to separate photos for the board that ran the length of the far wall. That was where all the victims would live until I solved this. So, no matter what I did, I'd see them.

All were stunning—not surprising as they were all sirens. It was the age-old argument, mostly by men who found themselves conned out of coin, that sirens were a danger to society. Even now, if I meandered down to West Riverend, I couldn't walk five feet without seeing men salivating over the rich baritone of Lenore Bastille at Adam's Rest or the lithe bodies that spun at Gomorrah.

Not a day went by without a report that a siren had been attacked or taken into custody for unfair swindling. I was of the opinion that if you were stupid enough to flaunt money and to try to grope a dancer, you deserved to be conned, but the law was the law.

It would be up to me tonight to run the route, so I jerked on my jacket and grabbed my bag. The fastest way would be the underground, and I would be able to avoid the cold, but conversations and the thought of them put an itch between my shoulder blades. I'd rather freeze on the people mover.

What once had been a small, single loop had expanded over the years so now the rickety station cars rattled from Riverside through Greektown until it reversed course to begin again. Scanning my pass, I gave the only other person in the car a nod and chose to stand and stare out the window as we pulled away from the station.

It was forever a comfort to watch the buildings, crumbling or splashed with paint, blur and meld until they resembled a creature about to take flight. The city of Detroit was, to me, a phoenix. Beaten, broken, burned, and still it rose to greet the day. Graceland had countered, over breakfast one morning, that those qualities also applied to the undead ghouls that pulled themselves from the banks of the Detroit River every so often. Still, as I studied the murals, half soaked in the shadow of an early winter night, from the window of the people mover, magic resonated in Detroit's bones. It was pure fay that lived in the brick of Oldtown, in the ghosts that ran across Belle Isle. At one time Detroit was a hub, an Ellis Island for those trying to escape the tyranny of my own ancestor and the first Pilgrim, Patrick.

"Hey, you got a dollar?"

I remained still, eyes on the blurred city. If I'd wanted conversation, I would have risked the underground. Still, I dug into my pocket and pulled out Graceland's dollar.

"Sure, do you—"

The words died in my throat as the person was directly in my space, face hidden underneath folds of rotted fabric. I hadn't heard them move.

"Thanks," they said, bloated grey fingers coming out to snatch it.

"I have a daric[11] if that will ease your way better?"

Their head lifted at that, and from the depths of the folds, I saw the ruby red eyes and the sharp line of white teeth that revealed themselves as the creature smiled. The compartment filled with the smell of honey and cinnamon, the delight of magic clear in the small space.

"It will."

The gold coin passed from me without remorse, but I knew, somewhere in the city, Graceland was having a conniption fit over the loss of some of his rarer currency.

"Kheili lotf dārid."[12]

Bowing my head, I eased down into the seat across from them. "My cousin Rashida would provide better conversation, I'm afraid, but you're welcome. You're a long way from home."

"No further than Hamtramck Station," they said. "That's where home used to be."

Sometimes that was the motto of Detroit—used to be. There was a time when the city stood on its own feet, arms swept out to welcome

---

11 Ancient Persian currency.

12 That's very kind of you.

everyone, to harbor. I saw the busted windows of buildings so far untouched by the rebuild, like gaping jagged mouths and empty eyes, out of the corner of my vision and sighed.

"I wasn't aware that any efreet were in the Metro Area."

Even though it wasn't a question, they still cocked their head at me, and I felt the magic around them crackle. I eased a hand down to the pouch on my hip, but found my wrist captured by strong, fat fingers.

"You don't smell like Allfather, so not a Pilgrim," they said, leaning close so the stench of crumbling mold overpowered the earlier delight. "Why would you care?"

"I can promise you there won't be an efreet left in Hamtramck if you don't let me go," I said, "betrayer to betrayer."

That eased the grip on my wrist, and the folds of cloth settled back. "My apologies, but you can't be too careful in the town of the Fitzpatrick's," they said and pushed up the hand wrappings. "My symbol."

The dying sun of the Vedic Pantheon bled orange and yellow against grey skin. With a nod I gripped my wrist, pressing a thumb nail into my palm until a bead of blood bloomed. Holding out my hand, we both watched as the blood moved across my palm, jumping into dots and lines around a heart.

"Bloodcraft," they whispered, leaning forward. "It seems you are the one far from home, child."

"Vodou," I corrected firmly. "I'll make my way down south this summer."

"A pilgrimage?"

"A crucible," I corrected again, thinking of the annual Laveau family dinner. "I need to earn my way."

"As we all do," they said with a sigh. "Perhaps there will be a time when suspicion doesn't follow us. I've heard the wind, Dyaus,[13] whispering of change. We can only hope it's for the better."

"Word is the Fitzpatricks are behind that," I said. "Vedic might be joining the loa in folding into the council."

---

13 The "Sky Father" deity of the Vedic pantheon. Similar to Zeus but less likely to turn into a swan and attempt to bang an unsuspecting mortal.

I expected a blistering dismissal, for his eyes to burn in red fury, but his shoulders lowered farther and he shook his head.

"Bound again. There was a time your gods and mine were proud that they spit in the face of Mother Eorthe and the Allfather when they abandoned us. Now it seems we will all be kept pets."

The station car jerked to a halt, and the efreet pushed to their feet.

"This isn't Ham station," I said.

The red eyes watched me from the darkness with a strange sort of gentleness, as if they were remembering someone else. "Child, I haven't lived there since the fires. I think I'll try my luck at the Watershed Backrooms."

Where a daric would get them plenty of opportunity to gamble. "There's a shelter near Wayne State. Harvest Heart. I could put a word in for you."

They stopped in the doorway, one clawed hand holding the struggling metal door easily. "Tell me, if you're so influential, what is your name?"

It was on the tip of my tongue, to answer the curiosity with the truth, but I saw the way their fingers played over the gold coin I'd given them.

"And give you control over my future?" I said, voice light. "I have no desire to be won by whoever you lose that money to tonight."

Laughter shook the folds of cloth as the efreet moved to the exit. "Smart witch."

The doors slid closed behind him, and I leaned back, letting my head crack against the cheap plastic, but I didn't hiss at the pain. A lesson, a reminder, that my treaty proposal was right. If I hadn't been touched by betrayer magic, he would have cowered or attacked at the whiff of a Pilgrim.

"Next Stop, West Riverend."

Things would change, I decided. But first I needed to see the patron saint of strippers.

CHAPTER 3

West Riverend, like my mother, was a reason I had exactly four grey hairs and a developing ulcer. Stubborn and resilient in its debauchery since the mid-seventies, even in its grimiest sections, it shone with neon.

The slush of snow from earlier in the week reflected flashing signs of lithe figures, twisting, beckoning. If I turned back toward the east, the lines of those desperate to get into the various clubs would stare back. Not looking for attention, I kept my head low, as I listened to the blend of conversations and music.

Gomorrah loomed over the rest of the strip as it had since Ms. Feather Glen opened it. Once upon a time, it was a church, and wasn't it ironic, Feather liked to comment, that it was still a house of worship? The massive stained-glass windows, emotive as a face, cast bursts of saturated color on the sidewalk as the lights pulsed in time to the music inside.

I took the sprawling steps at a jog, scooting around the complaining line when the bouncer saw me. As he pulled open the heavy oak door, I murmured my thanks and deftly slipped a green coin into his palm.

Another world, one perhaps closer to Arcadia, was what I always thought when entering. It was kept as one large room, most of the pews intact so patrons could sit and watch the fay onstage. Long-haired nymphs spun up in strands of jeweled cloth dangled from the ceiling, limbs pale as the moon and dark as its other side flashing out. Others frolicked, naked as dawn, down the aisles, wings fluttering. It didn't matter that it was Friday—the pews were always full. As I scanned the crowd, I realized it'd been too long. No one was familiar.

"You drinking?"

I jerked my gaze away from the crowd to study the man in front of me. Drunk on liquor and magic, both oozed out of him in thick, rolling waves of rotted fruit. I shook my head and went to step back, but he stepped with me, fingers snagging my arm.

"What, you're too good for me?" he asked and looked into my eyes.

His were red, bloodshot sure, but the pupils were a sharp amber. I stared back, unimpressed.

"You should really reconsider," I said and gave my wrist a jerk.

His nails, normal a moment before, dug sharp into my flesh, and as the lights flashed onstage, I caught his real form. Entrails swayed to the music from the disembodied head, the arms jutting out at broken angles from its cheeks. The leyak[14] frowned at the lack of response. "Come on now. Don't you like me? Just look a little longer."

I blinked hard as the stage lights flared out and his illusion returned. The longer I let this go, the worse it would get; eventually he'd shift, transforming his appearance into exactly who I wanted to see. Knowing that if he did, I'd murder him where he stood, I shifted my weight and gave a final jerk to give myself momentum. As he pulled me back, I brought my boot up and stomped where his entrails dangled. He crumpled, and I pulled out my badge so when he shot back up, claws outstretched, it was shoved practically between his eyes.

"Make my day, shifter," I said, voice calm even though my insides shook with grief and anger, "because I'll put you down permanently."

For a second, it looked like he might, but he straightened, pulling at his jacket. "My apologies, Pilgrim. I'll be going."

I watched until he was gone. It wasn't fear, but pure, unadulterated want that hit me, along with disgust—that I was that far gone that I could be seduced by a leyak assuming the form of my dead girlfriend.

"You always have a knack for losing me customers. Now you have to buy a lap dance."

I gave Feather a shrug. "You seem to be doing well enough. Full house."

"Praise Jesus!" she laughed. "Oh, you got some of your daddy in that pinched look. Easiest way to get under Rory Fitzpatrick's skin was to forsake his Creator's son."

"Why do you think I drew the short straw to come down here?"

Another laugh spilled out, bells ringing in the air. Feather Glen

---

14 A shapeshifter in Indonesian lore. Ugly as sin and twice as douchey.

was barely five feet, skin a milky blue that defied age. Spun atop her head were silver curls in a beehive that put the women uptown to shame. Her eyes, wide in such a small face, shone crystal blue behind cat eyeglasses.

"Word has it you don't...come down here, and that no one sends you anywhere anymore," she commented, face going serious in a way it rarely was.

That was when you could truly see the otherness. A fairy stoic was a bit like a goblin: sharp angles that light shadowed and glanced off. As the red light from the stage pulsed, I easily saw the sharp points of Feather's teeth.

"Is that word from your son? He tell you to expect me?" I asked.

"He's a good boy," she sighed. "Don't know how he got tangled up in the law. Where did I go wrong, do you think?"

"Letting him answer my parents' babysitting ad."

She grinned at that. "Your parents did right by him; I'll always be grateful for that. Now why are you here?"

"I'm looking into some deaths for your son—sirens. He says they aren't yours."

"I don't keep unregistered sirens. Everyone knows that," Feather said.

"Hmm," I said noncommittally, eyes going back to the stage. "I may have my father's work ethic, but I don't have his gift. People liked him, told him things—sometimes despite themselves—and never felt put out about it. All I can do is tell your lying, Feather. So, tell me the truth."

The words floated, wrapped in magic that smelled of crushed mint and candle smoke, and I saw the moment it found Feather's throat, the way her lips trembled to fight against it.

"Or?"

Not looking away from the stage, I shrugged. "Then maybe I haul every single girl in, make a stink. That one with the black hair, bet she's one. So's the one with the half-shaved head—sisters?"

"They don't want trouble. They stay onstage; they don't trick nobody," Feather argued, voice tight. "They got a right to work and be left alone."

She was as soft a touch as Horace, just wrapped in sharp eyes, and I gave a nod. "I'm not looking to lock them up, Feather. I just need to know if they knew the girls that died. I don't care if they have the proper papers—I should, but you don't make mistakes with your girls. I know you."

The moment of hesitation popped like a bubble, and even though it was obvious Feather didn't like it, she nodded. "You could have led with that. You can go in the back. Their act is almost over."

"I appreciate it, Ms. Glen."

"You're a good one, Brigitte, but if you mess up my girls, I'll bury you. Horace will help."

"He'd complain the whole time though," I countered mildly. "I didn't come here to mess with them—or you."

It was as much of an apology as we both knew I was capable of, and Feather waved it away with her dainty hand.

"Have them back in ten—and I'm sorry again about your mate."

Was it possible for bones to turn to steel? Because even if I wanted to, there was no strength to move my suddenly too-heavy body. "Girlfriend, Feather. Humans call them girlfriends or boyfriends or partners."

"Nothing friendly about what you two used to do to each other on the dance floor at Elysium," she said, laughing again. "You go see my girls."

She sailed away gracefully, but my own first step dragged, like being pulled through sand. Margot loved coming here during the day to write in the pews, surrounded by glitter and the lost shoes of customers and dancers. She would be silent and still, then scribble something down at a furious pace, as if she had to get it out at that exact second. I could leave her here after an entire night at Elysium, to fulfill my duties, and come back to find her chatting with the bartender or trying out the spinning cloths on stage with a dancer.

With curled fists, I moved through the crowd toward the back stairs, heavy stone that curved down to a basement converted into dressing rooms. Though empty of dancers, it exploded with stuff: feathers and glitter, cloth, and the heavy oppression of expensive perfume.

The plush carpet sank down beneath my feet and caught my

reflection in the large makeup mirrors. In the florescent light, I looked washed out, a sickly ghoul among the wild colors and textures.

"Ms. Glen said you wished to speak with us?" a quiet voice asked from behind me.

I turned slowly, and with care, slipped the badge from my pocket. Handing it over, I kept my thoughts to myself as the two sirens looked it over.

"Have you come to take us away?" the girl with the shaved head asked, the same voice from the stairs.

"No," I said and tucked the badge back into my pocket. "I don't care about your papers. I don't even need to know your names. I just need to ask some questions."

The tension in their bodies was palpable, producing a scent like rotted orange with the sharp slap of sea salt, and I prepared to bolt after them if they decided to run. Thankfully, they both eased by me to sit on the benches at one of the makeup tables. They were young, probably just on the right side of legal to be working here, and definitely sirens.

Like the corpse in the alley, I studied their eyes. Always a milky white line of the pupil, a fine slit that contracted and expanded in a field of black. There was a time, before the corruption, that sirens were the height of beauty for the fay: mermaids that sang and told stories for the weary, the lost, or the curious. My own ancestor, Patrick, after sending his siblings on their first pilgrimages to learn of the world's vastly different magics, created by those who'd strayed from the Allfather and Mother Eorthe, would lay in the water at night below the stars and listen to their song. It was there he and Seraphim the mermaid fell in love, where promises were made and would be broken, where peace would be shattered.

Henry, the oldest of the Pilgrims, jealous of Patrick for being the Creator's favorite, crept back to Ireland from the dark wilds of Europe. He watched, furious that his brother would throw away his objectivity to a creature of the fay. So, one night, when Patrick was to meet his Seraphim, Henry beat him there.

Disguised in his brother's cloak, he lured Seraphim to the water's edge, then struck. He'd learned of dark magic deep within the woods of Romania and grown stronger. From Seraphim's neck, he tore her very soul and shoved her out to sea. As she bled to death, she whispered a curse upon her lover's brother: if he would take away her chance of seeing the light of day ever again, she would do the same to him.

When Patrick called to her, and what came for him was not Seraphim but a monstrous creature, he nearly lost his life. Not knowing what his brother had done, Patrick began his legacy of brutality against magic.

Seated before me was the consequences of my own ancestors' anger and arrogance. Two shaking girls, who had done nothing besides be born and abandoned by a system that believed they held too much in common with vampires and vlkodlak to be deemed worthy.

With practiced hands, I reached into the pouch made of hog leather and grabbed a pinch of dill and lavender. Crushing it, I spread it under my nose, a thin line of protection.

"You don't have to," the girl with the shaved head said quietly. "We don't do that."

A melody crept up around my neck, Mama's lullaby whispered into my ear. "It's better to take precautions," I said just as softly, nodding to the other girl. "Can you speak?"

"She can, but she doesn't," her sister said quickly and gripped the girl's hand.

"Because she hurt someone," I stated blandly. "I'm not here to judge, but neither of you are trained, correct?"

Both girls looked at each other, then back to me, and gave twin head shakes. I rubbed at my ear, as if that would shake the sound of my mother's voice from it, and sighed.

"All right. I have a trainer; she'll take you two on. Feath—Ms. Glen—knows her, trusts her."

"We're ok, we're—"

"You're not," I interrupted. "It doesn't just go away because you don't use it. You can't smell it— Mama's peppers and my father's vanilla tobacco. Your sister not speaking will only amplify her other powers. I promise the trainer will help and get you papers, so if you two want to do something besides dance, you can do it."

"And what do we have to do in return?" the girl demanded, voice cracking.

"Did you know Francesca Domino, Lacey Calligan, or Abigail Donaldson?"

The way they tensed, backs going straight, told me what I needed to know. As did the lie that came out of the girl's mouth.

"No."

Taking a step back, I watched them twitch nervously as I leaned against the frame of the only exit. "I can explain why I asked, but I have a feeling you know what happened to those girls. Let me tell you something you don't know. Pilgrims, we go through these trials, endure all types of magic to prepare us. To see if Mother Eorthe or the Allfather deems us worthy enough to bestow a special gift. Mine? I can smell bullshit before it comes out of someone's mouth."

"We're not—"

"Don't finish that lie," I interrupted mildly.

Clearly frustrated, the girl lapsed into silence, her head moving to look at the wall. Her sister, the silent one, stared at me, as if looking straight through.

"You loved her?" she whispered.

It was Margot's voice, a curious sound that I could pick out instantly, whether we were in a crowd or not. Clenching my jaw, I reached deep inside myself for some softness. This girl didn't know what she was doing. Even her sister stared at her in shock.

"Yes, more than anything." Honesty always worked best with sirens.

"But you let her die…" the girl said, voice growing deeper.

There it was: the curse of Seraphim reflected in the expansion of her pupils, and if I was anyone else, I might have fallen into those depths. Instead, I lowered my head, took a deep breath through my mouth, and looked up.

"Was it a broker? Pimp?" I demanded.

"We don't know," the first girl said, shaking her head when I took a step forward. "But we were all brokered by Dillan Holloway."

If it was possible for this case to get more difficult, this was it: the epitome of "oh shit." Dillan Holloway, better known as Mayor

Holloway. Notorious party boy and all-around pain in the ass, he infamous for holding lavish parties in his mansion while some parts of the city barely had hot water.

"You're telling me Feather bought you?" I asked.

They both went pale, eyes bulging in fear, but I cut them off before either spoke.

"Doesn't matter. I'll get her in contact with the trainer I talked about," I said and turned for the door. "Delilah Navarro is the best. She'll take care of you."

"Pilgrim."

Turning back, I waited, brow raised, as neither girl spoke. Finally, the one with Margot's voice opened her mouth.

"Thank you."

With a sharp nod, I took the steps two at a time, the smell of mango shampoo flooding my nostrils. Desperate for fresh air, I shoved open the door back to the main chapel and almost nailed Feather.

"Everything ok?" she asked. "You look like you're going to be sick."

I was. I was going to stumble home, and after throwing up, I would stare at the paperwork I gifted Margot on our anniversary. I'd gotten it framed by her favorite metal artist down near Mexican town, and we both wept as she pressed her freedom to her chest. It hadn't mattered in that moment that Dillan Holloway made her spy on me, invade my life, made me fall in love with her. What mattered was that, after I bought out her contract, after she was free, Margot stayed. The pretty brass frame hung in our—my bedroom.

"I'm sending Delilah here, by the middle of next week. You should have told me you bought them, Feather."

"So you could what, throw them away?! Give them back to that pig?" Feather demanded, her voice a quiet hiss. "They're babies. He's dealing in babies."

"He always has," I spat out. "I wouldn't have made them go back."

"Your father would have. I don't have the proper permits to have them work off their debt with me. If Holloway's work contracts had been legally sound, he wouldn't have had a choice. You're in his shoes now, no matter what you think."

It would have killed him, had him coming home to stare blankly at the wall as Mama whispered to him, but yes, Rory Fitzpatrick would have followed the law. Pilgrim and human, because as a Devourer[15] he had to, couldn't risk corruption or the loss of power.

"I'm not my father, Feather. Remember that next time. Delilah will get them papers, wipe their records, and train them. Free of charge."

"You're a good girl, Brigitte."

My huff of laughter was more bitterness than amusement. "Yeah, well—I'll see you later, Feather. Tell your son at Sunday dinner to come see me Monday, early. I'll make time."

"Or you could come to dinner. It's ham this week. If I remember right, you like ham?"

It was an olive branch, and even though part of me wanted to break it over my knee, I nodded. "Sure. Can I bring Graceland?"

The mention of him widened Feather's eyes. "Of course! I'll have to clean, get Horace to help me dust. Does he like ham? Should I cook something else?"

Unable to help it, I laughed, and even though sometimes I swore I didn't have it in me, it was loud and genuine. "Feather, he wouldn't want you making a big deal. He doesn't think like that."

"Will he be bringing Persephone or one of his siblings?"

"No, Penny is still—busy. The rest probably are too. Nothing fancy, Feather."

"But should I put out—"

"Feather," I interrupted and placed a steadying hand on the fairy's shoulder, "ham's good. He's partial to red wine."

Instead of answering, she shooed at me and hustled off. I knew I should go home, purge the sickness from my gut, get the breakdown out of the way, but there was one more spot to check in before I crawled home. As the bouncer held the door for me again, I nodded and received one in return.

"Safe travels, Pilgrim."

---

15 One of the two paths chosen for Senior Pilgrims. The Allfather's blessing. A Devourer can consume magic from other creatures, stripping said creature of its power. Especially effective against fallen magics, this requires a pious and unyielding fortitude so that the Pilgrim is not corrupted.

My thanks were lost in the clamor of half-drunk nymphs, IDs out and spirits high.

I quickened my pace, barely getting my hood up as wet slop from the roof rolled over and slapped one of my leather-clad shoulders. Tomorrow this would all be sleek, glossy, and frozen, but with the hot gas curling through manhole covers and the masses of bodies, it was in a perpetual state of slush. Thankfully the walk wasn't long—the entrance tucked toward the back of West Riverend, built into the bedrock of the river.

Where Gomorrah proudly threw its inhibitions into the garbage, Adam's Rest was its prudish sister. Only those touched by magic could see the staircase that wound its way deep into the earth. McGavin, the sole proprietor of the Rest, claimed to hate humanity but was known to indulge a fascination with the *Turner Classic Movie Channel*. Judging by the thick gothic stone and lit torches, they were in a Phantom of the Opera mood tonight.

Two dusty red curtains served as the door at the end of the long, winding stairs, and I pushed them apart to a haze of smoke and my favorite bouncer in West Riverend. Oswald, all ten feet of him, had once ripped a vlkodlak in half after the beast started a brawl. Giving him a full smile, I handed over my badge and tried not to laugh when his faintly orange skin went bright red.

"I'm sorry, ma'am, it's a—"

"Formality," I finished for him, as I always did. "You're just doing your job, Ozzy."

The troll shuffled his feet at the nickname. "'ppreciate it, ma'am."

"What's going on tonight?"

"Well drinks are half priced, but—" He looked down at me with a frown. "—nothing you should probably drink. We got a new bartender—she's not partial to half humans or Pilgrims. Lenore is on tonight though—right about now, actually."

"Thanks, Ozzy," I said and handed him a slip of paper. "For your sister. See if she can solve this one."

Isadore, Oswald's sister, was the smartest fifteen-year-old I'd ever met—human or fay. She was also determined to be a Pilgrim, even though fay weren't eligible. Because I couldn't offer her more,

I nurtured her inquisitiveness by giving her riddles, and I hadn't stumped her yet.

"I better not tell her until she gets off school tomorrow. Last time she faked sick to get home," he said fondly. "Anyway, enjoy the music—but remember, no drinks."

With a tap to my temple, I moved through the club proper. It was an open, smoky space, but during the week, it was exponentially smaller, a hole in the wall more akin to Casablanca than an MGM musical. Along the far wall was a stage of sprawling oak where the band, the Nocturnals, were tuning up. They played the entire West Riverend, but Friday nights they belonged to Adam's Rest. Gillian Savage, the small, unassuming drummer, had for a time been part of the Pilgrims, a feisty junior who happened to meet Justin Savage, part-time musician and full-time vampire at Planet ComiCon.

We'd trained together, down in New Orleans. When Gillian met Justin, it was the first time in my life I'd stood nose to nose with my father in disagreement. Any Pilgrim who broke their oath—and letting your boyfriend turn you fell into that category—was immediately 86ed. It took some clever spinning of the code, and an extra kiss to the chip of Blarney Stone I'd received on my eighteenth birthday, for the great Rory Fitzpatrick to back down.

In the end, Gillian got to walk away to marry the man she fell in love with, and they started the Nocturnals. My ass got sent out to the arctic as punishment. While Gillian and Justin made themselves the go-to band for the West, I nearly bled to death on an ice flow after discovering a small tribe of yeti.

I rubbed my shoulder where the familiar phantom pain of claws stung and watched the band set up. Gillian must have felt my eyes, because her head snapped my way. Before she'd turned, they were a clear green, but the change had muddied them to a murky amber. Her grin was lightning fast, as was the way she leapt off the stage and instantly sidled up to me. Throwing her arms around me, she laughed happily.

"Oh! I haven't seen you in forever, Brig!"

Wheezing, I returned the hug with much less strength but all the same enthusiasm. "It's been a while. I—" I stopped, realizing the room had fallen silent, and over Gillian's head I found the entire room staring at us.

I only spared the others a flat look, eyes sweeping across the crowd until they settled on Gillian's husband. He gave me a shy smile as he pushed up his thick glasses—vision that even vampirism couldn't fix—and shrugged as if to say, "What can you do?"

I nodded and pulled Gillian back to examine her. "Gods, look at you! This life suits you, Gil."

The eternally young girl bit into her lip, sharp teeth leaving the full bottom unmarred. "It really does. I know you went through a lot of trouble for us, but this was where I'm meant to be."

"It was nothing," I said quickly.

Gillian shook her head. "Eventually you'll learn to accept thanks. You here on business?"

"Maybe I just came to see you play."

"Not with that look in your eyes. What's going on?" My instant hesitation dulled the girl's smile a little, but she nodded. "Right, it's against code to talk shop with Deep Europe," she said, more sad than bitter.

There was no argument for the truth. Deep Europe, the home of vampires, vlkodlak, and cursed magic, were treated with more suspicion and trepidation than any of the other fallen or betrayer magics. But I shook my head. "It's sirens, Gillian. Young girls being killed. I can't say more."

Even with such little information, Gillian's eyes welled up. The change heightened everything, especially anger and despair. My smile was soft as I gently patted her cheek.

"It's all right, Gilly. I'll catch them."

The vampire gave me a long look and smiled. "I honestly believe you. Always did. I—"

Desperate to avoid another compliment, I shifted gears. "You guys set up?"

"Oh, we set up hours ago, just testing…" she said. "You aren't talking about the band, are you?"

"No, but if it makes you more comfortable to ease into it, we can talk about the band."

It was hard, I knew, for Gillian to fully wrap her mind around the restrictions that came with the bite, with immortality. The suspicion of the magical community was a blip compared to the check-ins, the temperament tests, and the lack of privacy about feeding.

"We decided on the blood bank in Corktown you suggested; Morphosis is going to forward the paperwork to you. I think the idea of a shared familiar makes us both uncomfortable."

"Sharice sent me your paperwork," I said, voice careful. "She mentioned you took issues with some of the questions."

"They asked me whether or not my family is aware of my condition, if I have grudges. They made me go back to elementary school, Brigitte. They knew I bit a child in preschool."

"Temperament is important," I countered calmly. "I know it seems silly, Gil, but if we chart your history and triggers and apply a solid feeding plan, it's been proven that we can reduce incidents by nearly eighty percent."

"You don't need to sell me. I'm not a—"

"You are," I interrupted, "and that's ok. But you need to understand there are consequences to possessing the power you have now. I'm not here to judge you; that's not my job. It's to protect you."

"And everyone from me," Gil said, face tight. "We let Justin's familiar go. She's been compensated for her contract being broken early; everything is legal. We'll be feeding at the bank from now on. That's it."

"The treaty is in a couple days," I reminded her, "and I got Bernard and Bronson breathing down my neck, looking for anything to make me look incompetent or weak. I know you two aren't the problem, but I can't play favorites—not with Deep Europe."

"I know."

"It's not personal, Gil. Now get your cute butt back to your husband; he's missing you."

The smile she gave was blinding as she sped back to the band. I wove my way past the small circle tables to the bar. The whispers, the insults that were a little louder, rolled over me. When I was younger, I'd been a people pleaser. Pilgrimship had a way of bleeding that out of you.

Sometimes it seemed there was nothing left to bleed, especially in the face of change. It'd taken me years, but I'd scraped together the funds for rent, for staff, for training to run a record house for all the registered cursed creatures of Michigan. Off Leverette and Trumbull, the small, rented space made of ugly brick in Corktown, stood proudly. On its slightly too small sign, the word "Morphosis" was scrawled. Considered folly by my peers, it was a flickering hope to myself and Sharice Miller, a social work graduate from Wayne State, that cursed creatures could have a safe place when they needed it most.

A long way to go, I acknowledged only to myself as I approached the bar. As I slipped onto a stool, I kept myself half turned to see the room.

The lights swept low across it. Everyone sat up a little straighter, almost subconsciously, as the band stopped tuning. Slouched on my elbow, I watched the curtain pull back, the way the crowd leaned forward. Lenore Bastille, dressed in a slip of silver, her short, dark curls pasted to her head, leveled her eyes to the crowd and raised her arms. "The Angel of the West" was how her more devoted fans referred to her, and judging by the smug smile I could see even from across the room, it was clear Lenore liked it.

With her arms still raised, she snapped her fingers twice. The band, trumpet and piano began to play a mourning dirge, and she sang, *"As I walk through the valley of the shadow of death, / I take a look at my life and realize there's nothing left…."*

Despite myself, I grinned outright at the jazz rendition of Coolio's classic. McGavin originally hadn't let Lenore pick her own music, but it was obvious she'd finally swayed him.

"You drinkn' or what?" a voice demanded.

I spun in my seat and listened to Lenore serenade her way through the first refrain before answering the bartender's sharp words. "Water," I said, shaking my head when the small fairy moved for a glass. "Bottle, unopened."

If possible, the bartender looked more furious, and her eyes darted over to Oswald. Following her gaze, I rapped my knuckles against the wood and waited until the bartender looked back to me.

"If anything so much as mildly inconveniences Oswald, I'll kill you," I said easily, and took the bottle. "That's not me puffing up either."

"You're pretty friendly to the vamp and troll for someone who's murdered their people," the woman said, grabbing a rag. "They don't mind?"

"I think they understand it works both ways. I've lost people to rabid vampires, and no, I've never killed a troll. My father did, during the early days when they were eating people's pets."

"Is that how you sleep at night?" the bartender demanded.

"I don't sleep much," I offered, eyes narrowed. "Why don't we skip this song and dance? Reveal yourself."

Gritting her teeth, the bartender's fingers gripped the bar as she shook her head. With the music growing louder, Lenore about to hit her crescendo, I leaned nearly across the bar.

"I can see the seams of your illusion. It wasn't a suggestion. Reveal yourself now."

There was a shimmer of magic, the small sound of glass breaking as the façade fell away. The beady black eyes burned against the green cast of her skin with fury.

"Goblin, got it," I said, voice purposefully calm. "Explains the shitty attitude. Don't see many of you down near these parts."

"I'm a citizen, same as you," the woman informed me. "I got rights."

"You absolutely do, and is the other part of that deal is that you answer my questions. I'm investigating some deaths: girls, barely legal."

"You think I care about some human girls getting themselves killed?"

I slid the photos out from my pocket, turned them over, and pushed them to her. "They aren't human."

Sharp eyes flickered over the photos. She would remember these forever, I knew; it was why most goblins worked in the business district, because they never forgot. It was the same reason so few goblins worked police.

"They're sirens," I said.

"I got eyes," the bartender said and pointed one long spindly finger at one of the photos, "and I know trouble when I see it. You got trouble—terrible trouble here."

"Where?" I asked.

The goblin tapped the same spot on the photo and blew out a sharp breath. "Human's eyes not so good, ah?"

I shrugged noncommittally at the insult, because I'm not human—not totally, anyway. The original Pilgrims hadn't been plucked from the Allfather's rib or made from the seeds strewn from Mother Eorthe's hands. Patrick, Henry, Dimitra, and Elu were perfect balance, all the good and all the bad of both Creators, in bodies that could decay but took a hell of a long time to get there. The four had spread over the earth, bestowing knowledge and training on magically inclined humans, and those Junior Pilgrims helped them maintain a presence everywhere. There were dalliances, of course, children born between partners, but sometimes they had magic, sometimes not. It was only when the Allfather or Mother Eorthe chose that another Senior Pilgrim was born, a child from one of the four who was just as powerful, meant to combat the growing unpredictability of magic, the fracturing of pantheons. Mama used to laugh about the fury of the Allfather, the rain that poured for three days when I was born with Mother Eorthe's blessing. The first Conduit[16] instead of Devourer since the original four.

"Got a magnifying glass?" the bartender asked.

I shook my head; of all the tools I carried, magical and ordinary, that was not one of them. I noticed the vampire next to me had an empty whiskey glass, and I grabbed for it, unimpressed when he bared teeth at me. I flipped it over the spot the goblin had pointed out. Magnified, I saw she wasn't lying.

"Fuck," I hissed and shoved the photo into my pocket as I stood. "Thanks for the help."

"Ain't helping you," the bartender said, angling her head in the direction of the stage. "You going to tell her?"

How did you tell Lenore Bastille, the Angel of the West, that one of these murdered girls had been going under a false name? That the

---

16 One of the two paths of magic for a Senior Pilgrim. Mother Eorthe's blessing.

youngest, Lacey Calligan, was actually Annabel Lee Bastille, who'd broken Lenore's heart when she ran away from home last month. That while everyone had written off the baby Bastille sister, she was tortured and killed. I'd never met the girl, but the small tattoo of angel wings just underneath the left ear, the same tattoo that was under Lenore's right, was enough of an identifier.

"Not until I have something to give her," I said, rubbing hand over my face. "Do not mention her sister or what you saw."

Surprisingly the bartender nodded, and I gave one in return before I zipped my jacket. For a second, I just stood as Lenore wound her way through the end of the second verse of Taylor Swift's "Blank Space," crooning, *"Wait the worst is yet to come, oh no / Screaming, crying, perfect storm…"*

Giving a tense smile to the shadows of the stage, from where Gillian watched me, I made my way back to Oswald, who was surrounded by six pixies trying to convince him their IDs were real.

"I'm a hundred and three!" one wailed.

"Night, Oswald," I said mildly.

"Leaving already?" Oswald asked, absently swatting as one of the pixies flew up into his face.

"I gotta see a boy about a girl."

Oswald sighed and grabbed the pesky pixie by her wings, then set her back down. "Safe travels, Pilgrim."

"Thanks," I said, and waved to the mass of pixies pulling on his shirt. "And good luck with that."

CHAPTER 4

The look on Graceland's face as I knocked on the glass separating Ima Noodles from the street almost wiped the sickness from my stomach. However, as the shock wore off, he tilted his chin up and pointedly looked back at his date as if I didn't exist.

With a grin, I knocked again, and this time multiple tables turned to stare at me. I practically bit through my cheek to avoid the cackle in my chest as Graceland stood. In his tight grey suit, he looked like any normal businessman in the area—until instead of walking to the door, he phased through the glass.

I ignored the gaping mouths of the patrons and the wide eyes of his date and offered a wheedling smile. As if knowing what was coming, Graceland shook his head.

"I thought you were doing SheWolf?" I said. "Looked like an idiot asking for you there."

"It's almost as if I didn't want to be found," he said. "We just ordered dessert. What is it?"

"Nothing with pomegranate, I hope."

The amount of wither he achieved with a small shift of his eyebrows was impressive. If I weren't the usual recipient of his displeasure, I would've been dust. Instead, I notched up my smile.

"I need you."

His sigh could have filled the entire street. "You realize I was hoping for him to say those words to me tonight."

There was the barest amount of pain in his voice, and that, not the irritation, not the frustration, softened me.

"I know. And I wouldn't bother you if it wasn't vital, but—it's bad. It's all bad."

This time his sigh wasn't exasperation but acceptance. "Let me say my apologies."

When he turned, he threw up his hand as he hit the glass. He glanced back at me, teeth gritted. "I went through instead of using the door, didn't I?"

"I got you riled up."

"As only you can do," he said mildly before he phased back through.

I wasn't the only one that could rile him up, but I turned to give him privacy. His family infuriated him on a regular basis without making Graceland smile the way I did.

"Let's go," he said as he walked from the actual door this time.

I waited until we fell in step before I glanced in his direction. He seemed happy.

"So, when do I get to ask him what his intentions are with you?"

"Go read your smutty fan fiction, Fitzpatrick," he said and dug into his pocket. "Balls, it's cold."

As if agreeing, the wind howled, and I curled my hands into fists inside the silk lining of my own pockets. "I'll buy you a cup when we get there."

"It's bad enough that we're finally going back to Haven?" he asked, eyebrows disappearing under the beanie he tugged over his hair. "Suppose they'll remember what we look like?"

"There are reminders of you in the DIA—several well-endowed statues if I remember correctly," I offered. "Me, probably not."

"Nonsense," he said. "You look exactly like that cubism painting in the cafeteria, the one they probably appropriated."

There was a time when our banter would have been sharp as blades, meant to cut imperceptible slits until the loser fell apart. Now the laughter turned to hot steam in the cold Michigan winter, and I stifled the urge to slip snow down the back of his tailored jacket since it was only a couple more blocks.

The lights of the city were slowly being repaired or installed, but the old ones blinked above us, wind pushing at the battered metal poles, making them whine. Haven, tucked in the hectic blocks of Wayne State, was like coming into a different world. It was one of the pockets of the city that bustled, night students, magical and human, pouring from buildings.

We slipped around a chattering group of changelings and goblins on the corner, and I shoved at the rickety door of Haven. The bell immediately belted out the score to *Gladiator*. Luna and Gaia Darkchild, the werewolf brother and sister who owned the small coffee shop and the rooms below, constantly changed the theme. Done without the other's knowledge, it often led to loud bickering around the espresso machine. However, the twins both stared at me with identical dark hazel eyes from the counter as we shook off the cold.

"You two look like you saw a ghost."

The words made them blink, and as if coming awake, Gaia shoved at her brother, who dripped water on the counter from the rag in his hand. "Luna, you get my crossword wet, you're dead," she said, voice harsh, as she pointed a finger at me. "You might as well be; haven't seen you in months. You, what, getting coffee from Starbucks now?"

I glanced at the visible Starbucks cup on their back counter. "You seem to like it enough."

Luna dropped his rag into the bucket by his feet, hands scraping through his shaggy dark hair to pull it back. "It's a mixed bag. They put their employees through college. But anti-union? Gross. Their cups are prettier than ours though."

"Learn how to draw and ours will look good," Gaia said. "They just wanted an in with the magic community, but I told them I wouldn't end up like Teavana, swallowed up by the man."

"Psssh, you just knew Grandma would wolfsbane you."

Her eyes flashed red as Gaia glared at her brother. It made her wide, bronzed features fierce. "I'm going to drown you in the sink."

Unconcerned, Luna shrugged. "Then who would brew for you?"

Haven had belonged to the Darkchild pack long before a Fitzpatrick stepped foot in North America. What started out as a shop for herbs and ingredients for the magical community had evolved into a coffee house in the late eighties. Technically open to the public, few humans came here for the coffee, since it was often laced with whatever magic Luna was dabbling with that day, and its effects depended on if he liked you. A charisma shot might wear off right before a big presentation, or it might score you a second interview. Luck could get a lecture canceled, or it could end up with you finding a twenty that covered a parking ticket you weren't expecting.

While the coffee was drink-at-your-own-risk, the rooms downstairs made the Darkchilds their real profit. Five spaces, identical in size, that all held a long table and chairs where humans and magic clashed every weekend in battle, their field a board, their prize whatever the GM dictated. The Darkchild siblings, like their parents before them, had been able to evolve their business. While Luna and Gaia lacked human barista abilities, they were known in the city as the hotspot for *D&D.*

"So, you want a cup or what?" Luna asked. Then his eyes narrowed. "Or are you here for the game? Because they started already."

"I'll have a cup of the Irish, black," I said. "Get Graceland a 313[17]."

"Oh, for the love of Gods," he spat and stomped off to the small group of tables.

Luna and Gaia grinned at each other, all sharp teeth, as they nodded together. "You got it!"

Setting to work, Gaia ground the beans and Luna approached his minifridge, plastered in various band stickers, where thick rubber gloves hung from the handle. Looking more like it belonged in a dorm, it held some of the most powerful elixirs from the Darkchilds' vaults. Carefully, as if he were handling a newborn, Luna held up one of the various beakers to the light of the shop and his eyes flashed blue, the beta to his sister's alpha.

"This batch isn't ready yet; would it be all right if I swapped out the foresight for something else?" he asked me.

"Sure, just make sure it's nothing too embarrassing. I'm going to try to get him back to his date before midnight."

Luna nodded, tongue between his teeth, and went back to rummaging through his cooler. Gaia slid me a mug across the counter.

"You look tired, Brig."

"I am," I said honestly and took a sip.

If there was one thing the twins could brew, it was their cup of the Irish. It always smelled of peat moss and Gran's kitchen. For the first time since getting off the phone with Mama, I felt my shoulders relax.

---

17 Three parts grit; 1 part espresso; 3 parts passion.

"You sure you don't want anything extra in it?" Gaia asked. "We got some focus and patience ready. Your mother sent us a shipment of concentrated lion's mane from her Evermore stocks."

The mention of my mother's market down south made me smile, but I shook my head. Before I took over as Senior Pilgrim, I dabbled in everything the twins made. Research, I argued to my father. Really it was more about letting someone—well, something—else be in control.

"No, I'm good. Gotta work clean tonight," I said and accepted the second mug that Luna pushed at me. "What's the verdict?"

"A mixologist never reveals his secrets," Luna responded and wiggled his eyebrows. "But I think his date will be happy."

The twins both laughed at his joke as if it was hysterical, shoving at each other from behind the counter. Shaking my head, I went to the tiny table Graceland had chosen. He stared out into the city, watching people as he always did, confused and wistful.

"You ok?" I asked and plopped the mugs down.

"Yeah, it's weird with Christmas gone. The city seems to sink, doesn't it?" he said, eyes not leaving the streets. "Like the lights are gone, and I have this tugging in my gut."

"This time of year, it's always hard for you."

He turned from the window and expelled a long breath. "You'd think I be over it by now. How many centuries has it been?"

It was rhetorical, so I shrugged. "In the first grade, Alyssa Elder called me a slur. I bit her so hard she needed stitches. If I saw that bitch on the street right now, I'd do it again."

There was a second when he blinked, as if I'd struck him mute. Then his laughter had him leaning back. "I—I will never understand humans. Magic's erratic nature makes sense; humans are just meat with blunt fingernails."

It was true, so I took another sip instead of agreeing. He no longer looked like a lost kid, and we needed to get to work.

"So, we got a problem," I said and took out the photos. "This girl—notice anything by her left ear?"

"Her ear?" he repeated as he leaned forward to look, then shot back up.

"Yeah," I commiserated. "So, one of the girls is the baby sister to fucking Lenore Bastille, and I got two illegal girls at Gomorrah who say they got contracts with Dillan Holloway. They say that he had contracts on all the dead girls."

Instead of answering, Graceland rubbed at his lip. Finally, he grabbed his mug and took a drink. "You sure they weren't playing you?"

"No, but when I went through the files, I felt it. It was a beast."

"With no backup or wards, I'm assuming."

"I'm fine, *Dad*," I groused. "Holloway could have a backer or a client he can't control."

"Doesn't mean they aren't playing you."

"They're practically babies. I got Delilah coming to see them Monday."

"Even if they're telling the truth, Holloway is untouchable without evidence. Even *you* can't just haul him in," he stressed.

I tapped a fingertip against the picture of Annabel Lee Bastille. "These girls—"

"Sirens," he corrected.

"Girls," I repeated through gritted teeth, "deserve justice. They deserve to rest knowing they weren't forgotten about. We're going to have to pull Lenore in before this gets out."

"Ok then why—" he stopped himself, head drawn back, to side-eye me. "Shit, you want to do something illegal. Spit it out."

"Grace—"

"No, don't wheedle. Just rip the Band-Aid off," he demanded, hands windmilling to get me to continue.

"I'm breaking into the Manoogian Mansion. Tonight. You're helping."

The silence spread across the table, and I tried not to fidget as he stared. I felt as he attempted to poke inside my head, the small wisps of dead leaves and ozone curling into my nostrils. With a lick of my lips, I locked down the parts no one is allowed to see.

"You're getting better at that," he murmured. "Ok, so how are we doing this?"

"What?"

"Have you gone deaf?"

"You never give in that easy."

"Tis the season" he said bitterly. "I can't die, and if you do, maybe I'll be released from service."

"Doubtful. You'll just become Crisco's pooper scooper." I grinned at his bafflement. "Mama has a seeing eye gator."

"I don't think I'll ever fully understand humans."

"We say that about you gods too," I reminded him and tapped the photo still between us. "He probably won't have girls on the mansion grounds—even Holloway isn't that stupid. Records, though, he'd have those."

"Locked down, behind alarms and lasers and dogs," Graceland pointed out.

I leaned back in my chair, teeth digging into my bottom lip, and glanced around the shop. Gaia was balanced on the counter doing her crossword while Luna, still in his thick plastic gloves, gently poured a blue liquid into a Styrofoam container.

"Guys?" I said and watched as their ears twitched a second before they turned.

"Need a refill?" Luna asked, shaking the container at us. "I got a new mix. It's three parts rizz and one part blue raspberry lemonade."

"Nope, no rizz," Gaia said,."You pay bills, you are too old to say rizz."

Luna lowered the container. "Buzzkill."

"That's better," Gaia said.

"You know what we need," Graceland said. "You two have ears like bats and you gossip like Fates."

Instead of flashing her eyes, Gaia swung over the counter with a jar in hand. "Put a dollar in."

"What?" Graceland asked, baffled.

"You use a slur in this building, you put a buck in the jar. Had to start it when we got some dumb ass humans in here."

"I didn't—bats?"

Gaia grinned and shook the jar again. "Two dollars."

"It's not a slur, it's an animal!" Graceland argued. "Senior Pilgrim?"

"Are you serious? You're going to invoke mediation over two bucks?" I asked.

Whipping out his cellphone, he tapped rapidly, then shoved his phone in Gaia's face. "See? An animal. It's a human expression!"

"Humans are racists," Gaia pointed out.

"That's true," I agreed.

"For the love of—" Stopping himself, Graceland drew out his wallet and shoved the money into the jar. "Happy? Now can you help?"

With a nod, she slid the jar to her brother. "Manoogian Mansion huh? That's a tough nut. We got a shipment yesterday. Powder from Sunrider, says it took him years of trust building with the locals in Cairo. Luna will mix it up with some of the marigold dust Ms. Odette sent us."

"Has Sunrider caught up with Caja Scabbath yet? Last I heard she was in Egypt," I asked, thinking of the burglary.

"No idea, but you'd be better off hitting up Flippen since his sister is almost always in the wind. If Sunrider had, he probably would have mentioned it. He's got a bit of a crush on her," Luna said, eyes still on the jar as he held it up to the light.

"Luna," Gaia sighed and pressed a hand to her head, "that was told in confidence."

"Is anyone gonna say what that shit does?" Graceland pressed, pointing at the mixture.

"Nothing for you. You can make yourself invisible," Gaia said slowly, as if speaking to a child. "It will make Brigitte undetectable, visually, to humans, betrayers, and fallen. If they got fay magic, you know the drill here."

"No harm to thyself," I said, referencing the Darkchild oath to true fay.

"As for the dogs—well, you got the dog lord himself sitting across from you," she said on her way back to her crossword.

"Cerberus is my dog," Graceland pointed out. "Of course they like me."

The werewolf jumped back onto the counter and glanced at her brother. "Luna, are we considering dog a slur for us?"

Ignoring his sister and Graceland's indignant squawk, the smaller werewolf screwed a lid on a small jar of gold-streaked white dust.

Pulling the thick gloves off with his teeth, he held the jar up to the light again.

"It'll probably give you two hours max. Sunrider said the bones have to be old—older the bones, more powerful the powder. These are out of some tomb he got caught in," Luna said, more to himself than the room.

Gaia gently took the jar from her brother, face soft for once. "Luna, have you eaten today?"

Blinking at his still raised, now empty hand, Luna shook his head. Setting the jar next to the register, Gaia nudged her brother to the door that led up to the small apartment they lived in.

"You go on now. Eat what's in the fridge then take a nap," she said, making her eyes flash. "Alpha's orders."

Ducking his head, Luna waved to everyone, and in silence we listened to the sound of his feet going up the stairs. It was closing in on a decade since the hunters—ones not sanctioned by Pilgrims—tried to eradicate the Darkchild pack. I was an extremely angry sixteen when I helped Gaia carry a limp Luna from the burning building, his body covered in the various magical liquids and powders of their storeroom. The smell of magic dying, crackling, and suffocating had lived inside me since that night. It was the first and only time I'd seen my father dispense Pilgrim justice against humans.

Luna had been in line to be alpha, training for a day that was set long in the future. In the flash of gasoline, the light of a match, the Darkchilds' future line was reduced to the two twins and their grandmother. With Luna stuck somewhere between the past and the present, Gaia knew there was only one choice. So, the hot-headed younger sister who'd never wanted to be in charge accepted her role as alpha. Not that a true pack existed—it'd been years of only the three Darkchilds, no one to train, no one to mediate. Stagnation kept them profitable; with the insurance money, Gaia gave her mother and father a proper burial and rebuilt Haven. She didn't have her father's quick smile or her mother's shrewd business sense, but she had Luna. She wasn't alone, and they were safe.

"He's better," I told her with a gentle voice Gaia normally hated. "He's come a long way."

"I wish I could say I helped, but it was really Margot," the werewolf admitted, arms wrapped around herself. "We've missed you—I know why, but it's been hard not expecting the two of you to be in the corner plotting."

Margot took to Luna on the first visit. He was mute then, but Margot somehow understood, and afterwards dragged me there twice a week. Together she and Luna would paint or do puzzles, Margot chatting away, as I drank coffee with Gaia. Then one day, when Margot asked a question, Luna responded with, "Did you know if you mix two parts Mello Yello with one-part graceveil and one-part edible glitter, you can pass as a fairy for an hour?"

"I couldn't come back right away. It still feels like she's here," I admitted. "But it wasn't fair to you guys. Thanks for the help."

"Treaty is next week."

My lips twitched at the bluntness. "Really? I'd forgotten."

Taking the cue, Gaia dropped it and bagged the small jar. "That'll be fourteen fifty."

When I raised a brow, the werewolf laughed and held out her hand.

"I'm running a business, Pilgrim, but since you're on the blessed mailing list, I'll give you a promotional pen."

Fishing out my wallet, I handed her some crumpled bills. "What if I was on the cursed mailing list?"

Shoving the money into the cash register, Gaia sharply smiled. "Luna made a gum that makes you sneeze thirty times in a row. Safe travels."

CHAPTER 5

"Are we a hundred percent sure that we should do this now?" Graceland asked for the twentieth time since we were dropped off. "And why did I have to pay for the Uber?"

Even in the darkness, I imagined his face, brows pushing down as he complained. Letting that image keep me calm, I kept my gait steady as we passed into the Berry Historic District.

"Consider it a job expense, because you are so much of a coward that you already made yourself invisible, so if someone feels like it, they can call the cops on the lone weirdo wandering the streets."

"Penny handles my taxes; send it to her. You're walking with purpose, not skulking. No one is going to call," he pointed out.

"Doesn't make me less Black, Graceland."

There was a beat of silence, and from my left his voice came softly, "Humans are terrible."

They were no better or worse than their Creators, I wanted to point out, but that was a touchy subject with him. Around us the houses loomed like ghosts, casting historic shadows of a time past. It took lifetimes, but slowly the neighborhood had rebuilt itself. There were husks, shells of homes to remind the city of its fracturing in other parts of the city, but here, the anger bled away until only weariness remained. I glanced back towards Jefferson and shivered. It wasn't anger, but the despair of ghosts could cut to the bone just as quickly.

"Time to use the powder," he whispered.

The jar had been clenched in my hand since we got out of the car of some random college kid. In the faint light of the streetlamp, I paused. There were few magics I was hesitant about, but illusion magic, no matter how carefully crafted, was always tricky. Unscrewing the lid, I motioned for Graceland, and out of the darkness came his open hands. No more than a couple tablespoons were dumped out onto his palms; bone white streaked with thin lines of gold.

"Baron Samedi, Maman Brigitte, grant me passage in the spaces between. In offering, my soul, the flesh of my flesh, as my mother before me," I said and nodded to him.

From the shadows, he inhaled sharply, and the powder blasted from his floating palms. It swirled around me, instantly filling my lungs.

"You know, in the year I've been stuck with you, that's like the ninth time you've offered your soul up as collateral to various beings."

Glancing down, I grinned when I saw only empty space, but now on the same plane, I could see Graceland and his annoyed frown. "So what?"

"What's the plan when they come to collect?"

Invisible to the world, we crossed the street and stood at the end of the long, straight drive. The mansion, backlit by the various soft yellow lights of the lawn, looked to be watching us. From behind my back, I could feel the anxiety Graceland emanated. For all his bluster, I knew it wasn't for himself; it was for me.

"I figure it's like the Thunderdome," I said idly. "He must have given security time off. I remember last year he had two goons, humans that stood guarding the front door."

"Thunderdome?"

"Yeah, two men enter, one man leaves? You haven't seen *Mad Max*? Add it to the list," I whispered as we crept around the driveway to the back of the house. "You'd love the costumes."

There was a door, one I remembered solely because I fought my way out of it. Money wasn't the only thing that had bought Margot her freedom. Jiggling the knob, I cursed and dropped to my knees.

"Give me a sec—keep a lookout."

"So instead of just entering, we're getting arrested for breaking too?" he said from the darkness. "Where's your kit?"

Pulling a pin from my hair, I showed it to him. It was a finger bone, slender and glossy white even in the darkness.

"You had that in your hair!" Graceland hissed loudly.

"Keep your voice down," I admonished and silently said a prayer. I slipped the nail of the finger into the lock and almost instantly, it clicked, the noise harsh in the cold around us.

Shoving at the door, I clipped the pin back into my braid and motioned for Graceland to follow. The garage was empty of Holloway's BMW; it was Friday night—well, almost Saturday morning—but he probably wouldn't stumble back in until dawn curled over his boathouse.

"We need to talk about the fact that you took off all your protections but kept a human body part in your hair," Graceland whispered and tried the door that led to the main house. "It's unlocked."

"It was a gift."

He stood frozen in the doorway, mouth pulled in disgust, "Someone gifted you a finger?"

"That can crack any lock," I pointed out and tugged him out of the doorway. "It won't trip alarms either."

"Impressive, but it's still a piece of a body—whose body, I might add?"

We moved through the back of the house, through the ridiculous number of sunrooms that Margot and I once woke up in after a party Holloway threw. The way the morning sun glinted off the water of the Detroit River was almost enough to make a person forget how many bodies lay at the bottom of it. Holloway's house was the same.

"Harry Houdini. Bess, his widow, gave me it on my sixteenth birthday," I said fondly.

"She died in 1943."

Nodding in agreement, I pressed myself against the doorframe and looked out into the empty main room next to the stairs. "Didn't stop her from eating most of my cake. It always gets me that you can literally remember everyone's death day, but you haven't seen *The Lion King*."

"I've seen *Hamlet*, the original production," he reminded me with a haughty sniff. "I do not need to see cartoon animals prancing—"

I cut off his words with a slap of my hand over his mouth. Before he could bite me—or worse, lick me—a shadow passed by. It swept up the stairs faster than any human was capable of, not bothering to look in our direction. I dropped my hand and, with one last scan of the room, sprinted after it.

The pulse in my neck throbbed, heart in my throat as I took the stairs and stared up at the shadow on the landing. Even without features, I felt the curiosity that radiated from it as it cocked its head at me, but the minute my boot found the top step, it was gone again. Graceland stood at the landing, but I felt fingers, like winter, run down my spine.

"Go right, check out the rooms. See if you can find anything," I instructed quietly, and without waiting for his response, ran.

At all of Holloway's parties, the upstairs was sealed off by both magic and human guards. Saying a silent prayer, I crept, invisible, down the hall. Though steeped in darkness, the shadow was somehow visible, like staring into an abyss.

"Do you want to tell me what you need?" I asked, hand outstretched. "Maybe I can help?"

The shadow shook its head and pointed to the half open door behind it. Giving the shape a short bow, I skirted around it. The touch of fingers brushed against my spine. A warning even before the taste of leather and rot hit my tongue. I ducked and flattened against the wall as the door was wrenched open, the man nearly clipping my shoulder as he stepped into the hall. Invisible, I clenched my fists and waited as he took another step, then another. I was about to exhale when he froze, his head turning to the side, nostrils flared. From my angle, I only saw one eye, but that was enough to make my irritation at having to distract a guard turn like bad fish in my gut. Vlkodlak.

I eased back out of sight, moving to the desk to look out the window. The betrayer moon[18] shone back at me as I heard the first crack of bone in the hall. Of fucking course. I held my breath as he entered the room, watched the painful bending and breaking of his fingers, bones and claws bloody as he shuffled. He would be in pain, body slowly breaking and remolding itself over the next week, until the moment when the full moon wiped his mind. It was a sight I'd gotten used to, from the other side of Morphosis safe transition rooms, but those were people that wanted safety and support.

"I can smell you, Senior Pilgrim; he told us you'd smell different

---

18 A Judas moon during the night. It is the cycle of the moon that most effects cursed magic, heightening its power but making them more unstable.

at first, but it's a trick, like your power. I was warned you'd stick your nose into our business," he informed me as he took another step forward. "You shouldn't be scared."

Bullshit. Any Pilgrim worth their salt stepped lightly and with sharp eyes around Deep European magic. The home of Henry Fitzpatrick, betrayer of the first Pilgrims, brutal, savage and often a curse on already monstrous people, those who carved magic from marrow, who killed because it fed their magic. These weren't the cursed who lived in my town, victims that didn't want to be mindless, that took the precautions I'd crusaded for since I finished training. These weren't the true werewolves that the fay blessed in order to save them from annihilation.

These were what the Darkchilds called abominations.

Slipping off my glove, I curled two fingers into one of my leather pouches and prayed silently to my namesake.

"I can smell you too buddy, and let me tell you, it's not great," I said and became visible.

The vlkodlak's nostrils flared, eyes bloodshot and, like the shadow, he cocked his head. His olive skin was beaded with sweat, matted brown hair already patching across his skin. "You're just a little thing, aren't you? This won't be fair."

"If you walk away now, no harm, no foul."

His laughter rumbled deep in his chest, and my eyes dropped to his hands. They were curled, nails wicked.

"I will walk away, Pilgrim, with the taste of your blood in my mouth."

I had an insult—a real banger—ready, but as he lunged across the space, my mouth went dry. I lifted my hand from the pouch, pale-green dust thrown. It covered his eyes, and as he swore, I sidestepped, watching the powder change his eyes to pure white. With a sharp howl, he clawed at his face as his knees collapsed.

"Creature of magic, you have broken laws held sacred by people far wiser than yourself. By the rites of Mother Eorthe and the All-father, the violation of your magic is punishable by death," I said. "Thankfully for you, I'm feeling generous."

The vlkodlak gave one long groan before he went limp, and I

resisted the urge to kick him. Now visible, I was on borrowed time. My fingers danced over the dark wood of the desk, searching for knots, scars, anything. When nothing gave, I moved to the drawers—empty. Another flicker went down my spine, faster now, like an ice cube sliding down my back. Picking up the pace, I spread out what was piled on the desktop. Blueprints, uptown; a deal with Madam LeFore for several antiques; receipts for cigars, sex toys, renovations. Flipping the pages, I scanned quickly and felt my teeth set, the anger running through me.

"Did you find—oh, shit!" Graceland exclaimed as he gave the downed vlkodlak a wide berth. "You ok?"

Tossing him my phone, I spared the limp body of the creature another sneer. "Take pictures, check his pockets. I want to know if he's got papers to be here."

With a nod, he went about it as I kept reading. It wasn't until he held the phone out that I realized my hands were shaking. It was the unfortunate side effect to anger, always had been. Recognizing it, Graceland took the paper and read through it. Setting it down, he took my hands in his own and rubbed briskly.

"You gotta tell me what you see on that paper that I don't. To me it's just a list of building supplies."

He rarely gave out kindness, had once admitted to me he often thought he was incapable of it. I'd vehemently disagreed then, and I tried not to reject it now because my anger was palpable, poison burning my bones.

"I'll show you instead," I said, voice flat, and led the way to the door.

"You just gonna leave him there?"

"It's powdered absinthe, chalk, and bone. We've got time."

The house was settled. The shadow was nowhere in sight, and the magic clamoring for my attention, gone. Silent, I navigated the house as if it were my own and led Graceland across the back lawn that would have made Gatsby proud. It wasn't until my hands were on the heavy handle of the boathouse that I heard his sharp inhale of understanding. Nowhere in the house looked renovated.

"Brig, we should call Horace," he said. "If what's in here is what I think, he can help."

"Without proof or a warrant?" I shook my head. "Come on, coward."

Even though I led the way, I still reached back for his hand as we waded through the muddy blackness. His fingers gripped mine firmly as we went to the back wall.

"It's here," I said to the darkness. "I know you're here, you bastard."

"What?"

"Switch. Old Prohibition tunnels, small speakeasy. They run all over the city, but these ones run out to Belle Isle. He renovated them—I'm assuming to hold his girls and run them without the city knowing."

The silence broke when my fingers found the rusted hinge. Flipping it, there was a creak, then the scrape of the floor in front of me. The sound echoed past us, and Graceland's voice followed.

"And you know this how?"

The suspiciousness was expected, but the sympathy made my stomach clench as I took the first step. Around me, fluorescent light flickered on, following the length of stairs that spiraled down. That was new.

"Margot and I came to a couple parties down here."

"Ahh. When I was still working for your father. So, do you think there'll be liquor at this horror show?"

"Holloway doesn't party the way he used to," I said and took the last step. "Everyone in the city thought he was actually growing up. Turns out, he upgraded from playboy to flesh slaver."

The lights cracked on like glowsticks above us, and where once there'd been something akin to Adam's Rest on a slow night, there was now a hard-concrete foundation and rows of steel cages. The smell of blood and urine burned in my lungs, but what was in the last cage on the end stopped the acrid air in my chest.

"Is that a siren?" Graceland whispered.

"Go send for Horace."

"Brig—"

"Now!"

As his footsteps slapped against the stone, I stifled the urge to run with him. Instead, I forced my feet forward, slow and measured, to where the dead siren lay. She was young, maybe early teens, painted hands still gripping the cage, eyes wide and milky. The same slash as the one in the alley circled her neck, blood dripping down like crystals spun on a thin red cord.

"Oh honey, what did he do to you?" I whispered, tensing when I heard Graceland come back down the stairs. "She's got the cut on her neck, same as the others, Grace—"

The rest of the words locked up in my throat as water hit the floor. It was achingly familiar: soft plops in the summers when I would run in from the beach and drip onto Mama's floors, begging for lemonade. Turning my head, I gazed at the shadow from upstairs, realizing what it was. Here, it took the shape of a girl, long black hair pulled in front of her face and the smell of bog—decay and dirty water—filled my nose.

"I need ten seconds," I said desperately to the death omen. "Please."

The banshee radiated remorse as her bloated fingers peeled back her hair to expose eyes filled with water. Quickly, I pulled out my phone and snapped photos of the crime scene, trying to count the seconds in my head. At eight, I shoved the phone back into my pocket, just as the girl opened her mouth.

Through sheer force of will, I got my knees locked as her wail hit me, slamming me into the cage. Metal ripped at my jeans, but the pain only forced me forward to the exit. I just had to get to Graceland.

The first claw went in and out of my side so fast I didn't have time to gasp, the blow taking the air with it. My lungs were empty, but my tongue tasted damp fur, Mama's hand ground chalk and bone thick in my mouth. Shoving away, the world spun, and I stumbled back, catching myself on another cage.

The vlkodlak, face still covered in powder, licked clean the claw he'd slid into me. "I've tasted plenty of you, but nothing quite so sweet."

If I hadn't been actively bleeding out, I would have rolled my eyes. I hissed at the sharp pain and shoved my palm against the wound, feeling the wet gush against my hand. Even though the smell of blood and his fur turned my stomach, I lifted the dripping palm to my face and dragged it across. It stung my eyes, but I curled my lip up, tongue tasting it as I grinned.

"How about you come for seconds then?"

His eyes narrowed at that, nostrils flaring as he scented the air. "I've already killed you, Pilgrim."

He could've been lying, but from the amount of blood soaked through my shirt, I didn't doubt it. Still, I wasn't about to let him leave the bunker alive, so I shoved up my sleeve. Jabbing fingers into my wound, I bit the inside of my cheek, bringing the blood to my forearm. The red smeared in a sloppy heart shape, the series of dots and lines running horizontally.

"Do you really think drawing will scare me, Pilgrim?" he asked, amused.

"Maman Brigitte, Queen of the loa, accept the offering of blood and grant me short passage."

"You call to your gods," he scoffed, motioning to the room around him. "No god would step foot in this place."

He was right. Mother Eorthe and the Allfather would never wade through blood and death. That's what they created their children for, and when those children rebelled, they were never without either. The vlkodlak knew nothing about those children and what they were willing to do to be free.

"Maman, I must complete my duty. Grant me focus, no matter how bitter, and I will—"

"Enough!" he bellowed and took a step forward. "If you—"

It was as if his threat was swallowed up, step stuttering as he scented the air. "Healing."

I wasn't, not truly, but he didn't need to know that.

"That's because unlike you, I'm not cursed, dog."

It was like a switch, or a leash—the way his eyes went to amber slits and his body arched back before flying forward. I didn't even try to move, just steeled myself for impact. His body easily forced me down, my head slapping into the cement with a sickening crack. My vision spun with black spots as he rested a single claw against my throat.

"You've been more fun than the others. Haas was right about your power. It's too bad Roman wasn't here for you. He'd like your taste," he said as he slid the nail across my neck like a lover's caress. "You have spirit; perhaps, unlike her, you were meant for the bite."

I tried to speak, gagging, and he leaned up just enough that rotted air flooded back into my lungs. I twisted, flicking the blade hidden against my wrist with my thumb. Even as it cut into my own flesh, I screamed and swung. Blood rained down, hot and pumping from his throat. Again and again, I slashed, face turned slightly to avoid the splashes. He slumped on top of me, taking the rest of my air, but I held the blade to his face. The stench of death had already set in, as it always did with magic.

"Brig!"

The weight lifted was a relief, then pain arched like lightning through me. Frantically, I shoved my hands against the wounds, hoping pressure would relieve the pain. There were harsh whispers in my skull, and I shook my head, refusing to give the spirits a foothold.

"Brigitte! Listen to me, your lung—I have to—"

Graceland sounded miles away, like I was falling underwater. I tried to reach out, but pain came sharp and crystalline, pulling me up against my will.

"I got you! Hold onto my shoulders."

My fingers felt loose, but I managed, because he had me. He was warm. Graceland was never warm.

"I'm not," he grunted. "You're cold."

I hadn't realized I'd spoken. Shaking my head, I tried to focus. "My phone. Is my phone ok?"

"Hell, Brigitte, now is not the time to be worried about your nudes."

The laughter shook my body until it ended in a whimper. "Photos. I have photos of the scene. Recorded that fuck. For Horace. Make sure he gets it. Will is in my desk."

I saw his thick eyebrows collapse in confusion, then rise quickly along with his pitch.

"Oh, fuck no, you are not dying. I'm not about to be bound to Bronson for the last year of my servitude," he said as he shifted me to wave at the street. "Our ride is here."

"Is it a chariot?" I joked and spat a little blood from my mouth.

For a second, he stared, then sighed. "Damn, that would have been better. It's an Uber. Unfortunately for him, it's the same sap who dropped us off. Be quiet and try not to moan."

Gritting my teeth, I nodded when he placed me on the sidewalk and gripped the frame of the door to steady myself.

"Hi!" the driver exclaimed. "Small world."

Graceland pulled out four hundred-dollar bills. "If I give this to you, you do not look back here, and you blow reds."

The driver's dark eyes flickered to me, and I tried to give my best smile, hoping there wasn't too much blood on my teeth. It must have passed, because the boy plucked the bills from Graceland's hand and we were off.

Half sprawled against the seat and the window, I finally caught sight of myself and the pen sticking out of my chest. Reaching, I twisted it so I could see the writing. *Haven Emporium and Brew.*

"You couldn't breathe. I had to improvise."

"I should have taken Gaia up on that magic shot. Yours sucked."

"Do you know how much Starbucks charged me for that half-shot of luck? It's like the avocados all over again."

"Phone," I said. "Quit complaining about money."

He showed me the screen. "It's fine. I think I deserve the credit for that since I talked you into that shatterproof case."

"Sure," I managed to get out before hissing. "Grace, I'm going to pass out."

Grabbing my wrist, he turned the bloody painting of Maman's symbol toward himself. His fingers were like lava as they ran over the symbol, and from his mouth came a language I couldn't decipher. Struggling, I focused against the pain and realized why: it was tongues, the original language of the Allfather. Graceland's father.

His fingers settled my hand over my chest gently. "Sleep, you'll survive till we get home."

Heat curled around me, but not like lava, or the pain of a flash fire. There was no suffocation, only the relaxing of muscles, the tangle of limbs and straining kisses. It was the heat of promises murmured as we stared at the mural Margot painted on the ceiling. Death rides a pale horse, except it was Graceland on a unicorn.

"It's time to wake up," Graceland said, voice cracking like he could see what I'd dreamed.

"No."

"Did someone shoot her!?"

The voice was deep, but panicked, and pulled me from the dream like a gunshot. I gave my favorite bartender and only landlord a smile.

"Jesus, she's got blood all over her teeth! I'm calling an ambulance," Thaddeus informed us, hand coming up to touch my face before it dropped back to his side.

"No. Just help me get her to the backyard," Graceland said.

The words had me fully awake, and for the first time, I struggled against him. "No, no way, just let me die. I'm not doing it."

His quick glare stilled my fussing as he carried me through the bar, the kitchen, and finally out the back door. It was a small plot of land, the majority taken up by the garden Thaddeus tended religiously. Even in the winter, under his callused hands, produce bloomed. It was one of the reasons the Bearded Folly attracted impeccable Yelp reviews.

"Oh, this is going to be easy," Graceland said, voice surprisingly cheerful as he dumped me next to the carrots. "He's already turned up most of the earth."

"What?" Thaddeus asked.

"Hold her hand," he instructed, grabbing a shovel. "Keep her distracted."

Fumbling, Thaddeus gripped my fingers and pushed some of the hair from my sweaty face. "You got into trouble?"

Giving a tight nod, I squeezed his hand and tried to focus on him. His eyes were soft, brown like pond water in a full face graced with a glorious black beard. On one drunken night, after we buried Margot, I informed him I wanted to drag him by his dark curls to my bed. He looked as worried then too.

"Vlkodlak, Deep Europe," I pushed out around a pant. "Hunting sirens. Girls. Not sure why yet."

"It was for sport," Graceland said. "It's time."

"Graceland, I don't want to do this."

"You should have thought about that before you got ganked," he informed me.

The earth was soft and cool like a pillow, and I wanted to rub my face against it when the pain came, stealing my momentary peace.

"We're running out of time," Graceland said. "Shit, Brig, you got the flask? Thaddeus, grab it from her pocket."

The sun was starting to curl up in the corners of my vision, and I felt the pressure of a hand in my pocket. The hysterical bubble of laughter burst out as I remembered his quiet concern at my drunken brashness.

"It's nearly empty."

The sigh from Graceland was long suffering. "Of course it is. Do you have peanuts in the bar?"

"What?"

"Peanuts! He loves peanuts. Get me two bowls."

There was one last squeeze then Thaddeus was gone. I watched as Graceland, grumbling, unscrewed the cap on the flask and poured the contents on my chest. Hot pepper rum seared the wound on my side, and I gripped the earth, feeling it slip between the skin and nails of my fingers.

"I got the peanuts."

"Good," Graceland said and, as with the rum, just dumped them on me. "Now stand back as I bury her."

"Bury her!?"

Somehow, I managed to get my eyes open, giving a smile. "Thaddeus, it's ok. Trust me."

"Stand back," Graceland said again. "Good luck, boss."

The sun, all light really, peeled from my vision with each shovelful. The dirt should have felt oppressive, the weight collapsing my lungs, but I let the air go willingly. I tasted the earth, the spice of Mama's rum. Then, like my sight, it all faded to nothing.

CHAPTER 6

I was seven years old the first time the ghosts found me. They were in the walls, in the streets, in the very room I slept in. Dad was terrified, but Mama? Her face shone with pride. Within a week, she took me to the fields of our ancestors. Among the rows of peppers, I clung to her as we watched the ghosts crouch to examine the plants, to tend them, to pull them. She led the way, waded past the singing, the weeping, the bleeding as the beating sun left trails of sweat down our backs. The white paint of the main house had long since disappeared in the appetite of a great fire, but Mama poked through the rubble until she found a small doll made of straw. With care she handed it to me, and I pressed it to my chest, and we stared at the ruins of the house.

"What do you see, baby?"

"Hurt, Mama."

Clucking her tongue, she bent down to fill her palm with ash. "Yes, terrible sorrow. Your great grandfather lost his first wife here, his children. But can you not hear the songs, the joys, the tears our people shared together in triumph, in hope?"

"How can you hear anything besides the fire?"

"Let the fire burn away the screams. Let it cleanse you, Brigitte. Pain cannot sustain you. Hope, the promise of new growth—that will be the way forward."

Odette Fitzpatrick was an optimist, a ray of sunshine with a spine of steel and a heart soft for every living creature. I often wondered how she could stand in the face of everything she'd been forced to endure without flinching, and while I'd learned many lessons from her, there was one I never reconciled. Pain was never gone. Even after a bone broke, regardless of its thickening, strengthening, there would be days when it rained and the bone would throb, as physical a reminder as a scar.

Pain wasn't a reminder; it was a state of being. Agony raced along every meridian of my bones as I crawled from the open grave. The sun blistered me immediately, the scent of spice and heat bubbling my tongue, my lips. My legs refused to listen, one step twisting my knees to the dusty ground. I needed to get up, move, but my legs finally decided there was no way they would follow me again.

Footsteps approached, thundering, the sun too bright to make out anything but the shape of hands as they reached down for me. I couldn't find it in me to resist, to spit out the order to be left alone as they lifted. Neither man looked at me, firm fingers gripping my underarms but letting my toes trail through the dust. It was almost a relief to not have to walk, even though my shoulders ached, but when we crossed from the suffocating sun to the shady willows, I saw their faces. Rich ochre features, beautiful and gleaming, were marred by the coarse white threads that stitched their mouths shut, embedded like a tree that grows around things left behind.

I knew the punishment well, common amongst those who gave lip service to the loa during life, and almost in reflex, I licked my own lips. Neither of them paid attention, only lifting me higher as we approached the small cabin surrounded by the fields of waxy, bright peppers. The heat of the porch dripped sweat across my face, burning my eyes. As I struggled to shake my head at the blinding salt, the door creaked open. The soft, old, worn wood helped me slide as the men tossed me inside, but the pain still escaped like helium through a balloon. Blinking through hazy pain and darkness, I barely made out the throne and the man lounging in it.

A skinny man, much older than he looked, leered from under his black top hat at me. His fingers, long like his entire being, tapped against one of the various skulls that cradled him. Purple pinpricks glowed from the shape of his face as he tilted his head in my direction before settling into the endless black behind the half mask of bone he wore.

"Brigitte Laveau Fitzpatrick, ya soul belong *to* me," he said, voice echoing around the small room.

I opened my mouth to scold him, but my lips wouldn't move. Panic drove my palms from stabilizing on the floor to the plushness of my mouth. Coarse thread scratched under the pads of my fingers, a single line of stitches sealing my scream inside my throat.

"I've waited for this day," he sneered.

"Baron Samedi, knock that nonsense off!"

Around me, the world shifted, the shadow cabin cracking in half. As the pieces fell away, the space grew and brightened. It was a home, worn but clean, and—lips free—I grinned as Maman wielded a large cooking spoon like a sword against the man on the throne.

"Don't you chouk[19] while our baby is in pain!" she shrieked, slapping the hat off the man's head.

Ducking, he tumbled from the throne, disappeared, then popped out of the shadows next to me. He pulled me up as a shield, and I didn't bother fighting.

"Dezole![20] Dezole! Protect me, Pilgrim!"

As his fingers curled around my biceps, the healing was instantaneous, a pure shot of blistering rum that ran down my throat to sit warm in my stomach. With a laugh I turned my head and kissed his grizzled cheek.

"Baron, you did this to yourself."

"Damn right he did!" Maman crowed, still brandishing the spoon. "Unhand her, you fiend, so I can beat you properly!"

He did, shoving me at his wife and teleporting back to his throne. Casually, he draped himself across it and smirked at me when Maman dropped her spoon to embrace me.

"Oh, sweet child. We missed you."

"Wi nou te fe[21]," Baron said, wiggling his eyebrows and patting his lap. "Come sit."

"You stop that," his wife threatened with a wave of her spoon. "She doesn't have time for your flirting today."

Unrepentant, he tapped his fingers against the skull on his armrest. "Got ya'self in the shit this time," he commented, and his smile widened under his mask. "Take after me."

---

19 Poke. Haitian Creole

20 Sorry! Haitian Creole

21 Yes we did. Haitian Creole

"She has none of your blood," Maman informed her husband. "The Laveaus came from that night with that beautiful artist. She's the spitting image of me."

Maman, the Queen of the loa, wife of Baron Samedi, was as pale as the moon with hair as fiery as her temper. The way Baron told it, after he betrayed Mother Eorthe, he scoured the world for a queen and earned rejections from several fay, many of which came with a slap to his face. Dejected by the rather prudish reception, he sat on the edge of the world, a series of cliffs that the ocean crashed against. It was a fallen of the Allfather, a creature with one wing, who came to him. She was luminous, naked, with her hair spilling down like red fire, eyes like emeralds. She danced for him, skin the color of bone under the full moon, and when she held out a hand, he eagerly stumbled up. He got within a foot when she disappeared, and as he swung around, he felt a light hand on his hip. Some feet away, the fallen stood and, in her hands, was Baron Samedi's flask.

He expected her to drop dead the minute she drank, but she only raised her arms to the air and spun in a circle. Tilting her head back, she opened her lips and did what only Samedi of the loa could: spew fire.

I'd inherited plenty of Maman's traits: her name, her stubborn ability, but certainly not her looks. Only the tint of red in my hair when the light caught it right and the curve of our bottom lips saved us from looking like complete strangers.

"Oh, Maman," I said and kissed her cheek. "I missed you."

"Then visit more," Baron demanded.

I only raised a brow as he dug a hand into the two bowls of peanuts balanced on his lap. "As much as I love you both, I do not love being buried alive," I reminded him.

Maman nodded her agreement as she grabbed my hand to lead me to her kitchen.

"You need to eat. I just finished my stew," she said. "Your mama came to see me last week. I swear that woman spoils us—brought enough conch to build another island out here."

"Brought the rum too," Baron called from the living room. "But none of that left."

Rolling her eyes, Maman reached across her chipped table and took my free hand. "You're in a fragile state right now, sweet girl."

There was little I could hide from my mother, but there was nothing hidden from Maman. I could never figure out if that was comforting or not, to be seen through so easily.

"It was a monster, Maman. He was hurting girls."

"Is it betrayer magic?" Maman asked.

"The worst," I said softly and touched the delicate green veins against her pale skin. "It's Deep Europe."

"Ones allowed to exist are suppose'to be under control," Baron said from the door.

The stench of sour okra tightened my mouth—disapproval. I looked to him, poker face to poker face, but Maman, who wore her heart on her sleeve, pointed at him.

"She is not to blame for their transgressions."

He barely spared her a glance, purple eyes flickering. "I am blamed for what my brotha does, how followa's misinterpret our teachin'," he said, placing a hand over his heart. "When your fatha convinced us to join, we banished, we blood let, do our best to cut the cancer from our system. Why shouldn't you?"

"We should," I agreed, holding up a hand to keep Maman quiet. "He's right. These aren't my cursed—these are true vlkodlak."

The slimy smell of okra increased as he sneered. "You allowed Deep Europe to exist without jistis[22] for too long; is it any surprise that you let somethin' to fester, its rot will eventually reach your nose?"

"She is not the only one, Samedi," Maman warned.

"Of course not," he said with a wave of his hand. "But the rest gotten in line, wi? Look at ya partn'—his siblings refusin' to be collared, but they respect him. Respect you. I keep my fanmi[23] in line. There're whispers the Vedic and Yoruba are next. Soon ya will have tamed all betrayer magics to ya sense of morality. Yet Deep Europe left alone to become somethin' ma horrifying every cycle."

---

22 Justice. Haitian Creole.

23 Family. Haitian Creole.

"You aren't telling me anything I don't know."

"Then what ya gonna do about it?"

Maman brandished her spoon, arched it to slap into the wood an inch from her husband's head. "That's for the treaty and you know it. You've said your peace; now let her eat."

Snapping his fingers, he disappeared. My stomach turned, but I swallowed the stew, lungs filling with the heady heat of conch and clove. Maman eased her way back to her stove, anger forgotten as quickly as it came.

"He's nervous about the treaty," I noted.

Maman's snort was sharp as she tossed a grin over her shoulder. "He has been since the moment your father convinced him to join."

"Since you convinced him," I corrected.

"We can co-exist with our past Creators and still maintain our independence," Maman said. "You're nervous, too."

"If they reject me, it goes Bernard," I said, breathing out heat and my fears. "He embodies Deep Europe, Maman. The damage he would do—he would cause so much pain."

"Then don't fail," she said firmly. "There is something else; your breath held only pepper."

Despite the weight on my shoulders, I grinned. "I love you, Maman. It's going to be six months soon, but this whole business, it's like before—with Margot."

At that, her emerald eyes turned as hard as stone, her voice firm. "We gave you the gifts to survive that trial, just like your mama and daddy gave you the gift of life. You loved her, Brigitte, as fiercely as we are capable, but she is dead. We can't change that; your Graceland can't change that."

"I know."

"It's one thing to know and another to accept," she said, glancing down at my empty bowl. "It's a step that you finished the food so quickly."

Humming my agreement, I closed my eyes. The wind outside was gentle, taking the edge off the heat that bared down on the house, rattling the chimes on the porch. If only I could stay here, where the smell of yeasty bread and Baron's raunchy jokes lived.

"No, no, no!" Maman cried out. "No sleeping."

I kept my eyes closed—figured five more minutes then I'd get up and do what needed to be done. *Just a tiny rest and I'll do the chores,* I wanted to argue, but my lips refused to move. There were hands on my shoulders, the scent of pepper rum spilling over me, but even that didn't get my eyes open.

"I want you to stay, but it's past time, child," Maman whispered.

I turned my head to question, but my chair toppled backward. Flailing, I fell, eyes popping open, but not to the light of the kitchen. Infinite, empty blackness rushed up to meet me, slamming me back into the earth.

"We need to get her out!"

Yes! Gods, yes! I tried to scream, struggling with the weight against my chest. I clawed, but the scent of metal, dirt soaked with my own blood and sweat, greeted me. There was too much, bits in my eyes and mouth, choking, blinding.

"No," Graceland said firmly, voice clear despite the grave between us. "She's got to do it herself."

"What? Why?!"

"Nothing is free with Vodou; you earn what you ask for. You want kid gloves, go be a Christian," he snapped.

I was drowning; as I shoved dirt aside, soil filled my lungs, and I sank like a stone.

"Brigitte Fitzpatrick, I swear if you don't crawl your ass out of this shallow grave, I will burn your movies. Starting with *Simply Irresistible.*"

Shallow. It was shallow, I remembered and frantically pushed as the light of the moon washed over me. The air was sweet, and as I sucked in a harsh, uneven breath, I tasted clove. Strong hands lifted me, and I gave Thaddeus a grateful smile. He only nodded, dropped me to my feet, and disappeared back into the building. Music and chatter flowed into me as the door opened, then disappeared as it slammed behind him. *It's Saturday night,* I realized.

"I was gone for a whole day?" I asked, already knowing the answer.

Graceland looked me over. "Yep, we've got dinner with Horace and his mom tomorrow night."

Gods, all I wanted to do was sleep for a year, maybe two. Even though my hands shook, I pointed at him.

"You keep your uncultured hands off my movies."

He only smiled. "How are the ancestors?"

"The same. Ridiculous—amazing," I admitted, frowning when his smile grew. "I just crawled my way out of a grave. I'm allowed to be vulnerable."

"It was only three feet at the most. Come on up."

The sixteen stairs that wound around the spine of the two-story bar felt like scaling a mountain, and by the time we reached the foggy glass door, sweat stung my eyes. Graceland shoved the door aside for me, and without preamble or modesty, I stripped on my way to the bathroom.

The door remained open as I wrenched the handle on my ancient tub. In the hall, I saw Graceland in his chair, already cracking open a book from my shelf. Gratitude flooded my eyes, and a little sob escaped. When I was younger and he worked for Dad, he would have left my ass in the dirt outside, considered his duty done the minute I was topside. Now his small nod increased the pressure in my chest as I climbed into the tub. He wouldn't leave me alone.

The hot water slapped against me like fists, and I leaned my face into my hands. Tears, painfully salty, dashed against my raw lips, and my shoulders shook silently. I knew it was just a reaction, body grateful it wasn't dead, but in truth, part of me wished I was. That piece, jagged in my throat, wept.

CHAPTER 7

It was the high and holy Sunday sun that blasted me fully in the eyes when I rolled over in bed. My bedroom had the unfortunate luck of facing the street, so I'd equipped it with the thickest and, frankly, ugliest drapes I could find at the thrift store down on Fenkell. The eyesores of pinky orange and putrid green possessed the ability to make Graceland gag, which had only cemented the purchase.

Blinking at the spots in my vision, I hissed at the sight of not only an outfit folded on the chair by my bed, but my tacky curtains bunched next to it. I ignored the clothes and snatched my robe, the green silk one Mama gifted me last year, and considered the curtains while I wrapped myself up. They'd stay down until I was inconvenienced enough to put them back.

"Fuck."

I cocked my head at the invective, as well as the sound of furniture being moved. "Grace?"

There was another bump and a clatter of china, and I shoved at the sliding door that separated my small bedroom from the main room.

Graceland stared back, eyes slightly manic. Beyond him, I saw my desk was clear besides two trays of coffee, still hot with steam, and food.

"You made breakfast?" I asked and winced at how rusty my voice sounded.

"Yes—well, Thaddeus did before he left for the market, but I brought it up."

My favorite, French toast slathered in butter and bananas. For a second, I wanted to press the food to my chest; instead, I leaned forward and inhaled.

"Should I leave you two alone?" he asked, then nodded to my head. "Is that the sleep scarf Beafore sent you?"

My fingers touched the silk covering my curls. "Yeah, infused with birch bark smoke and lavender. Protection."

"It's nice to see you thinking about that now."

Gripping my coffee, I drained half, uncaring that it scorched my mouth. "Have you heard from Horace yet?"

"Yeah, he said they raided Holloway's. Said he'd catch you up tonight." He paused. "Damn, take a breath."

Cheeks full, I shot him a middle finger, expecting a laugh, but he just poked at his food.

"Graceland?"

"Your cousin Rashida sent a report. She beat Orunmila[24] in a divination contest yesterday."

"Hopefully for the last time," I said. "Yoruba gets accepted into the council, then she won't have to prove herself every time she needs something from them."

I pushed my foot into his, wiggling my brows. "You want to spit out what's really bothering you?"

Instead of answering, he brought a folder from his lap and slid it across the table at me. Delighted at his drama, I laughed as I picked it up.

"Did you clean off my desk just so you could set the stage?" I asked and flipped it open. The joy curled and died in a flash the minute I started reading. "Where did you get this?"

"Did you think Holloway wouldn't keep records?" he countered. "You're damn lucky I found this and not Horace."

"Graceland, I—"

"I don't want placations. I've long since stopped trying to put reasonable thought to human behavior, but what would your father think?"

Shame warred with anger as I stared down at the file. "It's what I had to do to free her."

"You told us it was just money."

"Did you really believe me?"

"No, but I didn't think you'd kill for him," he said and pressed his fingers to his temples. "Four people, Brigitte—they weren't fay. That shit will mark you."

---

24 Yoruba God of divination and fate.

It all marked me, didn't matter if it was supernatural or not. I kept my face impassive as I flipped from page to page, stopping on the picture of the four men I'd fought to the death.

"Remember how I told you about *Mad Max*?"

Cocking his head, he nodded. "Two enter, one leaves?"

With a nod I pressed my fingers against the paper as if trying to absorb the memory. "Except it was five of us. I didn't know when I paid him that those men had too. We all wanted someone. They wanted contracts transferred; I wanted Margot's freedom. They weren't good men, Graceland," I said and held up a hand. "I know that doesn't make it better. There's nothing I can do to make it better. We had the entire house as an arena. Last one standing. That's how I got my ribs broken, that busted cheek that I told you guys was from the rogue vamp. I took their lives."

"You broke sacred law. I know you bend it a lot, but Fitzpatricks don't break it."

"I was a reluctant Pilgrim at that point. I would have been chastised and sent away for a couple months, especially because I have files on all of them, recordings on them, on Holloway. They're in my safe."

"Was it worth it?" he asked and took a sip of coffee. "All of that, when she died less than six months after?"

From most people that question would have been a slap, an insult, but I knew he was genuine.

"Yes, because she died free. She got to choose," I said,

It was words he'd understand, better than anyone. The worth of choice was priceless when you grew up without it.

"I read the entire file," he said. "Go to the last page; I shoved some loose shit in there, figured you should see it before Horace."

"It's more girls than we thought. Sirens, fairies, pixies. All from overseas," I said, leaning over the list. "Which means they would be untraceable; he probably smuggled them over."

"He sold them to damn near everyone in the city, and kept records, I'm assuming to try to take down as many people as possible with him if he fell. Which he did, right into an early grave."

Graceland's tone, coated with bitterness, lifted my gaze. He was older—older than I could really fathom—but still, even after everything, his eyes were all emotion.

"And that includes me," I said and sighed. "I'm sorry I didn't tell you, but I would never drag you into that, not when you are so close to being free yourself."

"So, what do we do?"

Switched topics meant I was forgiven, and gratefully, I pushed my fruit onto his plate. A small peace offering, and his equally small nod meant acceptance.

"We can't follow up on this until Horace gives us the ok. So, we do pavement work on baby Bastille before Sunday dinner," I said.

"Holloway is dead. This can probably wait till after the treaty."

It's not a shock, more an inevitability since he decided to dabble with Deep Europe, so I stabbed another piece of French toast. "RIP, I guess."

He raised a brow at me, "damn."

"I'm not feeling generous, considering I had to be buried alive." I said and shoved the food into my mouth.

"Fair enough."

"I want to have a file ready for Horace."

"No rest for the wicked," he mumbled as he got up.

"Where are you going?"

"I've got some errands to catch up on since I was busying monitoring someone's dead ass last night," he said and patted his pockets. "Shit, I forgot about the paper."

"What?"

I took the scrap from him, studied the symbol on it. Three broken links, barely clinging to each other.

"I have no idea what this is," I admitted

"Maybe throw a query out to Brood Dragos?"

I shook my head. "I can't ask for favors until I secure them protection. But after, I will. Do we have a copy of the recording I made?"

"It's on your phone," he said. "Do you need me for anything else?"

I wanted to pull rank, demand he help me for the day, but he clearly needed space, so I shook my head.

"Take the trays with you."

"You don't want an excuse to see Thaddeus," Graceland teased, but took them. "He was really worried about you."

"Go away."

His cackle trailed behind him as he left, but I immediately reached for my headphones. Plugging them into my phone, I searched for the file, stomach going into my throat when the sound of my own ragged breath hit me first.

"You've been more fun than the others, Haas was right about your power. It's too bad my brothers aren't here for you."

"You have spirit. Perhaps unlike her, you were meant for the bite."

My breakfast came up so fast I didn't have time to open my eyes, just leaned toward the trashcan by the edge of my desk and threw up. In my ears I heard the splatter of my blood, the sickening crackle of death, my sputtered breaths.

"You've been more fun than the others, Haas was right about your power. It's too bad my brothers aren't here for you."

Slapping the screen, I pressed my forehead to the desk as silence swam over me. As my stomach rolled, I opened my eyes, studied the wood. Haas. Bernard Haas. Rage tingled in the tips of my fingers, burning away the sickness, but I still pushed it out in long sour breaths.

Not real proof, no matter how I already knew. Haas was a common name in Europe, as Bernard liked to tell people when he was in campaign mode, a common name that people could relate to, unlike the elitist Fitzpatrick. It was why he'd kept his father's surname—that and to punish his mother for holding onto her position far longer than most Pilgrims did, making it nearly impossible for him to get to Divine Arbiter. My failure would be his last chance, but the recording wasn't proof enough to eliminate him from the succession. I studied the symbol of the broken chains again before shoving it into my pocket and pushing to my feet.

I know I should have told Graceland, but there was too much rawness left in wounds long healed. There were times I still dreamed about waking up stuck in Holloway's house, clutching my ribs with one hand, as I waited to see if I'd survive till morning.

It took effort to lift myself from my chair, to grab my bag and shove everything I needed inside. I needed to work, but first I needed clothes.

Said clothes turned out to be a decently clean pair of jeans and a promotional hoodie for Gomorrah I'd gotten Graceland as a joke. Mostly hidden by my leather jacket, the magic woven into the threads randomly spit out bursts of color that even the beaten leather couldn't contain. It meant it was time for laundry, so with a sigh, I hauled the massive duffel of dirty clothes with me, waddled to the door, and promptly dropped it onto my foot when I saw the woman in my doorway.

"Ms. Bastille."

Without comment, she moved past me to examine the room, dark heels clicking against the creaking floorboards. She'd dressed in a suit jacket and skirt, a rich blood color that matched her lipstick. The glossy black curls she normally kept pinned were loose under a black, netted hat. *She was sublime,* I thought, immediately frowning. Without moving an inch, I silently inhaled and clenched my teeth against the heavy, cloying taste of desire in the air. Tricks of the trade.

"Do you mind if I smoke?" she asked, voice soft as she dug through her bag.

I shook my head, and she tapped out a single cigarette, placing it neatly on the desk as she dug for a lighter. I shut the door and moved for the matchbook I'd stolen from the bowl at the bar downstairs.

"Need help?"

Only her mouth moved, smile fast, as she lifted the cigarette to her lips. "If you wouldn't mind."

Touching the tip briefly, we watched each other as the cigarette flared. Blowing out the match, I inhaled a little of the curling smoke, giving the siren a slow smile.

"My pleasure, but you should probably stop trying to overpower me because all you're doing is making my headache worse," I said. "Also breaking the law, but mostly just irritating me."

Immediately, the weight of thick desire evaporated as she gently took a puff. Blowing the smoke up into the air, she gave me a side eye.

"You seemed an easy mark."

"And you've been around long enough to know I'm not. Maybe you just like to abuse your powers when they suit you," I offered, eyes sharp. "But I haven't hauled you in before, so maybe you only want justice for your sister."

That struck a nerve; her pretty mouth twisted. I nodded. "That's what I want, Lenore, for your sister and the other girls. So, what do you say we work together?"

Taking a swift drag, Lenore tapped the ash onto the desk. "I'd say it depends on what you have?"

"No please?"

"I haven't begged for anything in a long time, Senior Pilgrim," she said, "and I won't start for the Conduit of Magic."

The unwanted but earned nickname passed through me like a cold breeze, but my face stayed blank. It was true that because of my mother's magic I had been the only Fitzpatrick passed over by the Allfather during my trials. That while the rest were Devourers, blessed with the power to feast upon magic, to end it, I was a Conduit. It had been Mother Eorthe who gave me the ability to let magic flow through me, to redirect it.

"Word is Holloway is dead. That you?"

"Nope," I said, popping the P hard, "vlkodlak, the Deep Europe variety."

"Give me his address; I'll send him a fruit basket," she spat out.

"No love lost, then?"

Slowly, she licked at her lips, then ground the cigarette straight into the desk. "None."

"The name Roman mean anything to you?"

Mama would have slapped the back of my head at my directness, but the smell of rotted fruit that hung in the air, showcasing Lenore's anger, hinted I was getting somewhere.

"Maybe. Maybe he sniffed around Adam's Rest a few times. He kill my sister?" she asked.

"He helped. What I need is to find out what brood he belongs to and how he got to America. Think you can help?"

Lenore shook her head and rose as she grabbed her purse. "We handle our own problems in the West."

It was the exact pushback I expected. Leaning back, I crossed my booted heel over my leg. "Your sister was the only one who wasn't brought from overseas. There was a reason she was chosen. So you could walk out of here, or you could sit your pretty ass down and help me catch the bastard that slaughtered your baby sister."

As if made of paper, the siren fluttered back down into the chair, purse forgotten, hand clutching her throat.

"You've got a lot of information for not having her file."

"I'm good at my job."

"But she wasn't the baby, you know," Lenore said, face hidden behind the veil of her hat. "We had another sister. Eleonora was sixteen when she overdosed, after she dazzled someone at school, caused a fight where a boy was killed."

"I'm sorry."

"Words mean nothing without action," she said. "If I help, do I get to be there when you kill them?"

"No. I'm sure you've heard; treaties are next week. When I'm done, I'll contact you, and we'll go from there."

"So, we do all the work, and you get the glory?" Lenore scoffed. "Typical cop."

I'd learned a long time ago to let taunts roll off me, that if I went off the handle every time someone called me something, I would never stop screaming. But the curl of desire was a noose around my neck, a lover attempting to stroke behind my ear. Words could be forgiven, but direct defiance made me stand, palms slapping flat against the scarred desk.

People didn't realize that magic was painful, at least for those who weren't born solely of the fay. Sure, I'd earned my magic, had enough pulsing through my veins because of my ancestors, but it always burned under my skin. The room around us hummed, books chattering open and closed, as I silently pulled the magic from the room. Around us, the candles that dotted the space flared and extinguished, smoke curling toward the ceiling. It wasn't desire now that littered the air, but panic, and even that was sucked away as the glass I'd generously drunk from the night before cracked and exploded. The shards pinged against the desk, against our faces, but neither of us moved.

The scorching of my blood was worth the look of genuine fear on Lenore's face. Leveling my gaze, I gripped the edge of the desk to keep myself on the right side of sanity, ignoring the whispers of spirits wanting to hitch a ride now that I was vulnerable.

"It wasn't a suggestion to not use your power," I said. "Neither was my polite request for your help. And I'm not a cop."

Lenore ducked her head, running her tongue across her lips, but I felt her panic. I watched her eyes dart around the room, searching for clues, and if I hadn't been furious, I might have felt bad. I knew what it felt like to be nullified, to be cut off from something that reminiscent of your very soul. Akin to taking a step in the dark and finding it missing, the surprise would quickly turn to numbness.

"I'll get the information," she said quietly.

"Thank you," I pushed out, nodding to the door. "I'll come to you when I get back."

Clutching her bag, Lenore gave another quick nod and practically dashed to the door. As it slammed shut, I watched through the distorted glass as her shape moved down the hall. *A display of power had been necessary,* I reassured myself as I grabbed the duffle. I just wished it didn't cost me. I stared at the scorched floor, where the magic pulled into me had burned into patterns behind my desk when I redirected it.

I needed guidance—and clean underwear.

CHAPTER 8

Now approaching Poletown subway station," the prerecorded voice supplied happily. "This is home to our first and largest underground settlement. Built by both the Feller and Sullivan clans, it is a shining example of our ancestors' ingenuity and hope for a prosperous future in their new homeland."

Bracing for the stop, I gripped my duffle as the door opened. Bodies streamed around me and, like I'd entered, I exited last. Poletown station was my favorite, a marvel that dweorg[25] clans Feller and Sullivan designed and built in a little over three years. The transit system threaded underground across Detroit, creeping just past into the various surrounding cities and allowed magic—or those with a jade pass—to travel quickly. The Sullivans eventually migrated back to Ireland, but Rian Feller and his sons, Bogart and Gable, named after his love of black-and-white human movies, now tinkered and maintained the sprawling mall of shops and rails.

Even though it was underground, the artificial lights shone like the warm glow of a sunset and the trunks of trees that grew to the surface provided pillars of support. A lush walking garden ran the direct middle, splitting traffic so visitors could take a leisurely stroll from one end of the mall to the other, avoiding the manic pace of the outside lanes. That's where I spotted Bogart, sitting and nursing what looked to be a mead from the Bronze Aegis, the best pub down in Poletown and the only one that had a shop down here and above the surface.

As he tipped his mug at me, I kept my nod just as passive. That was about as nice as Bogart ever got, so perhaps I still had some luck. Moving to the outside path, I twisted through the crowd to my destination. The Missing Sock was, without a doubt, the best laundromat in the city, and while I wasn't allowed favorites, this was the only place I went for laundry—and fortune telling.

---

25 Germanic version of dwarf. Small and hardworking fay.

The outside walls were lined with fast spinning machines, but the middle of the room was one long table, and at it sat the three sisters. The triplets had names, but Cleo, Lannex, and Atris loved the drama of title. As always, they were arguing bitterly.

"I'm telling you it said extra bleach," Atris wailed and tugged on the cloth in question. "This is only white, not extra white!"

Snatching it from her sister, Cleo squinted at it. "If it were any brighter, it could be the sun."

"Put your glasses on, you blind bat," Lannex declared as she ripped it out of her sister's hands. "Our clients don't pay for extra white then get pit stains."

"Ladies," I said, keeping my smile small as all three heads whipped up from the offending garment.

Three sets of white eyes stared at me. All blinking at once, they shifted to a soft, milky blue, followed by identical grins.

"Our favorite customer!" Atris said and stood, cloth forgotten as she approached me, spindly arms wide.

"You say that to everyone," I said indulgently, but held out the duffle, which Atris snatched to her chest as if it were gold.

"No, she means it," Cleo said mildly, as she slipped on her large glasses. "No one else pays us properly."

"That's the problem with moving to America," Lannex lamented for the thousandth time. "There was a time we ruled the world, you know."

It was a statement, not a question, so I nodded and watched as Atris rushed my clothes to a machine. There was a time when listening to the sisters spout curses at the state of my outfits in ancient Greek made me blush, but now, as they squabbled and shook their heads, I laughed. Out of my pockets, I pulled a bag of thick silver coins and tossed down five. Immediately, Lannex turned them over and placed them between her fanged teeth.

"Oh, you have ones from Aegina! And Artemis!" Cleo exclaimed, coins practically pressed to her nose so she could see them.

"This is too much," Lannex said, sounding less impressed, but the coins moved to her hands. "You know the rate, so what do you want?"

She was the oldest by a whole minute, and the shrewdest. I flashed my sweetest smile, but it did nothing to crack the suspicious squint of her eyes.

"I need information on someone's death."

Atris, flighty and helpful, opened her mouth, but the hiss in ancient Greek from her sisters had her falling silent. Even Cleo looked nervous, rubbing her fingers against the bridge of her nose.

"You think we would break our sacred vow for money," Lannex said slowly, fangs bared.

"Yes."

The single blunt word made her lips twitch until her mouth was a full out grin. "Give me one more drachma and you have a deal."

It was an easy decision, considering Graceland possessed an entire stockpile of various currencies to blow through, so I tossed another one on to the pile.

"Who do you want to know about?"

"Annabel Lee Bastille."

Atris dropped into the chair next to her sisters, and Cleo took her hand. I stepped forward, but Cleo shook her head at my concern.

"They were friends. It was hard when she passed," she explained.

"It was so unexpected," Atris said, voice watery. "She was so happy, talking about going to Europe with Calvin and—"

"Calvin?" I interrupted. "She wasn't with Dillan Holloway?"

Atris shook her head like a wet bird. "She signed a contract for a year with him, doing escort work. Made great money, but they weren't together. She barely saw him once she met Calvin. She was going to move, after her year, to Europe. He wanted to marry her."

Pulling my phone, I selected the pictures Graceland had taken of the vlkodlak. "Is this Calvin?"

All three leaned forward, but only Atris shook her head. "No, he wasn't as harsh-featured. And when he turned, he was all black, threaded with silver, not that muddy brown."

Not Roman either. Maybe brothers, maybe just brood—either would be easy to track if I could get my hands on papers or a brood tree. Lineage was everything to the houses and broods of Deep Europe. Even minor ones had themselves charted, in the hopes that marriage or battle would raise their station.

"She was found on Belle Isle," I said quietly and brought out the file. "The one I found Friday was in Campus Martius, the second was Zug Island. Can you guys read through this, tell me if the police got everything right?"

"Are—are there photos in there?" Atris asked.

"Yeah. How about I help you with some clothes while your sisters look it over?" I suggested as she stood.

The youngest sister nodded, and together we made our way to the wall. The sound of the machines spinning, gears grinding, drowned out Cleo and Lannex, whose heads were low and together as they flipped pages.

"I should help them. It's always better when the three of us look, but—" With a shuddering breath, Atris leaned against a dryer. "She was my best friend. I mean Cleo and Lannex are my sisters, but Annabel Lee was—she was only mine, you know?"

"It must be hard sharing everything with them. Did Lenore come to you three when she went missing?"

Atris tensed, eyes hard, and I bit the inside of my cheek at the misstep. Placing my hand gently on her fragile shoulder, I softened my voice and tried to mend the wound I'd reopened.

"I'm not looking to make an arrest, Atris. I'm not looking to get you or Lenore in trouble. I just want to figure out what happened to the three girls. That's all, I swear."

Shuffling, she bit into her lip, looking toward her sisters before glancing back. "Promise?"

Without hesitation, I drew two fingers across my lips, then my heart. "Pilgrim's promise."

When she did the same, the binding magic glowed between us, sealing the deal, and she relaxed.

"Lenore came two days after Annabel went missing. Demanded we see if her sister was still alive. She—well, she tried to force us."

Which would have only made Lannex furious, I thought, but nodded. "She was desperate."

"My sisters would have thrown her out, but then she started crying. Real tears," Atris added quickly.

To make Lenore Bastille cry, one would have to practically rip her arms off, but Annabel Lee was her heart. It was local gossip that Lenore once nearly killed a boy who made a pass at her sister without permission.

"We looked. We couldn't see her."

"When was this?"

"Right after the new year."

"And when did she start mentioning Calvin?"

Atris's spine stiffened, her chin tilted high. "We didn't tell Lenore about it. She was already upset. But about a two months ago."

When I was drowning in sorrow and paperwork, I thought, and gave Atris a sad smile. "Let's go see what your sisters have to say."

The two were leaning back, arms crossed as they took us in. Atris's eyes went to the ground as she slid back into her seat, but I just stared at the other two.

"She blabbed," Cleo said to Lannex.

"As we expected," Lannex reminded her, looking at me. "But you made a promise."

"And I'll keep it," I assured. "What did you find?"

"Feather's son is a good cop. They said it appeared that she had been drugged, an overdose, but it wasn't drugs in her system."

"What happened?"

The quiet of the room was broken by the grinding of machines, but Lannex kept her eyes on me. "It was Deep Europe that perverted Seraphim, your ancestor's lover. Of course, with her it was a vampire, but a curse is a curse."

"You're saying a vlkodlak *bit* Annabel and it went bad?" I asked. "This looks like a hunt. I assumed claw slash?"

"Possibly, but if Calvin was such a beast, do you really think he would take fay, especially a corrupted one, as his queen without a bite? They do not consider themselves the cursed, Pilgrim; they see themselves as the future, the inevitable. Would a brood accept someone without that? Deep Europe respects nothing but power. Regardless, all we know for sure is she died in an extreme amount of pain."

"If it was the bite, then why slash her throat? What's the purpose of—" I stopped and nodded at the sisters' knowing gaze. "Because giving the bite is illegal, instant death without trial, but if they got caught hunting here, they'd get deported and face punishment by their own chapter."

"And is it not your distant cousin that runs Europe?"

That was a polite way of saying "Clean your own house," and I felt my spine tighten.

Lannex gave me a long-measured look, the kind that only creatures older and wiser could produce. "I imagine that doesn't reflect well on you, Pilgrim. Having unregistered monsters getting into your city, killing your charges, right before the treaty is decided. And when you are trying so hard for peace with those very creatures."

I froze, bones locked with a cold rush of panic, but I kept my face placid. "Who else knows?"

All three tilted their heads, but only Cleo smiled.

"Is that a demand, Pilgrim?"

I ducked my head. "No. I apologize."

"Accepted. It's important to remember my sisters and I see much of what remains invisible to others, on both your clothes and your future. Regardless, we have told you all we should."

Having avoided disaster, I stepped back and bowed my head again. "I appreciate your time and skill."

It was Lannex who sighed, her voice soft. "I will give you one more bit of advice, Pilgrim. When you go to Belle Isle, bring a seer. There is one at Harvest Heart; he will help you."

"I can—"

"Stretch yourself too thin," Atris interrupted.

"Your powers will be needed elsewhere," Cleo added.

"We will have your clothes delivered by the end of the day; wear the green dress to Feather Glen's. She will like that," Lannex finished.

"I'll bring you more drachmas next week," I said.

Lannex's face broke rank again to smile. "Safe travels, Pilgrim."

Unburdened from the heavy duffel, I should have felt lighter, but as I tapped out texts to Graceland and Bronson, all I wanted to do was sit, or maybe go pick a fight with Bogart. Anything to keep from falling down a path of more complication.

Instead, I checked the large map, then tapped my father's ring against where I wanted to go. The staircase next to me shifted, the ore lined steps glowing red, and I saw Bronson at the top.

"Got your text," he said. "What did I do to earn two visits with our illustrious leader?"

I wished I had a pithy comment, but my bones were heavy with weariness, so I just jogged the steps and motioned for him to follow me. Thankfully he did in silence, and we wound our way through the people to one of the various rounded pathways of Campus Martius. I snagged a small metal table, hissing when I sat on the cold chair.

"This isn't gonna take long, but you want something to eat?" I offered, motioning to the various food trucks.

"I want you to get to the point," he said, fingers tapping against the table. "You look like shit, and you smell like dirt."

"I had a nap, couple nights ago."

It took a second, but he froze, fingers stilling. Slowly, his eyes moved over me, as if searching for injuries.

"That was you, out at Holloway's?" he asked, voice soft. "It was that bad?"

The gentleness was old Bronson, the cousin who would clean my skinned knees and laugh as we raced down the street to the Darkchilds' or to Mama's garden. I could smell the heat on the summer sidewalk, the crushed herbs between clumsy fingers.

"I'm ok now," I said with a small smile. "Physically, at least."

His nod was brisk, face tightening. "So why am I here?"

Business. Family time was done.

"Holloway has been trafficking girls," I said, waving when he started to speak. "Fine. Sirens, fairies, pixies. The boathouse—he renovated the bar in the basement. It was rows of cages, Bronson. Blood and urine and death."

The air rattled from between his pursed lips, and he offered his hand.

"Show me."

The images punched at my brain, so I nodded and reached for his hand. He jerked immediately as I opened, letting the magic flow through me and into him. The copper-tasting horror, the rotting stench of decaying flesh, the wet, suffocating fear.

"Fuck."

I eased back, taking my magic with me, but he still stared at his hand as if he'd been burned.

"Vlkodlak," he spat out. "I'm assuming not registered?"

"Got it in one. They're from Deep Europe." I paused, then added, "They're with Haas."

His eyes darted up to mine. "As in Bernard?"

"He said his name, that Haas had told him about me, that he knew about my power, what to look for to see past the betrayer."

"You're sure?"

"I swear on Gran," I said. "Horace has a recording he got off my phone."

We stared at each other, dark eyes against light ones, and neither of us blinked.

"I believe you," he said finally. "He's been dabbling with things, not technically illegal but it's been going for a while— I thought when I was—"

"His second, you could temper it," I finished. "Ends justifying the means."

He looked lost, eyes blank, and I knew to be careful, couldn't demand answers or accuse. My fingers just touched the edge of his hand, and he placed his free one over mine.

"You can tell me, Bronson."

"I will when I get back. I've been documenting, in case it would help me if your father gave me the treaty, but it's too dangerous until you officially have the power of Divine Arbiter. We're going to need you at full power," he said, and rose. "My flight leaves for North Dakota in a few hours."

We. It'd been so long since it'd been we, and my mouth opened, ready to rescind the punishment, but he shook his head.

"Don't you dare. You make a decision, and you stand by it," he said. "That's what a Divine Arbiter does. You want them to respect you, you stand there and own the bad and good."

"Do you think I should warn Constantin?"

He stopped his exit, looking at me. "You're asking my opinion?"

The question should've grated but it wasn't said with malice, only genuine surprise, as if he truly couldn't believe my intent.

"I'm asking what you would do, Bron."

"I think you run the risk of him pulling out of your deal on something that you don't have proof is related. And if Haas is using this to make you look incompetent, we both know you aren't, so catch them and spin it."

That was as much of an acknowledgment that he believed in me as I was going to get, so I nodded again. "Safe travels, cousin."

"Safe travels, Brig."

I watched him walk away, the easy way he stepped to the left to let Graceland breeze past him. Neither acknowledged each other, and my cousin slipped into the masses of long coats and beanies. My resident pain in the ass, however, stalked up to my table.

"So, is this the part where you tell me why I have to go to hobo paradise," he demanded.

The bite of late January wind forced me to swallow my pithy comeback as we trudged through half-mushed snow. Hissing out a harsh breath, I nudged him farther onto the sidewalk as a car splashed by.

"Because shockingly, they might react better to someone like them than a nosy Pilgrim."

His huff was more offense than amusement. "That was a low blow. I'm nothing like them."

"You know, for someone who thinks he was so egregiously wronged, you have very little sympathy for the plights of others," I said mildly as I led the way across the street.

Disapproval crashed off him in waves, but I just gave a sharp look, one he knew meant "behave, or else." Harvest Heart was an unassuming storefront that moved around the city, looking like a vacant rental space. Staring into the empty grey walls, I gripped the handle of the door. For those not magically inclined, it wouldn't have budged, but to me it slid open easily, the rolling blast of heat shoving away the icy fingers of winter.

Inside, it resembled a doctor's waiting room, but each of the rooms beyond reflected the different homelands of various fay. I'd spent a weekend in the wet heat of a fake Congo once, trying to convince an eloko[26] that Detroit wasn't in need of its skills. It took two days, several solved riddles, and a deal that it could make a pit stop in Florida to see about bath salts, before it agreed to go back to its forest.

From behind the large round desk, the secretary, a nymph, peered at us from behind tea shade glasses. Her electric green hair was shoved to one side, and an elaborate braille tattoo rolled up the left side of her neck.

"Macie," I said in greeting.

The nymph narrowed her yellow eyes, painted lips pursed. "I keep telling them we need to get that door fixed. Supposedly no trash is supposed to be able to get in, but here you are—again."

"You see why I hate coming here," Graceland muttered under his breath.

"She's talking about me, you giant baby," I said and grinned at the secretary. "I don't see you choking, so I can't be that bad for the environment. Now judging by the way you *were,* when sucking that elf off in Elysium, that guy must have been pure garbage."

The fury rose so fast that the secretary was already out of her seat, hand extended for my throat, when the main door opened. Freezing, we all looked at Matriarch Kaia with varying degrees of alarm and amusement. The elderly nymph's yellow eyes swept over the scene as she shook her head.

"Marcie, sit down," she commanded as she folded her arms. "Are you harassing my people, Senior Pilgrim?"

"No more than usual, Matriarch."

With a snort more appropriate for a woman half her age, the nymph held open the door to the inner sanctum. "Well at least come do it where I can watch you. Marcie, please mark their visit in the records, and use their actual names this time. The other Matriarchs and I don't know who 'Graceland and literal half-human trash' refers to."

I pushed the air through my nose to keep from laughing as we

---

26 A chaos creature of African origin. Known to dwell in deep forests, they are vicious little shits.

followed, waiting until I could keep a straight face before speaking. "Graceland is his name, Matriarch. It's what he's going by now."

The elder stopped and turned to look at him. "How—dramatic," she said finally. She quirked an eyebrow at me. "Am I to assume you're going by the other name as well?"

"Not this week."

Sighing, she shook her head at the oddity of humanity and swept an arm out to the space before us. "You know the rules, but because you insist on breaking any set before you, I'll remind you. If you use magic here or provoke violence, I will be within my rights to kill you."

"I'm not here to cause trouble. I'm looking for a seer."

"As I've been told."

I ignored the irritation in the woman's voice, because my next words were gonna cause more. "Have you sent them out yet?"

The Matriarch sighed. "Yes, the two water sprites you requested were dispatched to Flint yesterday."

"I appreciate it."

"We don't often find ourselves helping humans with problems they created," she commented as she moved us through the lobby.

"The ones suffering didn't," I corrected. "You know better than most what damage those with more power than you can do."

"Your father was much more pleasant," she pointed out. "Easier to work with, certainly."

"And better looking," I agreed. "As I recall, you can't resist a full beard."

"Oh, you are a terrible child," the Matriarch scolded, but the corners of her mouth twitched.

"As everyone likes to remind me. Just point me in the right direction, and I'll be out of here quick."

"He's in Europe—said something called him to it. The boy has barely been out of Brightmoor, but the will of Mother Eorthe is elusive."

"He's a child?"

"He's still sane; of course he's a child," she said sternly, "Keep him that way."

Nodding, I moved to step away, but the Matriarch grabbed my wrist. The slender fingers were warm, but her gaze hard.

"He's fragile, Senior Pilgrim. Do not push him."

She never showed this much care for human children kissed by unstable magic. No one did, really; humans were fearful of anything different, and fay considered it perversion. The Matriarch released her hand, but I stayed in place, watching her carefully.

"Whose is he, Kaia?" I asked.

The woman's lips opened, then she shook her head. "I'm not sure what you're referring to, Senior Pilgrim. Have a pleasant visit."

With that, she moved away, her long bohemian dress swaying, and I ground my teeth, tongue pressed against the roof of my mouth. The fearful distrust of a Pilgrim's wrath was part of the job I hated, even if it was easy to understand. If the boy's mother or father was even still alive, there would have to be an investigation. How often had I seen the effects, people so addicted to the flow of magic inside them that they shot up and doomed their children to isolation, madness, or the kindest outcome—death?

The inner sanctum resembled a glen of Ireland, lush with green life, but as you branched off into the hallways they began to change, taking the shape of whatever the fay inside needed. This Europe reminded me of Snow White's escape, dark looming trees that crept toward us, bottlenecking into a single door. Ignoring the itch of anxiety between my shoulders, I pushed the door open and stared into darkness.

"I've lived in Europe," Graceland said casually, hand reaching out to touch the tall pines. "Why can't we be somewhere nice, water surrounding us, wine glasses? Why does it always have to be scary shit with you?"

"Venice is sinking into the sea and France has rats cooking in kitchens," I pointed out, wading into the trees.

Following, he kept close. "That's a children's movie—Rat Gooey or something."

I grinned. "You know the name; you're just being obstinate. You don't get paid unless you get it right."

"Fine. *Ratatouille*."

Humming approval, I pressed onward as branches scraped at my arms. The room was whatever it needed to be for whoever was here, but because I didn't possess the magic required, we were stuck dealing with whatever the residing magic created. This thick, dark forest smelled heavily of rich dirt and the metallic taste of blood. The panic of being under the ground and clawing to the surface flashed through my chest.

"Give me my dollar," Graceland grumbled.

Grateful for the distraction, I dug into my pocket and handed it over. "On your downtime, do you just roll around in money?"

"Do you realize how unhygienic that is? I mean—did you hear that?" he demanded.

Cocking my head, I listened to the quiet whine of a wolf that was sharp enough to penetrate the compact forest. Creeping forward, I kept a finger to my lips. There was a clearing beyond the dense pines; it dipped down to a still body of water, lit bright by the moon that hung low and orange in the sky. Along a bank more dirt than sand, a thin figure stood.

"Brig, he's practically a baby."

"He's who we need," I reminded him.

The boy watched us the entire way, eyes wide and dark. There was no fear, only curiosity in the tilt of his head, and when he smiled, more teeth than friendly, more specter than child.

"You would brave Europe for a broken child?" he asked, voice distorted. "A defective thing will be the great weapon against me? Foolish, Senior Pilgrim."

I didn't know the voice channeling through him, but clearly, they knew me.

"You seem to have no problem speaking through him."

"I wanted to catch a glimpse of you, Brigitte Laveau. This thing is merely a tool."

"You forgot the Fitzpatrick," I shot back.

"I did not. Patrick would have crushed you under his heel. I wouldn't have; I would have welcomed your gifts."

"You got no problem name droppin, but I don't seem to know yours."

"You've known me since before you were even created, witch."

I opened my mouth to press, but there was foam collecting in the corners of the boy's lips. Cursing internally, I gently held my palm to his forehead, feeling the heat pouring off him.

"This isn't real," I told him firmly. "You come back now."

Blinking, the boy reached out a hand and touched mine. "You're real."

I tapped fingers against the boy's palm to ground him. "Yes, and I need your help, but first I'd like your name."

"Martavious."

"I'm Brigitte. Do you think you can help me, Martavious?" I asked.

His eyes were unblinking as they scoured my face. "Some people here think you'll hurt them."

"Some people here are ill, Martavious, but some are right. I will hurt them when they give me no choice," I said.

His hand pulled back, but he didn't shrink away. "You could have lied. It's nice you didn't," he said idly, grabbing the small pack at his feet before smiling at me. "If I help you, can I get a cheeseburger and a milkshake?"

"Are you shaking us down for a cheeseburger?" Graceland asked, astonished.

Before I could respond, Martavious's eyes flickered to the man, and he shook his head.

"I don't work for free, even for fake gods," he told Graceland in a voice much older than his small frame as he hauled his pack onto his shoulder.

Without another word, he walked for the exit. As he took the world he created with him, the room went back to plain drywall, and I glared at Graceland.

"I didn't say anything!" he protested.

"Yeah, but what were you thinking?" I asked.

"That this could be a con; scrappy little kid clearly has powers, but how do you know he's a seer? In my day, seers had no eyes."

"Because assholes plucked them out," I reminded and tugged him along. "And *in your day*? While you're at it, do you want to yell at anyone else, tell some nymph to get off your lawn?"

He jerked his arm free to wave at our surroundings. "This is all fake! Creatures that can't deal with reality, so they get a free pass. Anyone with a sob story can come get a pat on the back and free stuff."

Even though his anger wasn't directed at me, I still jerked a little at the force of his rage. Holding up a hand, I waited until the small boy turned the corner before rounding on him.

"Just because you chose to go alone for so long, because you were strong enough to carve out a life, doesn't mean you get to judge those who can't, Graceland," I said, voice quiet but fierce. "There are people here, sure, that are living in a fantasy because that's where it's better. There are creatures who have nowhere else to go, were abandoned, are sick. It isn't our job to judge them; it's our job to protect them. If you learn anything by being in my service this year, I hope it's that."

"Your father wouldn't be doing this."

The twitch in my face was involuntary, and my left hand curled into a fist. "No, he wouldn't. He would have done it by the book and another girl might be dead by now. I *am not* my father. I'll never be able to eat sin, but I can damn well try to curb it."

"Senior Pilgrim!"

The high, cheerful voice turned both our heads. The girl with skin far richer than mine smiled with abandon, but it wilted as Graceland walked off toward the lobby.

"Did I—"

"He's just moody," I reassured her. "He'll get over himself."

Elle Feller's smile came back, the spitting image of her mother Rasha, stocky with long, coarse hair that curled without thought to direction. Today she wore a bandana—the same green as her eyes—trying to tame it, but curls spilled out as she glanced up at me, her face pinched in worry.

"I heard what he said. I—thank you for what you told him."

The compliment twisted in my stomach, but I nodded. "You guys ok here? Funding, I mean. Did that grant go through?"

"Yes. I'm not sure what we would have done without your help. There's only so much the city can do, and getting all the necessary supplies, the nourishment for so many—" Pressing a hand to her forehead, she took a deep breath. "Sorry, it just doesn't seem like it ever ends."

"If you need to take a break here or there, you do it, ok? Getting burnt out isn't going to help anyone," I said firmly. "Have you told your dad about working Morph yet?"

"No, only Hanna knows," she admitted. "I'm still trying to figure out how to tell them. I don't want them to freak out that I'm interning at Morphosis. I just keep imagining Dad telling me I can't do it and it clams me right up."

I dropped a hand onto the girl's shoulder, smile soft. "It's going to scare them because it's new, but if you need me to talk to them after you do, if they have questions, let me know and I'm there. But you tell them, ok? You're doing great things for those people—it won't matter to Gable and Rasha that it's cursed magic. You know that."

"I will," Elle promised. "Soon"

I wasn't going to bet on it, but I still nodded. "Ok. I gotta go make sure Graceland is behaving."

"You're taking Martavious out today?"

Ah, there was the guilt, because Elle looked at me with happiness, probably thinking I was taking the kid for a day trip.

"Elle, I'm—"

"Taking him to look for a body on Belle Isle, I know," she said cheerfully.

"How?"

"Because he told me. He's excited to be useful."

The thought that a child no older than twelve was excited to go body hunting made me grimace, but Elle laughed.

"You're too much like my parents sometimes. He's never been protected, so to try now, he wouldn't trust it. You can be soft with him, but he understands his gift."

"Kaia knows his parents," I pressed, "doesn't she?"

Elle's smile floundered before it tightened. "Yes, but it isn't my place and would be unfair of you to ask."

"Is either one of them still alive? Just answer that."

"Yes, his father," she admitted. "They found him locked in a car, strapped into a car seat. Had been there for nearly a week by himself."

It was rare, the feeling of uncontrollable rage that shook my hands, but now it happened for the second time in two days. Graceland would roll his eyes at my caution, tell me anyone would be angry about a parent abusing magic so badly that their child was damaged because of it. Having justification didn't make the lack of control feel better.

"I'll do the paperwork and monitor him today," I said, tucking my hands into my pockets. "But if Luna and Gaia will take him on, I want to place him."

"Is Luna...?" Elle almost asked.

"He's better," I assured her. "I was there on Friday. They could use an emissary; it's time. And living with them is better than him growing up here."

We both knew it, but Elle wouldn't be Elle unless she argued. "He's doing good. His test scores at school are reasonable, and he's eating well."

"How much time is he spending apart from other people? Will anyone even talk to him besides you and the Matriarchs?"

Elle didn't look convinced, the furrow deep between her brows. Reaching out, I placed a hand on her small shoulder. "I'll make you a deal. I'll offer him the opportunity, if he wants it, then I'll have Hanna bring him there when she goes for her lesson with Luna and Dr. Beafore. But I'm not making him leave if he wants to stay."

It would be a choice. Something he hadn't been given before, and I would honor it.

"Either way, he'll be back in a couple hours, Elle. I promise no harm will come to him," I said and, like with Atris, dragged two fingers over my lips then my heart in a Pilgrim's promise.

"You don't have to make it official. I trust you," Elle said, smile coming back. "Safe travels."

CHAPTER 9

Less than five miles and twenty dollars later, I leaned back and listened to the humming of the small boy strapped into the back. It took him what felt like seconds to power through his food, messily chewing, and I could practically feel Graceland's heart palpitations at the number of crumbs currently living in the back of the rental. Martavious seemed unaware, his hum soft, barely there, but I swore it was the beat to "Welcome to the Jungle."

"You are going to vacuum the car out before we return it," Graceland informed me as we slowly rolled across the bridge to Belle Isle.

"How did you manage to get a car so quickly?" I asked.

Scoffing, Graceland's eyes flickered to the back seat, watching as the boy shook off crumbs from his shirt. "I've earned a lot of favors."

"Do you guys want to know something?" Martavious asked from the back seat.

Glancing at Graceland, I waited until he shrugged to answer, "Sure."

"There's a lot of dead people here. I'm not telling you about all of them for a stale cheeseburger."

"You got a shake too," Graceland reminded him.

Rattling the cup, the boy sucked at his straw. "It was supposed to be strawberry. This tastes like vanilla."

I turned in my seat. The boy watched me with a slight smile, manic at the edges. I recognized the look; he thought he had us over a barrel.

"But you drank it all anyway," I pointed out, matching his narrowed gaze, "and we need you to help us with only one dead person."

"That's what they all say—just one—then suddenly I'm holding seances for twenty bucks in the basement of the Jeffersonian."

The bitterness in his voice permeated the car, and I crushed the lid of my own shake to keep my hands busy.

"Did you live there?" I asked.

Martavious stared out at the guard who checked Graceland's pass. The man gave him a wave, but the boy shook his head. "For a bit, until they decided I couldn't make them any more money. Then I lived in the park until Elle found me."

"Which park?" Graceland asked as we wound our way past the memorial fountain.

"None of your business."

Sighing, he shrugged at me, as if silently saying *you can't say I didn't try*.

"Park at the casino," I said.

The car settled in a parking space, and all three of us fell silent, staring at the freezing grey that weighed down the entire area. Mama had held my hand in this exact spot when we went to Belle Isle for the first time. On the then decaying island, while she communed with spirits, I traced plaques. It was something she insisted on, always carrying plain paper and charcoal, a way to honor and carry the past with you. So, while she whispered to long dead residents of the island of snakes, I wandered and added to my collection.

On a bridge of chipped concrete, I first traced the words *Speramus Meliora; resuget cineribus*[27]. Even at seven, the magic sparked off the metal for me, blue crackling arcs tickling my fingers in acceptance. Later, I had presented the paper to her, but she only looked at it seriously before folding it into a small square and tucking it into my pocket.

"It is yours to keep safe now. You must protect it."

The piece of paper, now almost two decades old, was still folded into that square and tucked in the pocket of my work bag. Reaching for the handle, I stopped and whipped around to stare at the boy, sudden realization hitting me.

"Wait, do you have a jacket?"

"This is why neither of us has children," Graceland mumbled.

Martavious raised a brow, but his fingers curled around his pack's strap like he was sure it was going to get snatched. "Nah, but it's fine. I run hot."

---

27 We hope for better things; it will rise from the ashes

Outside, the wind whistled like it was calling his bluff. He was mostly bones, but I knew the cost of pride, so I shrugged off my beaten leather and passed it back. "Put it on."

You would have thought it was gold, the way he cradled it to his chest, eyes wide on me.

"You serious?"

The suspicion broke something in my chest. Tapping the writing on my hoodie, hot pink magic shot out like sparklers. "Magic hoodie. Ugly as sin but it's warm as hell."

His dark eyes narrowed a little as if searching for the thread of a lie, but finally he slipped the jacket over his scrawny shoulders.

"If you wanted, I could show you more than one body?" he offered.

"We just need the one, kid," Graceland said softly and pushed out into the cold.

It bit down on us, sharp fangs that had us all shivering. Leading the way across the Isle, I forced myself to focus on the crunching of frozen grass under my worn boots, rather than watch Martavious try to burrow further into my jacket.

"It's kind of beautiful," Graceland commented as he wrapped his arms around his chest. "Cold as balls, but it's like that movie you made me watch, with the autistic witch."

"*Frozen*," I reminded him.

"Lotta used condoms laying around in that movie?" the young boy asked. "Because we've passed, like, three already."

"Thanks, kid," Graceland said dryly.

The amusement was enough to keep me from cursing out loud as the next punch of cold came off the water. It lanced through the hoodie, slicing at my chest, and I hissed as we moved down toward the crumbled path.

"Word is there's something special happening here next week," Martavious said.

He's fishing and thinking he's being smooth as silk, but I can see the way his fingers tap excitedly on the straps of his pack.

"Yeah, she gets to get her ass handed to her by the gods, kid," Graceland said, his eyes searching the horizon.

"Not the gods," I interrupted as Martavious's eyes went wide, "but their very powerful children and proteges."

"But Elle said you're cool, and you have a magical hoodie."

It was that simple when you were twelve sometimes. I can remember saying something equal to Horace growing up.

"Gotta prove I'm tough too," I offered as a flash of pain punched right behind my left eye. "Down there, Graceland."

Once upon a time, it had been an archway of thick limestone, but neglect and decay had left nothing but a haphazard pile that resembled a climbing structure. Past it was the steep decline to the sewer where Annabel Lee's body had been found.

"You can see?!" the boy said suddenly from behind me.

Shaking the feeling of pins stabbing, I moved so the limestone blocked us from the wind. "No, not like you. I can see pain. My mother, she can."

"She's alive?" he asked.

"Yeah, lives in Louisiana with my dad."

"Has an alligator," Graceland added.

Martavious squinted at him for a second, then his whole face lit up. "Crisco is a good name, especially since he loves your mother's pie crust."

We both tensed, our eyes finding each other in shock. As if he realized his mistake, Martavious's fingers clenched around the straps of his pack, ready to bolt.

"You can see that far. Can tap into their lives without ever having met them?" I asked, voice light again.

Nodding silently, Martavious shifted onto the balls of his feet, and I saw the way he braced himself, squaring his shoulders like he was preparing to be hit. It made me itch to reach out, but Elle was right: softness would not be trusted.

"Good. Then maybe you can tell me more about the scene than I thought," I said flippantly and turned to the empty sewer lane.

It was a choice. He could bolt, head back to Harvest Heart, or come down to me. Seconds ticked by, my watch a reminder that the day was slipping through my fingers when I had so much left to do, but

I remained still. Finally, a small body slid next to me, jacket brushing up against my side.

"She didn't die here."

The dull brown stain was still visible against the chipped stone, dried but still speaking. "I figured. The blood—it's a pooled stain, not splatter. She was left here, though. Was it because they wanted her found?"

The boy hummed next to me, his frame shivering in the cold, but his voice was warm, curious. "He felt bad. He didn't want to leave her here, but what choice did he have? She was supposed to be his wife, to help him lead his brood, but then it all went wrong."

"Can you see him?" I asked.

"Magic that wears two skins is always the hardest." He held out his fingers, wiggled them in the air. "He cried, held her until someone made him leave. His brother has a tattoo, he practically dragged him away, and I can see his forearm. It's three circles, but—"

"Broken," I finished and looked to Graceland.

Turning back, the boy stared up at the limestone, lip curled as his voice deepened. "Calvin, get ahold of yourself. It's only a bitch. We'll have Holloway get you another one, we'll try again."

"She's dead. You said she'd be fine. Stronger, you said," he croaked, voice weepy now.

"Obviously not; she wasn't strong enough to accept the bite. That should tell you she wasn't cut for brood."

"I loved her, Roman. I loved her so much."

Jolting at the names, I scrounged for a pen in my hoodie pocket. Scrawling it across my palm, I waited for the spark of something, but nothing. Disappointed, I followed as Martavious moved over the collapsed stone back to the jogging path.

"You thought you loved her kid; sirens do that. Get into your head. We'll find you someone else." The deeper voice rumbled out of Martavious, and he raised his hands like he was patting someone. "Let's get you back home, see if Gregor wants to go out?"

Writing the name onto my palm, the taste of blood flooded my mouth. That had been the one I killed. Licking my thumb, I rubbed out the name to erase the phantom pain.

"Neat trick," Martavious said as he turned back to me, eyes normal, voice evened out. "Is it the pen?"

"That's like asking if that trick you just did was because of your backpack," I said. "Is it the backpack?"

His grin was pure child, as if he'd forgotten to guard himself. "Of course not. Did I help?"

"You did," I confirmed, smiling back, then glanced to Graceland.

He had, as he usually did, stayed back while I worked the scene with other people. Most humans and creatures made him uncomfortable or were made uncomfortable by his presence, so he found stepping back worked. Now he was a long, straight line as he stared at a grouping of trees, jaw working as if he was chewing a large wad of gum.

"What is it?"

His eyes didn't leave the trees. "We got eyes on us. Get the kid back to the car," he said, voice pitched low.

So, whatever it was had hyper hearing. That didn't narrow it down.

"Graceland, tell me what it is, and I can help."

Slowly he shook his head, eyes unblinking. "Get him in the car. Say absolution and cover his ears."

It should have been impossible to feel colder, but the word absolution felt like ice shoved under my nails. Giving a curt nod, I reached out a hand for Martavious, who thankfully took it without argument. Everything inside me screamed to turn back, to help or at least not leave him alone, but this was above my paygrade.

Purposely, I kept our pace normal, simply a mother and child walking the Isle. If we didn't make a scene, we'd get farther before having to run.

"I can't see it," Martavious whispered as we crossed up the path.

"That's because it doesn't have a soul," I murmured back.

I expected that to only give him more questions, and maybe he would have given me the third degree if a shriek hadn't pierced the air. In one fluid movement, I hefted him onto my back and ran a dead sprint back to the car, lungs filled with jagged gasps. But my hands were calm as I wrenched the door open and dropped the boy into the seat. Following, I slammed the door behind us and hit the lock.

"Cover your ears," I instructed and dug into the bag I'd tucked under the passenger seat.

"What does it—" Martavious stopped as another shriek shook the car. "Covering my ears."

Nodding my approval, I gripped the rosary and a small jar. Pulling the cork with my teeth, I dipped my pointer finger into the silver liquid. Without hesitation, I drew on Martavious's forehead, then on my own. Plugging the bottle, I tossed it down and rubbed the rosary beads between my hands to warm them.

"Allfather, blessed are those who walk through the valley. Blessed are those whose faith sustains. Though I am fragile, your covenant protects me from all who wish harm upon me. Given with blood, nourished by faith. Hear my humble plea."

"Pilg—Brigitte."

Worrying at the beads, I spared a glance. "What?"

"It's breathing in my ears."

Dropping the rosary, I clapped my hands over the boy's ears and stared out the window behind him. The face that peered in was melted as if it had been touched by flame, but I knew that was simply how it had been created. Along the waxy wings were eyes of various colors, blinking at different intervals so one was always watching. There was no mouth, but I heard the scratching whispers inside my head. My vision wavered; nostrils flared in pain as I stared into its eyeless face.

"Cristo."

The word struck like a fist; the creature bending at the waist. Shoving Martavious down, I laid on top of him, hand over his mouth, and squeezed my eyes shut. It was seconds that ticked away like minutes, then the scream, like an animal being slaughtered, cracked the glass. Underneath me, Martavious shook, and I tried to speak, to reassure him, but my own voice was lost over the ringing in my ears. The force of the driver's door being wrenched opened had me up, blade at the ready—and meeting Graceland's eyes. The relief made my hand nerveless, blade dropping, and we grinned at each other as he slid into the driver's seat.

The wheels squealed against pavement, and I glanced out the

shattered glass of the car. The creature stood, wings outstretched, eyes watching us as it clutched the blinding light spilling from its body.

"You let it live," I said and pressed fingers against my aching temples. "Are you ok?"

"I'll survive," he said dryly, saluting the alarmed guard as we raced across the bridge. "You are paying for this rental."

He hadn't explained himself, but before I could ask, there was a loud snore by my feet. Martavious laid on the floor, a small cut above his lip, broken window glass arching around him, like flowers in a casket.

"I made him sleep," Graceland said without looking back at us.

"He's going to wake up screaming," I said idly, and scooted into the passenger seat.

"Better than being dead."

He was right, so I just studied him. Hair disheveled, the dark strands he carefully kept ordered hung in his eyes, and the rip in his wool coat had light pulsing from it.

"It cut you," I said, reaching out to inspect the wound. "How bad?"

Jerking away, the car swerved before Graceland corrected. Flipping a middle finger to a car honking as it sped past us, he pushed himself as far from me as possible.

"You know you can't touch it; I'll be fine."

"You let it live," I said for the second time.

"I tried, stupidly, to talk it down," he admitted.

"Wild guess: it wasn't interested."

His snort was laced with pure sarcasm. "Actually, we bonded over our mutual hatred of me. Figured we'd do coffee next time."

"Was it sent for you?"

His brows nearly disappeared into his hair. "Like sent as a hit? We're not the Mafia."

"Go to the mattresses?" I grinned.

"You do realize that it was 1530 the first time that phrase was used, not in your precious movies?" he said snidely.

"Do you want your dollar?"

"Fine. *The Godfather.*"

Fishing for my wallet, I pulled out the dollar and tucked it in between his outstretched fingers. As soon as it touched, it disappeared, joining his massive hoard of various currency he collected, I imagined.

"Are you ever going to answer my question, or are you hoping deflection will stick?"

"Maybe I'm just waiting you out. You'll be dead in a few hundred years, probably sooner with your line of work."

"Graceland."

"It's my fault that they're stuck in the first place. I accept that. I get you don't," he added as my mouth opened, "but going rogue and then getting soft, not following through, isn't acceptable."

It made sense, logically, but I'd seen Graceland in action; soft was a relative term. He must have caught that thought on the edge of my mind because he laughed gently.

"We should probably ditch the car. Our scent is on it."

"Is that thing still going to be there?" I said. "I can't have it on the Isle during the treaty, Graceland. If you can't do it, I'll call Penny."

Who would, despite her reluctance to walk the surface, kill the feral with glee.

"It won't be there," he said and steered into an empty parking lot. "Here's your stop."

There were lots like this strewn all over the city. Some legitimate, but this one was the ever more common "get mugged by a motley crew." Three trolls and two goblins, all dressed in black, had hats pulled down low against the cold or to hide their features, but I knew when I was being measured.

"You did a number on her, eh boss?" one of the goblins said, peering up through the window.

"Tell Hephaestus I'll pay extra when I come by next week," Graceland informed him as he slid from the car, hand pressed to his side.

The troll closest to me leaned over and opened the door. "Let's get you out, ma'am."

Nodding my thanks, I grabbed my bag and scooted past him. With a sigh, I went to the back and—without the adrenaline of fear—struggled to get Martavious over my shoulder. Stumbling, I made it a step when the weight was lifted. Blinking up at the troll, I watched him tuck the boy against his chest as if he were a baby.

"I got a newborn at home, 'bout his size," he explained, ears going a bit red. "It's not far to campus. I'll carry him for you."

"Campus?" I asked.

Eyes flickering to Graceland, the troll waited until he nodded to respond. "Yes, ma'am. The boss said to have passage ready to Dr. Beafore."

For a second, I just watched him, the lack of recognition refreshing. It was easy to forget, while I had files on every creature born or migrated, I lacked the reputation of my father. I dealt in trouble, and judging by the gentle way he cradled Martavious, he wasn't it.

"Thank you," I said and followed, glancing back to see Graceland still chatting and avoiding my gaze. "Do you handle a lot of Graceland's business?"

"Not really. Our real boss, Mr. Heph—his brother—usually takes care of it, but he's on vacation. So, if he needs something, we're sent out to help if we can."

As we reached the corner, I could see the bell tower of Wayne State looming over the campus and hustled to keep up with the troll. Around us, students alternated between shoving past us, oblivious, or gaping.

"Never finished school," the troll said, shifting Martavious a little higher as we crossed campus. "My dad, he worked down at River Rouge. Wanted me to follow him, so I did."

Same for me, I wanted to say. I grew up knowing I'd be a Pilgrim. Trained, bled, and took courses, all while secretly being relieved that Bronson was better at the job than me. Even before Margot, it was obvious; I didn't have the natural aptitude to be Senior Pilgrim. Thankfully, Dad, with the prodding of Mama, allowed me to stay low in the ranks. And when he found out about Margot, there hadn't been any disappointment, only a single lecture about fraternization. Of course, that was probably because Margot charmed them with handmade sweaters the first time they met. If I were to go into their closet now, I was sure they would still be there, hanging side by side, gathering dust.

"Do you regret it?" I asked.

Holding the door open to the science building, the troll shook his head and looked down at the boy he cradled. "Nah, I'm not smart enough for all this. After auto tanked, we had a couple lean years, but with Mr. Heph I make good money, enough that my lady and I could have a baby. Sure, we ain't going out every weekend, but we're safe, you know?"

I did know. I remembered staring into the face of a newborn cherub, my first year of street work, left in ragged clothes with a desperate note pinned to it.

"Senior Pilgrim Fitzpatrick! To what do I owe the pleasure?"

The entire lobby froze, eyes on me, as Dr. Beafore sped toward us. A large woman, her strong shoulders carried tragedy with poise. Her face was fierce, slashing cheekbones and dark eyes that remained appraising even as she swept me up in her arms. Wheezing, I squeezed back.

"Beafore, you're causing a scene," I managed.

Dropping me to the ground, she looked around, alert eyes surveying the students who quickly looked away. Satisfied, she gave me a smirk before looking up to the troll.

"Doing heavy lifting again, Leto? How's that beautiful baby, and your wife, of course?" she asked and waved for us to follow her.

"They're doing real good. The root you gave us for his teeth is a lifesaver. Alisha froze it like you said, and he actually slept through the night."

Humming her agreement, Beafore unlocked her office. "Good, good. If you need any more, my grandchildren can get it for you. Put the boy down on my couch."

The room smelled of cherries and tobacco, which meant, unlike me, the doctor had broken her promise to quit again. As if hearing me, Beafore shook her head.

"You tell my Gaia, and I'll bury your body so deep your mother won't find it," she warned with a glare that swung to the troll. "Why are you fidgeting?"

Having settled the boy gently, Leto stood, hands laced as he stared at the ground. At Beafore's scolding, the tips of his ears went red, but his eyes remained locked on the shaggy carpet.

"Per the second page, chapter fourteen of the treaty, when a creature of the fay meets a Pilgrim they must remain—uh, docile? So, the Pilgrim can determine if we're a threat," he mumbled, eyes flicking up for a second. "I didn't realize you were, but I promise I'm not going to do anything against the rules."

My heart melted in my chest, but Beafore jumped forward, a meaty palm smacking against the troll's ribs. It was a testament to her strength that the troll leaned back on his heels.

"Leto, you oaf. She isn't going to smite you for being alive," the doctor scolded, but her hand patted where she struck him. "Brigitte doesn't care that you once cheated on a test in middle school."

The troll's eyes came up from the floor, and I saw the genuine fear at the admission. "It was one question," he said faintly.

"Yes, yes, you heathen," Beafore said lovingly and waved to the door. "Go on, kiss your baby for me."

Shuffling past, he gave me a wide berth, the door shutting like a whisper behind him. Dropping into the chair Beafore had for her students, I wiped a hand against tired eyes.

"You got troubles; that's the only time you come visit anymore," Beafore said.

"Gaia said the same thing," I informed her.

"My granddaughter is a smart girl. You want some tea?"

Nodding, I watched the older woman roll her chair over to the small setup she had, the serving cart laden with cups and pots. It was almost therapeutic; the woman who could crush a desk to dust handled old china like she had been born to do it.

"He was actually afraid of me," I said and rolled my eyes at Beafore's snort. "You know what I mean. Most of the people I deal with aren't afraid, they're angry. It's easier to do the job when the job wants you dead."

"Of course. Then you can justify beating something up," Beafore said, taking a sip of the tea from the red pot. "Urgh, stale."

"Says the woman who used to pit fight—illegally, I might add."

Twisting her lips to keep from laughing, the werewolf daintily poured from her green teapot and handed the cup over to me. "I was a rebel. Plus, that money got us out of the Purple Gang's pocket."

It was a story few knew, that Beafore only trusted to Dad after years working together. How Beafore Darkchild's own father foolishly believed that in order to market themselves, they had to align with the mob. It was the only time in the Darkchilds' tenure that they allowed themselves to be run by an outside force. While Seb Darkchild was smuggling drugs for Capone and the Bernstein's throughout Michigan, sixteen-year-old Beafore was planning which colleges she wanted to go to.

For a time, it was nice, the ability to walk amongst the richest people in the city. Attending galas and parties without being looked down on. It only took a single silver bullet and a deal gone bad, her greedy father trying to double cross the wrong dealer, to make Beafore an orphan.

She was sold two days after her father's funeral, chained in silver and dropped off at a home where she'd attended one of those parties. She would be a servant, she assumed, and even though it scraped at her pride, she would happily scrub toilets if it kept her alive. That hope was extinguished as she was dragged downstairs for her first glimpse of the fighting pit.

It took two years of broken bones and screams that she could never scrub off, but Beafore Darkchild walked out of the pit with her family's debts paid. Since, she never forgot the taste of blood in her mouth or how it felt to be owned. Through sheer force of will, she rebuilt the Darkchild legacy, only to watch most of it go up in flames years later. She lost her husband, her only son, and the gentle soul of her daughter-in-law.

"Word is, you've got abomination troubles."

Dangerous waters. Treading carefully, I nodded. "Bad news travels fast."

"Would it be tasteless to say you've done this to yourself?"

"I mean, you just said it," I offered. "It isn't Brood Dragos or House Stoja."

"That you know of. You cannot make deals with devils and expect them to behave as angels."

"I tell Graceland that anecdote."

"And he'd agree," Beafore said. "Should I be concerned?"

"You already are."

"Senior Pilgrim."

My title, not my name, spoke volumes.

"I have names. Only first. I'm not sure what brood yet, but yeah, it seems we got wolves fr—"

"Abominations," Beafore corrected. "We are true wolf."

It was a moot point to argue semantics, so I only nodded. "Three vlkodlak. One is already dead."

"You need help with the remaining two?"

"You'll be the first to know if I do," I promised. "You heard about Tomes & Bones?"

"Of course, an original tome ruined, it—you think it's connected?"

I honestly had no idea, so I shrugged. "Seems a bit convenient that a tome on how to eradicate cursed creatures is destroyed the same time I have abominations in my town."

"Our town," she corrected.

The look we gave each other spoke loudly, but I respected Dr. Beafore far too much to tell her to butt out of official business. Smiling, Beafore pushed a cookie across to me.

"Who's the kid belong to?"

Matching her smile, I took a sip of tea. "Martavious. Doesn't have a last name, but…I'm hoping it'll be Darkchild soon."

Beafore's head whipped up as she scented the air. "He's not wolf. You know we don't take humans."

"He's a seer."

"Even worse," the doctor declared.

The tea was bitter, but I took another sip and let the idea sit in the room. Beafore was known for her dramatic bursts followed by mellow discussion.

"How old is he?"

"Almost twelve. He's living at Harvest Heart. I think if Gaia and L—"

The words petered out as Martavious jerked once, twice, before shooting to his feet, fists up. He whipped around, eyes wide, mouth open.

"Stay away from my friends!" he screamed.

Setting my cup down, I stood, ready when he turned quickly and threw a disorientated punch. I caught it easily, and he blinked at my hand overlapping his fist.

"I—what. Demon?" he managed.

"Close. It was a feral," I said and nudged him into the seat next to me. "Take a deep breath."

"His first instinct was to defend his friends," Beafore said casually. "Would that be you and Graceland?"

"I misspoke," Martavious said instantly, his dark cheeks flushing as his eyes wandered to the tea trolley.

"Absolutely," Beafore agreed, as she reached back to snag the tray of sweets he was eyeing. "You must have, because Graceland is notoriously unfriendly."

Gently, she slid the tray across the table, expecting, I'm sure, that the boy would immediately lunge for the small cakes. Instead, he curled his fingers into fists and tucked them into the pockets of my leather jacket. My heart hurt at the sight.

"You don't want one?" she asked.

"What do I have to do for it?" Martavious demanded suspiciously.

There were few who understood what it meant for Beafore Darkchild's eyes to go glassy. They glittered black as she pushed the tray a little further. "I want you to listen to a story. You can have as many of those as you want just for that."

It was like at the sewer, when I hadn't pressed, simply letting him make his own choice, but this time I could see his face. Emotions flew over his features as he blinked rapidly, but confusion and curiosity were what it settled on. His fingers slowly emerged and crept toward the closest cake, like he was waiting for it to be slapped away. When it wasn't, he quickly jammed it into his mouth. Satisfied, Beafore settled back in her chair.

"My people, our lineage, was the first to walk this land."

"Werewolves?" the boy asked, mouth full.

Her smile was kind. "No, we weren't always part of the fay. We were guardians of the land and sky, created and abandoned. We tended the Earth's gifts, taking only what we needed and giving back double that. Over time, when the fay were cast out of Arcadia, they came here. They were frightened by us, having seen what men across the ocean were capable of, but our leaders shared with them our places of safety and worship. Slowly the fay became more open, and North America was a beacon of magic, a home for all lost souls. Then men came from across oceans and our people, as they had with the fay, gave. But it was a mistake."

Eyes wide, cake forgotten, Martavious leaned forward. "Why?"

Beafore mimicked him, her elbows on her desk. "Because these men didn't respect the fay, or the lives of those who they saw as less. They learned the secrets of our nation and, under the guise of friendship, offered items with sickness in them. My people were decimated by plague and by force when they resisted. They cried out to the fay, and even though Mother Eorthe was silent, her children weren't. They hid many of our people, thinking perhaps if the conquerors couldn't find them, they would go away. It didn't work."

"They should have fought them!" the boy declared, then dropped his gaze. "I mean, that's what I would have done."

"They couldn't, physically. Many were nature spirits who had no means to wage war against steel and powder. But as the carnage increased, they knew they couldn't stand by, especially when Achak Darkchild grew ill."

"That's your last name," the boy interrupted.

"Yes, Achak is my ancestor. He was a guide to the fay when they first arrived, and they claimed him when his parents were killed. He was an emissary, representing both the Algonquin and the fay. When he became ill, the fay begged Mother Eorthe for a cure. When she remained quiet, they formulated a plan. Under the moon, the fay performed a miracle and brought Achak back from the brink. He was stronger, faster, and fully in tune with not only the fay, but the Earth itself."

"Like Captain Planet!"

Confused, Beafore glanced at me, and I grinned.

"Super old kids' show, savior of the environment. It's on repeat in the children's wing of Harvest Heart."

"Exactly," Beafore told him. "Achak knew the invaders would never stop, so to protect his people, he bestowed on them what we call the bite."

"So that's where werewolves come from," Martavious asked, eyebrows low as he contemplated. "That ain't what they teach us in school."

Beafore's laugh was genuine as she nodded her agreement. "There are many things that are brushed aside in the so-called name of progress. Not all wolves are like us; this was a gift, given to those who gave shelter to the fay. There are men across the ocean who claim to have the same, but ours is a gift that protects us. *They* are cursed, abominations that use power for brutality and are consumed by it—but we can get into that if you accept."

Martavious's eyes were careful, his body tense as he reached for another cookie. "Are you going to bite me?"

"If you wanted," she offered, and laughed as the boy's eyes went wide. "But why don't we start with an offer? My grandchildren, Luna and Gaia—they run a shop for all fay. If you'd like, we would begin to train you to be our emissary."

"Me?"

"Yes, you'd train under them, learn about our pack. You'd live there as you—"

"Elle wants to get rid of me," Martavious interrupted, his voice flat as his eyes slid over to me. "That's what this whole afternoon was, right? A test run to see if someone else could put up with me? I knew it."

Scrambling up, the boy grabbed for his bag, but I beat him to it and blocked the path.

"Elle absolutely did not want to get rid of you," I said firmly, ducking my head to keep his gaze. "I'm the one that wanted you with the Darkchilds."

"Whatever," he said, eyes already tearing up. "Just let me go."

"Martavious."

Beafore's voice stopped us both. Her hand held out something, and while Martavious scooted closer to see, I bit the inside of my cheek. It was a locket about the size of a silver dollar, cracked open to show off the pictures inside. In one half was a man, face grizzled in salt and pepper hair; in the other, a beautiful couple grinning at each other.

"This was my family. That's my husband, Johann. He had a laugh like a foghorn. The other is my son and his wife; this was right after they got married."

Surprising me, Martavious moved closer, reaching to run a finger over the photos. "They loved you so much. He called you Peony because it was your favorite flower."

Beafore's smile was slow but steady. "Yes, he did. They were taken from me, from my grandchildren, because of my arrogance. I didn't want to work with humans, had bad experiences with them when I was close to your age. I made the mistake of not having an emissary, thinking we were strong enough without help."

"They don't blame you," he told her, eyes still on the pictures. "They're proud."

Snapping the locket shut, Beafore dropped down to the child's level. "You are powerful, Martavious, and if you wanted, we would be happy to train you. This isn't charity; it's a job, and it won't be easy."

Without blinking, the boy stared back. "You promise?"

"Can I show you something?" Beafore asked.

When he nodded, she held out two fingers and swiped them across her lips, then across her heart.

"Do the same, then place your palm on mine," she instructed.

He did, and Beafore smiled.

"That's a Pilgrim's promise. Technically it's only for her to do," she said, waving in my direction, "but it can't be broken. So now that you know I mean it, what is your choice?"

With his fingers still pressed against the werewolf's, he nodded. "Yeah. I'll do it."

Beafore gave a solemn nod. "Then welcome, Martavious Darkchild. You have begun your first step toward becoming true pack. Now help me bag up the rest of these treats for you to take with you."

As he bolted past us, Beafore gave me a raised brow. "I'm assuming you can handle the paperwork?"

CHAPTER 10

I consider myself relatively brave in terms of dealing with scary shit, but under the stare of a pissed off Elle Feller as we pulled up to Harvest Heart, I shrunk in my seat.

"Oooh, you're in trouble," Martavious sang from the backseat.

I rolled my eyes at him but silently agreed. I got out slowly to give myself time to judge the glare. Thankfully, it seemed more bubbling nerves than righteous fury.

"You're late! Where is he?" Elle demanded, bouncing on her toes to try to see through the dark glass of the backseat.

Scrambling out, Martavious gave her a bright smile. "I'm a werewolf now, Elle!"

Instead of answering him, Elle crushed the boy to her and glared at me for clarification.

"We saw Beafore; she's agreed to take him on as their emissary. Hasn't told Luna or Gaia yet, but we started the paperwork. I can have it delivered here tonight so the Matriarch can finalize it."

"Martavious, can you go inside? I'd like to speak with the Senior Pilgrim for a minute," Elle said.

The formal title made me flinch, but Martavious spun around after only three steps.

"Wait, your jacket."

His fingers, chewed down to stubby nails, clung to the leather like the straps of his backpack, and I sighed. Gran would've approved. "It suits you. Keep it."

"This is the best day of my life," he informed the universe and ran inside.

"You are so lucky he's happy," Elle informed me and crossed her arms again. "You told me he was going to help you with a body."

"He did."

"I know what happened," she said flatly.

Shooting a glare behind me, I turned back to do damage control, but she shook her head.

"It wasn't Graceland. We have nymphs that live on the Isle."

"So, you had them watch me?" I demanded. "After saying you trusted me? Cool."

"It was about his safety, not your pride."

"Then you know I protected him," I said and jerked a shoulder back toward the car, "as did Graceland."

Shuddering out a breath, Elle nodded, but didn't look any happier. "And if he hadn't, that feral could have killed the two of you. Then you took him to Beafore, even though I told you I wanted him to have a choice, that I would discuss it with him."

This was about the time I would normally bail on a conversation. I was an expert of the good ol' Irish goodbye, the up and walk away, but Elle was near tears. Sighing, I pinched the bridge of my nose, trying to relieve the pressure in my head.

"Elle, he's not yours. I know you love him, but we both know you aren't set up to take him yourself. He isn't going to forget about you."

That had the tears falling, and before I could get out an apology, she launched herself at me. Strong arms wrapped around me tightly, and, shocked, I looked to Graceland for help. When he only laughed behind the car window, I glared and awkwardly patted Elle's back.

"I'm sorry I got mad, he's just—he's such a good kid," she said into my hip.

It was hard sometimes to remember that Elle, for all her poise and maturity, was barely on the cusp of being an adult dweorg herself. I resisted the urge to rub at the phantom pain in my shoulder, feeling ancient, like at any moment I might just crumble to dust. Instead, I tilted Elle's chin up so she looked at me.

"It's fine. He's lucky he's got you, Elle, and it's not like you can't visit him. I'm sure your sister wouldn't mind having a wing woman."

Elle laughed as she stepped back. It was common knowledge that Hanna Feller was head over heels for Luna Darkchild. Everyone knew it, besides Luna.

"If I'm there, maybe she'll get more than a broken sentence out of him," Elle agreed and glanced back toward the building. "Do you think we could wait till tomorrow night to move him? I'd like to be there."

I shouldn't have. Technically, a Pilgrim was supposed to oversee all foster transfers of any magical being, but with Asim and Moira with me tomorrow, I didn't want to send an out of towner.

"I trust you to handle it. You can take him yourself. Treaty start Monday night. I'll do a check in after first talks."

"Oh, we can do it tonight! It's just I have a shift at Morphosis, and I—"

"It's fine, Elle. You can do it tomorrow. I'll have the paperwork delivered in a couple hours. I'm actually headed to Feather Glen's in—" I stopped to check my watch, swore. "—like right now, actually, so I'll have Horace sign it too."

"Ok. Good luck at the treaties," Elle said, smiling softly. "We all talked about it this morning. Even if it doesn't go through, you have our support in an appeal."

The shock at her easy words was a gut punch, but I gave her a nod and grabbed the car's door handle.

"What am I, your chauffeur now?" Graceland demanded.

"Just drive," I said blankly. "I have to change, but I didn't bring it. Shit."

"I got the green dress. It's in the way back. Some harpy delivered it to me while you were off signing that boy into servitude."

The sharp bite of his words had me blinking back to reality, but Graceland just waved a hand at me, telling me to settle down.

"It was a bad joke; why do you look like you got sucker punched?"

"If the treaty fails, Harvest Heart will stand with me in appeals to Mother Eorthe. They won't let it be immediately turned over to Bernard."

"And that surprises you," Graceland said, brows raised as he turned onto Woodward. "You've done more for them than her. She's a deadbeat mom."

"Graceland."

"Oh, please, when's the last time she even responded to one of your prayers? Like, we know she exists, but I've never met her."

"You've also never met a sasquatch, but I assure you, they are very real," I informed him and twisted my way into the back to get my clothes. "It's not that I don't understand why they're grateful, but there's a chasm between being thankful and standing up to your Creator. It's—humbling, I guess."

"Good. Maybe that will keep your head from getting any bigger."

Ignoring him, I stripped and slipped on the simple sweater dress. The thick green wool pulled at the skin of my arms, and I immediately pushed the sleeves up. Staring down at the faint scars on my skin, I thought about it. It hadn't been a lie—a sighting of Mother Eorthe, even among Pilgrims, was rare. Juniors were all given small gifts passed along by her chosen handmaids. I'd gotten my power from the source and suffered enough for it.

"Still thinking about getting that tattoo?"

"Always," I lied and scrambled back into my seat. "What do you think of a raven?"

"I think they mind their own business too much to be on your body," he said blandly. "Plus, blank canvas is better for saving your life. Doubt Maman is going to like her symbol drawn over something else."

It was an argument we had once a week. Nodding agreement, I stared out into the city. It was Dad who'd moved us north, to strengthen ties that had been ignored, but he had never felt like this was home. Mama was the same; she enjoyed the art and markets, but the South called to them. They'd been surprised when I hadn't moved back with them, instead choosing to cement myself here. Somehow, Detroit had seeped into my bones, sorrow and hope tangled together. Graceland saw darkness when all the artifice of the holidays had been stripped away, but I preferred it. Without the blinding lights, you saw the cracks in the sidewalks, the things left behind.

"Ok, your silence is depressing me," he complained. "What are you thinking about?"

"Honestly, I'm depressing myself," I said around a laugh. "Oh, you passed the house, the one with the red door."

"The house with the red door," he said in a thick European accent.

Snorting, I held out a palm. "Easy, *Taken.*"

"I didn't promise you a dollar," he said, as he reversed.

"Cheapskate."

A few years ago, this had been a tired neighborhood, but slowly, like a lot of the city, it was waking up. Feather's house was a tall brick monstrosity, complete with a single turret, and affixed to the top was a stone gargoyle wearing a pirate patch.

"Do you think she has it enchanted?" Graceland asked.

I shrugged. "You could insult it, see if it spits at you."

"Hey! Jack Sparrow sucks!" Graceland called up to it.

The gargoyle didn't move, but the front door did. Horace poked his head out. He was dressed in a cream-colored sweater and brown slacks—and, from the pinched look on his face, it had been Feather's doing.

"What did you say?" he asked.

Graceland jerked, face going red, but I just laughed and took the steps quickly. Giving Horace a once-over, my grin widened.

"Nothing. Nice sweater Bukowski," I teased.

His heavy sigh was punctuated by pointing at Graceland. "It's his fault. I had to dust too; do you understand how difficult it is to not crush her figurines with these hands?"

"How is this my fault?"

When both of us stared, Graceland rolled his eyes.

"You guys are so dramatic. It's not like—"

"Graceland!"

Feather flew into the room and immediately grabbed his hand. Sneaking a glance at Horace, I mirrored his grin as his mother dragged Graceland to the kitchen.

"I have three different wines for you to try, all reds, because a little bird told me that's what you prefer."

As soon as we were alone, Horace peeled off the sweater and tossed it into the chair next to him. With a huff, I pushed it to the arm and plopped down, letting my eyes fall shut.

"You've had a busy couple days," he probed.

Cracking open an eye, I nodded. He was so gentle that he still blushed when his mother made raunchy jokes, but I'd seen the damage his fists could do. It was a strange dichotomy that, without fail, made me want to shield him.

"How's the city dealing with not having a mayor?" I deflected.

"Tremont Johnson is interim right now, special election next week. He's probably a shoe-in."

Frowning, I sat up and stared, confused. "You like Tremont. Shouldn't you be happy?"

"He seems clean, which means he's either not or won't be after enough time in office," he said miserably.

"That's strangely pessimistic of you, Chief. Isn't it just as likely that he continues to be a proper civil servant?"

"That's oddly optimistic of you," he countered. "Did dying make you nicer?"

My smile always came naturally with him. "No. I'm just tired."

"You've been busy today," he said. "Would have thought you'd be at home studying."

I shrugged. "I'm prepared, *Dad*. I got a lead—major one—on your sirens. Do you want me to tell you, or do you want to pretend that Holloway overdosed?"

I was well aware that he wanted everything, but he also lived by the rules of public opinion.

"It's not going to make him less of an asshole," Horace said. "Hit me with it."

"He was trafficking, not just sirens from overseas, which I'm sure you figured out from raiding his place. That's the good part. A lot of those girls we can find. But the three dead, they were bought from him so vlkodlak could hunt."

"Hunt?"

"It's a thing, in Deep Europe: annual hunts, hunting for sport. I think there's an official one coming up in Romania in the spring. But, ah—I imagine they get bored between and by the rules they set."

"They have rules for hunting?"

"Not talking about animal hunting, Chief. Whichever brood or house holds the hunt has designated areas, boundaries set by magic. If something or someone comes within those borders, they're fair game. If the, uh, prey gets out, then they're free to go. It's how they solve a lot of servitude contracts: let the family who participates choose a member, and if they're successful, the whole family's free."

"Jesus."

Nodding my agreement, I saw the grief that washed over his face. He scrubbed at his eyes when two beers appeared on the small coffee table in front of us.

"Thanks, Ma," he called.

"Use coasters," Feather yelled back.

Shoving one to me, he took a swallow. "The dead one we got in the morgue—he one of them?"

"Yeah, brothers. Three of them. I'm gonna send out for brood trees tomorrow morning, and this doesn't go beyond us, but I think a Pilgrim is involved."

Perhaps it spoke highly of my organization that Horace choked on his beer and set it down too heavily on the table. We both watched as the glass splintered.

"Not one of yours. Your father was too careful—you're too careful."

"I appreciate the support," I said and ran a hand over the table, the glass going smooth. "It's a Fitzpatrick, technically. Bernard Haas."

He watched me, eyes quiet, but I saw him thinking, methodical. "You're sure?"

"No, but I've gotten whiffs," I said. "I know you know this treaty is one of the big ones. Divine Arbiter is going to allow me to choose the direction of not only the Pilgrims but magic for the next cycle, and I'm swinging for the fences by trying to bring in Deep Europe and—" I stopped, considering the words carefully. "I'm going to integrate the fay into the Pilgrims."

He didn't move, like a giant slab of stone; then he blinked once. "Did you just say—"

"Fay, yeah. I pass these talks and the Creators give me permission, I'm integrating. It's vital we allow equal voices as Junior Pilgrims. It can't just be humans, not when our city is so interwoven with magic, with fay."

"That's a lot to shoehorn into one treaty."

It wasn't outright disapproval, so I nodded. "Our people deserve to see themselves reflected in their leaders who protect them. I want to be trusted."

"You don't hear me complaining," he said. "But it won't happen overnight."

"Twenty-five years is a long time," I reminded him. "And I've got at least one more cycle in me after that, if not two. If I can keep Haas from killing or discrediting me, that is. Hell, rumors are that's what happened to his mother."

"Then this isn't something I can help you with. This is bigger than me."

Again, I nodded my agreement. "Bronson has more info for me. When he gets back, he's gonna give me what he's got. Which leads to our next issue: the second body is Annabel Lee Bastille."

When Horace didn't respond, I continued. "She's got the same butterfly tattoo behind her ear that Lenore has. I went to the spot she got dumped, brought a seer. Your guys tagged her as Lacey Calligan."

"It was the ID she had on her. We're still waiting for her system run to come back."

"One of the brothers tried to give her the bite. It went wrong, and he killed her. I'm trying to locate them, hence the brood tree—"

"Wait, I thought you said they brought these girls to hunt?"

"She's the only one not brought over. She had a contract with Holloway. Best guess? She caught someone's eye."

"Give me the names."

Bottle frozen halfway to my lips, I raised a brow, but Horace didn't budge, his face set.

"Roman, Gregor—that's the one I killed—and Calvin. He's the Romeo," I said and winced at the slipup.

"You're the one that killed the wolf on Holloway's property?"

"Did I?" I asked back and looked around. "Are we recording this conversation, officer?"

"Is that how you ended up being buried? Apparently, Thaddeus quarantined that part of his garden. It killed the bulbs he put in yesterday." Horace took a slow sip of beer.

"I'll re-bless it when I get home," I dismissed easily. "Yeah, he was pissed I knocked him on his ass. It was self-defense, but yes,

I'm going to write a report to the council. I'll drop it back with my babysitters before I leave."

I didn't have a personal issue with Madison and Malloy, the overseers to the Senior Pilgrims, just that their position often meant more work for me.

"As your previous babysitter, I take offense to that."

"You're still my favorite," I assured him. "I just hate that I have to write a report and then be chastised for stepping on your toes because I didn't call you first."

"You always were a terrible dancer."

"Horace."

"First, we both know I asked for your help, so it shouldn't bother you. Second—" He ticked off both fingers as he glared. "—you should have called me before, but you're about as stubborn as your father. The only difference is you aren't scared of dying, which is stupid, because you got responsibilities."

I placed the beer down, squaring my shoulders for a fight. "You think I don't know that? I'm up to date on paperwork. I got two trips planned after the treaty, out to the west to make sure things are squared away for the year. I'm doing the job."

"Yeah, and nearly getting eviscerated because you're too proud to call for backup, telling your partner to leave a dangerous scene. That's you being responsible? Because Graceland could have taken that wolf easily."

"And he could have been given another ten years servitude!" I practically shouted, out of my seat and stalking back and forth before he could cut me off. "He could have been punished, and if you think I'm going to do anything to jeopardize his chance at freedom when he's this close, then you're an idiot."

My steps were quick, sharp stabs, two forward before I swung around to take two more. "And do you really think that I'm going to call the police, so I can put you in an uncomfortable, illegal position? I wouldn't do that to you, not after how hard you worked to get where you are. Feather would have my head!"

"She's always wanted me to be a little more rebellious," he said, face placid.

The sudden intrusive image of Horace in aviators and a leather jacket brought laughter bubbling up, but I pointed a finger at him. "You're a bastard."

"He is!" Feather called from the kitchen. "He's the product of a night of fervent love with many men."

I expected Horace to fluster, maybe yell out a few choice words for his mother, but he only watched me, eyes soft.

"You. Are. Not. Expendable," he said. "Not to me, not to your parents, not to the city. I mean, seriously, if Bronson was in charge? You know what, forget I said anything. I'm not wishing that into existence."

How did I tell him that I knew? That sometimes knowing was the only reason I got up in the morning instead of just pulling the covers over my head?

"I have a feeling things are going quiet for a bit; they are gonna take a chance to lick their wounds, mourn their brother. But I'm seeing Lenore Bastille as soon as I'm through talks. I gave her some crumbs. I'm betting by the time I get back to the streets, someone will either bring them to me or me to them."

Nodding his agreement, Horace grabbed his beer. "Just keep me in the loop. I'll send someone to pick up your report from The Bearded Folly."

"Excuse me," Graceland said.

We turned, and everything but laughter drained away. Over his carefully tailored suit was a truly hideous black sweater. Clearly handknit, it held a giant pentagram in the middle.

"Stop laughing," he hissed, eyes cast back to the kitchen. "She's being gracious. Dinner is ready, you heathens."

"That's suspiciously nice of you," I mentioned as I got up from the couch.

"I can be nice," he said, but his grin quirked at the edges. "Plus, she made you one too."

CHAPTER 11

Laden with leftover ham and three bottles of red wine, I steadied Graceland on our way to the car. Dinner had been equal parts ridiculous and hilarious. Feather, apparently not reassured by my relaxed attitude about Graceland coming (and in what Horace said was a fit of madness), baked three different dinners. Graceland, in his demonic sweater and wholly unused to the amount of attention and care being directed at him, turned an alarming shade of red and stuttered his thanks. If it hadn't been for Horace and me, there was a good chance we would have been there all night, listening to Feather praise him.

"She bought wine, named after me," Graceland told me for the fiftieth time. "Didn't even know they had that."

Nodding, I juggled the plate of ham to my other hand so I could steady him. "She found a child of Dionysus on Tinder. Said the date was shit, but she's an alchemist opening up a new bar downtown. Let her try some of the stock."

"I am drunk," he said happily.

"You are," I agreed and shrieked as we were sprayed with water. "What the fuck!"

Swinging us around, Graceland pointed at the gargoyle. It stood in the same spot upon the turret, but its head was turned away from us, like it was hiding, "I knew you were enchanted, you filthy pirate!"

Pulling Graceland toward the car and out of range, I listened as he threw curse after curse at the statue, which turned back to glare. Shoving the food in the back, I opened Graceland's door and dumped him inside. Even though my sweater, black with Maman's symbol across it, was stuck wet to my back, it had been a good night. Probably the best I'd had this week. Sliding into the driver's seat, I leaned back and closed my eyes, listening as Graceland whispered insults to the gargoyle, his face mashed against the window. In a minute I would have to move, put the keys in the ignition, and drive us home. *Two minutes,* I promised the universe silently.

"Brig, I need your help with something."

"My least favorite sentence," I said with a sigh and cracked open my eyes. "What?"

He was sober. Eyes no longer glassy, but sharp as they watched me.

"Well, that buzz didn't last long," I commented and reached for the keys. "Regardless, we got a busy day tomorrow."

I let the car purr to life and raised my brows in question.

"It's a—" He stopped and motioned downwards.

"That sounds like a doctor's problem. Do you even have issues like that?" I asked, suddenly curious.

"What? No! It's an underworld thing, making sure the ferals stay dormant for at least a couple days."

It wasn't that I didn't want to help—actually, no that's exactly what it was.

"Graceland, it's almost midnight," I whined. "Can't one of your siblings help? We need to be up and ready early."

"I can be ready in minutes," he said smugly. "I'll make sure you have breakfast tomorrow."

I paused. "I want Iggy's Eggies[28]."

"Deal."

He accepted my terms too quickly, but I didn't have time to question it, because he was already unbuckling. Scrambling out, I grabbed my bag from the back seat.

"You know nothing will hurt you down there," he said, amused.

"I've already died once this week. I'm taking precautions," I said. "So how do we get down there?"

His grin was a flash in the dark street as he turned and led the way. Several houses down from Feather was an empty plot. Once upon a time it was grand as hers. Then it was a crack den. The city had pledged that the homes razed by fire and soaked in despair would be bulldozed, one section of the city at a time. Now it was

---

28 Baller breakfast hole in the wall (literally) on W Grand River.

an unassuming flat piece of dirt with a tiny sign sticking out of it, announcing that it would be a community garden.

"I'm surprised you'd get your feet dirty," I mumbled, but followed him.

With his back to me, Graceland straightened, hands raised to chest level. His palms were out, and I squinted in the darkness to try to see the ritual. The first crack of bone had me jerking, and he cast an apologetic smile.

"Sorry. Getting old," he joked as he turned his thumbs unnaturally inward toward the back of his hand.

Underneath my feet, I could feel magic older than time itself calling to me. It was a language I couldn't understand, but as the ground shook, I didn't have to know the words to feel power. Slowly, as if each individual grain of earth was being picked up, the ground rose around us. I wanted to reach out and touch it, but Graceland was already moving down. Blinking, I tried to force my eyes to focus, but he was gone, disappearing into the abyss.

"Uh, Graceland? You're with passenger, remember?"

"Oh, shit, sorry," he called from the hole. "Hold on."

Like a heartbeat, red pulsed slowly from the pit, exposing compact stairs. Still hesitant, I took the first step as if I'd pass through it. It was stable, but I could feel the heat increasing as I descended, beads of sweat popping along my hairline.

"You got a thermostat down here?" I said, fanning myself when Graceland glanced over his shoulder.

"Dead people get cold easily," he explained.

It was only a couple steps, but I could feel a stitch in my side and my knees wobbled. "I hate traveling between."

Nodding his agreement, he tapped against the final stair. "That's because you're not supposed to."

As his foot touched it a third time, the stair expanded. I didn't understand his next words, but the earth went clear before bleeding into a violent riot of colors. It was glass, stained in streaks. Upon the pane was a boy, wings half burned as he fell to the earth. His panic was etched in a pale peach face, as was the single hand he had outstretched to the sky. My heart squeezed in my chest, and I couldn't help my mouth.

"Jesus, Graceland."

Shrugging, he stared at the scene. "The irony of that statement. Follow my lead."

With that, he took a step, dropping straight through the glass and out of sight. Even though logically I knew this wasn't going to kill me, my body wasn't onboard with the idea of taking a step into the unknown. Sucking in a deep breath, I took the step.

Of course, it was too much to expect that I'd do it gracefully like him, but I hadn't expected to plummet. The skirts of my dress spun around me and, going on instinct, I tried to grab at something to slow myself. My hands clasped around air, and I let out a curse.

"And you call me dramatic," Graceland said blandly.

Cracking open an eye, I realized I'd landed. The ground underneath was stone, cobbled pebbles that wound a path through moonlit grass. The farther we walked, the more his shoulders relaxed.

"It's a lot nicer than the last time I was here," I said.

"Penny has been doing renovations. Fire and brimstone isn't in style anymore," he said and grinned at the gate in front of us. "My peanuts!"

There was something to be said that he considered the massive three-headed dog bounding toward us something small. When I'd been here the first time, tucked in the skirts of my mother, I had been terrified, but as the dog knocked Graceland to the ground, I only shook my head. Usually the heads were in disagreement, but it had been a long time since they had seen their dad. They slobbered in unison, bumping against him as they stumbled.

"Oh, my baby girls!" Graceland cooed, hands disappearing into the thick black fur. "Have you been good? I bet you have. Eating all your food and everything, right?"

"They've figured out how to open the fridge," a snide voice commented from behind the dog. "I let them stay up past bedtime too."

Stepping around the mass of dog, I grinned at Graceland's wife. Penny smirked back and held out a hand for me.

"Come on, let him spoil them."

Graceland gently pushed the dog away. "No, I need her help with something. You too."

"How specific," Penny said, deadpan, and waved a red-nailed hand at the dog. "You can give them a couple minutes. That's an order."

"You can't order me around," he complained, but was already petting his babies again.

His wife's snort was a loud dismissal. "Who's been watching your kingdom because you threw a temper tantrum?"

Without waiting for a response, she pulled me with her through the gate. As soon as the door shut, she dropped my hand and stalked forward. On four-inch black stilettos, she slid gracefully in a well-worn pattern of nerves.

"He's ok, right? He doesn't call like he should, but I know it's just after Christmas and how hard that is for him," she whispered worriedly, her voice much higher than the throaty one she'd used before.

She was a stunning woman, tall and lush, her hair long and loose, flowing down her back as dark as the River Styx that ran through their home. Her eyes were a bright violet that turned a wicked black when her wrath was incurred. Draped in red velvet, to everyone in the underworld she resembled a poison dart frog, beautiful but deadly to touch. Right now, she looked like a little kid, teetering in her heels as her teeth worried at her red lips.

"He went on a date," I offered.

It was like the sun coming out, a flower opening to the day, the way she jumped and clapped her hands together.

"A date! Was he cute?" she demanded, then lowered her voice. "Oh, Brigitte, our boy is growing up."

Before I could respond, Penny held up a hand, back straightening as she licked the lipstick off her teeth. I watched her face go blank until it was the same arrogant angles that got her the job of Graceland's wife. The transition was nearly seamless, except for the fact that her left hand trembled a bit as the guard stepped through the door and into her personal space.

"Queen Persephone, there is a message in your chamber. Athena is demanding a response," the man said, voice low.

"Thank you. I'll take care of it immediately," she answered and nodded in dismissal.

The guard's eyes swept over me, but he turned and left. As soon as he was out of earshot, Penny gripped her hands into fists and let out a harsh breath.

"You are the Queen of Hell," I reminded her quietly. "You could make them keep a farther distance."

"If I do, I'll never stop," she said, laughing nervously. "Then eventually Graceland will come home and everything will be through text message."

"And listening to him bitch is worse than panic attacks," I agreed.

Her second laugh was more natural, and she pushed her hair off her neck. "Exactly. What a pair we make, right? Our family thinks we did it to spite them, but we saved each other," she said seriously. "Plus, if I keep pretending I'm a badass, I'll eventually be one, right?"

"You've conquered armies with only a butter knife. You are badass."

"Quit hitting on my wife, Pilgrim."

Whipping around, Persephone threw herself into Graceland's arms. They were a perfect set. He was the only one she trusted to touch her, and she was the only one who could make his face serene. He pressed his cheek to the top of her head and breathed in. It was lilac, I knew, because he often marveled at her ability to smell like spring when surrounded by hell.

"I miss you, asshole," she said and slapped his chest before cuddling in again. "There is no one here that understands the intricate nature of Mel Brooks."

"Because *Spaceballs* is so deep," Graceland teased. "I missed you, too, Penny."

"Tell me about your date," she demanded.

Rolling his eyes, he dropped her back onto her heels and glared at me. "Judas."

"My star," Penny said softly, using a nickname only she could, "she loves you the same as me. We want you to be happy."

"Most wives don't—"

Grabbing his chin, she narrowed her eyes. "Oh no, mister, don't you deflect. If you don't spill the beans, I won't tell you about the charming gentleman I met."

Graceland was stunned for words, and his wife patted his cheek.

"He was quite kind," she mused and smiled shyly. "It was just coffee in the meadows, but he accidently touched my hand, and it was ok."

That single word made him beam. "I'm proud of you Penny."

"Tell us your business; then we can talk about your date."

I could see how torn Graceland was, the way he glanced quickly between the path I recognized as the way to Purgatory and his wife. Gently, I nudged him to her.

"Just tell me what you need done, and I'll go take care of it myself. You two can catch up."

"No. I have to take you myself," he said and reached for Persephone's hand to squeeze again. "I'll be back in a couple minutes."

Frowning, the queen looked to Purgatory, her eyes going shockingly wide, as if she was seeing what Graceland's business was. "My star," she said lips curled as she shook her head, "that's against the rules."

"I'm a rebel." He shrugged. "Plus, we make the rules now, don't we?"

"Anyone want to clue the human in?" I wondered out loud.

"Nope," he said smoothly and wrapped his arm through mine.

Giving Penny a nod, I let myself be guided up the winding path. It was rougher than the other two, stones uneven and grass growing up between the cracks. Weeds grew high along the edges, and I couldn't help but smirk.

"Too lazy to hire a gardener? With your money hoarding I'm sure you could afford—"

The words got stuck in my chest as I caught the smell of the wind: mango shampoo. At the end of the path that led to purgatory, I turned to Graceland blindly, my eyes already full of tears. Words, questions took root in my throat, wrapping around each other. I wanted to push them out, demand to know, but fear and hope strangled them. Instead, I gripped his fingers, clenching and unclenching, the cold he emanated keeping me from falling to my knees.

Nudging me toward the massive arched door, he smiled. "Go talk to your girl."

My fingers ran against the simple carved door, and I inhaled another gulp of sweet, fruit-filled air. "She's really going to be there?"

"I'm a trickster, but I'm not that cruel," he said and pushed the door open for me. "It just took me awhile to find her."

Had it always been this hard to move my limbs? It felt like dragging a body across the threshold, but the door snapped shut as soon as I forced myself through. I was in a park, a conglomeration of different ones from places I'd been, and directly in the center, the Woodward Fountain. It was one of the last places we'd been together, eating lunch on its steps, and I'd just listened, with eyes closed and the sun beating on my face, as Margot complained about the cold modern architecture.

There were people everywhere, some milling aimlessly, while others circled the fountain like mall joggers. In the center, though, sitting on the ledge of the fountain, was a face I saw whenever I closed my eyes for too long. Shoving through the crowd, the desperation building in my chest, collapsing my ribs, so certain that as I ducked under someone's arm and came back up, Margot would be gone. I cleared the last person, and only empty space separated us. I froze in that emptiness, simply watching, eyes hungry. She was writing, tongue tucked between her lips, as her blue hair blew around her. She'd done her hair a day before she died, a rich indigo she said would be trending within a week. It made her skin milky, her veins more prominent, and I remember how I worshipped them with my lips, tracing them all over her body.

When we lowered Margot into the earth, Cosmo debuted the hair color of the season, splashing models all over the world with indigo manes. None of them looked as good, but that wasn't the point, Margot said. A muse wasn't in it for ownership, but the glory of seeing the birth of creation.

Squeezing my eyes shut, I prayed that when I opened them, we'd be back in our bedroom, that the humming of voices and footsteps would sink away. A hand, gentle and soft, caressed my cheek, fingers tapping at my freckles. Unable to resist, I opened my eyes and, helpless against it, began to cry.

"Love," Margot said, her voice a squeak, "you can't do this to me. You cry, I'm going to cry, and then everyone here will start. We'll drown before I get to kiss you."

The laughter came as quickly as the tears, and I let Margot pull me in. Her lips tasted like home—cheap gum that has jokes written on the wrappers. Sinking into her kiss, I tangled my fingers into her blue hair, anchored myself for the first time in a long time. I swayed, or maybe we both did, but neither of us drifted as Margot's hands came to rest on my shoulders. Finally, when I couldn't find breath, I pulled back but kept my hands in her hair, cradling her head.

"I can't—" Stopping, I inhaled, and my bottom lip trembled. "I don't—I think my brain is broken."

Laughing softly, Margot tugged at the collar of my dress so that our foreheads rested against each other. I wanted to close my eyes again, but she might've turned to mist or never have existed in the first place, so I just stared, breathing in her air.

"I missed you."

I don't know if it was Margot or I that said it, but we both smiled at each other. I licked my dry lips as she reached out, fingers connecting the freckles on my face with imaginary lines, and I let out a quiet sob. *Constellations; you have constellations,* she would tell me when we were tangled together in our bed.

"Graceland said he couldn't find you," I said. "After you died, I asked him, and he said you were gone. He told me he'd keep looking, but I figured—"

Logically, I knew that being fay, there was no way she'd be chosen for true nirvana, but if anyone deserved that it was Margot. So I'd believed that, tried to be grateful that she was somewhere beautiful.

"I hid from him," she whispered.

It was like falling into the Detroit River, through the ice and suffocating in the cold. I pulled back, letting my hand drop from her.

"What are you talking about?"

"I knew you'd come here," Margot said, voice unbearably gentle. "I knew once you found me, you'd never leave, so I hid. He found me because I'm ready."

"Ready to see me?" I asked confused.

"Ready to move on," she said and pointed to the gate at the far end of the park. "I've been granted Elysium."

It was heaven for magic, surrounded by music and shade from the hot sun that burned people away in the pit. I took another step back, wrapping my arms around myself as if to warm my skin.

"So why am I here?" I demanded and tried to ignore the hurt slicing chunks out of my insides.

"Because we didn't get to say goodbye," she said. "Because I love you, but you can't follow me here. There's too much left for you to do."

"I could talk to Graceland—now that we found you, maybe he can grant me a boon. I'll be in his debt or Persephone's, but we can pull an Orpheus. I can bring you back."

A numbness built inside me as the tears began to rush up again, and this time when her arms banded around me, I just remained still.

"You can't, even if they wanted to. They can't grant that for fay. If I came back, I wouldn't be me, Briggie," Margot managed to get out around her own tears. "Please don't hate me."

It had been what kept me going—the idea, the faint hope of holding her again, of being us again. Now I felt completely untethered, like I was outside of myself. She'd be gone. Gone. Gone, and I was wasting time.

"I could never hate you," I murmured.

The words only made her sob harder. Around us, everyone turned to stare, broken momentarily from the trance of Purgatory, and as Margot predicted, they began to cry too.

"Hey, hey," I repeated and finally got my limbs to move as I shook her gently. "If you want me to leave, you gotta stop crying. Otherwise, I'll end up in the pit, sweating my balls off while you're living in paradise."

She bobbed her head. "We both know you wouldn't end up in the pit."

"I got too much blood on my hands for Elysium, baby," I told her and saw something flicker across her face. "Is that why you think I hate you; Graceland told you?"

"You killed people for me," she said.

There was a time when I would have caught her wobbling bottom lip with my teeth, given a nip before kissing it better. This time I just touched it gently with the tip of my finger.

"Yeah, and I'd do it again in a heartbeat. I'd kill as many people or fay as it took if it meant you'd be free."

"I wasn't worth your—"

"You matter. You have always mattered," I interrupted. "You are a person, Margot. Just because no one saw you, the real you—that means they were messed up, not you."

Her smile was as radiant as the first time we met. It blinded me then too.

"How can I just walk away?"

A chasm cracked in my chest. It was through sheer force of will that I didn't let it split me in two, didn't collapse into pieces on the floor. Instead, I inhaled the smell of mango one last time and smiled.

"I'm going to close my eyes. You're going to kiss me and walk away. Don't look back, and I won't open my eyes. When I do, you'll be gone. Simple as that."

"Simple as that," Margot repeated.

We stared at each other for a second, eyes searching, mapping out each other's faces. Slowly, I let my eyes drift shut and tried to stay still. It felt like an eternity, then soft fingers traced my freckles again.

"Margot, please," I begged.

Lips replaced the hands, kissing across my face before finding my mouth. Desperately I kissed back, curling fists at my sides to keep from reaching for her, keep from anchoring myself to the world again. It was over too soon, her lips pulling back, and when I chased them, I met with air.

There were footsteps, but everyone was moving again, humming, talking…and I couldn't track Margot anymore.

"She's gone, Brig," Graceland said from behind me.

I kept my eyes screwed shut, as if by keeping them closed, it wasn't over and maybe there would be another kiss, another chance.

CHAPTER 12

Ok, real talk. How do I look?"

Turning my head lazily from the airport bench I had declared mine, I pushed up my sunglasses and grinned. Graceland had changed from his jeans and faded Metallica shirt to a suit. It was cut skinny, a deep bruised plum color that clung to him, and at his throat, a glittering green scarab held a black tie.

"I think if you weren't married, I'd drag you back into the sketchy airport bathroom," I teased.

He scowled but I only wriggled my eyebrows at him. He'd been through two costume changes already in the time it had taken my parents' plane to land. Now, as we waited in the DTW baggage claim, I wasn't sure I could take a third.

"I want to look official," he explained as he tugged his collar. "Today will be the first time I've seen your father since I was transferred to you, and I want him to see I'm taking this seriously. I'll change."

Grabbing his wrist, I pulled him to a stop and went up on tiptoes to fix his tie. Even though my fingers worked quick, I kept my voice gentle.

"I was just teasing; you look great. You know both my parents love you."

He went stone still under my hands, and I glanced up as I dropped back onto my heels. Maybe he didn't.

"Oh, Graceland."

Flapping a ringed hand, he grabbed his bag. "Let's pretend that didn't happen. We need to focus on the treaty."

It was his turn to look like a little kid, eyes looking everywhere but at me, so I dropped it.

"Thankfully, after we Uber to the hotel, we have a couple hours before we meet with Asim and Moira. I want you on the Isle, keeping watch. If we're lucky, maybe—"

"My babies!"

My mind went completely blank as I stared at the medium-sized alligator that pulled my tiny mother through the luggage claim. Odette Laveau Fitzpatrick in her flowing dress and braids couldn't possibly have convinced any airport security she should be allowed in the building, much less on a flight, with that creature. The alligator—Crisco, my brain supplied—came to a halt by us, casting his eyes up at Mama lovingly, who threw him what looked to be a raw chicken leg.

"You be good now," she told him and opened her arms to Graceland. "You look so handsome!"

His panic snapped me back to reality, and I pointed to the alligator and mouthed *she saw you through him.* Nodding, he returned the hug, gently patting. But with Mama, there were no half measures, so she only squeezed tighter, rocking him back and forth. When she did pull back, she gripped his face between her ringed hands and dragged him down for a proper kiss.

"Mama, stop kissing my partner."

With a glare that could turn someone to stone, she did. "Brigitte Marie, you apologize. This man keeps you from the jaws of death every day of your life!"

"Sorry, Mama."

"Forgiven," she said, just as easily. "Now come here. I need to hug you."

It was impossible to stay irritated with Odette Fitzpatrick—my father could attest to that—but I tried even as I clung to her hug.

"Mama, where is Dad?"

"Oh, he's waitin' with the car he ordered, I'm sure cursin' me with every breath. I'm lettin' him get honked at," she said. "Crisco will take us to him."

The alligator, recognizing his name, uncurled from his spot. Patting his head, my mother grabbed the handle to the harness he wore around his belly.

"Mama, we were gonna order an Uber."

"I don't want some baby drivin' us. I remember what you were like getting your license."

It wasn't worth arguing the intricacies of ridesharing, so I focused on what was in front of me. "I don't think Crisco is allowed in here," I said and glanced at the crowds around us.

"Soundin' like your father," she sniffed as she and Crisco led the way back through baggage claim. "He's a sweetheart, and it's not my problem people are narrowminded."

"Places have rules, though, and—"

That had her laughing deep, hip-bumping Graceland, who steadied her as she bounced off him. Batting her eyelashes at the tall man, she grinned. "Everyday she's soundin' more like Rory. I adore it. Tell me, Graceland, she this dedicated to rules when I'm not here?"

"Well, I mean—" Graceland sputtered, eyes moving to me.

The crowd turned at her peal of laughter, shifting away as they saw Crisco charge toward the exit. "That's what I thought. Oh, there's Rory!"

Dad's gaze was equal parts exasperation and devotion as we came toward him. I was incredibly familiar with that look, and I nodded in agreement as his eyes moved from his wife to me. Mama gave him a firm pat on the butt before she moved to help Crisco get into the back seat, and we both shook our heads.

"Hey, Dad."

"Hey, yourself," he said, green eyes narrowed. "What's this I hear about you dying?"

"Rory," Mama chided, voice strained as she hefted Crisco's front half onto the seat. "You promised to talk normal before you became a worrywart."

"I said hey," he argued as he turned back to me. "Well?"

"It was for a case."

Unsatisfied, he turned to Graceland. "And where were you?"

As Graceland tugged nervously on his tie, I rolled my eyes.

"Making sure that I didn't die for real," I said and nudged him to the car. "Stop being a bully and get in."

At the insult, my father's neck went a little pink, as if being a bully was the worst thing he could be. "Do I at least get a hug?"

"Do you deserve one?" I asked.

"Oh, he's missed you horribly," Mama called from the back seat. "Send my handsome son back here!"

When no one moved, I tugged at Graceland's wrist. "She's referring to you, Romeo."

"Dette, stop flirting," Dad told her, but gave Graceland a small smile. "She'll keep badgering you, so go on."

Being with the Fitzpatricks was a bit like being inside a hurricane. There was a center of calm, but around it, a blistering speed of talking, arguing, and poking. I always said it was a good thing Mama and Dad never had more than one of me, or we would have really descended into chaos. I leaned against the car as Dad finished with their luggage, swinging it like it weighed no more than a piece of paper, and took another deep breath. It was also love, fierce and loyal, and if I didn't get in the car, I might start crying from the sheer relief that came from being in my parents' company.

I twisted in the passenger seat to stare at my mother and Graceland, who was suspiciously quiet. Crisco had lounged himself across my mother's lap like an enormous cat, and poor Graceland was pushed up against the glass, eyes watching the alligator like he might leap across the small space.

"You wanna switch spots?" I asked.

"No, no, I never get to see him," Mama complained and reached a hand to pat the man's arm. "We are goin' snuggle and tell each other your secrets."

"What if I want to snuggle, Mama?" I tried again.

"Then you can come visit more," she informed me as she turned back to Graceland. "Did you know she used to sleep with a giant stuffed bat? She was determined to be a vampire. Drove Rory crazy."

"Oh, my G—" I swallowed the last part as my father got into the car, shaking my head at her. "Mama, I didn't want to be a vampire. I went through a goth phase."

"Hush, we're gossipin'."

With a huff, I turned back around and caught Dad grinning at me. When Rory Fitzpatrick smiled it was like a small boy: pure.

"What?"

"We've missed you," he said simply before starting the car.

I felt the same and gave his hand a squeeze. The calm contentment was almost enough to make up for the fact that Mama and Graceland were cackling to each other in the back.

"Where are you sticking us?"

"Oh, you know, budget cuts, so just the penthouse at the Siren."

While Mama gave a happy noise, Dad just raised his eyebrows in surprise. He probably would have preferred I rented a house for them out in Mexican Town where I grew up, but I wanted them closer to the Isle where I could have eyes on them.

"How's retirement?"

"Boring," he muttered, eyes cast back to his wife to see if she was listening. "I know your mother worried, but somehow golfing doesn't provide the same high as chasing perps."

"Imagine that," I deadpanned as I shared his grin.

I'd inherited his sarcasm and humor, which often left Mama scolding us both. Together though, we could rib each other.

"Is that why you two decided to come?" I asked. "Get some excitement?" His hesitation made me turn to look at him, noting how he kept his eyes on the road. "What?"

"I wanted to be here for your first negotiation. You might need help."

The last word bristled against my skin. "Have I been doing my job?" I asked, voice flat, this time not for a punchline, but because I was furious.

"Of course you have, but—"

"You think I can't handle this," I finished for him.

The sudden silence from the back had me crossing my arms and sinking into my seat. Here, the lecture from my mother would begin. I could practically hear the way her mouth opened to demand I apologize.

"Dette, I got this," Dad said softly. "Did you know that for my treaty, we went to appeals?"

There hadn't even been a whisper of appeals in the paperwork I'd studied for weeks, trying to ferret out nuggets of wisdom from Gran and Dad. Leaning back in the seat, I watched him carefully.

"It's not on record."

"No, it's not. It was an embarrassment, and it happened before transparency was rewarded. I was eighteen and a fool when I took over. By the time the treaty came, I was nineteen; I thought I could march in and make demands. If I'd had someone to help me, to guide me, maybe that wouldn't have happened. While I was sweating over appeals, Gideon was golfing."

Uncle Gideon, professional disappointment and Bronson's father. Long before I was even thought about, he'd been Divine Arbiter, and even though he was fifteen years older than Dad, he lacked both the dedication and the temperament for the job. He served until Dad was barely old enough and abdicated the second he could escape.

"I'm not here to overshadow you; I'm here to help."

I knew that deep in my bones, Dad wasn't Gideon. I'd heard the stories of Dad setting up deals only to have his brother swoop in at the last second and charm his way into glory.

"It's not about you stealing my thunder, I just—" I set my jaw, sighed. "I know you didn't want me to take over—but after what happened in Alabama with Bronson and…Margot—I don't want you to think that I don't take this seriously."

"She's been prepping for months," Graceland offered from the back seat.

"I have," I confirmed, chewing on the inside of my cheek, "and I know my proposals backward and forward."

"Oh, I know that look," he said as he maneuvered the car into the valet area for the hotel. "You wait till I'm parked."

I wished the ride was longer, maybe infinite, because while I knew he loved me, would and had defended me, he wasn't going to agree. The thought made something in me shrink, that for the first time in our lives we might truly be at odds with each other.

"Spill it."

"I'm going to ask for loosened restrictions on true fay, not indiscriminately," I rushed to say as his eyebrows rose. "But the Darkchilds and the Fellers—they don't need me in their business 24/7. I have files of similar requests from other states. Hell, in North Dakota they practically have a changeling on payroll. We aren't at war, and if we're going to cohabitate, they should be treated the same as humans, like citizens, because they are. When you and Gran fought for integration, that was a decision to accept magic could coexist—would coexist—with humans. This is the next step."

When he stayed silent, I curled my nails into my palm, letting the pain sting before I unleashed my other bomb.

"I want to put a motion forward to let fay into the Junior Pilgrim program."

Everyone stopped breathing and looked to Dad. I knew the magnitude of my proposal, the ramifications, and what he would say.

"You would undo our first tenet, the oldest one we have, the entire reason we exist?" Dad asked quietly.

"We exist to monitor magic, to be a balance—so why can't magic help monitor itself?" I demanded, voice cracking already. "They have just as much stake in it as us. I've brought statistics; I have candidates I think would thrive. We could expand our program and maybe people wouldn't be afraid of us."

"You're already seen as too sympathetic toward magic," he reminded me.

"Through no fault of my own," I countered. "I didn't ask to be a Conduit. We can't all be Devourers."

I expected him to counter, ready to keep doing battle, but he only opened the door and exited in silence. I swallowed hard against the rush in my ears as I watched him walk away. Age didn't matter, and neither did the fact that I knew he wouldn't agree; the rejection stung bitterly.

"I'll talk to him, baby," Mama said and squeezed my shoulder. "You go on and get ready."

Silently, the same as my father, I got out for the valet. I'd expected him to tick off all the reasons it couldn't work. That was how we discussed, how we fought: with facts. Now that he'd changed the rules, I felt like I'd taken a step in the dark and found a stair missing. Giving my mother a kiss on her cheek, I waited until Crisco led her away before I punched the panel of the car.

"Is breaking your hand conducive to getting your dad on your side?" Graceland asked, smoothly passing the valet money.

Pressing throbbing knuckles to my lips, I glared, but he looked back, unrepentant. I could rid myself of the pain. It was easy with minor wounds to let the magic flow over it like cold water. But I let the crunch of bone stay.

"I want you to find out about everyone that's on the Isle," I told him. "We meet in the casino in two hours."

There was the expectation for him to argue—we both knew that. He would jest about how I was a taskmaster and I'd jab back, like a ballroom dance where we knew the steps perfectly.

"You got it," Graceland said. "The Devourer thing was a cheap shot."

He disappeared. The first few times he'd popped out of existence, I'd nearly jumped from my own skin. Now pissed and itching to hit something again, I welcome the solitude. I hadn't meant it as an insult to my father, merely a fact. There had been a time I was viciously jealous that it was the Allfather that chose to bestow his gift on Dad and Bronson, while I'd gotten mine from Mother Eorthe. Too much betrayer magic in me to be able to cleanse others of their magic permanently, I'd been patiently told.

Swallowing the taste of bitter root on my tongue, I trudged back to Woodward. Moria and Asim would have everything brought to the island, organized, and ready, but I still felt the panic crawl across my skin.

When it was just Detroit, it was easy. My people, my problems. Being Divine Arbiter meant considering the needs of every city, every country, every single documented creature. Hundreds of thousands of reports read, tagged, and filed. But what if it didn't matter? What if, despite all my research, both gods looked at me like they had the first time I'd stood in front of them, an easily dismissed child?

The guilt of not completely hating the idea had me pressing a hand to my stomach. If dismissed, I could have my own life again, be free to disappear, maybe just travel like Gideon. A horn shrieked down the street, and the allure was crushed under the heel of my boot as I hopped onto the Q-Line. I understood my necessity, and I could never destroy what Dad and Gran built.

It was the music from *Rocky* that chimed from the bell as I shoved through the doors of Haven. I'd given up on trying to shut my brain off on the quick trip, knowing I needed to keep busy if I didn't want to turn into a blob. The frazzled look on Gaia's face as she looked up from the small boy currently wearing Luna's rubber safety gloves and glasses was enough to dissolve my nerves into a laugh.

"What have you done?" Gaia asked, but I wasn't sure it was to me or the boy standing in front of her.

"I'm 60% sure that it's stable!" Martavious declared happily.

"Fantastic!" Luna said from behind a welder's mask. "We'll take it to the alley, test it but—oh, hey, Pilgrim."

That had Martavious's head whipping up, the bottle in his hand dropping due to his surprise. With a sigh, Gaia shot forward and caught it before it hit the floor.

"Focus," she demanded, eyes flashing. "Pilgrim, what do you want?"

"I came by to check on things before I have to go to Belle Isle," I explained. "Anything exploded yet?"

"Don't jinx it," Gaia warned, holding up two fingers as if to ward my words off. "Take it outside, you two."

"You got it, Alpha!" Martavious chirped and saluted before Luna pushed him toward the alley exit.

Luna snorted at that. "Yeah, Alpha, you got it."

As soon as the door closed, Gaia simply sat on the floor. Amused, I leaned over the counter and watched her suck in a huge breath.

"You alright down there?"

She glanced up, and my smile died at the tears running down her face. Without thinking, I hopped the counter, my arms going around her.

"I'm fine," she said, her voice choked, "I'm fine."

She didn't struggle to escape my hold though, just leaned in and pressed her face to my shoulder. We sat in silence for a couple moments, both listening for an issue outside.

"Luna likes him," I said softly.

"Luna loves him," she corrected, voice muffled. "He hasn't gone away at all today, Brigitte. He's been focused and alert since the boy told him that his shoes were cringe."

Good tears then. I laughed as I heard an excited yell from the alley.

"Did Elle prep you about—"

"Yes," she interrupted, pulling back to scrub at her face, "would have been nice if you or my grandmother warned us that we would be adopting a literal child, because what the hell do I know about kids? But I've never been afraid of a challenge."

No words had ever held more truth.

"He's already asked if we're sure twice," she admitted and waved a hand towards the register. "Wanna sign off on the papers and make his day?"

"I'd love to. You should splash some water on your face."

"Alpha?"

We both turned to see Martavious at the end of the counter, sharp eyes ticking from Gaia's face to mine.

"What did you do to her?!" he demanded.

Even as part of me mourned how quickly I'd lost being his favorite, I grinned at his readiness to square up.

"It's a good cry," I explained and waved the papers at him. "Want to read the proof?"

His eyes moved quickly, fingers tapping where the straps of his backpack usually were. "Those my papers?"

"Technically, they're mine to file, but you'll get copies—Martavious *Darkchild*."

He fingers curled into his shirt and he looked at Gaia. "Are you sure?"

Gaia silently stood, her hands wiping her face. She moved with purpose until she was in front of him. From the alley, Luna came back in.

"Did it explode or was it brewed right?"

Martavious's head dropped. "It exploded. But Luna said it was close."

"Look at me, Martavious," she demanded.

Swallowing hard, he looked up. "Yes, Alpha."

That got a snort out of Luna, but Gaia only narrowed her eyes.

"You better get back to work until you get it right."

It took a second before he realized he'd gotten the answer to his question. The smile that split his face was huge. He stumbled forward, arms open, then gripped them back. With a sigh, Gaia nudged him past her but ruffled his curls. Looking to her brother, I watched the twins share a smile.

"Brigitte?"

I looked to see Martavious digging into a smaller cooler bag next to his backpack under the counter.

"Senior Pilgrim," Gaia corrected without turning, "an emissary always addresses by title unless given permission."

"You have my permission to call me whatever you want," I said, biting the inside of my cheek. "What's up?"

He held up a second vial. "Wanna taste test?"

"Not a chance in hell, kid," I said with a grin.

"You're cutting it awful close," Luna mentioned as he motioned for the vial. "You got what, a little less than two hours before you gotta get wrecked?"

"Which is why I'm here procrastinating. Moira and Asim will have all the physical stuff ready. I just need to show up and bleed."

"They're going to hurt you?"

I turned to a nervous Martavious and saw the corner of my jacket peeking from his backpack. I could've lied, but he would've seen it.

"I gotta earn my keep, but I promise they won't take anything I'm not willing to give away."

"Martyr," Gaia muttered.

"I'll remember that when you're complaining about parent teacher conferences," I said sweetly. "I'll see you guys."

I managed roughly ten steps in the cold before I saw Graceland leaning against an illegally tinted Escalade up the street. Without a word, he opened the back door. I give him a strange look but quickened my pace.

"You running chauffeur now?"

"Just get in."

For once I listened and slid in next to a grim looking Moira, which didn't worry me as much as Graceland's lack of banter. He slid into the driver's seat. Through the darkened window I could see we were headed to the Isle.

"Do I get a hint?"

"We got a Brood," Moira said.

"Oh shit. Hit me."

"Brood Vasile."

Shit. Shit. Shit.

"That's not possible," I argued weakly. "They don't exist anymore, not since—"

"Patrick killed Henry. Yeah, turns out like most heroic myths, that one's wrong," Graceland said.

"Which one was wrong about you?" Moira asks.

"I don't have enough time in the world," he replied with a dismissive wave. "Got us the Brood Tree from Alexei Haas himself."

"With or without his father's permission?" I asked.

"You know that answer to that question. Alexei is smart enough to keep himself safe. He knows his father better than all of us."

"Ok, give it to me."

"It's at your apartment, where it's going to stay," he said firmly. When I opened my mouth, he quickly cut me off. "You have bigger concerns right now."

"I need to do your hair," Moira said, "and you're changing either here or in a public bathroom."

Mind racing, I turned in the seat so she could reach my braided bun. "Just do half up, half down."

Moira drew a small bag from her pocket. "I will, but your mother and I have been practicing over Zoom for months. She sent these. It will only take a couple minutes."

I stared at the three beads in various shades of purple threaded through thin black silk. Mama wouldn't have wanted to do it herself, afraid she might transfer something to the beads or take the magic from them accidentally.

Fingers twisting at my braids, Moira lightly unrolled them from the bun I'd done for the shower the night before. I let her gently move from braid to braid, turning them in her palms, separating. It was reminiscent of sitting and watching Mama as she braided, twisted, and maintained her own glorious hair. On the times when she could get me to sit still, I would marvel about how she'd go out of her way to spare me the pain of a twist or the pull of a micro braid. Even though Moira's hands were a little clumsy, it still felt therapeutic, a grounding rod so I didn't drown in my own thoughts. Even still, tiny threads of doubt curled as she threaded the silk and beads into the braid closest to my cheek.

"Vasile. I'm gonna have to talk to Dad and Gran, but with just the tree—do you think it's compelling enough to ask the council's favor, force Bernard to admit it?"

"I think—and this is just wisdom from someone older and frankly better looking than you—you need to focus on passing your talks with the council before you go courting favor," Graceland said.

"I hate to admit it, boss, but he's right," Moira said. "All done."

I glanced into the rearview mirror and gently touched the silk-threaded braid around my bun, the three beads at the front like a tiny crown. Mama never missed.

"She'd be proud," I told Moira. "Give me the clothes and let's do this thing."

CHAPTER 13

Belle Isle was shrouded in mist as we pulled off Jefferson onto the bridge. Thick and grey, it slithered up the windows, wrapping around the mirrors, squeezing until the faint whine of metal could be heard. Graceland sighed and hit the wipers, but the fog thickened across the glass.

"Moira, tell your guards to stand down," Graceland said. "They're blocking my sight."

Nodding, Moira pressed her hand against the glass. "Nathair.[29]"

The mist smeared with the next swish of the wipers, the path ahead winding. When I looked through the tinted window, I could see the fog around us shuddering, millions of spectral snakes curling over each other in tight bundles. Behind us, the path disappeared, the impenetrable barrier following us like hell at our heels.

"You're the one who said 'don't take any chances with security,'" Moira reminded him.

"How much did you have to pay the white lady to take the night off?" he asked as he maneuvered us to the casino.

"I let Asim handle her," Moira admitted. "He's better with ghosts."

"More patient," she meant. He would have taken the time to explain the situation, whereas Moira would have flashed her badge and booted the vengeful woman from her spot.

We parked, and even in the wet fog I smelled it: Arcadia and Eden, minerally clay and tart apple. A reminder of the past and what was at stake.

The short jog up the steps to the casino at least kept me warm as I held down the skirt of the dress Moira picked out, so the frigid wind didn't lift it. The midnight-colored top resembled a double-breasted vest, tucked at the waist, but the bottom was free-flowing lines that

---

29 Snake, Gaelic.

fell just past my knees. The sleeves of the dress shirt, the color of ash, flowed as well but narrowed to tight cuffs at my wrists. Even though it wasn't from my closet, it fit perfectly and smelled faintly of earth and lavender.

Asim was holding down the bar when we got into the casino. Four glasses—hopefully of scotch—were laid out on the gorgeous marble bar top. I grabbed the one closest to me and took a sip. Vernors.

"Seriously?"

"Scotch after we kick ass," Asim said.

"I absolutely refuse," Graceland said and tapped the counter. "Two fingers. Neat."

There was a flicker, a shadow moving. From the ether, a glass clinked against the marble. I reached for it, but Graceland slapped my hand away.

"Get."

"You get," I grumbled and grabbed my Vernors. "Any last advice from the peanut gallery?"

"Try to stay on our allies' good sides—which is everyone besides the sirens and the elves," Moira pointed out. "You are not going to convince either of those groups to like anything that comes out of your mouth."

"Moira, we should be trying to appeal to everyone," Asim reminded her as he rustled through his papers. "I've done some research, and Valeria likes Dove chocolate, which—"

Digging into his pocket, he slapped a bag of chocolates onto the table, and my brain simply gave up. I laid my head on the cool marble bar, trying to smother the laughter, but it rattled me and our glasses.

"Asim, you broke her. Did you really think a bag of slightly melted chocolates would broker peace?" Moira asked.

"To be fair, I once gave Persephone sixteen chicken fingers and it stopped a war," Graceland pointed out while dodging the napkin thrown at him. "I'm just saying, it can't hurt."

Blindly feeling for the bag, I pulled it toward me as I lifted my head off the counter. "If this works, then Asim doesn't have to do paperwork for a month."

"What if it doesn't?"

"Nothing. This isn't a competition," I said, eyes trailing to Moira's watch. "Shit, it's time."

All the amusement evaporated, oxygen pulled from the room into our chests. For a couple seconds we stood, staring at each other. This was what we'd trained for, months spent on the floor of my apartment quizzing each other, arguing, laughing over absurd cases. It had been the perfect distraction from the fact that the left side of my bed was cold.

"Well, enjoy being under a microscope. I have six episodes of *Hannibal* and half a banh mi sandwich at my condo," Graceland said.

"You're not coming?" Asim asked.

"Sadly, I am an abomination, so I'm not allowed," Graceland explained, not looking sad at all as he left.

They watched him leave, both Junior Pilgrims looking unnerved, but I just grabbed the folders from their hands and led the way toward the ballroom.

"Stop worrying. I knew he couldn't come," I said quietly. "He won't be allowed tomorrow either."

Their shoulders loosened, but they remained silent as they turned the corner to the ballroom. The doors ran floor to ceiling, intricately carved and lined with gold filigree. With my hand on the handle, I could feel the power in the room beyond, but I didn't hesitate. The door creaked as if made from ancient wood, and for a second, the smell of ocean air crashed against me. Then the door closed behind us, jasmine and bound leather taking its place.

The space was vast—and empty.

"Where is—"

I shook my head to cut Moira off. This was the first test. Passing off the folders, I stepped forward and dragged my right foot in an arc against the marble. Palms up, I curled my fingers and stepped back, pulling the magic into existence. It was like dangling from a cliff by my fingernails, but I refused to release, instead sweeping my left foot out in a matching pattern to my right. The clash of ocean salt and decaying earth, fresh ash, and cold crisp air slammed into my lungs. It burned and froze there, crackled when I exhaled. Magic was inherently stubborn, but the same could be said for me.

Above me, the chandelier shook, but I only rolled my shoulders and lifted one arm, lowering the other so one palm faced the sky and one the earth. If it was any other performance, I would have bitten the inside of my cheek, used blood to help. But they would've known. From the ground, tendrils of magic, a thorny green, speared through my palm, and I felt the split of my flesh around it, letting it in. It wove through my bones, up my spine, through the other arm, and came through the other palm like a tree bursting from the earth. I bent my toes inside my boots, anchored the best I could, and waited for the truly painful part. The air went still, not a whisper of breath, of the crowds bustling in the lobby. Then, around me, I heard the first crackle. I stared forward as the council flickered in front of me, ignoring the hairs beginning to rise. There was one loud crack—like twigs snapping, a rib breaking—and blue lanced through the air. It struck the green tendril, turning it gold as it raced back through the path already created. It seared, holy and righteous, through my blood and out the palm into the floor. My arms dropped limply, but I didn't blink as the Council stared out at us.

"Welcome, Pilgrims."

They were like statues of ivory, ember, and onyx draped in gowns and suits running the spectrum of jewels. On the far end, the pale blue nymph clad in sapphire was the first to smile.

"Senior Pilgrim Brigitte Fitzpatrick, it's a pleasure. That was an excellent display of power." she said kindly.

"Thank you, Master Ives."

The sound of disgust from the elf, draped in emerald on the far end, had the entire room turning to look at him.

"Impressive? My people could have done that in adolescence. And the way she simpers immediately—humans."

The last word was so filled with vitriol that I smiled twice as big to match it, my voice syrupy sweet. "Considering, Master Farrow, that elves live far longer than humans, I would be considered an adolescent, so thank you as well."

The elf gaped at me, brows crashing together, but the dweorg next to him let out a loud laugh and slapped him on the back.

"Oh, I like this one! She's got fire in her," he declared. "But can you handle your drink?"

"May I approach the council?" I asked.

When the dweorg nodded, I held out a hand, thankful when Moira placed the proper paper into it. Moving forward in quick steps, I handed off the paper with a bow.

"As you can see, Master Braun, I have confirmation from the Feller clan that I did indeed best Rian Feller in a shot contest. Thirteen to eleven."

"Narrow margin," he murmured as he read. "What about in dwarven cask mead?"

"Master Braun, no one, dweorg or otherwise, is beating Rian Feller in cask mead," I said seriously.

The man's laugh echoed as if they were inside cavernous walls. "Honest. I approve."

"You approve of everything," Valeria, next to him, tsked, and examined her ruby nails. "She isn't as impressive to look at as her father. Perhaps because of her mother?"

There wasn't an audible gasp, but the entirety of the council turned in unison toward the siren. It was well known, the distaste the fay held for betrayer magic, especially sirens who had been taken away from Mother Eorthe against their will. If Master Valeria had said that in front of Dad, that would have been the end of her, but I was still unproven.

"Master Valeria, it's unbecoming of someone of your beauty and power to insult my mother."

She tapped her blood-colored nails against the dark wooden desk. "Do you think that obvious compliments thrown at my feet will win me over?"

"Use the chocolates," Asim whispered.

Ignoring him, I clicked my tongue. "Of course not, but I thought it tacky to say I assumed you were smarter than to let trash dribble from your beautiful mouth. What lipstick is that, Kat Von D?"

The scarlet lips in question curled into a nasty sneer as she rose from her seat. "You think you can—"

"Enough."

The fairy directly in the middle, skin dipped in ember and wearing the color of a dying sun, shook her covered head. "Valeria, you are a fool if you think yourself above the power of the Laveaus in their country of worship," Elliana said, her eyes of kaleidoscope glass shifting as she examined me. "Pilgrim, I apologize for my colleague's behavior. We will send a gift to your mother."

Ducking my head in respect, I kept my face solemn, despite the victory. "Thank you, and I apologize, Master Valeria. I didn't come here to insult you."

The siren didn't respond with anything besides a snort, but the man to her left, wearing a suit the color of deep-mined amethyst, clapped his onyx-colored hands together slowly.

"Excellent. It was almost believable, Pilgrim. I did hear your associate, by the way—hand over the chocolates," he demanded.

"Chocolates!" Valeria exclaimed, her eyes wide as I brought the bag to him. "Those are my favorite!"

"And if you hadn't behaved poorly, maybe you'd have gotten them," the man said as he selected one from the bag.

"Perhaps, Master Darrius, they should be shared?" I suggested with a smirk.

With the chocolate partway to his mouth, he matched my smile. "Yes, I suppose," he said and offered one to the troll next to him. "Calla, chocolate?"

Calla took the tiny thing between his large hands, fumbling at the wrapper as he asked me, "How is your father?" He popped the entire chocolate, foil and all, into his mouth.

"He would want me to say retirement suits him, but he's bored out of his mind."

"Yet he handed down his position to you," Elliana pointed out. "We were under the impression your cousin Bronson was to be his choice."

Don't tense. I could hear Graceland in my head after hours spent training with him. If I showed any weakness, they would exploit it.

"My cousin wasn't ready."

"And you were?" Calla asked.

There was no slight in the troll's voice, no reason to believe he meant to imply they thought I wasn't. Slipping my hands back into my pockets, I gave a slight nod.

"I was willing to shoulder the responsibility."

"That's an interesting way to answer the question, Pilgrim," Ives said softly, head tilted. "Your overseers seem to think you can. Do you think you're ready?"

"Yes," I said firmly and glanced back at my Junior Pilgrims. "Can you pass out the statistics, please?"

There was no hesitation as they approached the long desk, silently handing out folders. On the way back, Asim pressed the final one into my hands, which trembled only slightly as I took it.

"On the first page I have the statistics from my father's final nine years and my first year. As you can see, under my father, there was a significant decline in crimes committed by fay. This was due to my father's ability to follow law and maintain it. As you can see in my time as Senior Pilgrim, there's been a decrease in crime against fay while maintaining my father's level of fay-committed crime."

"Your point?" Farrow demanded.

My look was frigid but my voice placid. "The Pilgrim's job is to protect the fay and humanity. To do that, it's necessary that the treaty be modified. We need to acknowledge that many of the laws written keep the fay separate."

"For a reason," Darrius reminded. "There are fay that could, and often do, cause serious harm to humans. Your father's ability to devour served both communities well. The original laws may not be popular, but they serve an important purpose."

"I agree they're important, but we can modify them to better serve our people. For instance, my work providing blood banks for our vampire population has led to a 78% decrease in attacks in Detroit alone. We're down to almost no forced changes anymore."

"Those are not fay," Valeria snarled. "They are abominations!"

"Some would say the same of you," I replied without malice.

For the second time, the council went silent and turned to the siren. Her face was nearly as red as her dress, but I raised a hand in apology.

"That isn't a slight, Master Valeria. But not every vampire is to blame for your people's curse, nor are they responsible for the curse they wear. They're citizens, and often our most disenfranchised. If I arrest a siren who is turning tricks, taking wallets off men because she was abandoned and never trained properly, how does that help her? How does that change her life?"

"Do all sob stories turn you so easily?" Farrow asked. "A criminal chooses to be criminal, fay or otherwise."

"And how much time do any of you spend on the streets?" I countered. "When was the last time you left your true home in Arcadia? The last time you saw how your people live in slums while you pretend to have their interests at heart? And you wonder why they stray, why they turn to other gods?"

The smell of bitter, burnt greens hit me, and I gave a short nod at the reprimand from Mother Eorthe.

"Perhaps this is too personal for you, Pilgrim," Valeria suggested, nails under her chin as if in deep thought. "After all, you weren't shy about being involved with a member of the fay, a muse. A reformed criminal. Am I remembering that right?"

At the mention of Margot, a breeze swept through the room: bergamot and jalapeno. A warning, but not for me. The seven all sat back, sharing glances of wariness, but it settled me down. I had no idea why Mother Eorthe would chastise the council for that, but I'd take it.

"Yes, I was involved with Margot Masterson. While we were together, I ran my own business, was only considered a Junior Pilgrim in the sense that I had passed my rites. I was brought in only when my father needed help. Moira and Bronson were his subordinates, so I didn't break any rules."

"What about after you became the Senior Pilgrim?" Ives asked, voice soft.

"We had already broken up by then," I lied to the nymph. "Six months later, she died."

"In your arms," Farrow said, narrow face sharpened by suspicion. "Are we supposed to believe that was just a coincidence?"

"Prove that it wasn't," I challenged.

The seven murmured to themselves, and it was only Braun that gave a firm nod. His thick fingers pushed the pages of my report aside to the final sheet.

"We aren't here to put her on trial for personal relations," the dweorg stated. "We aren't here to dispute differences of opinion. Our job, as handed down by our Mother, is to deem her power worthy of Arbitership of the entire world, and to hear suggestions for both Creators to consider. Your files are impressive, and there is no doubting you have the skills to continue, but would you be open to a suggestion?"

"Of course, Master Braun," I said.

"Be honest with us."

Genuine confusion rushed through me, and it showed, because Braun's face softened as he poked at the folder in front of him.

"Valeria would have been much more amicable if you told her about what you're doing in Detroit. Trying to find the killer of sirens."

"She's what?" Valeria demanded, but her voice was weak as she pushed the papers aside in her own folder. Quickly, she scanned the paper and glanced up. "You actually care about my people? That wasn't lip service?"

For a minute, I didn't move, because if I did, they would see my surprise. That file had not been in the folders when I looked them over, which meant one of the Juniors had slipped them in. I would've bet money on Asim.

"Of course I do," I said. "That's my job. I know that my father focused on policing the fay, and it's important, it really is. But it's also important to protect the fay. That's what I want to focus on in my first tenure: protection and…I'd like to put up for discussion inclusion of fay into protecting themselves."

The entire council fell to silence as they looked to each other, as if someone could give clarification to my words.

"Explain," Darrius finally said.

It wasn't a straight denial, so I jumped in full force. "If we could train fay, all walks of fay, in the same manner we do Pilgrims, as an organization we would be equipped to do so much more. A siren, for instance, would be more open to listening to a siren Junior Pilgrim than me, and—"

"Let me see if I understand what you're saying," Farrow interrupted. "You would pervert the fay's wild nature to make your job easier."

"Their nature is already changed, Master Farrow. They live with humans, love humans, follow our laws. These are not the pixies, trolls, and elves of Arcadia. The world has changed, and we need to evolve. If you would just look at the candidates I have included in the folders, you'll see this isn't about distorting fay; it's about respect. If we show that we aren't dictators, everyday fay won't have a reason to fear us."

Shoving the entire folder to the floor, Farrow leaned to look down at me. "And then you'll have lost your power over them,"

"Why can't respect work as well?" I countered. "I recently met a troll who was terrified of me simply because I'm a Pilgrim."

"Well, he must have been a criminal then."

Praying for patience, I shook my head. "He was just an everyday person who is used to the old ways, where we kicked in doors and used force. We already bring in fay to help us on cases, for information or supplies. Imagine what we could accomplish together."

"It sounds like you're running for office. That is your problem, not the Creators'."

It would've been so easy to crush the elf's neck, but as with everything, I refused to do what was easiest.

"And you're laboring under the delusion that the fay are still the same from when they first passed through the veil. Why do you insist on being difficult?"

"Difficult?" Farrow sneered and shook his head. "Do you know how many times one of us has heard the same olive branch speech in our lifetimes? You are either lying or stupidly naïve. Your history is littered with the bodies of our people and your own, based on so-called cooperation. Our Creators had to create your organization because of the blood soaking the earth from the very ideas you propose."

"That's not what—"

"Our own mother hid from the perversion created by the brutality, the blood of man and fay," he interrupted, chest heaving. "In your own chapter, you've seen it yourself, native peoples decimated because they trusted. Your job is not to blend but to maintain, to balance. Your own ancestor, Patrick, made the mistake of trying what you are asking, and I would assume you wouldn't be stupid enough to make the same mistake."

"Master Farrow—"

"We will submit this proposal," Elliana interrupted, but her face was bland. "I wouldn't suggest you have hope for it."

In the end, it was all I could ask for, that it was sound enough to pass to the Allfather and Mother Eorthe, so I nodded and moved on. "There are also several smaller proposals and requests, including but not limited to reestablishing pack lands for native werewolves. Several national parks have been closed recently, and I've had teams map out the grounds. It's a start toward reconciliation of our more… disenfranchised packs."

"You think resources should be wasted on fools, those that allowed themselves to be browbeaten into submission, even after the gifts we bestowed?" Farrow asked, incredulous.

All right. I changed my mind. He was getting strangled to death.

"Watch your tongue, elf," Ives said carefully, the nymph's normally soft voice a slap of icy water. "Those 'fools' are my people, and perhaps it would be prudent to remind you how often you whine for more resources for your own, then turn around and gloat about self-sufficiency."

Color tinted the tips of the elf's ears, and I hurried to speak before the council could erupt on itself.

"Master Ives, I know nothing we do will ever be enough, but these parks, they're beautiful. If we declare them preserves under treaty law, you'll never have to worry about them being taken away."

"Which means they're up to me to protect," Darrius said, resting his chin on an open palm. "What do I get out of it?"

"Typical dragon," Ives muttered.

It was, but I managed to contain my smile. "You get to place some of your charges at the entrances and lines of each reserve. I know for a fact many of the chimera and hydras you've rescued are working breeds. We'll give them a job; the packs can tend them, and they protect the pack during moons and training."

Darrius's smile was toothy as he nodded. "I accept."

"Wait a second." Ives argued, pale blue fingers raised to stop him. "This is sounding more like appeasement than restitution for my people."

Darrius raised a single brow at her. "It's called compromise, darling,"

"My people have compromised enough—*darling*," Ives countered.

"It is mutually beneficial," I admitted but raised two fingers as if to make a Pilgrim's promise when Ives opened her mouth. "But I didn't finish. We all know how many wood nymphs and gnomes have been displaced because of the wildfires out on the coast. We offer them sanctuary in return for caretaking the land while the packs are away. It would then fit reserve guidelines, but both you and Darrius would have final say in any changes. Which means your people have a voice. If the land can be maintained for ten years, the full responsibility transfers over to the packs, and under divine law cannot be obtained by anyone else."

"Clever girl," Darrius praised. "I accept. Ives?"

The nymph gave a long look, and I couldn't help but wonder if the dragon felt the crackle of nature magic, leaves crunching. Finally, Ives smiled.

"Yes, I accept the terms. We will go over the formal proposal together and contact you when the reserves are ready, so you can oversee the transfer."

It might have seemed small, but I shoved down the urge to fist bump. This was a step toward inclusiveness on a scale unseen within the fay. I wanted to exhale my nerves, but I just gave both a small bow before turning to face Braun.

"There is a request that I included from the Feller clan for you, Master Braun. They would like to welcome three more human students into alchemic study. Tomorrow, I'll submit the same request to Master Heron. They've asked for your blessing specifically, so I've included detailed reports on the three humans for you to make a fair assessment."

"Many thanks, Pilgrim."

Bowing again, I turned to Calla who, for the most part, had watched and listened in silence. "Master Calla, there was a request for you as well from the Yukon. The coterie of giants and yeti have filed several grievances concerning missing members. They think the Pilgrims aren't taking it seriously enough."

"And are you taking it seriously enough?" the troll asked.

"Very much, sir. I've sent three agents out there, and they've assured me everything looks normal, almost migratory—like the members moved on to better areas. With your permission, I'd like to accompany you up there myself, in the spring, after you've finished traveling. In the meantime, I will forward all my findings and reports to you."

The troll's mouth pursed as he reached for another chocolate from the open bag in front of him. "Yes, inform the coterie of our arrival date," he said seriously, though his beady eyes sparkled. "I look forward to seeing you in the field."

"Likewise, sir," I said, and faced Elliana.

The oldest of the group, her smooth, sharp face didn't show it, didn't show much of anything as she waited for me to speak.

"Your daughter wishes to speak with you."

The fairy's head reared back as if she had been slapped. "That is the request you've chosen as the most pertinent, the worthiest of my attention?!" she demanded, her ever-changing eyes flashing. "My daughter, a peddler of debauchery, a traitor to our kind, wishes to have a word?"

Feather Glen had warned me, months ago, about this when she came to ask for the favor. She had been so adamant on how badly it would go; it was almost like she was trying to talk me out of it. It didn't matter that Feather saved girls' lives, got all manner of fay off the streets—got them employment and schooling and training. She was a disappointment.

"She's sick," I said simply, "and that was a request, to inform you."

"Sick?" Elliana questioned softly, then shook her head. "What is my proposal?"

I'd been prepared for it by Feather, told fiercely by Horace not to get my hopes up, but bitter disappointment washed over me at the dismissal. Straightening my spine, I swallowed the venomous words I wanted to destroy her with and made a snap decision.

"This is for both you and Master Valeria, now that I realize my mistake about not releasing information about my current investigation. There is a brood trafficking both sirens and fairies from overseas into North America. With your permission, I'd like to open a formal investigation with Bernard Haas."

"Absolutely," Valeria said, eyes snapping over to the still silent fairy. "Is there a problem?"

The fairy tilted her head, her kaleidoscope eyes shifting over me. "How do you know this isn't an isolated incident?" she asked.

"It's not," I said flatly. "I have a ledger of at least twenty fay that have been taken from overseas and placed in Detroit alone. I need more time, but I know three of the buyers are from Deep Europe. Vlkodlak."

"Why would they buy what they could get in Europe?" Elliana said skeptically.

"They weren't paying to own them; they were paying to hunt them."

My words seemed to break the council as they stared out bleakly at me, looking for the first time like they weren't all powerful. It was the effect of staying inside Arcadia, far away from the truth and corruption. Only Darrius, familiar with those who would hunt many of the fay beasts he rescued, nodded.

"Even if Elliana doesn't give her blessing, I will," he said firmly.

Having the two votes gave me the power to use whatever means necessary, which meant I could go toe to toe with Haas to demand and obtain the truth, even if I didn't become Divine Arbiter.

"You would go against my wishes?" the fairy asked, voice soft but not gentle.

Darrius's yellow eyes flickered with heat, forked tongue coming out to wet his lips. "I've seen innocent creatures brutalized, and if I can lessen that I will."

"Our people are dying, Elliana," Valeria reminded her, fingertips pressed to her glossy lips. "Perhaps truly we have been away from this world for too long if your answer isn't immediately clear?"

The fairy's shoulders dropped, wings folded down as she nodded. "You have my approval."

Bowing, I drew my fingers across lips and heart. "You have my word; everything I do is in the best interests of your people."

Slowly, as if the world had suddenly halted, each raised a hand to their lips and mirrored me. Magic pulsed between us as the bond was formed, tingling like mint on the back of my throat, and the air burst with the scent of rain. A blessing.

"You have succeeded Senior Pilgrim. We will mark the record," Elliana acknowledged as she nodded to the door. "You may leave."

Behind me, Asim and Moira moved first, then stepped back and respectfully bowed as I moved for the door.

"Pilgrim, wait!" Farrow demanded.

The insistence had my subordinates' heads jerking up, but I turned slowly, one brow raised.

"You did not provide me with a request," he informed me.

Delight turned my lips just slightly as I weighed words and consequences. "I apologize, Master Farrow, but I've already been dismissed. Maybe next time."

With that I swept out of the room, smothering a grin as the elf cursed and my Junior Pilgrims jogged to keep up. Closing the giant door behind them, the light and air of the lobby crashing over me, I laughed.

Asim and Moira watched me with amusement and irritation, but the amount of relief that seeped from me kept the giggles coming.

"Brigitte," Moira started to lecture, but even she grinned, "did you have to do that?"

"Absolutely not, but damn it felt good," I said. Feeling too good to worry, I nudged Asim. "You ok?"

He nodded, but his brow was furrowed. "They aren't like I expected."

"Me either," Moira admitted. "I didn't expect them to be so—"

"Terrible?" Graceland interrupted as he approached. "They're like most beings with too much power—stuck up, narcissistic, petulant children."

He was more casually dressed, suit replaced with well-worn jeans and a Bayside t-shirt. The hair he usually spent hours crafting was chaos.

"Does that include you?" Moira joked.

"Oh, without a doubt," Graceland confirmed with a wink, "which we can all discuss in earnest later. But for now, I need to borrow your boss."

"She's your boss too," Asim informed him.

"As she loves to remind me," he said and shooed them away.

Leaning back against the cool pillar, I gave them both a nod, waiting until they were halfway across the lobby to speak.

"It went better than expected; they gave me permission to get the truth from Haas," I said mildly as I chewed at my thumbnail. "I didn't get cursed, if that's what you're worried about."

"That's a disgusting habit," he informed me but leaned on the same pillar. We were practically breathing each other's air. "Your cousin Mercutio sent a missive. He wants approval for a yeti patrol for outside of Kushva.[30]"

"Which I can't grant until I pass tomorrow and only if they will mind him," I say but grinned, "what else?"

"Alexei needs to speak with us."

"When?"

"I figured we have some time tonight to—shit."

As if pulled by a string, my head snapped in the direction he'd frozen. Coming toward us was probably the most beautiful man I'd ever laid eyes on. Carved from marble, tall and pale, with perfectly coiffed hair the color of sunshine. Normally, I would have fanned myself dramatically for Graceland's benefit, but there was something about the man's smile, just the wrong side of mean, that made me wary.

"Lucy! Long time."

It was like a puzzle, and as Graceland tensed like an antelope ready to run, the nickname was the last piece, clicking into place.

---

30 In Russia. By the Urals Mountain Range. Cold as balls.

Smoothly, I quickened my pace so I was in position to take the man's outstretched hand.

"Brigitte Fitzpatrick, Senior Pilgrim of North America."

Instead of taking my hand, the man dropped his, eyes going over my head to look at Graceland. "Still working for a Pilgrim, Lucy? That must sting."

I could have easily dropkicked him in the junk, though I wasn't sure he actually had any. "His name is Graceland." I informed him.

He finally lowered his gaze to stare down his nose at me. It was so reminiscent of Bronson that I curled my hand into a fist and resisted the urge to punch him in the throat.

"I can tell you're tense, but Lucy and I go way back. Like brothers," he assured me, smile growing.

Clearly, he hadn't spent much time around humans, because he thought he'd dazzled me, but his smile was fake and toothy.

"Exactly like brothers. I know who you are, Mike." I said, grinning when he winced at the shortening of his name. "I also know that while you're here, you toe the line. Should I go pray to your father, tattle that you're not playing nice?"

The wind rushed by as he took a step forward, and I stepped to match, the smell of candle smoke and steel surrounding me.

"I'm all for dick measuring, but I assure you, if you mess with me or *Graceland,* I will not hesitate to send you back to your comfy desk job in the sky. So, test me, because it's been a hard week," I said, voice dripping with fake sweetness.

"You shouldn't be so quick to alienate allies, Pilgrim, especially when you're already corrupted," he said, jerking on the lapels of his jacket as he spared his brother a glance. "You must have gone truly soft, having a human as a guard dog."

Point made, he spun on his heel and stalked away. Shoving I hands into my pockets, I scrunched up my nose when Graceland remained still.

"Pretentious dick," I muttered.

"Brig, you shouldn't have done that," he said, but his lips were curled up.

"Angels are the worst," I said, then winced at my mistake. "Sorry."

"We really are," he agreed, shrugging as he faced me instead of his brother's back. "He was always the upper echelon of douche though."

"You rebelled against Heaven," I pointed out, leaning against the pillar again.

"And he once leveled an entire city because of butt stuff."

"Do those things even out?" I mused.

"No, he did it because it disgusted him. All I wanted, ever wanted, was our father to see me."

The way he said it, flat and toneless, stopped my speculation. His eyes were back on the lobby, as if seeing far beyond Belle Isle, and my own vision tilted, shunted to grey. Pushing back against the pillar, I tried to get my mouth open, to tell him he was bleeding his magic through me, but my lips remained pressed together, vision shifting and blending until I went blind.

CHAPTER 14

The Children of Creation watched from their heavenly perches as the Allfather crafted humans from blood and bone. They were beautiful things, fragile but chaotic in a way that spoke to these holy children. As the world began to grow in front of their multiple eyes, so did their desire. It was Azrael, the oldest of them, that crept from his post first, walking the surface of the earth behind his father's back. The humans were easy to manipulate: a whisper in the ear, a dream given—spilled over into their waking lives. Unable to keep it to himself, he shared the knowledge with his siblings.

By the time the Allfather found them out, entire sections of the world were corrupted, humans bowing and bending to pantheons of various vices and virtues. Azrael was nowhere to be found, but his siblings had already renamed themselves. Shedding the shackles of the past, the first fallen chose the mantles of Grian, Aroni, and Amun,[31] to name a few, power growing the more humans bowed in their temples. Unlike the betrayers of Mother Eorthe, who despite their rebellion and expansion still held their breath when their mother's name was spoken, the fallen held no such faith. They'd been dismissed from Heaven; what did the Allfather matter when they had everything in their own hands?

It took centuries before Hades heard the whisper of his father in his mind, and at first, he thought it a dream, something he'd become prone to now that his worship was slowing. When it continued, he confided in his brothers, only to discover Poseidon and even Zeus felt the touch of their Allfather.

The three set out to the edge of the world where sky met land, to the place of their dreams, and sat. Time passed, but it didn't matter; they sat in silence, waiting. Finally, their father came, and

---

31 Grian, Irish Sun Deity. Aroni, Yoruba Nature Deity. Amun, Egyptian Invisibility Deity.

the only thing Hades thought was that his father looked old, his umber face weary, but when he rose, out of habit, to offer an arm, he was blocked by another figure. It looked like a human man, but his eyes were far too black, an abyss Hades found familiar, and from his back sprouted wings. They weren't the threaded vines of his brother Dionysus, or even the sparking blue of Zeus; no, these were feathers.

"Michael, he means me no harm," the Allfather said, voice tired. "You may go."

Without hesitation, the man—no, the beast—turned back to the mists, disappearing. Hades glanced at his brothers, who looked as disturbed as he felt.

"No free will," their father said, snapping his fingers, and a throne appeared. "It's something I'm trying out."

"We will not submit to that," Zeus told him, "if that's why you called us here."

The Allfather's laughter was light, like when they were children and did something funny.

"No, I don't suppose you would after what I've allowed you to do."

"*Allowed* us?" Poseidon spat and took a step forward. "Everything we've done has been in spite of you."

Not sparing his fuming child a look, he turned to his quiet Hades. "Do you have a proclamation to spew as well?"

"I'm waiting to see what deal you mean to offer."

The laughter was loud, delight for when they got something right.

"You always were the one to see the bigger picture when your siblings thought only of pleasure," he said fondly. "That space you've built, the underworld, what is the capacity?"

"Enough," he said, "as much is needed."

"I require use of it."

Poseidon took another step. "How dare—"

With a heavy sigh, their father snapped his fingers, and the mighty god of the ocean liquefied to a puddle of water. Holding a hand up at the other two, he shook his head.

"He'll come back when we're done."

Both brothers stared at the small tide pool, swallowing hard. It was Zeus who dared speak. "Only if we agree to whatever you're doing now, I assume."

Their father's smile was sharp, knowing. "You're so much more than even I gave you credit for. Tell me, how many children have you abandoned around this earth? Perhaps you take after me more than you think."

Zeus's face remained placid, but the air around them crackled.

"It will take more than insulting comparisons to make me lift a hand against you," he said. "I'm not foolish enough to leave you alone with my brother."

"Disappointing."

"We're good at doing that to each other," Zeus agreed.

For a second, their father's hands tightened on the arms of his throne, but then he smiled.

"A dual offer, then. Mother Eorthe and I have come to a new agreement, which means for now I can no longer—" He paused, lips pursed. "—recycle material when an experiment doesn't give me the results I'm looking for."

"You want me to sort the ones you kill then," Hades guessed.

"No, no, recycling means no killing either. If I create them, I must allow them to die without intervention. Waste of time."

"I don't understand."

The laughter this time was bitter, and not from his father but his brother. Hades looked between them in confusion.

"She finally outplayed you," Zeus said. "And let me guess, you'll send that golem you created—what have you named this batch?"

"Archangels."

Zeus laughed again, pressing a hand to his chest as if to contain the brittle noise. "You'll send the Archangels to decimate us all, even those of us who have done nothing but good, unless I kill your mistakes and Hades hides the bodies."

"Your children will be safe as well; everything you've created will remain. A mutually beneficial partnership."

"A boot on your neck is not a partnership," Zeus corrected.

"I accept," Hades said quietly.

Both Zeus and their father turned to stare, but Hades only stood taller.

"Brother, I—"

"I will not have everything we've done, every freedom we've given, every creature we've birthed, be ripped away because of pride," Hades told Zeus. "We are parents, and the time has come to sacrifice for our children."

And they did. How brutal to watch the various creatures their father claimed to love come to them, fall to them, and be placed. No explanation to fearful and confused children, only the swing of blade, a splash of life across the volcanic rock of the underworld, a soul for the Styx.

So, when the earth above his throne room split, the world curling back, and a creature hit the ground, Hades barely moved. Instead, he watched the night sky, frowning at the various falling stars he saw before the earth shut like a tomb.

It was only when the creature sniffled that Hades turned to it. It looked like a human boy, no older than fifteen. From its back were broken wings, the right barely a stump, while the left dangled at what had to be an excruciating angle.

"You've fallen, child," the god mused as he approached and set his palm on the boy's shoulder. "Believe me, I know the pain of being abandoned. He'll expect me to judge you, kill you. But for now, if you kneel for me, you'll be safe. Might be food for my Cerberus, but then again, you could surprise me."

The god expected the boy to shake, to tremble as all others had in his presence. Expected a tear-stained face when he tilted the small chin upwards, but all he saw was a sharp grin and coal black eyes.

"No, I think I've had enough of kneeling," he said, his voice like bells. "Perhaps you'd like to?"

Shaken, the god took a step back, eyes flittering to the few feathers left on the broken wing. His throat went tight in memory. Holding out a hand for his blade to come to him, he kept his eyes on the beast, but the boy was surging forward, his own hand up. The sword of bloodied bone shook in the air, tilting back between them.

"I am Hades, worshipped for longer than you've been alive, bastard son. I promise you do not want to do this," he warned.

The small thing, thin and fragile, only grinned, dark eyes glistening. "Hades," he said, testing the word on his tongue, "I like that name. I think I'll enjoy being Hades."

The blade shook in the air, cracking at the hilt, and Hades took a step forward. "Enough games, abomination! You think you're special? We rebelled first; you aren't special, just another unloved creature."

A scream split the air, the bone breaking free, and it shot across the room. Hades stumbled back, staring at the soaked blade in his chest. Within seconds the boy was upon him, ripping it from his flesh before shoving it back in. Again and again, thin fingers now slick with glowing ichor slammed bone into the thick chest of the god. As Hades fell back, hands burst from the ground gripped at his robes, skeletal fingers digging deep into his flesh.

Standing over him, the stained boy raised the blade over his head and grinned.

Gurgling, the god held his hand out as if to block the blade.

"What are you?"

"What I am now doesn't matter," the boy told him, voice sweet. "What I am going to be is a god."

With that he brought the bone down, splitting the god's skull. Dropping to his knees, he immediately began feasting upon the grace flowing from the wounds, drenching himself in memory and power.

"Little one, who did this to your master!?"

With drunken movements, the boy turned only his head, watching as Zeus and Poseidon took a step back at the sight of him. He'd drunk so gluttonously that it poured from his lips down his neck, staining his simple covering with celestial ichor. With a grin, the boy fluttered what was left of his ragged wings and saw the fury in the God's eyes.

"Archangel," Poseidon said with disgust. "Just a will-less savage. Did Father send you here?"

"Poseidon," Zeus said, reaching for his brother. "Wait."

The taller god didn't listen as he strode forward, pulling his trident from his back.

Standing, the boy turned fully, the long piece of bloodied bone in his hand. "He never loved you as much as Hades," the boy considered, "but I suppose killing you will at least make him pause."

"Poseido—" Zeus started.

The boy moved like shadow, flittering in and out of the space around the god, the sword of bone slipping like a needle into his flesh. Roaring, Poseidon swung away, the tiny pinpricks of a hundred small wounds beginning to drip down his skin. Lifting his trident, he turned, searching.

"Face me!"

There was nothing, and then the boy was right behind, a shadow of whispers.

"You're the weakest of them. Is that why Father never mourned your loss?"

Turning, the god tried to grab for him, but the boy dissolved to darkness in his meaty palms. Dropping the trident, the god raised both hands. From behind him, the River Styx churned, the black water gurgling with the force it took to pull it from its current. As twin streams of dark water curled from the banks, bodies in various states of decay began to slough from it, slapping against the volcanic rock.

The water poured over the child, who cried out. Falling to the ground, the archangel felt the sharp edges of the ground pierce his palms, his bare feet. For a second, he was falling through the air again, watching the rage-filled face of his favorite brother, his wings burning like autumn leaves when a bonfire starts. Wiping the water away along with the horrors it carried, he stood, eyes ticking in his sockets as he took in the room. The god strode forward, trident at the ready, but it didn't stop the smile that curled up the boy's face.

"I like that trick," he said happily. "But they didn't"

Snapping his fingers, the bodies stumbled up, bones cracking, flesh slapping against stone as they struggled forward. Poseidon turned and reached for his trident. The bodies lurched from all sides, and despite the few he skewered, they overwhelmed him. Fingers dug into flesh, and as they began to tug the god toward the river he'd just controlled, bursts of celestial light leaked through the wounds. It only made the dead more feral, rabid as they pressed decaying mouths to the holes, trying to capture grace once more.

"You know why they're so willing?" the boy asked eagerly. "Because your brothers took this from them. I'm going to give it back."

There was a teetering moment, the god on the edge of the Styx, when he might have thrown off the bodies; then a hand came from the depths and latched around his ankle. Like a pillar crashing to earth, the god toppled, bodies going with him into the oily black depths.

"Brother!" Poseidon screamed. Then his head went under.

Immediately, the water began to pull again, running quickly down the path, leading further into the underworld. As the boy turned to the last god, Zeus only stared back.

"You wanted him to love you."

"I did," Zeus said honestly, "but he didn't. You won't goad me like my brothers, child."

Tilting his head, the boy studied Zeus, then nodded wisely. "Morning Star. That's my name."

"You can't keep the name the Allfather gave you—not if you want free will."

"I didn't want free will. I wanted him to get rid of the humans," he said, eyes glassy, finally looking like the child he was. "They betrayed him by worshipping you and all the other false gods. I only worshipped him."

"And killing us will make him love you?

The laughter was beautiful, bells ringing in the wind—even as Morning Star wiped the excess ichor from his chin, licking it from his fingers.

"No, I can't make him love me—but I can kill everything he still cares for."

Shooting forward, the boy swung the sword, but it sliced through only air. Blinking, he turned in a quick circle, then glanced up. Above him, Zeus flew, wings of pulsing blue light flapping gently.

"He never took our wings, child; you truly must be fallen," Zeus said sadly. "You aren't the first, only the latest."

Reaching behind himself, the god plucked a charged bolt from his wings. It crackled and pulsed, growing into a full bolt.

"I've killed enough of you over my lifetime to know."

Pain. He thought he knew pain, but as the lightning struck him, it seemed to rattle his bones, cracking through marrow that left celestial blood boiling. It was same pain as the minute he knew he'd lost the war, when Michael's boot crushed his ribs and he fell.

The ground was unforgiving in his failure, the air snatched from his lungs as something broke in his chest. He looked up at the god, arms wrapped around his waist as if he could stop the shaking, the burning, the agony. But it wasn't a god—a giant eagle stared back at him. In a moment of stillness, both heads tilted, then the bird screamed, talons outstretched. Unable to force his spasming arms to move, the boy was defenseless as they pierced around his eyes. As the hallux squeezed to meet the other talons and he heard the wet squelching of his crushed eyeballs, he couldn't scream as his throat convulsed. It was only when the bird pulled his eyes from his body and the flapping of wings filled the chamber that the first gasp of pain left the boy.

Blind, he fumbled, fingers only finding loose rock, feet stumbling. Spinning around, he heard the approach of wings and tried to run, but felt the slice of talons across his back. Falling again, he pressed a hand against the blood and celestial heat, as if his slippery fingers could hold the essence he just stole.

"My brother, Hades, would have hidden you. He thought I didn't see, but I know my brother's heart. It could only withstand so much useless death. He would have shown you mercy, but you don't know what that is, do you, child? And with me, you never will."

A bloodstained hand shot forward, fingers grabbing the eagle's throat. With one quick pluck he took the eyes of the bird and dropped the god to the ground. Shoving the eyes into his own sockets, he blinked rapidly, taking in the screaming god rolling across the volcanic rock.

"He told us about you three," Morning Star said, new blue eyes sly, pupils blown. "How as children the three of you would watch the world below, pinch people and things between your fingers, pretending to move them around. You've always wanted what he built."

Zeus stumbled to his feet, hands still pressed to his eyeless sockets, but he spat blood in the direction of the voice. "I have so much pity for you, child, how much hatred you had to harbor to overcome the lack of will he gave you. He isn't your father; he's your master and you are a slave."

"Enough."

Zeus grinned at the first quiver of panic in the boy's voice. Dropping his hands, he laughed. "Even now, you cannot be sure it's not him forcing you to do this, can you?"

It was a single swing of the bone sword that felled the god, sending his head rolling, but the small boy slashed again and again.

Exhausted, Morning Star sat amongst the carnage and waited. It was days before the rest of the pantheon came, ready for war, armor gleaming when they descended upon the throne room. By then the new Hades, wrapped in a robe of shadow, lounged on his throne of bones, the head of Zeus under impatiently tapping fingers.

It wasn't war but submission; if he had bested their strongest, they knew they stood little chance, so begrudgingly they kneeled. He had no desire to restrict them, so long as they left the underworld to him. He had plans.

So, with wrath and blood, he built Hell for his father's humans, where the screams that rivaled his own when he fell echoed, and the smell of sulfur and brimstone burned in his lungs. As for his father's creations, he offered them freedom, kept them feral, and set them upon the world he wished would crumble. He fluttered through identities the way they flittered through human's lives. The demons had balked at the name Hades immediately, so it was Satan who led them, who fed them.

While his demons tricked and corrupted, he did his research. One by one he found his father's discarded favorites, coming to them in the night at all corners of the earth, taking from them not just their lives but their celestial power. Drunk on it, he changed Hell again, letting the demons have more say in the corruption, while he spent more time on the surface.

He caused destruction and decay, setting off disasters and death. It never failed to spark his curiosity what a single promise, a fleeting thing like wealth or beauty, could get him from humans. On earth he changed his name again; Satan was too harsh for the fragile humans, too scary, so he became Lucifer. It was perhaps that simple evolution, a grabbing for more power, that led him to her.

It was in Lothal that he followed the whispers of a champion, a fierce bronze statue of a woman whose temper was as quick as her blade. He was sure she must be celestial from the way humans worshipped the rumors of her deeds. He was proven right when he found her in the filthy alley, the bodies of the ferals he sent ahead at her feet and her dagger ready for him.

He scoffed at her arrogance and took a step, letting the dagger touch his throat. She was nearly as tall as him, but he still tilted his chin to try to look down at her.

"I promise you don't want to do that."

"These your dogs? How about you give me your coin, and we'll go our separate ways." she shot back. "I'd hate to damage that face."

Irritated, he shoved her dagger aside and took a step. The woman grabbed his wrist, and he froze as power slammed into him. The woman's eyes went a brilliant violet. It was warmth, energy pushing them back several feet as dust blew upwards around them. There was pain, but it was fleeting as power flowed like heat against frozen limbs. Memory swept over them, and they nearly collapsed into each other with relief.

"Morning Star."

"Lilith."

The names rolled over them, as if coming home but finding everything inside was someone else's.

So, he told her everything, because she had been his sister. The first to raise her blade for him and the last to fall from Heaven for him. They sat on the hill overlooking the sea, gazing down at the ship that she'd taken over when she'd first awoken on Earth. He expected her to be thrilled, to rejoice in his brutality against their father, to laugh as he described Hell. Instead, he was stunned as she took his hand between hers and pressed it to her cheek.

"You've been in so much pain," she said. "Let me show you something."

For the first time in millennia, he let himself be led, her touch grounding him, keeping him from the shadow. They passed through the villages on the hills, people greeting them warmly—or, rather, Miss Lily. She kept her body rigid from their touches but handed out coin and smiles to the children, nods of welcome to the men and women who glanced up from their work.

"Lilith—" He stopped as a child patted his leg. Pulling back, he moved more quickly. "Are these your worshippers?"

Her laughter reminded him of when they were little and he said something foolish, or accidentally dropped his sword in training. He felt a flush at his ears, and fury rose in his chest.

"Steady yourself," she said. "This is where I live when I'm not on the sea. They are just people."

Just people. What a strange thing to say. She seemed comfortable here, her body loose, daggers tucked into her belt. Lucifer wondered, suddenly feeling far too exposed, what he looked like to the people watching. A pup following its mother?

"They only want to make sure I'm all right," she murmured to him. "Have you forgotten how often we'd watch the other angels as children? It's curiosity, Morning Star, nothing more."

"Lucifer," he corrected. "I cannot keep what's given and expect to be free."

She turned back to stare at him, violet eyes soft. When the small cabin door open, he stepped back, but Lilith only smiled at the woman who nodded to her before ducking down the path back to the village. For a second the two gods stood, watching each other, and Lucifer wondered if she could see straight to the core of him.

"I am so sorry," she finally said, "for everything you've felt you had to do alone. Come on."

Confused, he followed into the darkness of the room. It was modestly furnished, a small bed, a basin, and a crib. Stunned, Lucifer kept himself against the wall as Lilith moved easily to the crib and plucked the bundle from it.

"You have a child?"

Shaking her head, she pressed an ear to the bundle's chest and sighed. "No, she belongs to no one."

Creeping forward, as if it might jump from his sister's arms and attack, Lucifer peeked. It was a little girl, a small pale thing with a shock of white hair. He must have a made a sound, because it opened its eyes—yellow eyes. Not human.

"She's half human, half fay," Lilith said. "Every so often, this village finds someone like her dropped on a doorstep, or on the cliffs, or in the forest, and they bring them to me. Here, hold her."

There was a tremble in his chest—fear, he realized—as he was passed the small thing. He hadn't felt that fear in a long time. The small girl blinked at him wisely.

"She's very sick," Lilith said. "In a few weeks' time, she'll be gone."

Head whipping up, he studied his sister and considered her matter-of-fact tone.

"Well, do something about it," he demanded. "Fix her."

A small hand, no bigger than his thumb, poked out from the cotton wrapping and gripped his finger weakly. He rubbed his other fingers across the soft skin gently.

"She's a half-breed, Lucifer. Mother Eorthe does not want her. I sent word, and it's silence. When they're healthy, I can usually find a nymph or some forest creature to take them in. No one wants a dying thing."

"I don't care that it's a half-breed," he said, tightening his grip on the bundle. "It's a child. It goes to Heaven if Eorthe won't take her. She's done nothing wrong; she goes to heaven."

"Mor—Lucifer, you know that's not how it works," she chided gently. "She will go to you."

He wished he could disappear, turn to shadow, and go watch the horrors men inflicted on each other. He wanted the rage in his veins to purge the panic, the fury to make him stalwart. Then the small thing coughed.

"You knew this would corrupt me," he said firmly. "You knew."

"You were already changing, my star," she informed him, her smile knowing. "You are tired. No one, not even the great fallen, can sustain that much hatred for so long. It isn't corruption; it's free will. You have the choice here. I will not take offense if you give her back and disappear again. If that is what you want, you have it."

Even as children, she'd been able to see his heart. How often had he sat before her, nerves and fears spilling out while she stroked his head and listened? Love. He'd wanted it desperately, and she'd always given it, even at the cost of her place at their father's feet.

"I'll go to him."

So, he went to the place where land met sky, the same place Hades made the deal to save his own children. It took three days, but it wasn't his father, only his voice— the oldest brother who had fought against him. They watched each other like they were in combat, until Metatron saw the babe pressed to his brother's chest, the same ribs that Michael had kicked.

"You've brought us a child? You think a mistake has been made?"

That voice taught him and his siblings, gently explained how to parry and stab. It sang on the days when rain was thick in the air, a deep rumble that made the littles sleepy.

"Yes. She's only a baby," he said as he held out the child. "She cannot have been rejected on purpose."

Metatron stepped back from them both. "She isn't my father's creation. She has no place with us."

The finality of that brought tears, wetness that Lucifer thought would never come again. The last time he'd begged at the feet of his father, asking for one soft word. He stood firm, the girl still outstretched, her little feet kicking as he pled.

"Please, brother, she is a—"

"You are not my brother," Metatron interrupted him. "You are the same as this creature: an abomination. My father has no words for you, and this child has no place in Heaven."

The tears dried, and rage sprouted like weeds tangling, but then the baby's fingers curled around his shaking hands. Taking a step back from his brother, he wrapped a large hand around the child's back, tucking her safely to his chest.

"You are wrong. Our father is wrong," he said simply and turned away.

So, he and Primie, as he named her after listening to how humans named their children, made their way back to the cliffs where Lilith sat. The three sat in silence, staring out at the water until Primie's worsening cough broke the silence.

"So, there is no place for this one?" she asked finally, her finger stroking the child's head.

"No."

"Let's make one then."

It had always been her way, to state both the impossible and the small in the exact same way. His protector, his council, and the force that kept him going. Smiling, he laid his head against her shoulder. It seemed like a lifetime since there'd been a place for him to rest.

"How? Where?" he said sleepily, thinking of all the ludicrous places she might come up with.

"Hell."

All comfort fled, the illusion of safety a broken thread, but Lilith caught him before he could flee. Pulling him down, she cradled both him and the child.

"I fought beside you because you were right, my star. What you are doing now, saving this child? It's right."

"What I did before wasn't." He knew that now, maybe had always known. His hands felt like they were soaked in blood, crusted under his nails no matter how he washed. "I should have just left."

Gently, she pushed him away and stood. She was tiny against the expanse of the ocean behind her, but her face was that of a warrior.

"Then atone for it by doing, not running. If we're going to build an afterlife, we need the others you spoke of. If they won't join us, then you release them and we'll find more, wake them the way you woke me. You are not a ghost, no longer a devil; you are a true god," she told him. "You will be seen by mortals and save those who are unseen by the other Creators. You will need a trusted name."

And so, he reclaimed the same name he'd once stolen. As Hades and Persephone, they traveled the earth to find the others who rebelled. The names, the power of belief growing as the pair started answering prayers, fed and strengthened them. As powerful as they'd ever been, they swept through city after city, looking for the gods he'd allowed free reign since killing their parents. Some already walked other paths and had begun forging ideologies and followings for themselves; others joined the betrayers against Mother Eorthe, blending into hybrids of the pagan and the divine. To each, regardless of whether they followed him, Hades bestowed a blessing, reminding them there would be places for their followers if they wished.

In the end, with a pantheon of ten, Hades, Persephone, Athena, Ares, Hermes, Dionysus, Artemis, Apollo, Aphrodite, and Hephaestus entered Hell.

There was a deep shame that followed Hades as they battled their way through the pit. He had been gone too long; both the feral demons and those he had once controlled fled to the surface to prey upon the mortals. There were stragglers, but the ten carved through them. It was only when they made it to his throne that he broke. The lake of fire, the stench of flesh being tanned, had him wishing he had never come down here.

The others didn't even seem bothered, simply watching bodies blaze in a lake of fire beyond. It turned the shame to resolve. They would be fair, he told them firmly as he released all the souls he'd captured, letting them cease to be. In another life, each one of them had embodied something for their father, he explained. They were inspiration, war, love—and they would do that for the humans and fay alike.

They released a collective grumble, but Hades held firm. The humans would give offerings, he told them, and in turn, each could grant boons as they saw fit. There were humans and fay that had been cast away, just like they had, he explained, and he showed them Primie. That cemented it, Primie blinking at them all wisely from underneath a small sunhat. Together, the ten resculpted the pit that he had been cast into so long ago.

It held four sections. The first, Purgatory, often resembled whatever its occupants thought of as a place for time to slip away—sometimes a park, other times the DMV, and, on rare occasions, a hospital waiting room.

The second, Asphodel Meadows, was simply a place. Neither good nor bad, it existed with a blandness that represented its occupants. It was a sparse place, one that only rarely had new visitors.

The other two sections, Elysium and Hell, were the most populous. Hades hadn't wanted Hell to continue, but it had been Persephone who raised her voice in disagreement. There was evil in the world, both fay and human. To pretend there wasn't, or to offer an easy out based solely on believing in a high power, was wrong, she argued. In the end, Hell was rebuilt beyond the long, flowing river of black, filled with bloated bodies.

Persephone ruled there, rarely speaking of it. She wrote reports, sending them out to the others, but only Hades read them. The others had been content, after they rebuilt, to go back to the surface, to walk the earth and gather tribute, while Hades and Persephone remained below.

Elysium, which Hades tended, was paradise. Aphrodite helped build it, a lush world of life and love in a place where there had only been blackness. It was there he laid Primie down, in a cradle of twisted vine and flowers, to sleep. It was another kind of death, as if he was hitting the solid ground of the pit for the first time, to walk away from the cradle and let the nymphs who resided in the tree that shaded her to sing her into dreams.

For a time, there was peace. The pantheon grew, fought, and loved under the guidance of Hades and Persephone. On his own, despite the suspicion of his own pantheon, he visited the others who'd chosen to follow different paths, who took names like Ushas and Nirrti,[32] in order to learn how they lived. The fire of knowledge inside him from Metatron's dismissal never left, and while his siblings were content with their new lives, it seemed his curse was to continue to seek, to try to feed the still throbbing ache of his past. Time stretched, blurred, and became non-existent to the God of the Underworld as he returned to Elysium to tend the garden, to guide his family.

Then he made the mistake of going back to the surface.

It was done for Persephone, who found the longer she spent in the Underworld, the less she wanted to leave. Athena, the wisest of them, demanded after centuries that Persephone must spend at least half of the year among the other gods, among the people. She had no defense against it, so at the end of winter her hands would begin to shake, and she would press her face to Hades's neck as he led her to the sunlight.

---

32 Ushas, Hindu Goddess of the Dawn. Nirrti, Hindu God of Decay.

The world was blinding, the same as it had been when he arrived with Primie, but as he blinked away the spots, he saw Athena. She was a fierce woman, who despite her intelligence also held a heart of fury, preferring to give and take with the swing of her mood. However, it wasn't the god's pinched face that clenched Hades's heart, but the woman behind her.

She was human, tall and skinny with brown hair and large dark eyes. She clung to the back of Athena's dress, gnarled hands staining the white fabric.

"That woman," Hades said, hands still around Persephone. "What's wrong with her?"

Athena barely spared a glance at the woman. "Some fool married a nymph. They've both died," she said absently. "Plague or some such. She's begging me to take her to the underworld, but your father has already claimed her."

The rest of the pantheon had taken to referring to the Allfather only in reference to Hades. They had rejected him in the first place, they reasoned, and now that they were gods rather than angels, they didn't need a father.

"They'll be separated?" he asked, even though he knew the answer.

"Please, please," the woman begged as she crawled forward, "please, let us be together."

It was Persephone, tensing in his arms as if she had already realized what he was about to do, that sealed it. Gently, he peeled the goddess away from him and knelt beside the woman.

"You may have safe passage to Elysium," he said, offering his hand. "Come with me."

"Hades, you cannot—"

The older woman's words were swallowed up as a spear of light pierced the air and struck the ground. The air went still, the earth quieted, and from the light was the face of Hades's favorite brother, the one who cast him from their home.

Michael had wanted to slay him instantly for his blasphemy—but that wasn't why he was sent, he admitted with quiet rage. A lesson would be bestowed, a punishment for trying to steal what belonged to the Allfather. He was to be bound to a family. This family was one born of Mother Eorthe and the Allfather, created to balance the world their children inhabited. He would be an advisor and a student, unable to be a god again until he was released from their service. The only good thing about such a small punishment, Michael sneered, was that the house Hades built would fall apart in his absence. He had no one with his level of power, no true family that could inherit his throne. It would be the end of him.

The panic that had lain dormant for so long gushed like fresh blood in his mouth, but a hand, slight and clammy, found his. Persephone didn't spare him a glance, but squeezed his hand as she addressed the Archangel, voice haughty and honed like the blades she had practiced with as a child. They were wed, she informed him, which meant that while he was gone, she would rule completely. With her chin tilted high, she told her older brother that her first act was that the woman already granted passage to Elysium was safe.

There had been a moment, a glint in the Archangel's eye, but in the end, he led the way back to the light. Squeezing Persephone's hand, Hades let her go and went back into servitude.

CHAPTER 15

Graceland filled my vision, staring at me with horror in his eyes. Blood, thick and fresh ran from my nose; more irritated than scared, I swiped at it. My vision was my own again, but pain knocked in my skull.

"Haven't done that in a while," I said calmly and slid gracelessly to the floor, tucked behind the pillar, hidden. "Next time you want to mind meld, Spock, give me a heads up, yeah?"

There was nothing angry or accusatory woven into my words, but I saw the way he tensed, his eyes wide. We'd only done it once before, when he let himself be kidnapped so I could find a hideout of a gang of goblins. That was basic, seeing through his eyes to find the hideout, but it led to a headache that blinded me then too.

"It's ok," I reassured him, tilting my head to stop the fresh rush of blood. "I used to get nosebleeds as a child when I first started seeing ghosts."

Jerking a handkerchief from his pocket, he handed it to me, and without preamble I shoved it up my nose and grinned at him. For a second his face was blank, then he pressed his fingers to his eyes, trying to pinch his own amusement.

"You showed my father that same thing," I said idly. "Took him fifteen years to get it. Guess I'm special, huh?"

The distressed noise was quiet, as was the shake of his head. "It wasn't my choice."

The lightness I'd tried to inject vaporized in my own horror. His shame had displayed without his consent because I'd poked at his brother.

"I haven't seen Michael since the day he brought me into your family's service. Do you think, maybe, sometimes it's better to let things die?"

He'd tried so hard to scrub the angel part from himself, but unlike his siblings it remained carved into his ribs. When he'd gone "soft" under the tutelage of the Fitzpatricks, the ferals began their search for him upon the earth and decimated everything in their path to him. He held the same quiet sorrow when we drove away from the feral earlier, the failure to fix his mistakes like a weight that pulled his head down to stare at the floor. The question hung in the air, and I tried to find an answer that would help him.

"Graceland, it's ok, I've—"

"Stop. Just, for right now, just this time, let's not, ok?"

I swallowed my words of comfort for him and held out a hand. "Help me up, then."

"I could tell the minions and your dad you needed to rest," he offered, thumb coming up to touch the blood under my nose. "Tomorrow is going to be a long day."

I felt his gaze, the disapproval, but just rubbed a hand across my face. Pulling the smear to my ear, I pressed my palms together.

"Maman, I've been blessed with knowledge through pain and humbly ask for anything you can spare."

"Brig—"

Giving him a quick shake of my head, the rush of heat hit my stomach, spice tingling my tongue. With shaky fingers, I touched my cheek and felt only skin, not the sticky coagulation of blood.

"Blessings, Maman."

Graceland's gaze was sharp. "You're actually ok?"

"I tried to tell you," I said kindly. "You trusted me with a gift. Joyous or painful, it's a gift."

"You still look tired," he commented. "I can tell the minions you're busy. I'll even show you how to silence your phone so you can sleep."

Instead of answering, I tilted my head toward the lobby. Following the direction, Graceland and I stared at my dad, dressed in a navy suit, in deep conversation with Darrius Alger. If it had only been Dad, I knew Graceland would have gladly come with, but even the sight of the dragon consort moved him toward the bar.

"I'll prep the minions."

Sighing, I nodded and stepped fully into the lobby. They were complete opposites, my fair-skinned, burly father, and the willowy grace of the man seemingly carved from precious onyx. As I approached, they both jerked to stare as if they had been caught plotting.

"Gentlemen."

"Senior Pilgrim, what a pleasure it was to see you take my peers to task," Darrius purred as he raised my hand to his lips. "I was just telling your father what a refreshing experience your introduction was and how interesting a Divine Arbiter you'll be."

"I appreciate any opportunity to be refreshing," I quipped, softening my smile. "Thank you for backing my request."

"You didn't hesitate about placing my people," the dragon countered. "My charges are often neglected because they have no voice with which to protest the mistreatment done to them. You cared; that is something not easily overlooked, even by those who hate you on principal."

"He told me about Farrow."

It was a small sting, the softness of my father's voice; the hesitance made Darrius look between us.

"I think, perhaps, I hear a cocktail calling my name," the dragon said and tipped his head to us both. "Give your beautiful wife my number, Rory, and I'll have you both come to visit. I'd like to meet this Crisco you told me about."

Gracefully he slid away, smooth hands tucked into his purple suit. Focusing on his retreating back, I tried to think of something to say, which only made the tension worse. The floundering was such a rarity that it made my skin tight. Growing up, Mama and I butted heads via shouts and sparking magic. Dad listened in silence, endured the boil and flare of my temper, then walked me through the problem.

"I'm sorry."

I blinked stupidly, mouth open. "For what?"

His raised brow made me grin, and the tension fell away. We both knew Mama's favorite phrase, designed to get a full apology from someone.

"I wasn't angry, and I trust you. Did you really think that—about Bronson? That I wanted him over you?"

I hurt him. Not intentionally, but it was clear how deeply it cut.

"Yes. He wanted it."

"And you didn't," he said, lips flattened. "That's the only reason I trained him."

Choice. He'd given me a choice. Gods, was it possible for me to crawl back into bed, restart this day, this week, this year? My own father, who hadn't been given an option, who, until he met Odette Laveau, rarely smiled under the weight of his station, gave his only child freedom.

"Did Mama—"

"No," he interrupted with a shake of his head. "There are few things your mother won't fight about, but she respects the rules."

A child must be born. The Fitzpatrick line had to continue; regardless of orientation or want, a child had to be produced. There was a woman Bronson held a contract with, ready to surrogate for him as soon as power was transferred. Then I was given everything. While it was a constant worry I'd heard from the overseers since I'd taken over, the idea of children wasn't even on my radar. My father, the traditionalist, had been willing to go against his own nature to give a choice.

"Dad—"

Hands callused but somehow soft took mine, squeezing gently. "You are the light of our lives, Brigitte Marie. I'm not delusional enough to believe that will keep you safe, but we're here if you need us. It's not a burden to have help."

Another misstep. Independence was taught to me from adolescence, but whenever I'd fallen, they were there with wisdom, with love. It was hell being wrong.

"Well, shit."

His laughter was infectious as he let me go. "I need to pick your mother up for dinner. She's excited about the reservations you got us to Preacher's Son."

"Send Chef Christian my love," I said, "and tell Mama to behave."

"Funny, she told me to tell you the same," he said, patting my cheek. "I'll be here tomorrow."

Instead of the irritation of being managed I'd felt earlier, it was relief this time, an understanding that my father's attention was not a judgement but a safety net for a high-flying act. My team was watching us, so I just nudged him to the exit before turning to the bar. This time I grabbed the glass Asim had set out and drained it.

The heat in my throat was soft, and I ran a thumb across the lip of the glass before nodding to the others.

"Are we prepared for tomorrow?" I asked.

Asim flipped his folders open. "I think so. Magic is always more forgiving, since they all live in our world."

"You should be sleeping," Graceland interrupted.

"Which I will in—" I glanced to my watch. "—five hours, give or take."

"I know Rory put them on the council, but I'm not sure how comfortable I am dealing with demons," Moira said and poked her stirrer at Graceland. "I'm surprised you haven't complained."

"Take it up with Penny. I don't make the rules." He shrugged. "They can't possess you unless you ask them too. If you're stupid enough to do that, then Darwinism."

"What?"

Snorting, I motioned for the folder. "Ignore him. He's reading *On the Origin of Species.* He's been using that as an excuse for everything. We have to include them. They possess power that we can't fix, so it's better to monitor them than do nothing. Shinoda abided by our rules, allowed us access to information we wouldn't be able to touch. We've saved lives using it, and if everything goes well tomorrow, the ones I've chosen will be able to give us the same."

"Shinoda is cohabitating with his host though, right?" Moira asked. "So it's not as ugly as possession?"

"It can be," Asim said.

The entire table went silent, and my own fingers froze over the papers in my hand. That was how I'd found him for the program, and though I would never have begrudged him, I knew he wore shame like sackcloth over losing his brother to a demon. It was why he kept meticulous notes on everything, including a file on his brother who had never resurfaced, despite our best efforts.

It was his detailed reports that I shifted to break the tension at the table. "Do we have specific demands for each of them?"

It took a single beat for him to shake the grief from his face. "Besides your big one? No. They will have requests for you though. I've included various breaches in pacts made by both the Pilgrims and their own kind. It's likely that they will try to make it seem like they are being victimized, but in truth they have triple the number of offenses of our peers."

"But there are still humans and Pilgrims abusing magic," Moira pointed out.

"There always will be," Graceland said casually. "Those who have power always want more, and those who have none will do anything to get a taste."

"How poetic," Moira said dryly.

"I'm not the one whose kind shoots up pure magic to get high, who doesn't care about the fact that they are pregnant as long as they can stay high, and who curse their children to unstable magic," Graceland shot back.

"No, you only tried to usurp Heaven. I can see where you'd think junkies are the real threat," Moira drawled.

"Guys, enough," I said, hands coming up in appeasement. "I think we're done for the day. Obviously, we're all tired. Rest up."

Draining my second glass, I set it back on the bar top and grabbed the files Asim pushed in my direction. "I'll study tonight, and we'll regroup in the morning. Bright and early."

When nobody argued, I knew it had been the right call to make. Graceland led the way back to the SUV, and I gave him a shake of my head as he opened my door for me.

"What a gentleman."

"I didn't try to usurp Heaven."

"I thought we weren't talking about that," I said mildly and buckled myself in. "Is it my turn to remind you that Moira is a traditionalist? You won't change that."

"Why'd you choose her?"

"Because she reminds me of Bronson."

Graceland's disgust was evident as he put the SUV in D. "And that's an admirable quality?"

"They both believe—truly believe—in our original tenets. Magic is dangerous and needs to be controlled to keep humans safe. There's comfort in knowing they will do the job to the letter of the law, even if I think there is a world of grey."

"It makes your job harder."

"It makes my job more well-rounded," I corrected. "I'm not looking to have yes men. I know I'm not perfect, Graceland. I will never be able to devour magic, and sometimes that's needed. I want to be an open hand to help, but I won't deny that my other is ready as a fist."

"Then wh—"

My phone chose that moment to blast a trumpet that had us both jumping. Punching the accept button, I grinned at Graceland.

"Speak of the devil."

Bronson gave an unamused noise. "I can only imagine what you were saying."

"Surprisingly singing your praises. Got an update?"

"Pack Santee remains as irritatingly insular as usual."

It was true that the western packs were known for their isolation, which I couldn't begrudge them. If I consistently got fucked by anyone not pack, I'd probably do the same.

"I managed an audience with Chatan Santee. He admitted that he and his council met with three vlkodlak, but he tried to tell me they were from Brood Vasile," He said with a disbelieving laugh. "I clearly explained why that was impossible, which—as you know—put Chatan's back up."

Graceland glanced at me with raised brows, and I tapped my head against the headrest.

"Did he say why they came?"

"He wanted formal documentation from the Divine Arbiter before he would disclose the entirety of their meeting, but it seems this brood is searching for a cure."

"I passed today, just have to get through tomorrow," I offered but chewed on the inside of my cheek. "I'd like you to come back home."

The SUV jerked, but I ignored Graceland's stare to focus on Bronson's noise of dissent.

"You just sent me here," he reminded me. "I want to finish the job. I have a meeting tonight with a contact. I'm getting these vlkodlak, and I know Pack Santee is hiding something."

"Bronson I—I have it on good authority that the brood I'm following here is Brood Vasile."

"That's—"

"Impossible?" I interrupted. "Yeah, I know, but how many times have we said that in our lives? If it turns out that it's true, then we've stumbled across something buried from Gran and both our fathers. We both know they can't be cured, but there's nothing more dangerous than hope."

The silence crackled between us, then Bronson spoke, his voice soft but firm.

"That's more reason to stay here and get more information. Give me forty-eight hours; by then you'll be Divine Arbiter, so if I need you to come break down doors you can."

"You're putting a lot of faith in me."

"You've never given me reason not to," he admitted. "Safe travels Brig."

"Safe travels, Bron."

I set the phone in my lap and just stared as Graceland looped The Bearded Folly looking for parking.

"Why do things always have to get complicated with you," Graceland complained. "Can't even get a good spot when I'm with you."

"It's not my fault you're shit at parallel parking," I said as I closed my eyes and leaned back. "I need food and a twenty-minute power nap. Then we are going to be up late."

"Fine, but you'll eat whatever I decide to get."

CHAPTER 16

Even before the street came into view, I smelled the spice, the burst of herb and flower, that even on slow days Eastern Market exuded. They were slightly less busy than usual because of the chill, but stalls were still being examined and erected, and the low hum of business was evident.

The city towered over the squat expanse, brick splashed with color depicting the history of Eastern Market, the graffiti welcome in a place so devoted to celebration. Moving past the building, I rounded the brick, eyes scanning the nymphs arguing over the arrangement of their flowers, the troll carrying crates as a goblin woman spouted out numbers from her clipboard at him. It was rare for there to be trouble here. In some parts of the city, like West Riverend, there was always someone looking to start something, but Eastern Market held a firm armistice even with the gangs. I wouldn't have to do much besides enjoy the low laughter and the smell of produce as it was inspected—if I managed to locate my mother and Crisco.

This was one of Mama's favorite spots, the bustle, the smells, a way to bring life to a city that sometimes felt clinical and cold. As a child, I'd been dragged from booth to booth, listening to Mama barter, trading advice and her own goods in exchange for shiny eggplants and freshly plucked chicken feathers.

On the edge of the small throng of vendors were a series of patio tables, most empty because of the sting of cold air. There Mama sat, surrounded by an already full cloth bag and at her feet her trusty gator.

"Has anyone given you trouble about Crisco?" I asked in lieu of greeting.

"I'm sure I've gotten looks," she responded and held her cheek out for a kiss, "but that's their problem. Excellent dandelion bitters from the gentleman closest to the exit today."

"I'm not late, I want that on record," I said and patted her arm. "Want to take a stroll?"

"Of course. I got here early. Couldn't sleep."

I tucked her arm in mine and steered us toward the first row of vendors. "Nightmares?"

"Worries. I feel somethin' between my toes, like sand you can't quite shake," she said, "I had your father take us to Tomes & Bones after dinner last night. Fabulous meal, of course. Christian rarely misses."

"They got it all fixed up?"

"The buildin', yes. Chantelle is still a little unsettled. You find out who did it?"

"It's on my list, Mama, but I've been a little busy."

"No one says different, but Chantelle is a friend. She mentioned Caja—no use trying to get that girl on the horn, but you go see Flippen. He'll know about what's stolen."

"And I can check your markets while I'm at it?" I said, amused.

"You could use the walk in Evermore," she said, "especially after passing over last week."

I nodded and patted her hand when the scent hit me: the sweet rolling of rot, cloven and damp. Trying to keep my breath even, I let my eyes wander but kept my head focused forward. The market was thrumming; gnomes selling kitchen gadgets, a troll moving crates, the human selling dandelion bitters frowning at his phone.

"Baby, you've gone quiet."

The scent was still there, screaming at me. As we turned the corner the thread of orange hit me, and my feet stopped.

"Mama, you got your flask, right?"

She scoffed. "Of course." She stopped and her nose wrinkled. "Ah, an intruder. I'll give you two space."

"Can you give us time?"

Mama's grin was lightning fast, and I should probably have been concerned about how much she enjoyed chaos. Letting my hand go, she lifted the sleeve of her flowing dress. Against her rich obsidian skin were what looked like tiny pearls, as if she could unbutton the skin of her forearm, but I knew better. The tiny rods of bone sprouted from her radius during one of her own mother's experiments. It had been painful, Mama admitted, and terrifying, but it had made casting easier.

Dipping her fingers into the lip of her flask, she traced damp skin across the bone pearls, winding a pattern like string art, the sting of rum suffusing the air that went still around us.

The silence was instantaneous, and when I pulled my gaze from the patterns, I found myself being stared at by everyone in the market. All manner of fay and human stood unblinking, eyes the same milky white as Mama's.

"I appreciate it, Mama."

"Best not to have witnesses in case you need to kill him," she agreed and went back to strolling with Crisco.

I would not be killing him. The Creators would probably frown upon it if I Eighty-sixed another Pilgrim. Taking the next corner, I tasted the thread of orange again, just pungent enough to keep the clove from numbing my tongue, and at the far end of the vendors I saw Bernard Haas.

He was a rough-hewn man, tall but not overly large. His face was a mashup of features: prominent nose, thin lips, heavy brows, light skin.

"Cousin."

Bernard glanced up from the flowers he was studying. "Ah, Pilgrim Fitzpatrick. I heard congratulations are in order after your first day of talks."

"I'd accept them if I thought you meant them," I said back just as plainly. "What are you doing here?"

"The same as you: waiting my turn to prove my worth," he said and pulled out his wallet. "I'll take the winter roses."

When the elf behind the counter only stared ahead, Bernard frowned and looked around. With a sigh, he tucked his wallet back into his pocket. "A handy trick. Is it supposed to intimidate me?"

I smiled and I leaned in despite the fact that no one else could hear me. "Bernard, I don't need tricks to do that. If you know I passed, then you also know that I was given favor to ask you for records on a rogue brood in my city."

"Brood Toma," he said easily. "I've already sent the papers to the overseers, and they should be sending them to you."

His lie killed the hint of orange, and I pressed my tongue to the roof of my mouth to keep it from going numb from the stench of rot.

"It would have been faster to just have the papers sent to me."

"It would have," he agreed. "If that's all you require, Pilgrim, I'll take my leave."

I let him get one step, then two—which was growth on my end.

"Bernard, stop."

He did, but only turned his head to show he was listening. My smile sharpened as I lifted my left hand and watched his lift as well. As his body tensed, I spun on my heel and watched him do the same so he was facing me.

"You think I didn't come prepared." I tsked, reaching into the pouch on my belt. "I don't need my mother's power to make you cautious." I held up the twisted bundle of hair tied tight with coarse thread. "You laid your head in my town, yet you're arrogant enough to lie to me about the brood."

When he remained silent, I exhaled through my nose. *Fine*. "Speak."

"I will tell the overseers of this overreach," he threatened.

"But will you tell them you lied to your Divine Arbiter, that you've lied to three before me? Brood Vasile. I want answers."

It was panic, a burst of copper and cold coffee on my tongue as he paled in front of me. His eyes darted around but I smiled still.

"I already killed one of them, and *when* I am Divine Arbiter, I will bring balance to your doorstep with blood if you choose that path. You do not hold the ear of *any* of the Fitzpatricks any longer."

There was fury beyond fear at my insinuation about Bronson, and the bundle of hair in my hands ignited. With a sigh, I dropped it under my heel. I'd known it wouldn't last long, but I'd hoped for a chance to force a confession.

"You are a child fumbling for its first steps," he spat, "and I will enjoy watching you tumble, *cousin*."

"I expect the papers, Bernard. The real ones. On my desk in forty-eight hours."

"But are you ready for the consequences of what you're asking?"

he asked, his smile returning. "How willing are you to sacrifice for knowledge?"

Around us, people began to move, finishing sentences or tasks that hung suspended. Time was up. The thrum of the market rushed in to fill the vacuum, and Bernard didn't spare me a glance as he moved for the outside.

"Dick," I muttered under my breath and made my way back to the patio area.

Mama sat, her feet swinging as she chatted to Graceland over bags of food. As I approached, both their heads came up.

"I got you a bagel sandwich and some fruit." Graceland said.

I nodded my thanks and glanced at the dress bag on the seat next to mine.

"Were you rude?" I asked. "Is that why Moira's not here?"

His laugh was all I needed to hear. Ignoring the food he'd laid out, I unzipped the bag. It wasn't something I would have chosen for myself but, like the first dress, it was a perfect fit. The pale gold flowed, full sleeves cuffed by flowers that smelled fresh even though they were stitched.

"I can smell the flowers from your dress, Alexander McQueen. It's a bold choice for the meeting today," Mama said.

"She's worried that it makes her look weak," Graceland commented.

Before I could punch him for digging in my thoughts, Mama grabbed my hands, tugging me to face her. It was something she'd done whenever I questioned myself.

"What have I always told you?" she demanded.

"Never try to dye my eyebrows."

For a second her mouth ticked up. "Brigitte Marie."

"Power doesn't come from the opinions of others; it comes from inside yourself," I recited.

She leaned forward and pressed a kiss to my cheek before grinning devilishly in Graceland's direction. "She did try dyein' her eyebrows once; burned one of 'em right off."

"Mama!"

Her laugh was loud as she gathered her bags. "I'll leave you to gameplan, but watch the clock."

I checked my phone and sighed. "Time magic."

"There are consequences for any magic," she dismissed with another touch to my face. "I'll see you for dinner tonight."

Graceland watched as her and Crisco toddled off, then tapped his chest. "Does my suit make me look sallow?"

"You don't need a reminder that you're beautiful," I countered and brought a cuff of the dress up to smell the flowers. "Fitting, I suppose, that it's got magic woven inside it."

"Moira does know you," he pointed out and tapped my plate. "Get over here and eat."

"I know she does. I just wish she trusted me," I said and quickly snatched a strawberry from his dish.

Instead of the squawk of outrage I expected, Graceland lifted a second plate from his lap that was filled with fruit.

"I know you too, fool," he gloated, "and she does trust you, but Rory saved her life. Moira wouldn't set that aside just because he stepped down."

I knew that, just like I was aware that Moira had watched me grow. She'd witnessed every teenage tantrum, every mistake, and now I was her boss. There was a chip firmly rooted there.

"She'll fall in line," he said. "You inspire loyalty, Brig. The Darkchilds, the Fellers. Hell, I guess even I like you a little."

"I'll make sure to tell the consorts that, see if it gets me a leg up," I said. "Update me on Alexei."

"Subtle subject change," he said with a grin. "He apologized for being unable to speak last night. He sounded worried."

"I can ease some of that when we talk today. I insinuated that it was Bronson, not him that gave us the Vasile information. I'm not happy about the level of redaction on the tree. I want to know who these three bastards belong too."

It had been over bowls of Thaddues's marvelous French onion soup and fresh rolls that we'd unrolled the brood tree along the floor of my apartment, ready for a long night of studying. It was to Graceland's delight and my frustration that the night ended early because names were blackened, burned away, blocking paths just as they started.

"They're not bastards, but you're gonna wish they were."

"But—" I paused. "Wait, how did you get this information?"

His grin sharpened, reminding me for the first time in a long time that he was, in fact, the King of Hell, the destroyer of man, the attempted usurper.

"You think my girl doesn't know how to interrogate? We were warriors of Heaven. It took her a minute, but she found the vlkodlak you ganked in Purgatory. He wouldn't give her much, but she got the name on their branch that was burned away: Magnus the Mad."

"I'm getting real tired of saying that's not possible. Is he still alive then?"

"Oh yeah, and absolutely batshit if his son is to be believed. Which, grain of salt, because Persephone says the one you killed was pretty feral himself."

"Because Vasile is feral," I pointed out. "That's the curse of having Henry Fitzpatrick as your brood elder. Power and madness in equal measure."

The other Fitzpatrick's culled that line when Patrick killed Henry. The entire brood he'd built had been slaughtered, his legacy of darkness ground under the full might of the other original three. It was the only period of reform within Deep Europe, if you could call it that. It forced the other broods and houses to quiet their savagery for centuries.

"Do they have any other siblings? True siblings, I mean, not bites?"

"A sister, but she doesn't leave her father's side, so it's just the three. Well, two, since you ganked the one," he said.

"And whatever emissaries they sent to the Dakotas," I corrected. "Bronson can handle them, but the fact that Annabelle Lee Bastille was bitten—ehh."

"You don't think they're looking for a cure? They're looking for a queen?"

I took a bite of my bagel and contemplated that. "What if the girls they killed are tests? Judas moon week, in the land of true wolf."

"That's speculation, Your Honor."

Snorting, I nodded. "I need to do some research. Ask Beafore's blessing to speak freely with Chatan."

"You'll be Divine Arbiter," he argued. "You can do whatever you want."

"And that's why you have no friends," I pointed out. "Just because I have the biggest dick doesn't mean I have to use it."

"What an image," he deadpanned. "Bernard give you anything else?"

"Besides poorly veiled threats and saying I was gonna fail? Nah."

Graceland nodded. "Amateur. In my villain era, I would have been a great antagonist to you."

"You still are," I assured him and checked my watch. "We need to head out so you can help me into this dress."

As we stood, he grabbed a bag from my mother's chair. "Here."

"You got me a gift?"

"No," he scoffed. "Your mother left it for you. Said it should help you look presentable."

CHAPTER 17

"I'm not late!"

My words bounced back at me as I burst into the empty lobby of the casino on Belle Isle, but when I turned left toward the bar, I saw Moira and Asim waiting. It probably said something about me as a person that the obvious nerves on their faces made mine settle. Asim's hands, normally fidgety, were filled with folders, so instead he moved from foot to foot. Moira was less obvious, her hand finding her favored feather earring.

"I'm not late," I say again, voice pitched lower.

Both jumped a bit; the jerk of Moira's hand and Asim's wide eyes were better than any placation.

"You literally have ten minutes until you are," Moira pointed out.

"Which is enough time to thank you for this beautiful dress," I said smoothly, "and for you to say how gorgeous I look."

"I love the braids," Moira admitted. "Your mom?"

"Little bit of Mama, little bit of magic," I admitted as I touched my half swept-up box braids. "I'm not usually fussy about using magic for quick style, but it would have been nice to have the time with her."

"It balances the dress; the threads of gold are A+," she said and glanced around. "Where's Graceland?"

"I'm here," he announced as he leisurely strolled in. "I wasn't running when I'm not invited to this anyway."

"He's mad that I'm getting all the compliments today," I said and laughed when he gave me a look of disgust. "Could I interest you guys in a drink before we do this dance? Not Vernors this time."

"I have a flask in my pocket," Asim admitted.

"Give me a sip," Moira muttered. "Hopefully, this group can stay on task easier."

"Fat chance. Anyone want to take bets on which one insults me first?" I said, only half joking as I led the way to the ballroom.

"I could insult you now," Graceland offered, "get it out of the way."

I laughed as I reached for the handle, but my amusement died the second my fingers made contact. The sharp needle of pain filled the flesh of my palm, bee stings and venom. My nostrils flared as I inhaled the magic, familiar and horrifying. Instead of pulling the door, I dropped my hand and looked to Asim.

"I forgot one of the folders in the car," I lied. "Could you run and grab it? We'll wait."

Without hesitation, he left, and I opened the door the second he disappeared from sight. When Moira didn't follow, I glanced back.

"You need to trust me on this," I told her, then turned to Graceland. "Ugly business."

The only tell he gave was a ticking of his jaw, then he nodded and went after Asim. I clenched my teeth at Moira's pause, watching her glance around, but finally she took the step and the heavy door locked behind us. It echoed through the ballroom, and I turned to the consorts to discover my instincts were correct.

Daniyal Badem—or, more accurately the demon wearing his skin—stared out at me like he had the day I saved Asim's life from his own brother. Behind me, Moira let out a startled breath, so low that no one should have heard. The demon grinned regardless, red eyes glinting where brown should have been.

"We meet again, Pilgrim," he said. "A surprise, I'm sure. But where is your other one? Daniyal and I were looking forward to seeing him again."

The rest of the consorts looked uneasily at him, then to me, waiting for an explanation. It was obvious having a child sitting among adults made them all uncomfortable, especially one more demon than human now.

"Where is Shinoda?" I countered.

The faint twitch, a single pull of his bronze cheek, expressed displeasure at his bait not being taken. "He retired inside a nice woman in Barbados. They coexist," he said and shivered at the thought. "Disgusting, but I was next in line."

"Even though you've broken magical law by taking a child."

The demon tsked at me as he leaned forward. "You haven't done your reading. How did the fay let you pass if you don't even know the age laws? Fourteen and up now."

I knew the rule. And I hated it. "You broke the law before it changed."

"Retroactively forgiven. But perhaps this is too personal for you. If you'd like, I could write a suggestion for you to step down and abandon your quest to become Arbiter," he said, voice warm and earnest as his eyes focused on something behind me. "Perhaps a recommendation for your peer to take over—she has been in the program longer. Looked over again and again, Moira; I could change that for you."

"And I could bind you to an eternity in the pit," Moira said sweetly.

It was impossible to completely stamp down on my smirk, but I managed to keep it small as the demon's head tilted unnaturally. The hands of his host gripped the desk with vigor, beginning to shift, black rolling up the skin as nails slid out to sink into the wood.

"Enough, demon," the woman to his right demanded. "She passed your test; if you cannot control yourself, you will leave."

It was like a switch flipped, and once again it was a young man looking out at me. The rest of the consorts settled back, and I forced myself to get down to business despite my heart bleeding for the boy inside him and the brother outside the door.

"Before we begin officially, I have documentation for Master Heron regarding the approval for more alchemists under the Fellers," I said and brought the folder to the table, passing it to the man on the far end.

His eyes, an unnatural amber from the consumption of too much magic, watched me silently as his entirely mechanical left arm flipped through the pages.

"The Fellers will be pleased," the woman who had rebuked the demon said. "I also heard about the minor treaty you negotiated between Master Darrius and Master Ives. I think you are an excellent choice."

"Thank you, Master Amalia."

The woman nodded as she laced her fingers together. "That being said, it is unorthodox not bringing two Junior Pilgrims with you. We would like to know why."

They would've heard a lie the minute it left my lips, but even if they couldn't, the demon would've corrected me. Sparing Asim was worth the potential mark to my record.

"It was my decision to keep him from this meeting when I felt that it wasn't Shinoda representing the demonic."

Amalia's brows raised. "The magic spoke to you, even from the hall?"

"She truly is a Conduit of Magic," Heron murmured, hand still moving the papers in front of him.

It wasn't unheard of, to be able to read magic like a person's face, but it was rare, even for a Pilgrim. For me, it was always there, an imaginary friend Mama encouraged and nurtured, but it was cemented by Mother Eorthe when I passed my trials. As a Conduit, magic flowed through me, each with its own flavor on my tongue and skin.

While the others twittered nervously to each other, the consort of Vodou and I gave each other quiet smiles. Hesta was wrapped in a dress of flowing cotton, her Bantu knots a crown from which the rest of her curls flowed down her back. She received the position when Mama refused, as she loved to say, to sit behind a desk and bicker. Hesta graciously accepted both the title of consort and every teaching Mama was willing to offer.

"A child with her pedigree is bound to be powerful, more than either parent," she said, voice deep behind richly painted lips. "Does this other Pilgrim have an issue with the demonic? If so, you've chosen your third poorly."

Did disappointment count as an insult? Tamping down on the thought, I nodded my acknowledgment.

"Asim Badem is an excellent Pilgrim, as I'm sure you'll come to realize when you look through the information I've provided for you. Many of the concessions originated from him. If Shinoda were here, I would have allowed him to join us."

"Pilgrim," the demon chastised, "you're going to have to say it eventually."

I wanted to crack my neck to dispel the tension, but without moving my body, I lifted my eyes to him. "That demon—the host he took against the law is Daniyal Badem, Asim's little brother."

Unlike the fay, who were mostly equal in terms of power and reach, the consorts of magic were all humans, chosen and trained by whichever brand of fay or Creator recognized the potential. Dad used his first treaty to begin bringing betrayer magics into the fold, to give Pilgrims the ability to consult and dispense justice without recriminations from their various deities. Vodou were the first to agree to negotiate terms, then demonic, and finally seers. Despite their power, those of natural magic still eyed them carefully—betrayer and fallen magic, after all, had been built from those too wild to be contained by either Creator.

It was obvious that the rest of the consorts, besides Killian on the far end, were disgusted as they twisted to stare at each other. The seer barely looked awake, his shaggy blond hair falling to one side as he supported his head with his hand.

The demon grinned and leaned over the middle of the table at me, red eyes set in a too-young face.

"I think I perhaps remember a law," he said, tapping fingers against his chin. "Yes, a law that states the Pilgrim in question must follow all tenets of the code in order to gain magic's favor. And if I'm not mistaken, one of those is providing two allies of worth."

It didn't matter that he couldn't die—I was gonna beat him to death. I'd climb over the top of the desk, grab him by the throat, and pound until my fists broke. I would—

"Oh!" Killian laughed as he lifted himself from his hand to peer at me. "Your father was powerful but predictable. It's interesting—the entire time you've stood here your future, past, it keeps shifting around. Messy, but exciting. Talk yourself out of this one," he demanded and glanced to his peers. "She's going to."

"It's true that I've broken the law, and thus should be denied magic's favor," I said, smile growing as Killian pouted. "However, there is a caveat. If I perform each of your magics, even in the most basic manner, then you can still bestow blessings on me and pass me along to the Creators."

Killian slapped his hand against the desk. "Didn't I tell you?" he gloated, beckoning me forward with his hand. "Do me first!"

"Killian," Hesta said, her voice firm but kind, "she has to do oldest to youngest magics."

"Oh right, course, course," he conceded.

"The oldest is mine," Amalia said. "What will you provide for Wicca?"

"Yes, do tell us, Pilgrim; will it be a poor attempt at purification again?" the demon asked. "We both know how well that went for you last time we saw each other."

"Silence, beast," Amalia demanded, hand outstretched. "You will have your turn."

"If it pleases you, Master Amalia, I'll create life."

All the consorts straightened in interest, eyes sharp, as I approached the long desk. With practiced movements and light fingertips, I drew along the lines in Amalia's palm, words flowing with each trace.

"Grounded, rooted firmly in the earth like all life before it, I will nourish and be nourished by the elements of my maker. Water, giver of life, quencher of thirst, I ask for your blessing upon what I've planted. Air, breath of life, the unseen but the felt, I ask for your blessing. Fire, cleanser of life, the eater of the overgrown, I ask for your blessing."

Pulling back, I pushed the woman's hand closed until it was a tight fist before placing my palm over it.

"As I will, so mote it be."

The smell of jasmine flooded the room as Amalia opened her hand and stared at the small, budding flower growing from her palm. With gentle hands, she rubbed a finger over its petals before giving me a nod.

"You have the blessing of the Mother Eorthe," she said. "She's impressed."

"Basic witchcraft," Heron said, voice as tight as his lips. "It requires no deft touch or danger."

The scent of flowers soured, the small bud rotting in Amalia's palm. The woman shot Heron a glare and closed her hand.

"The fact that you think danger equals something impressive is why you're more machine than man," she said stiffly, nodding for me to move on.

Up close, his amber eyes were more orange, the pupils not full circles, as if they had been eroded away. Despite the otherness, it was easy to see the general indifference on his face. Slipping my hand into my pocket, I took out a vial and passed it to him. The silver liquid bubbled at his touch, and as he raised it to the light, it turned a violent red.

"Did you anticipate failing?" he asked, voice curious now as he gave the vial a shake. "Is that intelligence, or a lack of faith in yourself?"

"I prefer to call it careful planning," I countered. "As you can see, I made it myself. It could be stronger, but my time with the Fellers and Darkchilds has been rushed as of late."

Popping the cap off, the man tapped the liquid out onto the half oval of his thumb and pointer finger. As soon as it touched his skin, it turned to a loose blue powder and, as if he was licking salt after a shot, his tongue ran along the line. He hissed at the burn but offered his first grin.

"Not bad for a novice. Crafting luck is ambitious, but you have excellent teachers. You should have soaked the lead just an hour more."

Nodding, I let out a relieved breath. "I was worried about that. The *Grimoire* says two days and fifteen hours, but to be honest, Sir Isaac Newton's handwriting is getting illegible."

"I'll send the Fellers laminated copies I have," Heron said. "You have our blessing, Pilgrim."

"Thank you, Master Heron."

I moved back up the table and bit down on a laugh when Hesta shook her head.

"You know you have our blessing. If I even tried to test you, Baron and Maman would have my head. Only they are allowed to judge you," Hesta said, eyes sharp as if daring the other consorts to say something. "Besides, coming back from the other side is testament enough."

"That is against the rules," the demon reminded. "You cannot play favorites and expect—"

Suddenly the room bloomed with the burn of hot peppers and rum. While the demon touched fingers to his tongue and the other consorts coughed, Hesta and I inhaled deeply.

"Our loas have spoken," Hesta informed him and motioned for me to continue the journey.

"Thank you, Master Hesta," I said and moved to stand before the demon, but he shook his head.

"Do the boy first. To fail at the end is more poetic," he said.

Not responding, I simply stepped to the seer. He wasn't truly a boy, but the way he lightly bounced in his seat belied his excitement.

"You've done well so far," he said as he offered his palm. "Are you going to read my mind or give me a reading?"

"I confess, my skills as an oracle are lacking," I admitted.

His bouncing stopped, eyes flickering to Hesta. "But I've heard about your mother, and I thought—"

"My mother is much more powerful in the ways of the mind than I am. She devoted herself to it. I will, however, do my best to impress you."

"All I can ask, I suppose," he said, disappointed.

"May I?" I asked, motioning to his hand.

When he nodded his agreement, I pressed my palm against his and laced our fingers together. The tug was instantaneous, but from his side. He was pulling my past, my present, and fragments of my future into himself. Tightening my grip, I inhaled and held tight. It was a trick taught to me on the rare occasion I'd been left with Graceland as a babysitter. I'd demanded he teach something new, something my parents couldn't or wouldn't.

After a brief war of wills—and a bribe of my Halloween candy—Graceland explained the art of compartmentalization. It was something warriors of all cultures did, he said, in order to continue in battle after a grave injury or watching those they loved die. It required a stubbornness, an extreme force of will, to block out all distractions, all but what was needed for survival. A warrior could be bleeding out and fight with the power of a thousand men—and if applied properly, the skill could be used outside the battlefield.

It was a useful trick to learn, but I'd never mastered it, as Graceland loved to remind me. He still had the ability to get his fingers into my mind, to pry open places locked down, but occasionally, I surprised him. Killian was easier to deal with by spades, and I watched with delight when he came up against the block in my mind.

His eyes met mine, full of confusion, then mischief, fingers tapping along the edges of the barriers set up, looking for weak spots. For a second, I swore the lyrics of Smashing Pumpkins floated through my head, but then he let me go.

" '*Bullets with Butterfly Wings*?'"

The flash of his smile blinded as his head pumped up and down. "Do you think that's too obvious? Because I was going to go with *Today*, but like, that song gets stuck in your head and I'm not him," he said, jerking a thumb at the demon.

"It could have been worse."

Killian nodded his agreement. "An interesting way to showcase our magic. You have our blessing."

"Thank you, Master Killian," I said, smile falling as I turned to the last consort.

Would it have broken Asim to be here, to listen to the demon speak in a distorted version of his brother's voice? Moira might think him capable, but she hadn't been there when Asim was training. He'd kept it together during the day, but at night I'd hear him weep, muffled and choked.

"What could you possibly offer me?" the demon asked. "Perhaps your soul? I would give you my blessing then."

"I have something better than that."

"Better than your soul?" he scoffed, looking to the consorts as if they would share in his disbelief. "What could that be?"

"Your name, Samael."

Above us, the chandeliers rattled, bulbs flashing bright before they shattered. Lifting a lazy hand, I cast above us, glass hitting the rippling purple barrier like rain against a roof. There was no pleasure on my face, but inside I was ecstatic at the panic cast across the demon's.

"What deception is this?" he demanded.

"I'm good at my job. Did you really think that I was going to just let you go after what you did?" I asked and let my smile show, feral and toothy. "You've left a trail, a signature, Accuser of Edom."

"It changes nothing," he said quickly, eyes darting toward the exit.

He was going to bail, disappear into shadow, and it might be years before he surfaced again. Quickly, I took the second vial from my pocket and held it up. The liquid, pure white, shone like diamonds even in the low light.

"Samael."

The use of his name hunched his shoulders, but he looked from the exit back to me. I could see the exact second he realized what I was holding, his nostrils going wide as he inhaled. His eyes flitted back and forth, and a thick stream of drool spilled from the corner of his mouth. The air fluttered around him, the shadow of half charred wings painted against the wall.

"This is what I have to offer you, demon," I said and tapped the vial with my nail.

There was music in the air, as if a high sound of a trumpet had barely escaped from the loose lid of the tube.

"Give it to me. I give you our blessing," he said immediately.

"I want to make a deal," I said sternly, pulling the vial back. "If you agree, it's yours."

"I agree to whatever terms you set."

"I want the boy back."

The entire room went silent, breath held as they stared out at me in shock. It was a well-known fact that humans rarely survived possession, especially those possessed for extended periods. The untrained human body couldn't contain that much pain or magic; it was an anomaly that Samael had been able to stay in the host's body this long without decay. That was all the hope I needed; if he wasn't visibly rotting, that meant Daniyal was still in there.

"And you'll let me go?" Samael asked, eyes still locked on the vial.

"For now," I agreed, ignoring the disapproval of the other consorts. "Give me the boy, you get the celestial grace, and you get to walk away."

"You have a deal."

Approaching the desk, I went to place the vial on the surface but found my wrist trapped. The clawed hand dug in as the demon pulled me closer. The other consorts scrambled backward as the scent of sulfur swept through the air. With his free hand, the demon reached forward to stroke my cheek, but I slapped it down.

"He will wish to be dead," he said, voice quiet against shiny, spit covered lips. "You aren't giving him a gift, but a curse."

"I'm not doing it for him," I said succinctly. "Cristo."

The demon released me, snagging the vial as he was blasted backward to hit the wall. He hit the plaster with a sickening crack, but everyone watched the darkness erupt from his chest, a beast of shadow with eyes of fire. It snarled at us, wings flapping as it scuttled along the edges of the light cast from the ceiling. While the consorts kept staring, I ran for the boy.

He was smoking, clothes and hair singed, but as I pressed two fingers to his neck, I sighed in relief. A pulse fluttered, faint and unsteady, but it was there. Muttering a prayer of thanks, I turned to my partner. Moira stood the same as she had in treaty talks, one step back, but her mouth was a thin line of anger.

"Lecture me later," I told her and grabbed the boy's arm. "He's alive and needs a hospital. Get him and Asim to Henry Ford and ask for Heather Bedford. Tell her what happened and tell her I'll be there as soon as I can."

She wanted to argue, that much was clear, and I prepared to slap her back down with rank. Finally, she just heaved Daniyal in her arms and, without another look at me, walked away. The door locking behind her snapped the consorts back to reality, but even they didn't speak as I dusted the sulfur powder from the front of my dress. It wasn't until I moved back to my spot that someone managed to find their voice.

"How did you manage to get celestial grace?" Heron demanded.

"That's what you want to know?" Amalia practically shouted. "She released pure evil upon the world."

"Evil has always walked the Earth, White Witch," Hesta snapped. "She saved that boy."

"Did she?" Killian asked. "Fallen magic is rarely comforting."

"I'm right here," I said firmly, back straight and standing tall. They all jerked around to stare. "I asked for the celestial grace from Graceland, King of the Underworld. It gives an impossible high, but

I laced it with nightshade. It won't kill him, but it will keep him weak for at least a year, which gives me enough time to track him. When I find him, I'll bind him, and if Graceland or Queen Persephone are unwilling to kill him, then I have other ways. As for Daniyal, the host he was accompanying, he'll either recover or he won't. If he becomes a danger, I'll put him down. I do my job. You can question my methods, but I don't let other people clean up my mistakes."

They seemed struck mute by my words, studying me with varying degrees of contemplation and trepidation. Only Hesta grinned with pride, the air ripe with hot peppers. Vodou understood the balance of risk and reward, of doing ugly things to save those in need.

"Maman is pleased," she said, "but Baron wants the truth spoken."

Impatient bastard. Licking my lips, I steadied myself.

"While I realize that was an unorthodox start, I do have my formal proposals prepared." I glanced back to the folders on the floor where Moira had dropped them to take Daniyal. Shit.

"Uh, well, I will leave you with the paperwork, but the most important topic I'd like to discuss is the integration of betrayer magics into our fold. I've worked incredibly hard with the Vedic and Yoruba pantheons, as well as Brood Dragos and House Stoja, and all are willing to submit themselves to—"

"You speak of Deep Europe?" Killian interrupted, head tilted.

I could do this. "I understand trepidation, but these are old broods and houses; truly, the fact that they even spoke with me is huge. The promise is that they will submit, follow the guidelines set by the Creators, as long as the Pilgrims provide protection to their people as we integrate other houses and broods. I won't lie and say it won't be hard or bloody, but this is a step to the future."

"Is this a joke?" Master Heron asked.

It felt like a slap, but I only curled my fists and pressed forward. "No, I realize that Deep Europe has been largely ignored by both my grandmother and father, but I firmly believe that with the help of Brood Dragos and House Stoja that—"

"Pilgrim."

I stopped, eyes to Amalia, and recognized pity. She folded her hands together and shook her head.

"It seems word has not reached you. Brood Dragos and House Stoja were slaughtered last night. A coup."

The words bounced off me, the breath stuck in my lungs. Months, chewed nails to the quick, using words like moves on a chessboard… so much time and effort reduced to ashes thick on my tongue. Death. Bodies that would have fought of peace, for change, sacred halls of creatures older and wiser soaked in blood. *Fuck.*

"My apologies," I forced myself to say. "I hadn't heard."

"Hmm. A shame," Heron said.

A mistake. Huge and engulfing. They didn't see the months of careful negotiating, only the fact that I was uninformed and wanted to bring in creatures clearly not in consensus with themselves.

"Truly, Constantin Dragos was a good man who would have been a great leader for all broods," I stated, eyes never leaving the council as I pushed on. "But we aren't here for hypotheticals. The Vedic and Yoruba pantheons have proven themselves. Rashida Amari, Senior Pilgrim of Africa, was an incredible help in negotiations, and the guidelines set are nearly identical to the ones my father created for the loa."

"Did you consult Bernard Haas, Senior Pilgrim of Deep Europe, when you approached Brood Dragos and House Stoja?"

I felt my eyelid tick and shook my head at Killian. "No, my cousin Bernard would have considered it a waste of time."

"Perhaps with age there is wisdom," Amalia pointed out.

Fear curled coldly into my throat, and I could feel it all slipping away, grains of rice that would clatter to the floor, that could cut into the skin of my knees as I desperately tried to collect every single piece.

"It wasn't a waste of time," I said, voice concrete despite my insides shaking. "It was a leap of faith. Knowledge can be earned in pain."

The smell of iron and conch filled the room. It wrapped around me like shackles, an anchor, a prison.

"Maman and the Baron have spoken," Hesta said. "You have passed to the Creators."

"Excuse me? The loas are not the only—" Amalia's rant stopped as jasmine and lilac replaced the punch of spice. Her jaw was tight, but she nodded. "Mother Eorthe agrees."

"And you've already impressed Killian and I," Heron pointed out, "though, if I could possibly meet with your partner later to discuss celestial grace, I would be most grateful."

"Of course. He'll be delighted," I lied, making a mental note to tell Graceland to behave. "But about the Vedic and Yoruba—"

"You've passed," Amalia said again, "and I think you should take your victory today. We will review your proposals in private and send what we deem worthy to the Creators. You may go."

I'd misread her fury, I realized. Wicca had been the first magic taught to humans by Mother Eorthe, the first compromise given by the Allfather, and I should have recognized the threat she felt by being overtaken by magics she considered perversion. Bowing to them, I backed up a couple steps and waved a hand, letting magic pull the door open for me.

Leaning heavily against the same pillar I'd collapsed against yesterday, I closed my eyes.

"Two minutes," I whispered to myself. "You get two minutes. Then you have to change and go."

"How about I keep watch and you can take five minutes?"

Not bothering to open my eyes, I nodded to Graceland as I slid to the floor. "We got Asim's brother back."

"Yes, I assumed the unconscious child smoking like a campfire would be your doing," he said mildly. "Finally pawned off that grace I gave you, huh?"

The laugh warbled out of me as if caught in my throat. "Graceland, how did my father do this for so long? I mean...he did this for almost fifty-five years, I barely feel like I'm hanging on to this one year. There's always something, always something."

"He had your mom, a good bottle of scotch, and—worst case—several punching bags. You'll be fine."

"Dragos is gone. Stoja is gone," I got out before I started to weep. "I failed. So many people I've killed. Oh Gods, Graceland, I failed."

"Take your five minutes," he said, hand briefly touching my hair. "Then we'll figure it out."

CHAPTER 18

Hospitals rank third (below the Secretary of State[33] and the yearly trip to the Laveau mansion) in my top five most hated places. At least Henry Ford on Grand Boulevard was better than most. Through winding hallways painted light pastels—a far cry from the stark white walls of other medical wards—I studied the framed pictures that dotted the walls. They weren't inspirational posters or the bland, mass-produced seascapes that insidiously seemed to find its way into any business. They were paintings, some crude, some surprisingly good, all done by children.

The one across from where I waited at the nurse's desk was of an octopus. Its head was lumpy, something perhaps a hat could fix, I thought, preferring to focus on Jonathan Age 6's drawing rather than the people who occasionally ran by or the voices that yelled over intercoms. Maybe a sombrero with as many tassels as the octopus had arms.

"How is it you'll stare at that dumpy octopus like it holds the secrets of the universe, but I can't get you to go to the DIA with me," Graceland demanded.

"Because I'm not going to that modern art trash exhibit. If I wanted to see a trashcan painted in red, I could just walk down any alley back home. And it will be authentic, because it's blood."

"That's the point! It represents how we as a society have become disassociated with violence!" Graceland protested.

Motioning to the picture on the opposite wall, I shrugged. "And that octopus represents the indecision of man. See, I can do it too."

"I miss Margot," he muttered, then froze. "Shit, I'm sorry, I didn't—"

---

33 Secretary of State aka the SOS is the equivalent of the DMV in Michigan. Making it sound fancy does not in fact make it any less of a miserable experience.

"You meant it," I corrected, voice gentle against his panic. "It's ok. She would have loved that stupid trash exhibit."

"Would have bored you to tears with details," he said softly.

"Fitzpatrick?"

Jerking away from the octopus, I was surprised to hear warmth. I shouldn't have been. The tall, willowy woman with kind blue eyes and hair perpetually pulled back tight always had that effect.

"Dr. Bedford."

"Heather," she corrected firmly and reached for my hand. "You need more iron and sleep."

"I'll try to eat some spinach with dinner."

"Sleep," she repeated. "Iron and *sleep*."

"You could always give me something to dose her," Graceland said. "Otherwise, she's going at top speed till she drops."

I rolled my eyes, and she gave him a knowing smile as she reached to squeeze his hand. It was always brief—those who touched Graceland knew his preferences—but she frowned and brought his hand up.

"You're just as bad!" she declared. "I understand the pressure this week, but no more alcohol and at least six hours of sleep."

"I didn't realize I was back in Hell," he said.

The fist she raised was small, but the look in her eyes was determined. Taking a step back, Graceland lifted his hands.

"Hey, do no harm, remember?" he joked, jerking his head toward the hall. "How's the kid?"

Heather let out a sigh that spoke for itself. "It was touch and go for a bit, but he's stable. Unconscious, with lesions on all his major organs. Ribs are broken, and that doesn't account for the other bones that have obviously been broken and healed without proper medical attention. He makes it through the night? He's going to recover, physically. Mentally, I can't give you anything. Your associates wouldn't tell me what did this, said to wait for you."

"Demon," I said, wincing when she paled. "Samael, Archangel."

"You're sure he's gone then?" Heather asked. "Because that boy didn't come from magic, and people don't survive this kind of damage from even normal demons."

"He's gone. I can promise you the boy is clean, and it won't be back for him."

She didn't look convinced, but before I could reassure her, Graceland piped up.

"I'll keep watch tonight," he said, nudging me. "Only you need to be available tomorrow for the Senior Pilgrim meeting."

It wasn't that it was a bad idea, but Graceland was not the person to volunteer. Normally, it took wheedling, bribes, and pulling rank to get him to do anything. Even as he moved down the hall, both of us eyed him carefully.

"He's gotten softer," Heather commented.

"Don't consider him a saint yet," I said. "Have there been any outbursts?"

I wouldn't have asked in front of Graceland, because there was no way he would have kept that from Asim. Worse, he'd feel obligated to take care of what he would assume was his failure.

"One. He made the machines short out when we first got him hooked up, but as soon as he heard his brother's voice, he settled down. Nothing else."

Magic, unstable and perverted, tended to lash out on its own, uncaring of the damage it left in its wake. It was my worst fear, to send the boy here only to have to immediately kill him. One outburst, especially something with no casualties, was passable.

"If he gets out of control, can they take care of it?" Heather asked.

"This is Graceland we're talking about," I reminded her.

"I'm not talking about his power. If the kid goes south, can they do what needs to be done?"

"That's not very Hippocratic of you, doc."

Heather stared. "Right now, until he wakes up, he isn't a kid, he's a vessel."

Even though it was a true statement, I bristled. It was reminiscent of the way Margot was treated, as if she would hop up from the bed to strangle them because she was fay.

Heather saw it in my expression. "This isn't Margot. This boy had a demon—an Archangel—inside him, Brigitte. I have a right to be cautious."

My breath was a hard exhale. "I'm that easy to read?"

"You hate hospitals," she said and shrugged. "When we were together, you must have told me a thousand times."

There were few people who could make me feel properly chastised, and my hand rubbed at the back of my neck. "Gods, I was a shitty girlfriend."

"Yep," Heather said, grin flashing as she checked her watch. "I got a meeting in a couple minutes, but I'll make sure to check in on him before my shift ends."

"I appreciate it."

It was a quick exit, like our relationship, but I lingered, eyes still on the octopus before moving to Room 116. Graceland was already slumped in the comfy chair, legs stretched out as he snored softly. The other two glanced up, having felt the shift in magic, but relaxed slightly when they saw me. Moira looked the same as when she stood over me in the ballroom, face tight and wary as she clutched my leather bag. It would have still been tucked into the back seat of Asim's rental if she hadn't thought the potions and artifacts inside were going to be used.

Forcing that thought away, I looked to Asim. His face was blotchy, eyes swollen and red, his giant hands clenching and unclenching at his side.

"Dr. Bedford says he's got a good chance," I offered, even though it was technically a grey area. "You ok?"

His choked noise, part laugh but mostly sob, propelled me across the room. Immediately, he crumpled, and I swayed to keep him upright. He had a good hundred pounds on me, but I didn't complain, instead bringing his head down so I could run my hand over his hair.

"I'm sorry, but I couldn't take a chance," I whispered. "I knew I could get him out, but I couldn't be sure how you'd deal with it."

There was a fear, small like a seed in my chest, that he wouldn't understand why—or worse, that he would and still be angry. As his arms tightened around me, I realized it was relief, not fury, that shook his shoulders.

"I would have broken down," he admitted against my shoulder. "I would have ruined everything."

I didn't placate, because we both knew it was true. Instead, I pulled him back, giving him a little shake till he straightened.

"What matters is we got him out," I said firmly. "You can stay here as long as it takes. I don't want you worrying about the rest of the treaties or what's going on back home."

"Thank you."

"We got him out. That's what matters," I said again.

"Is it?" Moira demanded from across the room. "Forget the treaty, forget protocol, everything's copacetic because a demon isn't wearing Asim's brother anymore? Let's not forget you let the demon go, or that you literally took the hardest road to get the council's approval. It's reckless and—"

"Hallway. Now," I interrupted.

Her mouth opened again to argue, but Graceland, whose eyes were too clear for him to have been sleeping, spoke.

"You should remember who you're speaking to, Moira. She isn't a child anymore and, like it or not, she's your boss."

"I can't believe you're ok with this," she shot back at him. "One of your brothers, free."

"Samael was always a tit. If she gave him even a second of pain, I don't care how the job got done," he said casually, eyes lazily drifting over to me. "Lacing it with nightshade was inspired, boss."

"Nightshade," Moira said, voice faint.

"She always has a plan. Sometimes it's reckless, but it's never shit," Graceland said and closed his eyes again. "Remember that next time."

"I—"

"Hallway," I repeated.

The older woman followed behind me, docile now. Shutting the door, I leaned against it and crossed my arms as the other Pilgrim stood there.

"Not that you wouldn't regardless, but you have permission to speak freely," I said.

"I'm sorry."

It wasn't what I expected, but I nodded as the other woman began to pace, fingers worrying at her earring.

"I should have trusted you, I do trust you, it's just—"

"I'm not my father, and you don't trust Vodou," I finished for her.

"Why aren't you mad? You don't look mad."

Maybe I would have been filled with self-righteous fury if I had cemented Deep Europe on the council, if I didn't have the blood of generations on my hands and more questions than answers. "We would be having a very different conversation if you hadn't had my back when it counted. You did what I asked, even though you didn't want to. You may think that I don't know how much you miss my father being in charge, and maybe in time you'll get to the point where you view me in a similar way, but for now, the fact that you respect the position is enough."

It was all I had, and I hoped it would be enough of a compromise. I understood how hard it was for her, to watch my father retire and to see the power struggle between Bronson and me, but that was done.

"Understood."

Just like that. I always marveled at Moira's ability to discard and move on. Shaking my head, I shouldered the bag she held out.

"I'm going to my mother's markets to grab a few things, but my phone's on. Keep me updated."

"Ok."

I should have had a pep talk prepped for times like this, but as everyone seems fond of reminding me, I wasn't my father. So, I held the door for Moira and stared past her at Daniyal in his hospital bed. With Margot, I hadn't gotten a chance to find her room. Even though it felt like an eternity, it was only minutes of compressions and injections.

If I hadn't forced myself, I never would have left the doorway, forever stuck staring into the past. My footsteps were drowned out by the sounds of machines, of squeaking shoes and mumbling people, but I compensated by pressing each step harder. It made me feel a little more real, but it wasn't until the fresh air spilled over me when the lobby doors slid open that my chest loosened. The faint scent of antiseptic clung inside my throat, but I swallowed it down and dug through the side pocket of my bag.

Before the mad dash out of my apartment this morning, I'd packed several artifacts I thought would help, but it was one of the many mini liquor bottles in there that I grabbed. Twisting off the cap, I took a huge swig. Cheeks full, I pushed my foot against the cement in a wide arch, one palm to my stomach and the other raised in the air. With as much force as I could muster, I spit the vodka into the air, an arching spray that caught in the heavy sunlight. Glittering, it hung suspended in front of me, booze-soaked crystals shooting rainbows in random direction. It would have more impressive if I could've spewed fire like Maman or brought people with me like Mama, but it would do. As I stepped forward through the jewels of alcohol I found myself not in the crowded parking lot of a hospital, but on a flowered path that led to a row of shops. Healing magic rolled over me, and I wiped at errant tears of relief. It was always different depending on the injury—a warm fire, a soft light. This time it was cool, like stepping into a stream of water.

Nevermore, the original market lived in constant twilight during the reign of Marie Laveau I. It was only when Mama inherited her third of the market that she argued viciously for the white arts to be represented, to expand their business beyond the realm of Vodou. Circe, the eldest Laveau sister would sneer and say it was only because Odette was the baby of the family that she got what she wanted. However, everyone knew it was because she was the most powerful and the favorite of both Grandmother and our loas. So, Odette built Evermore, a market for those who needed ingredients for the softer magics. The More Markets now held everything from specialty spell-casting apps to chickens for sacrificing.

The truth was, I hadn't really needed anything from Evermore; I merely enjoyed being there. White magic slipped into the bones like warm broth, and the heavy wards here meant I didn't have to glance over my shoulder. The smell of fresh cut flowers with the bite of nutmeg provided a pleasant mask for truly complex magic. Mama would not have left loopholes for her sisters to pry into this place. She'd spent months crafting the fountains of holy water, the wards of pure salt placed inside underground pipes that ran the perimeter. Within each shop she buried satchels of sage, crisp from the flame, and the bones of her favorite pets, providing comfort for them and protection for the owners. Even now, in the distance I could see the ghost of Croissant, her favorite possum, doing his patrols around Panacea Potion Shop.

It was a side to Mama only those close to her understood. Most thought of her as a madwoman or as the corruptor of the Fitzpatrick line. She liked it that way, enjoyed catching people off guard. It was a game for her, a chess match that others only realized they were playing when they were beaten.

It infuriated her sisters that they were denied entry to Evermore. They'd assumed that once Mama was back up north, they could crack it open, but that had been nearly twenty-five years ago, and they'd never even scratched the surface.

They would know, however, the minute I stepped into Nevermore. Circe and Tilde Laveau would descend like vultures, and there hadn't been a time in my life where I'd come out of Nevermore not feeling picked clean. So, I took my time to enjoy the plucking of harp strings, the sound of fountains rushing up and crashing down. I stopped to give Croissant a pet and picked up several bottles of Briar Heart[34].

There were several ways to Nevermore, paths that Mama crafted to make the descent easier for those who needed more traditional ingredients but weren't interested in the razor balance of pain and power Vodou demanded. I'd tried them all, but the one that gave the best chance of at least getting business done before my aunts found me was also the most dangerous. Turning the corner, I ducked into the alley behind Empath Records and stared at the large, double-wide coffin. It was traditional, black with tapered feet, and when I cracked it open, the red velvet inside released the scent of decaying books and dust.

There were other ways, I reminded myself as I pulled the lid off. It gave a mournful wail like in the old Universal horror movies. Mama had an acquired sense of humor. Stepping inside, I pulled the lid back over myself. It locked into place, leaving me in blinding darkness. There was no escape now; it only opened from the outside. Crossing arms over my chest, I whispered a prayer and fell into the abyss.

---

34 A potion used to help those with weak or damaged magical links.

CHAPTER 19

Being a single inch from the spikes of a rusted iron maiden was not on my bucket list, yet here I was, staring at metal tips that brushed against my eyelashes as I blinked. Having traveled this path, I knew the amount of movement allowed: one centimeter to the left, head tilted back until my neck was straight, arms tight to my side. The hardest part was getting my hands unfolded as I bulleted through the air.

I'd slid out through the bottom of the coffin and into the device, a hand into a mitt, the fit just as tight. Sharp metal teeth tore at the flesh of my arm, a reminder I hadn't pulled it tight enough to my hip. Thankfully I'd had worse, because I didn't have the space to hiss in pain, my bottom lip already caressed by a thick silver spike.

With a tentative shove, I pressed my booted foot to the bottom. The door swung open, and if I wouldn't have been speared, I'd have scuttled back. Flippen Scabbath, proprietor of the shop, stared at me, his ears perked up and large eyes wide.

"Surprise," I said and stumbled out.

Though smaller than me by nearly a foot, he steadied me with a solid green hand, setting a book back on the shelf.

"Always doing things the hard way," Flippen scolded and motioned for me to follow. "Your mother mentioned you might come by, but I didn't think it'd be so soon. Got a new shipment today, and I'll give you first shot at it. We need to hurry though; I'd say we got about ten minutes before the wicked witch of the west blows in."

"Would that be Circe or Tilde?" I asked mildly as we moved through the crowded aisles.

Indiana Bones: Magical Artifact Emporium was one of the oldest businesses in both More Markets, specializing in nothing and containing everything. The Scabbath clan were one of the more nomadic branches of the goblin tree, and while Flippen took after his grandfather in managing the shop, the rest of his family were spread like rice in the wind. His brother, Xander, was somewhere in South Africa, and Caja, his sister, had gone dark a month ago in Deep Europe after a stop in Egypt. They sent treasures, powders, curses, and anything else they thought Flippen might like back to the shop, but it'd been years since they'd been home.

When their grandfather passed away three years ago, he sent out letters to each family member, but quietly held the funeral alone. Afterward, he followed his grandfather's wishes, which granted Flippen free reign of the shop and everything in it. So, he knocked down a wall, bought the space next to them, and expanded. He renamed the shop in homage to his grandfather's favorite movie, lived above in the tiny loft, and placed Hogarth Scabbath's ashes next to the cash register in a replica of the Holy Grail.

He admitted to me only once, when we were signing transfer paperwork, that he was unsure if he could do the place justice. Now, as he plopped several jewel encrusted boxes on the counter in front of me, I couldn't help but smile. He'd made this place a home.

"All right, we got beetles from Egypt—Sunrider sent me a box, told me if I didn't sell them before they died then Gaia and Luna could grind them up. These guys got about a week left; you can have them for free. If you don't use them, dump them at Haven."

Poking a finger at the hissing box bedazzled in red rubies, I grimaced. "What can they do for me alive?"

Normally, when a goblin grinned, it put everyone on edge, razor-sharp teeth set in a face that allowed the smile to curl back behind their ears. The effect was dulled by the old man glasses perched on Flippen's young face.

"So, I have no experience with your human pets, but Reddit says dogs are the best, most loyal."

Mama would have something to say about that, but I shrugged. "Sure."

"I can guarantee these are better. They imprint on whoever sees them first. They don't live long, which may account for the fierceness in which they protect their owner."

"Flippen," I said slowly. "They're beetles."

Nodding hard, his glasses slid low. "Yes. Burrowing beetles."

The grin that spread across my face matched the goblin's in sheer delight. "Are you saying what I think you're saying?"

"Have you seen *The Mummy*?"

I tapped my fingers against the box. "Have I seen it? You mean the most gorgeous fictional couple to grace the screen since Bogart and Bacall?"

The goblin's laugh was sweet, another departure from most of his kin. "Can we all agree that Evie and Rick O'Connell are goals?"

"It's nice to have someone get my references," I said. "Graceland is getting better, but he's so self-righteous about it."

"So, nothing's changed," Flippen pointed out.

"Fair enough," I laughed. "So I could set these up as a trap, and anyone who isn't supposed to be there: bam! Skin-burrowing, flesh-eating monsters?"

"Theoretically, you'd have to make sure someone didn't come in by accident, because they don't discriminate. I had a lady wear them around her neck to and from her walk to work. Guy tried to jump her and ended up eyeless in less than two minutes. Had to testify," he said with a disgusted shake of his head. "That's why I stopped selling them; too much collateral. I figure you'll do right by them, or Luna will."

It was as close as he would come to saying that some magic wasn't meant to leave its homeland. His family would have gasped at the notion that knowledge wasn't meant to be shared completely, but they only saw the find, the excitement of discovery. Flippen saw the results.

Gently, I lifted the box into my bag, nestling it at the bottom. "I'll just take them to Luna. Best to let the experts handle it."

"Fair."

As he moved to grab another box, I worried at my lip. "Flippen?"

"Yeah?"

"You heard from Caja?"

It was always a sore subject. He knew his family couldn't help but keep roaming, even though he was often lonely.

"Not lately. She sent me an invoice for something she sent to

Tomes & Bones a month ago, but it was backdated—probably changed hands multiple times to avoid customs. It got there recently; got the receipt. Why?"

"Can I see the invoice?"

He didn't have to. There was nothing illegal here, and even if there was, it was my aunts' job to monitor that. Still, I smiled when he nodded. With a snap of his fingers the paper dropped to the counter.

"Did T&B file a complaint?" he asked, pushing his glasses up. "I can always take it off their hands if the weapons fragments weren't up to snuff."

And he'd do it at a financial loss to himself because he cleaned up his family's messes.

"No, nothing like that. They got hit. Ms. Vale said spear tips and other fragments got taken. Bane Tome got smoked," I explained as I checked the invoice. It was various bits and bobbles, but one word stuck out.

"Flippen, is this right?" I asked, jabbing at the paper. "Longinus?"

"Longinus lancehead," Flippen read and shrugged. "I mean, Caja always checks her documents before she sends. Is it a human relic? Important?"

"Is the lance that pierced Jesus's side important?" I repeated in disbelief. "The last of the five sacred wounds? Flippen, if this is right, that's one of the most powerful fragments in creation."

For a second, he only blinked at me, then snatched the paper to bring it closer. "Longinus lancehead, Antioch, Turkey. I know a couple traders out that way; I'll send word to them and to Caja again. This is the Spear of Destiny we're talking about, yes?"

"The tip of it," I agreed, panic settling in my stomach. "I mean, there are replicas everywhere, so it could be nothing. I don't want to jump to conclusions, but I've never seen one written as Longinus in a buyer's agreement."

"A way to hide it?"

"No, that was the name of the soldier who did the deed. It's a human thing; there wasn't any magic in him or the spear. It was the blood and water that poured from Jesus that blessed or cursed it, I guess. Caja wouldn't have cared about it since she's more focused on fay magic but—"

"Dangerous," Flippen finished for me.

"Cursed," I agreed. And missing. Not a great combination regardless of if the thieves knew what they had. "I'm not sure it could even be touched without disaster. Maybe with enough wards and gris-gris[35] but—"

We stared at each other in nervous silence, but there was nothing more we could do. Finally, he tapped the box in front of him.

"This is actually something I've been holding onto for you."

Lifting the lid, we both stared at a tiny pair of earrings. Two studs of burnished copper held together by a fragile chain. They sang, a quiet melody, and their warmth rolled over me.

"They belonged to Boudica," I whispered.

The Queen of Witches, a Celtic woman born of privilege and stripped of even her base humanity by the Romans after the death of her husband. Boudica led her clan, the Iceni, on a bloody but ultimately doomed crusade of vengeance. It was said, after her people lay dying around her and her blood seeped through her own hands, that Mother Eorthe took pity on her. Rather than let the body be desecrated as it had been in life, Mother Eorthe buried Boudica inside a willow tree. The earrings and her torc, a stiff necklace of gold, were said to have been stripped from her to allow her to return to the earth naturally. Mother Eorthe cast them aside, uncaring about the objects of man, but because she touched them, they were blessed.

"Where did you get these?"

Flippen shook his head. "I wasn't sure if they were real. They've been silent for everyone, but I figured if they sang for you then it was legit."

"It's a battle cry," I whispered and stroked the chain. "Mournful but proud. How much?"

"I'll give you a discount. One forty."

That price probably didn't cover the cost of the expedition, but if I

---

35 A charm or amulet often used in Vodou or African magics.

was the only one who could use them, they had little value to anyone else. Pulling out my card, I slid it across the table.

"You wanna see what's in the third one first?" he asked, tapping the card against the counter. "Too rich for your blood, but it's cool."

I was going to have to eat ramen just for the earrings. "Sure."

The third box, adorned with a shining emerald sun, barely contained the dark magic inside. Where the earrings were warm, this box seeped cold, the creeping of winter under a loose door. It stung as it crept up my bones to rattle my fingers. Nestled inside the rich green velvet was an orb, carved delicately from glass with two indents perfect for hands.

"No way."

Flippen nodded. "My brother found it, almost took him under before he got it into a lead-lined box."

There were things far more dangerous than demons. Demons' compulsions made them predictable; you could barter with them or outsmart them.

"You can't sell this, Flippen," I told him, voice cracking. "I'm not having this loose in North America."

"You don't dictate the rules of Nevermore, niece."

Both of us tensed at the haughty voice of Circe Laveau. With the skill of a magician and the hands of a blackjack dealer, Flippen slid the earrings and my card across the table. I let both fall into my open bag before turning to face my aunt.

"Auntie, what a pleasure."

The snort was a tiny, ugly thing, pinched like her face. Where Mama's face was lined with joy, mouth split by laughter, Circe was a prune of proud irritation. She resembled the old sepia photographs Mama kept of our ancestors. Her hands, lined with black tattoos in place of rings, folded over her stomach as her head tilted to inspect me.

"Have you ever truly meant that, I wonder?"

"Maybe when I was nine and you took me bogy hunting," I admitted honestly.

She gave a fleeting smile, as if the memory came and was swatted away. "What are you doing here?"

I could've lied, but Circe Laveau, while a heinous bitch, was not an idiot. Leaning against the counter, I dropped the smile.

"I'm restocking."

"What are you doing in New Orleans? In my market?" Circe demanded.

"You aren't the only Laveau here," I reminded her, giving a slight wince when my side stung. "And I'm not afraid of your party tricks."

"I'll show you more than tricks, little girl."

There were no qualms about pain and power with Circe Laveau. She'd traveled to the darkest corners of Vodou, to loas that our Baron and Maman despised.

"The treaty is this week. I'm not here to spy on you, Circe," I informed her. "I have bigger concerns than *my mother's markets.*"

With Tilde, that would have been enough to make her to stomp off in a huff. Circe's lips barely twitched as she sank her nail deeper into her palm and the pain in my side flared.

"Nevermore is mine. What sells here is my decision; what goes on here is because I decree it. It's time for you to run back to your mother."

If I hadn't died earlier in the week, the shooting pain in my side might have made me hiss, but I wasn't raised by wimps.

"I have more shopping to do," I said and gave Flippen a nod. "I'll see you around."

I marched past her, but found myself pulled to a stop, bony fingers latched like a shackle.

"You will go where I say."

Fury, hot Irish temper and Creole rage, drove me to slap her hand down, "Try your manipulation somewhere else, witch. You own nothing—not this family, not our legacy, and not me."

The words hung in the air, and Circe raised her hand, loaded with immense power, to strike. I could have moved, but only tightened my jaw as the hand swung down. There was a phantom push of air, then we were feet from each other, the smell of boiling peppers and sour okra filling the room. Maman had spoken, and she was pissed.

My chest heaved, lungs pressed against my ribs, and I saw Circe in the same state. It was probably the only time we looked related, the set of our anger burning in dark eyes. Neither one of us would go against Maman, but that didn't mean we were going to hug it out.

"You have ten minutes, then I want you out of my market," she spat and spun on her heel.

The shop's door slammed shut, setting the attached bell rattling. My sigh held the still foul air, and I nodded to the expanse of the shop.

"As soon as the treaty is complete, a family dinner," I murmured to a place no one else could see. "I'll even bring Mama. Is that acceptable?"

Fresh air and turned earth, rich against my nose, made me bow. Mama was going to kill me.

"She let you go pretty easily," Flippen commented from behind his desk.

Maman or Circe? I wanted to ask, but with raised brows I slid my shirt up to show him my ribs. Below the last one was a sharp shallow cut, and along the inflamed line, perfect finger-shaped bruises dotted my skin.

"Great ghosts, she would have pried you apart!" Flippen's face twisted as he shoved his glasses up.

"Nah, my mother would have murdered her if she'd really hurt me. This was a warning," I said and dropped the shirt. "I should be more concerned with the fact that I got my mom stuck going to dinner on our family's grounds."

There were few places Mama was unable find the light in, but her ancestral home was a place seemingly made of total shadow. Even her eternal optimism flickered there, like a candle being suffocated by glass. It would hurt her, and that tore at me worse than the fingers of the spirits that tried to get inside the cut Circe gave me.

"Let me see the orb again."

Silently, Flippen pushed it back to me. The orb shrieked when I touched a finger to it, putrid yellow smoke shoving against the glass before it shuttered backward, as if trying to escape.

"Spooky the way it whispers, right?" he asked.

Besides the high-pitched squeal, I hadn't heard anything. Carefully shutting the lid, I gave the goblin a long look.

"It isn't talking to me, Flippen."

He blinked at the box for another second before his eyes jerked to mine in realization. Pushing a long finger at it, he nodded at a wardrobe to my right.

"Put it in there."

Silently, I took it to the ancient monstrosity, the wardrobe bigger than me by feet, almost black with thick coats of uneven lacquer. The scent of decay—not the richness of earth, but the rot of flesh—rolled my stomach as I slid the box onto the shelf, right next to a large jar of eyes that stared directly at me.

As soon as the doors were shut, it was like a string being cut. I saw by the way Flippen rubbed at the bridge of his nose that he was ok.

"I won't sell it," he promised, shoving his glasses back into place. "It's got wards inside it; nothing can get out."

I'd felt the magic holding everything inside, knew there was blood spread over that wood, hidden under age and coats of stain. Still, precautions should be taken.

"Will you accept protection?"

He frowned. "If you think it's necessary. I'm not interested in being possessed."

I wouldn't have pressed it on him; goblins and dweorgs were both incredibly resistant to magical influence. He wasn't disoriented or aggressive, but better safe than sorry. My free hand went to my hair, where normally a curl woven with binding thread would reside. When I touched nothing but hair, I realized my mistake. After Margot, I'd shed everything kept for protection, ripping off every bracelet, charm, and talisman after the funeral and tossing them into my trunk at home. They were laying there now, some still stained with blood.

No thread, so I'd improvise. Rubbing at my laid edges, I pulled a hair. Easily, I tied it around his thin finger, the little reddish-brown bow festive against his green skin. Afraid I might spook him, my fingers moved slowly over his hand as I spoke.

"Any energy that serves as its own master, you are unwelcome. There are no vessels for you here, no body or essence prepared for habitation. You have been given notice and nothing else will follow. If you choose to linger, you will cease to be."

Behind us, the wardrobe gave a single shudder before it fell still.

Flippen's eyes went huge behind his glasses as the knotted hair around his finger snapped clean off.

"Please tell me that's good?"

"It's good," I assured him. "If you need to do anything inside the cabinet, I would wait a couple days. If you handle the box again, I'm going to suggest setting sage out to burn before you do."

"You got it," he said, head bobbing. "You should probably head out before the wicked witch comes back."

He was right, but my feet felt too heavy, dragging along the uneven cobblestones to the alley opening where the totem to Detroit stood, a flittering, half shredded curtain separating me from my city. Nevermore, despite its dark corners and dangerous potential, was like seeing the past. Draped in eternal twilight, the sun always on the cusp of losing its battle to stay, the entire market whispered nostalgia. Despite the modern upgrades, the air smelled of hay, of pitchfork metal, of magic so curious it was dizzying. Circe preferred to remind those who came to Nevermore there was a time when magic, and those who practiced it, were hunted. The pull of wood smoke and the faint cry of souls before they were put to the flame was hypnotic.

My aunt had a lot in common with demons, I mused as I parted the curtains to step back to reality.

CHAPTER 20

It was a rare occurrence that I found myself dreading the company of my parents, but there was no way I could look Mama in the eye after making the deal with Maman. So, I slunk to Haven like a coward, promising Mama in a hastily written text that I would still pick them up for dinner. The theme to *Jaws* played from Haven's bell as I shoved inside and glared at the twins behind the counter.

"What crawled up your—" Gaia stopped and glanced to where Martavious was scribbling something. "—butt."

"Gaia got a parenting book," Luna said and held up a vial to the light. "Apparently boundaries are important."

The irony didn't escape me, but I was too irritated to smile, so I shoved the box of beetles Flippen gave me in their direction.

"Gift from Flippen." I told them.

"Our favorite." Luna said, nodding to his sister, "you wanna tag it?"

Gaia shook her head, "The kid needs to learn. Martavious, grab the checklist in your red binder, start going through it."

I settled onto the stool and accepted the mug she pushed at me, sniffed it.

"It's just a house blend," she explained, "you don't get a cup of the Irish until you have better manners."

"You'd be grumpy too if you ran into Circe Laveau."

"Don't you let your mom catch you not calling her Auntie," Gaia warned and grabbed her own mug, "but I'd be downright snarly."

"So normal then?" Luna muttered.

Gaia rolled her eyes at her twin's back, "Got something from Flippen so it couldn't be all bad."

"True, I think—"

The words simply evaporated as I turned to check on Martavious.

Cross-legged on the floor he was for lack of a better word, snuggling the beetles. They hummed, scuttling up and over his shoulders and down his arms.

"Can I keep them?" he asked, beaming.

Gaia and Luna looked at me with twin expressions of wariness.

"They will mind him," I wheedled.

"There's what, five of them?" Gaia said and glanced at her parenting book. "How about you keep one?"

"Deal!" he says and quickly held the only colored scarab, it's vibrant green body wiggling. "I'm keeping Graceland Jr."

For a second, all of us just stared, then the three of us burst out laughing. Through my own tears of delight, I saw Martavious look a little baffled. Then his warm, small smile crept across his face, like he'd just realized it was ok to do.

The *Jaws* theme jingled again and a breeze of cold air had all of us turning to see the actual Graceland. Wrapped against the chill, he stared at us as if we were alien creatures, which of course only made us all laugh harder.

"What the absolute fuck?"

"Swear jar," Martavious said brightly, placing his beetle on his shoulder. "A dollar please!"

"What?"

"I'm a child, Graceland," he reminded him. "Boundaries are an important step in my development."

That only made the god look more baffled, and he turned to the Darkchilds and I for interpretation. Because I knew the twins wouldn't, I took pity on him.

"Gaia's reading a parenting book, and this menace…" I said and gently nudged him with my hip, "…is proving he's too smart for his own good."

"I'm gonna go to college, or trade school, or—Disney World," Martavious said, eyes cast to his guardians, "which you are funding with your language, so, dollar in the jar."

"I lose money every time I come in here," Graceland said but took out his wallet. "If I wanted to go broke, I'd go to Motor City Casino."

"And Caishen[36] would have you escorted out," I said. "Take our usual table, I'll grab drinks."

"One more year," he grumbled as he moved along.

"Luna, can I get—" I stopped as I turned.

The werewolf was gazing somewhere in the distance, swallowing hard. Immediately Gaia was at his side. Martavious watched, frozen and confused, eyes flickering between us.

"Luna," Gaia said and snapped her fingers in front of his face, "you still here?"

It took a minute, but he blinked, then shook his head like he was ridding water from his ears.

"I think I should lay down," he said, voice thin.

"Yeah—I—Pilgrim I'll be back with your drinks," Gaia said. "Martavious, lock the door."

"I'll do it," I offered and patted the still worried boy on his shoulder. "It's ok. You go along with them. Gaia will explain."

He did, trailing behind as Gaia led Luna through the door up to their apartment. Sighing, I locked the door and flipped the sign to closed before heading to my table.

"Heard you caused some trouble this afternoon," Graceland said and crossed his arms. "Should I chastise you?"

"Didn't realize I had a morality chaperone, Dad."

"If I were your father, I would have drowned you at birth," he said without malice. "I have news for you."

"Isn't that Hermes's job?" I teased. "Am I being billed for this delivery?"

"You can't afford me. You want bad or good first?"

"For once, I'll take good."

"We're in hour two and the kid is still with us, without a single flareup. Moira and Asim will watch him till tonight, then I'll take over. He's not awake, but at least he's not dead."

I waited for more, but that was all he gave me. "Why did I expect the good to be great?" I asked.

---

36 Chinese folk god of money; he has the power to grant prosperity or take fortunes away.

"He's had a demon wearing him for longer than most could survive. The fact that he's alive is great," he corrected. "Samael isn't going to be easy to find—or kill, for that matter. He's older than me and has a lot fewer moral and ethical hangups."

"Impossible. But speaking of old shit that causes trouble."

I slid my phone across the table and watched him easily enter my password, which I'd never given him.

"You use the same password for everything," he muttered as he read. "This the list Caja sent Tomes & Bones?"

"Yeah, got it from Flippen. See what I'm worried about?"

"That it really is mostly junk, I mean—wait." He glanced up to me. "You think this is legit? Come on, could she really have not known she had the real Lance of Longinus in her grubby hands?"

"Caja isn't interested in anything Allfather-related. I don't know why, but she disappears after she sends it, it gets here, Tomes & Bones gets robbed. There is no trace of anyone or anything on the cameras, and the Bane tome is destroyed. Lot of work—lot of *magic*—for junk."

"But still, Brig, that's a tall order for a couple vlkodlak."

I nodded my agreement. "True, but not that hard for Vasile. You on good terms with your more aggressive siblings this week?"

"We're fine," he said, eyes narrowing. "I'm gonna warn you to tread carefully with what you say next."

He truly was so much better than he thought, better than most of his siblings, who would not have hesitated to harm him or humans if they wanted something powerful.

"You said it yourself: no vlkodlak could get in without being seen. A god, however, would have no issue. I got an awful lot of them in Detroit."

"None of my siblings cares about a god killer, Fitzpatrick," he said, but frowned. "They barely recognize him as it is."

"God killer?"

Normally, when he looked at me like the stupidest creature he'd ever encountered, I felt the urge to boot him in the dick, but I just stared back, eyebrows raising for explanation.

"What, you think it's just a weapon?"

"I figured one of your siblings stole it for money," I informed him bluntly. "All of you could kill with a snap of your fingers, but you're greedy fucks."

"Wow, *offended*—but accurate," he said. "Use your brain, Brig. My father took a piece of himself, to make a version of himself, that he then had sacrificed to himself. The other four holy wounds merely drew blood. That's magic enough, but that lance—it killed him. It killed a god."

Well, that was a horrifying thought. "You really think it could kill the Allfather?"

"I know it can," he corrected. "It's his major fuck up, one he can't fix with a rainbow. But I also know that no one has seen the real thing in forever, and most likely Caja got conned. I'm not even sure regular fay or humans could touch the thing much less use it, you have to be bound somehow to the Allfather. I think we have bigger concerns, but if you want, I'll send word to Ares and Athena, see if anyone knows something."

"I'd appreciate it. You're probably right, but—"

"You have terrible luck for causing chaos," he finished. "Yes, I'm aware.

"Hmmm."

"No sharp retort?" he asked and sighed. "Disappointing."

"Why didn't you ever try to find it then? To kill him?"

He froze, the arrogance bleeding out, but he still gave an aborted shrug, "Because I never wanted him dead. Now that you're done picking scabs, you want your bad news?"

"Fair's fair," I agreed.

"Brood Dragos and House Stoja have been completely razed. Word came from Alexei. It's an absolute bloodbath right now, no harbor for members. Brood Toma and House Ballen have already taken their positions as the oldest now."

"Ballen doesn't surprise me, but I'm getting really fucking tired of hearing Toma's name," I said and pressed fingers to my temples. "They weren't strong enough to be behind what's happening here, and they certainly aren't strong enough to take head brood."

"Shell game."

"Exactly," I agreed. "What are the odds that Toma is Vasile?"

"I'd say you'd win money at Motor City. So what do we do?"

I wanted to do a million things, but he was right yesterday when he directed me to stay focused.

"I was right?" he said, surprised. "Are you actually admitting that?"

"Get out of my head," I said but shrugged, "I suppose you have to be once in a lifetime. I need to be Divine Arbiter before I can do anything of consequence."

"Which means proving yourself to the Creators and their right hands."

"Tomorrow's problem. I have to go disappoint my parents first."

"I think I'll skip that."

"Coward," I said, wishing I could do the same as I dug through my bag. "I need you to do something for me. Take these oils to the hospital. Asim will know what needs to be done with the briar heart[37]."

"I can do that," he said, taking the bottles and looking them over. "You gonna be ok?"

I shook my head. "No, but when has that ever stopped me?"

His smile, a small, twisted thing, helped me roll my shoulders back and stand. Time to face the music.

---

37 Briar Heart, a potion that helps repair links to the magical world that are damaged. Made of yarrow, sage, rosemary, and one red Kool-Aid jammer.

CHAPTER 21

Of course, sometimes the world gives you a solid. When I arrived to see my parents at their hotel room at the Siren, it wasn't anger I was greeted with, but exasperation.

"Your mother drew a white lady here," my father muttered.

I knew he was talking about a ghost, a wife, a lover, a sister, a daughter brutalized and clad in white, exacting revenge on those who wronged her, but I couldn't resist teasing.

"Oh no, not a Karen!"

My father's lips twitched as he held the door open. "You joke, but she's refusing to leave until, and I quote, 'the real Senior Pilgrim gets here.'"

Sighing, I shook my head. "Gotta speak to the manager if you want anything done. Tell Mama to stop collecting strays."

My father's laugh followed me as I toed off my shoes and went for the bathroom. I knew this ghost well.

Renee Garrel, a fragile stem of a woman, clad in a white silk dress and matching mask, confronted her husband in the bar downstairs about his numerous affairs on New Years Eve 1919. Humiliation, his and hers, forced them from the party early, and as the fever pitch of their anger clanged down the hall, it was punctuated by the slamming of their hotel door. After that came the muffled sound of a slap and one long, piercing scream that cut off with the precision of a conductor's hand.

It took three days for them to discover her body, still draped in the opulent gown of silk, her face bloated, tongue thick and dangling. At that point her husband had already fled back to his native France. The exact location of Renee's final resting place was speculation, but I could confirm that her soul currently wailed from the other side of the bathroom wall. Mama, to her credit, was sitting on the floor outside the bathroom, softly trying to convince Renee to settle down.

"Mama, this isn't a drunk girl's bad night. I got this," I said and pounded my fist against the wall. "You chose to be stuck here, Renee! I know for a fact on at least three separate occasions you've been given the option to move on!"

The sniffling was loud enough that I was sure the spirit was trying to get through the walls, but the magic of the room kept her contained to her side.

"No one's ever offered to help me," she sobbed pitifully.

"Do you want to pass over?" I said, voice sweet. "I can do that right now."

In the bead of silence, I put a fist into my mouth to keep from laughing. I almost choked on it when the spirit spoke.

"You are a hateful woman, Pilgrim!"

"Keep it down for another two days, then you can go about your business. But if you try to drown anyone else, I'm going to have to get rid of you."

"Room 213 is cheating on his wife."

"Let her drown him," I told her firmly. "Go cry on the other side of the room."

The wails settled into sniffles. I shook my head and offered my hand to help Mama up.

"Harsh," she commented.

"Sometimes you have to be," I reminded her. "You taught me that. Harsh but honest can be just as effective as nurturing."

As Mama's grip tensed in my hand, I realized the solid the world had done me was over. Feelings flashed across her face, and I recognized the fear and fury in equal measure.

I could and had withstood anger, often thrived on it, like fire in the forest. But Mama's pain was quiet and deep.

"Mama, I'm sorry."

My words cracked the air, genuine and fragile. Her head snapped up, and I pressed a hand to my heart. So many thought she was a powder keg, ready to blow at any moment, but in truth, her anger was easily drained away when she was faced with receiving a sincere apology.

"Dette?" Dad asked before turning to me. "Brigitte, why are you sorry?"

"I told you to go to Flippen," Mama said, dropping my hand. "so I'm partially to blame."

"No, no, you aren't," I replied, rubbing my palms together nervously. "I lost my temper with Circe. I brought family dinner on us."

"Family dinner," Dad said faintly. Then his hands fisted at his sides. "When?"

I winced. "First thing after the treaty. All of us."

Do you know what you've cost your mother?" he asked, voice quiet but building. "How badly you've hurt her because you had to throw a temper tantrum?"

Hanging my head, I looked at my feet, feeling ten again when I decided to try to fly off the roof, so sure my magic would protect me.

"Dad, I—"

"Stop. Stop and think for one minute, Brigitte Marie. Your actions effect other people. Your mother had a year, a whole year, until she had to step foot in that house again. You know how we plan, how long it takes to prepare, and now we're expected there in less than two days," he told me, slapping a fist against a bedpost that splintered under the force. "Did you even think about your mother when you opened your mouth?"

"Rory, mon cher, that's enough," Mama said.

Those simple words made him quiet, but his fists remained clenched. Slowly, as if she'd aged years in minutes, Mama swayed toward me, and as I had as a child on days when she was in this state, I held out my arms. She let me hold her and brought her ringed fingers up to hold my cheeks.

"I'm sorry, Mama, I really am," I said, pressing her fingers to my lips so she could feel the words as I said them.

"I know you are, baby," she said. "I'm just glad—"

The words cut off as she tilted her head, lips moving as she dragged her hands across my face and down my neck. Her head cocked further, ear coming closer to my chest, as if she heard something. Her hands slipped past my shoulders, and I realized too late what she felt.

"Mama, it's not—"

"Shut your mouth."

My jaw clicked shut as she found my side, nails ripping the softness of my dress until the air kissed the savagely bruised cut.

"Rory, come here. Now," Mama demanded, waving a hand behind herself. "I want us both to see this."

He came without hesitation, stepping forward to look over her tiny shoulder, and I saw his eyes widen, the cast of green that rolled over his face. I couldn't tell if it was from Mama's magic or seeing me hurt.

"What happened?" he asked.

"It's not a big deal. It will heal in a couple of days," I assured them both. "She didn't even—"

"She harmed you, tried to get inside you," Mama interrupted, fingers tracing over the lines. "She tried to kill my daughter."

"Mama, it's not—"

This time, instead of being cut off, the words simply didn't exist anymore, as if they'd been caught in her fist. I tapped at my throat, but she simply shook her head and stalked, magic seeping off her to stain the carpet in ugly, mottled patches.

"My own sister," she repeated as she spun back. "If you hadn't been strong enough, she would have possessed you. She actually attempted it."

"Dette," Dad warned and took a step toward her, "you need to calm down."

It was the exact wrong thing to say, which was a bit refreshing for me, because sometimes they were too in step. For Dad, being thrown backward into the dining set, it was not. I saw him mouth a curse, knowing it was his fault for wading into her magic, knowing it would always defend itself and her. He shoved off the wobbling table and approached her again.

"Dette, it's time to be done."

"Done?" Mama repeated flatly, head shaking, braids rattling. "It will be *done* when I tear her apart with my own hands."

Pulsing, the thick, bruise-colored stains of magic grew across the floor, white symbols rising from the void of them. Wards that fed Mama's magic as she continued her jerking movements hummed, deep voices of those long dead. Placing a hand against one of the wards, Dad closed his eyes, muttering in Gaelic. Instantly the wards slunk back, the carpet returning to normal, but as he stood, he found himself face to face with his wife.

"Dette," he warned.

"You will not interfere," she told him. "No one will."

Lifting a hand, wards began to draw themselves along her skin. White scars and silver lines glowed, crisscrossing and arching, until they reached her collarbones. The air crackled, and cursing, Dad took a step back.

"Maman Brigitte, I *demand* an audience," she boomed, voice shaking the room's windows.

Dad stepped back until he was in line with me and gently tapped my throat. Grateful to have my voice back, I gripped his hand.

"Dad, it's not—"

"There are finger marks along the wound," he said back. "I need my pack. Eyes on her till I tell you otherwise."

Mama was at the center of her wards now, hands up on either side as if she held scales. Talking to what looked like empty air.

"I have no right?!" she snarled, one hand tipping down. "Have I not given you everything? Have I not bled and starved and learned? I will have an audience!"

Next to her, a ward exploded, dark magic cracking like shards of metal, and I ducked as one whizzed by. Glancing back, I saw Dad gently slide the epitrachelion, a vestment of cloth, around his neck.

"You will not stand in my way," Mama warned. "My child has been harmed by my own kin. I will wear her blood myself—and yours if you interfere, Maman."

Another ward fractured at that, the magic directed at her, and it sliced through her favorite cotton dress and soft skin of her side. Blood poured forward from the wound, running down to the carpet. She merely wiped a hand through it, then rubbed it on either side of her eyes.

"She tried to possess my child, to take my only child," she said, voice slurring slightly as magic poured into her and out through her wound. "You've let this go on too long, Maman."

Dad shoved me back, and before I could argue or follow, he tossed a vial at my feet. It shattered into fragments and released a puff of sea salt and lavender, a barrier against betrayer magic. Pressing a hand against the energy separating me from my parents, I watched him approach the wards.

Throwing down more vials, barriers sprouted up, the wards detonating once they realized they couldn't escape. The barriers held, but cracks formed as hands, black with vicious nails, began to pound against them.

Wading through the center, he looked every bit the warrior he was remembered as, skin glowing against the shadow of insatiable magic. Slapping hands against my ears at the sound of nails shrieking against glass, I winced, but he continued forward through the stench of moon drenched bayou, through the whispers of the spirits ready to attach to Mama.

He must have silenced his footsteps, I realized, because it wasn't until he reached Mama that she whipped around. When her ward-covered hand came up to strike, he slapped it down and pressed his palm to her forehead.

The room shook, shivering like the world had gone cold. My ears popped at the rush of magic, but I pressed my palms against the barrier as he said something to her, lips moving tenderly in contrast to the fierceness of his eyes. It was a vacuum, sucking past me and through my skin as the wards screamed. This was an act of magic I could never attempt, had only seen Dad fully accomplish. Purification demanded complete faith even at the cost of everything else.

Sure, I could nullify small areas like I had when Lenore pissed me off, but even then, I had to redirect that magic somewhere else. This was far beyond a simple parlor trick; this wasn't snuffing out a candle but erasing an inferno. My knees gave way as what was left of my magic was ripped from me through the protection barrier. It shot like shrapnel to Dad, who opened his free hand in preparation to catch it. One by one the other barriers collapsed on each other, dragging white light over the shriveling hands of spirits trying to breach the floor. It pulsed as they disappeared, sunk until all that was left was unblemished carpet. As my magic hit his palm, it was absorbed with no acknowledgment, his attention completely on Mama.

Much like the high one could get from absorbing magic from

someone else, being on the opposite end gave a rush. Instead of a tingling buzz, it was a deafness, cut off from everything, a numbness deep in the marrow. Dragging myself to my feet, I focused on my father's still-moving lips, his thumb coming down to trace under Mama's eye before he cradled her cheek.

I got a single sluggish step before I stumbled against the wall. Dad pressed a kiss to Mama's mouth, but there was no passion in the inky black stream of magic coming with him as he pulled away. It curled like steam, smelled of blood. Quick as a snake, he reached into the air, fingers wrapping around it before he slammed his fist shut.

As soon as his fingers went tight, Mama fell limply to the floor. There was no hum in the air, no scent of lilac, no magic. Finally, he leaned back on his heels, closing his eyes as he swept his fist to his mouth. This was magic taught to him—one that he hadn't passed down. My body shuddered in solidarity as he swallowed the poisoned magic.

I'd asked once what magic Dad did, when I was too young to fully grasp Pilgrimship. Mama had set me on the counter, her lithe fingers tying the laces of my small shoe, and with serious eyes said, "Sin. Your father eats sin."

It had never been an avenue offered to me, but watching his eyes go from emerald to onyx, skin veined with sick black, there was no way I could be bitter about it. It was less than thirty seconds, but pain, not magic, radiated from him as he took a bracing step backward.

Mama lay across the floor, hair and dress like contrasting arcs, but she was breathing. I went for Dad, catching him as he stumbled. My own knees shook under his weight but held, and when he looked at me, it was with clear eyes and a grin far too boyish to fit the situation.

"Never thought I'd say this, but I think I'm ready to retire," he admitted.

I snorted. "You mean temporarily nullifying Mama isn't as much of a rush as eighteen holes of golf?"

He rubbed at the back of his neck with his free hand, a gesture of nerves I rarely saw—and which Mama adored.

"It's not just your mother."

"Yeah, you got me too," I agreed. "It's like cotton in my ears."

"It's the entire building."

Blinking, I tilted my head, sure I'd heard him wrong, but his sheepish smile moved me to the door, swinging it open to glance down the hall. I assumed it was only their room, but the entire hall was filled with the same eerie absence. Turning to chastise him, I stopped as he picked up Mama. It was as if he was handling glass, his massive hands incredibly gentle as he tucked her head to his neck.

"She'll be all right?" I asked.

Rubbing his cheek against hers, he nodded. "She needs to sleep. She'll wake up embarrassed, but fine," he said. "I guess I can't be mad at you. The Land of Laveau gets what Laveau wants—though maybe give me a warning next time."

"I shouldn't have lost my temper."

"She shouldn't have tried to possess you. I'll have to talk to Baron about—" He stopped and sighed. "You need to make Baron aware."

"You just said you wanted to retire," I reminded him. "Mama hasn't lost control in a long time."

"She always knew you would bear scars, but she would never allow you to bear the ones she has," he said, his lips pressing to his wife's forehead. "She's had a lifetime to come to terms with the fact she'll always have passengers, but for her sister to do try to do that to you... There's no greater fear for her."

With soft hands, he laid Mama on the bed, grabbed her bonnet, and lifted her head to protect her braids. Tears burned at my eyes, but I just grabbed a water bottle from the minifridge and set Mama's medicine bag on the end table.

"You should rest with her," I said, "and I'll deal with the hotel. I've got a little bit of time now that dinner is shot; I'm sure having the future Divine Arbiter owe them a favor will go a long way."

"Brigitte—"

"Hey, you're not the one that has to explain, console, and placate for the next hour," I remined him. "No lectures."

His sigh was deep, but he turned back to the bed. Grabbing my shoes and bag, I slipped into the hallway. It was unblemished, but too empty, hollow in an uncomfortable Motel 6 kind of way. *It had been a long time,* I thought again, *since Mama had lost control.* There had been moments in my childhood when her hands would shake and her voice would distort before she locked herself away upstairs. There were spirits that lived in Mama, not by her choice, but because Therina Laveau, her mother, had forced them into her youngest child. To Therina, power was more important than sanity.

"Ok, what the hell just happened?!"

My fists came up, automatically ready, but immediately dropped when I saw Graceland in the doorway to the bathroom.

"Be more specific," I suggested.

"Why did I see a dweorg bartender snatch an entire shelf of whisky and go through a trapdoor as he yelled about the end of days?"

"I thought you were at the hospital, seeing the sick, tending to Asim."

"I was," Graceland said. "I thought a drink would be a nice end to the day and—do I smell bayou?"

Waving my hand, I led the way to the door. "Good catch. Come on. We need to go explain to the manager on duty that everything will return to normal in a couple hours."

CHAPTER 22

It wasn't an hour, but nearly four before magic slowly crept back into the Siren hotel. Maybe I should have sent Dad, because I'd had to do most of my apologizing staring down the elven concierge over the barrel of a shotgun.

When Graceland and I finally escaped the hotel, my own magic was still vacant. There was nothing needling under my skin for the first time I could remember. I couldn't really be sorry that I refused to let Dad do the task. The frustration was my penance for bumbling into the looming Laveau family dinner.

The city was relatively quiet, the midweek slump heightened by the cold. It was easy to forget, when surrounded by tall buildings, that Detroit is so close to the water—at least until that wicked wind whipped through an alley.

"I canceled your dinner reservations at Grey Ghost," Graceland informed me.

"That's the real travesty," I complained, rubbing at my arms as if the friction might bring my magic back faster. "Got anything new?"

"Your cousin, Luciana, is retiring. She submitted her papers as soon as you passed the second test. Her daughter has flown through her trials, Allfather blessed."

It was not unexpected. I began keeping tabs on the child as soon as Dad began casually mentioning retirement. We were expected to produce offspring to whom we could pass along our titles, the Fitzpatrick children carrying on as Senior Pilgrims of the chapters. Long before me, it had been an albatross for those who were forced into relationships with people they had no attraction to or interest in.

It was Monte and Nora Fitzpatrick, twin Pilgrims who found their way to Arcadia through dreams, that paved the way for the rest of us. They lay at the foot of Mother Eorthe's massive willow and told her about their significant others. Monte spoke of how his Raphael painted the most glorious landscapes of the fay, weaving tales of painted hills more vibrant than those in Ireland. Nora told her of Natalie, a shy weaver who shared Nora's desire for a love without physical completion.

The love they professed touched Mother Eorthe, who never forgot the way her favorite son looked upon Seraphim. While she could not change the fact that a child must be born, that the line had to continue, she made a pact with the Allfather. A Pilgrim who didn't want an entanglement would offer a rib and Mother Eorthe would offer a safe place in her willows for the child to grow.

Luciana had no interest in romance, no disdain for it, merely an absence of need. So, when she reached her early thirties, she visited the Creators and offered one of her ribs. From that piece, Maria Fitzpatrick was born. She was a viciously bright child, and even without formally meeting her, I knew Maria would run her chapter with the same passion her mother had.

"My cousin's territory is a hell of place to take over as your first task," I said. "We'll go over whatever new data we have and send it along."

South America struggled with an excess of demonic possessions. Graceland claimed it was because the oppressive, wet heat that threatened to drown its inhabitants called to them, reminding them of the original pit. The lushness of the continent's forests, untapped and sparsely inhabited, left a lot of ground for them to hide. The corruption had often laid waste to villages, but within the last ten years, Luciana and her appointed Juniors had successfully implemented outreach programs to educate her people about the dangers of both demonic magic and possession.

"I'd tell her to watch for Samael," Graceland said. "Artemis says her hunt was interrupted by a demon puking grace. She winged him."

"That's why she's my second favorite of your siblings."

We both looked at each other and spoke in unison, "Persephone's number one."

"And I won't forget it," I agreed. "Where was she hunting?"

"Venezuela, out near Castillo Negro."

I made a mental note and led the way back to the people mover.

Thankfully it was deserted, because I wanted to spread out on one of the benches, no matter how gross Graceland thought it was to lay where other people sat. I needed to stare at the ceiling of the moving train and put my thoughts in order.

"I imagine Luciana would love to take a major demon down. One last jaunt before she settles down. She's too much like Dad to—what are you doing?"

While I had stepped through the open door into the mover, he was just standing at the cusp, head cocked. With his long fingers, he held up a hand to the air between the doors, and we watched the blue magic ripple and flicker. I felt actual panic in my throat.

"Graceland, my magic. I don't have my—"

The words were cut off as the door shot closed and the car rocketed from the station. I tumbled to the floor, nearly hitting my head on the pole. Gripping it, I popped to my feet and stared in horror out the window as Graceland and the main station disappeared. If I'd had my magic, I would have smelled the trap in heartbeat.

The city whizzed by, and I turned in a circle looking for a threat. Normally this would've been the moment I would dip my hands into my pouch, but instead I went for my pocket. My fingers curled around the switchblade; though it held zero magical properties, it was a wicked little thing.

"Pilgrim."

Whipping around, my hand left my pocket, blade out. I almost dropped it as I stared at the right hands of Mother Eorthe and the Allfather.

They stood side by side, equal in height and awe. Before, Michael had resembled an annoying businessman, but in his armor, shining gold, wings a soft white, it was as if he'd stepped off a canvas. It wasn't his true form, but I was well-versed in their vanity, having been with Graceland for so long. Archangels, while not as ugly as the feral seraphim on Belle Isle, were creatures of war, built for ultimate destruction.

Phoebe, dressed in a simple, hooded white gown edged with purple, should have looked diminutive next to the broad angel. However, magic surrounded her, born of pure creation, and it made her the more formidable right hand. Her disapproval would be a lash of wickedly logical and cold—not self-righteous—fire.

"I'm curious," she said, voice lilted, "what you could accomplish with such a tiny blade and no magic?"

"Nothing to you, but if something else was gonna try to take me down, I'd at least make them hurt for it," I admitted and put the blade away. "Now, if I had my magic, it'd be a different story."

"Amusing, the faith you have in your magic," Michael said, hand resting on the hilt of his sword. "Doesn't seem to have helped in your championship of Deep Europe, did it? Do you think your subordinates will doubt you now?"

Upper echelon of douche indeed. "Possibly. Do your siblings doubt you for not finishing what you started with Graceland?"

There was a moment when his mask flickered and I saw a flash of a dozen furious eyes. Then he was beautiful again, his smile in place.

"Do you think yourself truly qualified?"

"Are you?" I asked back. "An agent of war at a diplomatic summit?"

It wasn't that I expected him to smite me right there, but I thought he'd do more than clutch his pommel harder. Disappointed but impressed, I gave him an almost friendly smile.

"I think that out of my cousins, I'm the most equipped to handle the stressors of the job," I said. "I have no family to worry about; my mother and father are quite capable of taking care of themselves. I have the best record of case completion, but also the highest percentage of de-escalation success."

"Your cousin, Francis, is more likeable."

If I'd had a drink, it would have been spat on the floor. My laughter made them both jerk in surprise, but I nodded in agreement. "It's true, yeah, but Francis also has been known to fudge his reports. Once during a battle, he lost an eyebrow—fire-breathing bunyip[38] got him. He was so offended that it hadn't let him pet it that he tried to say his eyebrow was shaved off by a jealous lover. So yeah, if you think Francis can do it, call him up."

---

38 An aboriginal creature that lurks in swamps and billabongs. Loves to devour women and children. Also likes Dave Matthews Band.

"Rashida is as qualified as you, and older," Phoebe pressed.

"We're within single digit percents of each other on everything," I agreed. "Plus, she's in her late thirties, which means she's had more experience in the field. Problem is, she doesn't want it."

"And you do?" Michael said.

"Hell no," I said. "I don't want this position, but it was given to me by my father. He wouldn't have done that unless I was the best option. He knew, like I do, that Rashida loves her chapter, her home, her husband, and now her babies. She couldn't take care of her people the way she demands of herself if she had been tapped for this. I would never force that on her."

"But it was forced on you," Phoebe pointed out kindly. "You've given up quite a bit."

"A muse," Michael scoffed.

Oh, he was good. Almost as good as me at finding those hidden, unhealable cuts on a person's body. It gave me nearly as much pleasure to give him a lazy shrug as it would have to punch him in the face, because indifference forced a scowl from him.

"Everything I've given has been of my own volition," I informed them. "And so far, despite a stumble, I'm guessing I'm three for three."

"Confident," Phoebe murmured.

"Cocky," Michael countered.

I didn't feel it, but I grinned at him to fake it. "Maybe, but I also work my ass off. I know both of you know the hours I've put in; the Allfather and Mother Eorthe can always see me, so it's foolish to pretend that this all comes natural."

Surprisingly, it was Michael who nodded. "For all your faults, of which there are numerous, you are honest."

"Blunt," Phoebe agreed and held out her hand. "May I?"

I couldn't stop the dread curling my toes inside my shoes. We'd practiced, Graceland doing his best to replicate from Dad's journals what it felt like, but the second Phoebe's hand touched mine, it was clear nothing could have prepared me. It was like having fingers rubbing, clawing, prying against the faults of skin and bone, searching hungrily. The nails walked up my spine, pressed against the back of my neck, pressure forcing my mouth open as I tilted back. It wasn't pain that struck me blind, sound ceasing, but an overload of senses. Flashes of color, memories shoved into each other so fast that they blurred.

The fingers retreated slowly, creeping, leaving in their place darkness and a rush of sound. A ragged noise rattled in my ears—my own breath—as I struggled against the darkness swimming at the edges of my vision. Rubbing at my face, I considered if cursing would get points deducted. I had no idea if this would have felt as horrible if I had my magic. As the train jerked to a halt, I stumbled again.

"She tells the truth. She has followed the code—not to the letter in the footsteps of her father—but she is more like Patrick than any of them," she said, eyes searching me. "You see my mother's creations, don't you? Truly see them?"

"A human acting like another human isn't admirable," Michael sneered as his long fingers caught my wrist, wrenched it away from my face. "I prefer to see for myself."

This time it was pain, white hot, blistering, that collapsed my knees. He held me easily by the wrist, lifting so I dangled as he searched for corruption. It wasn't fingers but heat, fierce and celestial, pouring through me, finding the cracks of skin, eyes, mouth to spill out. It scrambled blood, and I bucked, a fish on a taut line.

He was searching through memories, through cases, like an obsessed customer at a record store. If there was something, he would ferret it out. The pain somehow hit its crescendo, the sound of trumpets and carnage filling my ears. Jerking harder, I slipped through his grasp and fell.

"Fuuuuck," I said to the disgusting, sticky floor, uncaring now about the Archangel's deductions.

"I think that's enough," Phoebe declared.

"I haven't finished," Michael disagreed.

His hand reached back down, and I didn't have the energy to fight, his fingers squeezing just under my chin. Almost instantly the burn was at the base of my spine, quickly skittering upward. Unraveling, like old wool. This couldn't be defended against, even if I had years to prepare, the pain that somehow felt fresh and lived in at the same time.

"You will give up his secrets, Pilgrim."

I should've opened my mouth, gotten words out, but instead the voice of another man, syllables clipped and chilled, permeated through the train car.

"Enough, Michael."

Once again, I tumbled to the floor, but this time he stepped over me, long legs eating up the distance to the door of the mover, where I could make out Graceland. Even slightly blurred by the haze of pain, I could see what was left of Graceland's wings. They were charred, the tips of the feathers streaked with black. Outside of his memory, I'd never laid eyes on them, and I could smell the bitter burning as if they had just been destroyed. Next to Michael's full spread of glorious white dipped in gold, Graceland's should have looked weak, but they were survivor's wings, ragged and alive.

"You would sully even this ritual? You truly have no respect for my father, do you?" Michael spat, hand going to his sword.

There was a sharp gust of air filled with smoke, and Graceland was behind his brother, his own weapon drawn. A war sword, built from bone, rust-colored from the blood that soaked it.

"You're a hypocrite. Who do you think sent me, Michael? Would I have been able to break the seal of this train unless *our* father knew you were torturing her, not searching her?" he countered, sword unwavering as he pointed it at his brother. "Did you think you'd find a weakness of mine, that I'd be stupid enough to leave that for you to find in her?"

There was another flutter and Michael turned, the point of Graceland's sword poking him in the chest. The façade of beauty was chipping away from his face as he stared down his youngest brother. Like stone crumbling, it fell away until all that remained were two creatures so alien that Phoebe took a step forward, placing herself in between me and the beasts. She let her wings come out, brilliant butterfly wings edged in gold and dipped in watercolor purple.

It was a nice sentiment, but I wasn't going to be protected. Stumbling up, I swiped at the wetness near my mouth, staring at the red streaked across my arm. Dipping fingers in it, I quickly drew and said a silent prayer to the Allfather. I nudged Phoebe aside, holding my arm out for the angels to see.

"Hey, douchebag!"

Both creatures turned, and I swallowed hard. Hundreds of eyes surrounded by putrid skin, two bodies seemingly made of them, blinked. The only thing familiar were wings, one pair full and blinding white, the other barely hanging on.

"Mother Eorthe, I think this needs to be a tag team effort," I muttered, "just in case the Allfather is sitting on the bench or something."

The eyes all swung up to stare at my raised forearm, and Michael let out a low hiss as his wings lifted him. Slapping a bloody palm against the glyphs scrawled on my arm, I bit down on the inside of my cheek, letting the blood fill my mouth as I prayed the Creators were watching. Michael only made it a few more feet, then, like a flashbang, light pulsed through the room. Behind me, Phoebe hit the ground, but I remained standing, fingers dug into the writing, eyes squeezed shut as light burst behind my eyelids. I spit the blood in my mouth onto the floor and heard it sizzle, the magic eaten to secure the veil I sent Michael through.

"Brigitte," Graceland said, voice gentle as he peeled my clawed fingers away from my arm, "open your eyes."

Letting them crack open, my vision swam for a second, little bubbles of light and shadow popping; then I saw him. He was in his jeans and T-shirt, hair tousled as if he had been sleeping, not about to start another war with Heaven. Gently, he patted my cheek before he moved around to offer aid to Mother Eorthe's right hand.

I turned unsteadily to watch him help Phoebe up. She looked as stunned as I felt, eyes wide as they swept over him to my arm.

"You—but you have no magic. What did you do?"

"I prayed," I explained and scrubbed at my arm, blood flaking off. "Enochian. Celestial language, the little I know. Thankfully, the Creators were in a good mood."

Phoebe gave a sharp nod before she looked to Graceland. "He was torturing her?"

"Yes. He would have burned her out if it meant getting a leg up on me," he said, casting me a grimace. "Sorry."

"I suppose we're lucky good old dad sent you here," I joked, but sobered when he flinched.

That conversation needed to be held without company. Forcing myself to relax, I gave the other right hand a small bow.

"I guess that answers your question of what I do without my magic," I said and dropped onto the closest bench.

"Praying to the Creators," Phoebe said, pleased. She motioned for my hand. "Let me."

Cautious, I nodded, skin jumping even though her touch was gentle. Healing magic, aloe and mint, flooded into my mouth. I'd planned to do minor healing once I got my mojo back, but this was beyond my capabilities, like an empty cup being filled with cool spring water.

Pulling away, she smiled genuinely. "This will make your parents worry less," she explained. "Every child, no matter their skill or age, will be worried about by their parents. Besides, you have a busy night ahead of you."

"Research," I agreed. "I could use that magic for my hangover tomorrow if you wanted to share?"

The fay seemed to bite down on her amusement, patting my cheek before she turned to Graceland. For a second, they seemed to size each other up; then, as she had with me, Phoebe pressed her palm to his cheek.

"You've done both the Pilgrims and Mother Eorthe a service today. That will not be forgotten, fallen child of the Allfather. Mother will be told about your brother and your bravery."

Giving us both a nod, she pressed her hands to her own chest and murmured. The air flooded with the scent of flowers on the wind, and she was gone. The mover groaned, the doors closing, and continued from the station at a crawl as if exhausted.

"I think that went ok, all things considered," I said, eyeing my unblemished skin. "Also, I think I'm a little high on healing magic."

When Graceland didn't laugh, I glanced up. He was staring straight ahead, his hands rubbing at the air behind his shoulder.

"What's wrong with you?" I demanded.

When he didn't respond again, I almost told him to cut the usual drama, but his hand trembled as he stroked his shoulder again. Fear slammed into my ribs.

"What did she do to you? I swear to the Allfather, if she hurt you, I will—"

"She healed my wings."

Words caught in my throat as the raw ones tumbled from his. He was the only one of his pantheon that kept the remnants of their wings. For the others, it was as simple as removing the nubs of bone, discarding them with the same ease they had their father. Even Persephone had plucked hers away, though she admitted that she helped care for Graceland's charred stumps, cleaning the delicate few feathers left.

Jittery on healing magic, I bounced forward off the bench, swaying with the train.

"Well, come on then, show me!"

The gust of wind pushed me back, but I didn't blink, as the scent of fall, decaying leaves and the crisp bite of tart apple, filled the room. Feathers the color of a sunset, rust and gold, overlapped each other. Woven throughout were the barest hints of oranges and yellows that held onto strong frames the color of fresh ink. They weren't healed—they were brand new.

"Is this how they looked before?" I whispered, hand coming out to touch a feather.

"No, they looked just like Michael's," he said, voice hoarse as he bent his wing in to touch it himself. "These are better."

They were soft, but when I ran my fingers down them, the feathers crunched like leaves under the heels of my boots.

"Why did you lie?" I asked and tucked my hands into pockets to resist the urge to stroke them again. "You told him you were sent here."

"Who says I wasn't?" he asked, folding his wings back until they disappeared, taking the scent of autumn with them.

"I know your tells, fool. You flinched. So why lie?"

The mover jerked to a stop, and we both blinked at the dying light that came through the opening doors. Corktown. Home.

"We've got work to do," Graceland answered.

He walked quickly, long legs leaving me behind, but I jogged after him. The street was quiet, the afternoon spinning its last threads of sun and heat. As I closed in, I caught the hem of his shirt. It slowed him, but he still didn't look at me as we dodged the passing people.

"Graceland, why is this such a big deal?" I demanded. "Michael was breaking the rules."

"And what do you think I just did?" he asked quietly, biting at his lip and then licking the wound. "I stepped into a ritual, threatened to kill an Archangel, and disrupted one of your talks, then Mother Eorthe's right hand gave me wings. You don't think that will have repercussions?"

For me. He had done it for me, and now he would probably be kept from going home, from spending his days tending the gardens of Elysium and watching reruns with Persephone.

"I could have taken him," I offered, but even to my own ears it sounded fake.

The snort that came from him was genuine amusement, and he finally looked at me. "He would have turned you to dust so fine you wouldn't be visible, but I appreciate the sentiment."

He had been so light moments earlier, childlike as he felt the new feathers. Now, with his shoulders hunched, mouth drawn, he would hate to hear it, but he looked old. We turned up the street, and there was Thaddeus outside the Bearded Folly, the same as he'd been the other day.

Without a word, he held his cigarette out to Graceland.

"Not in the mood," Graceland said.

"You might be surprised." he said. With his free hand, he held out an envelope to me, "I certainly was when I was told to play post office."

Confused, I took the envelope as Graceland snagged the cigarette.

"What?" he said, blinking stupidly at it.

Thaddeus shrugged. "Your wife said you had a hard day, so she'd make an exception."

"Smoke it out here, I don't want the temptation in my place," I told him and shoved the envelope into my pocket. "Meet upstairs when you're done."

I didn't wait for his pithy response, just headed in through the restaurant. There were a couple weekday regulars who waved, and

I nodded back, snagging a basket of fresh bread from the expo line on my way upstairs. Shoving a roll into my mouth, I closed my eyes and reveled in the everyday magic that was yeast and flour.

That pleasure died when I opened my eyes to darkness. Blindness. Shit.

CHAPTER 23

I touched my fingers to my eyelids, sure I must have closed them for some reason. Fear curled in the pit of my stomach as I turned and stared into the abyss. It was only when the gentle hum of wings rubbing together found my ears that irritation replaced the panic.

"Are you serious?" I called out to the void. "I don't even get a drink before this starts?"

My voice echoed back, over and over again.

"You realize if I hadn't lost my magic, none of these little parlor tricks would've worked!" I shouted. "This was supposed to be tomorrow! Is this because I expelled Michael?"

When there was still no response, I gave into the childish urge to stomp my feet, then started forward. Or backward. Or whatever direction. Arcadia was like that, ever shifting, like masks being tried on and discarded just as quickly. The darkness lightened just at the edges of my vision as my eyes adjusted, and I rubbed my palms against my pants hoping to feel something, but it was cold and blank.

"I just want it on record that I should have at least been able to finish my bread before this," I muttered, but it echoed back at me as if I'd yelled it, bouncing off the bright wall up ahead.

It wasn't until I was right up on it that I realized it was flowing color, a blend of pinks and oranges spilling down into infinity. Glancing back at the dark, I sighed and stepped through.

The scream caught in my throat as I fell, limbs scrambling against the light for purchase. Mama would have laughed hysterically, held out her arms like she was flying. I had too much of my father in me for that, so I scrambled like a wet cat, breath locked in my throat.

The damp clay rose to meet me, slapping hard into my chest, and the trapped scream popped from my lips. The warm, slick earth clung to me as I rolled to blink at the hot, baking sun.

"An unorthodox entrance," a female voice informed me.

Under my fingers, I squished some of the finest clay known and struggled to my feet. Mama would've killed for some of it for protection ointments.

"You can take some with you."

It was rare that I had the opportunity to look down at someone, but the woman was several inches shorter than me. When I first met Margot, with her legs tucked under her, it was this woman's face she was sketching. A face deep with the lines of time and life, draped over eyes entirely too wide and childish to belong. She was dressed simply, robes of yellow belted at the waist, but around her head was a crown of intricate jeweled flowers.

Ducking my head, I stared at the clay dripping off me and gave a bow. "Mother Eorthe, I apologize. I hadn't realized flying would be part of my test.

I couldn't tell what her raised brows were trying to say, so I offered another bow.

"You did much better than the last time I found you here."

Because it was true, I grinned. "I was arrogant."

"Oh, you're still arrogant," she told me. "Now you have the skills to back up your recklessness."

"You know, the stories always talked about your humble grace, Mother Eorthe. Do you hold in all that snark just for me?" I asked.

"Terrible child," she chastised, but didn't correct me. "Phoebe speaks highly of you, and I've been watching you all week. You've done your father proud."

It was the highest compliment I could've asked for. "What about you?"

"Greedy thing, aren't you?"

"I've been accused of narcissism."

Shaking her head, she touched gnarled fingers to her crown and pulled a small gem from it. It was a small citrine, no bigger than a baby's fingernail.

"I think you've done well despite yourself," she said, thumb rubbing over the gem. "I've received the documents you asked the consorts to pass along. You have a lot of confidence in your ability to successfully change something that your superiors built."

There was anger, hidden well in her voice, but I refused to bend under it. "I don't think I'll be doing it alone or in a vacuum. We'd do it together."

"Together," she repeated and shook her head. "You're young, but you've never struck me as naïve."

"Change isn't naïve."

"You think it's that easy? Wave your hand and it's done?" she snapped. "How comforting it must be to not understand. My children, millions lying dead upon the ground, their blood and hopes and futures seeping over my bare feet. You think you've experienced pain? There is no greater death than watching your children suffer. And you would incite change after peace has been so hard won because?"

"Stagnation isn't peace. We can be better; we can grow together," I implored and turned my hand, palm up, for her to take.

At first, I thought maybe contemplation had halted time around us, dust spinning in place, but then she dropped the citrine into my palm, and I knew it was resignation. In my palm, the stone glowed next to a pair of simple clay beads.

"One for you, one for your mother."

Curling my fingers around them, I sighed my disappointment.

"You won't even consider it?"

"I already have; the pantheons you want for the council are approved. They will be allowed on a trial basis, and if they mind the Pilgrims, in a year's time, they may serve on the council. But the rest—if you want to convince me that Deep Europe will bend the knee, you'll have to show me."

"How?"

Her smile was sharp. "I'm sure you'll find a way to surprise me. Your Allfather is through the gate behind you. Use the stone to open it," she said, head dipped in a goodbye. "Safe travels, my Divine Arbiter."

I wanted her overwhelming approval, I realized. After what I had done everything these last few months for, I wanted to be recognized as a Conduit worth her salt. But I was allowed to continue, so I took the opportunity. Facing the gate to Eden, I tried to settle my expectations; most people considered Mother Eorthe the easier touch. I turned back to her.

"Phoebe never asked me. About Holloway, about killing those men."

Her eyes were unflinching, her hands laced, but her voice was curious. "I don't taste guilt from you, Brigitte."

Something flickered in my bones, a warm rush of tea and jasmine. My magic.

"I don't feel guilty," I said, and realized I meant it. "It was the right thing."

"Then I have no reason to ask," she said simply, "but do not take that as carte blanche. Go."

The heavy arch of flowers was far too lush to survive in the oppressive sun of the desert, but here it stubbornly sat. Along the middle, stones of deep ore shone, and in the center rested an empty shell. Pressing the tiny stone in, it swelled until it was as fat as my fist. The gate whined, metal grinding as it opened for me.

The first step sank, moss cushioning footfalls as I moved into the garden. The gate was already gone, vines tangled over the spot where it stood. Eden was a paradise, but the lack of an escape, the high, encased ceiling of tangled vine and flower keeping light minimal, tightened my throat.

It was night again, the sounds of insects humming songs to each other and to the foliage. There was an itch, a compulsion under the nails of my fingers to reach for the fruit and flowers that hung ripe and rich above me. I ignored the trap, pressing deeper, following the path carved for me. There was heat here, not the blazing, baking sun, but full and heavy with humidity.

The path ended in a clearing, a beach of barely lapping waves and rounded structures. Tide pools, I realized, moving closer to the bent frame of a man peering inside one.

He was dressed simply, scratchy material that smelled heavily of incense. Like Mother Eorthe, his face was lined with age, each one carved from a time before I could even fathom. As he turned, his eyes sparkled with mischievousness better suited to a wild creature of the fay than a god.

"So, she let you through! Can never tell with that woman," he mused as he motioned for me to come sit. "Isn't it beautiful?"

The crystal-clear water settled, and despite myself, I was charmed. There were punches of color, vivid teal and emerald anemones that small fish peeked from.

"It is," I agreed and stretched out like a child on my stomach to stare, nearly shoulder to shoulder with him. "Did you think she would reject me?"

"Even though she blessed you, she appreciated your father's conviction to protocol. She likes to lecture about my…experiments, yet she isn't going to take a wound for her own. I've learned that ending a mistake allows for less mess than letting them run wild," he answered, and dipped a finger into the water. "Oh dear, it's time."

Opening my mouth to question, I stared in horror as the scene in the pool changed. It was clouds of red, blood pumping up until there was nothing visible. With a heavy sigh he stood, dusting off his tunic as he moved to the next closest one, plopping down with the same fervor he showed before to investigate.

But I was stuck, eyes frozen on the clouds of blood, and beyond the rose-tinted water there was nothing, an empty pool.

"Come along, it will drain in a minute, and I'll try again tomorrow," he called, hand waving me over. "This one is almost ready for life."

Numb, I got to my feet and moved to sit at his side. This time I didn't sprawl like a child delighted by the wonder of creation, but crossed my arms and legs. He didn't seem to notice as he stared into the clear water.

"How is he?"

The question was so quiet I almost missed it, but it made my hands clench. Looking down, I watched the tide pool for a couple seconds. Inside my silence, he seemed to understand and dropped his hand into the water, swirling it a bit. The world inside shivered, and from the bottom, an anemone began to grow, bouncing along with the movement of the water.

"You've done incredibly well this week, keeping everyone on their toes," he praised even as he frowned. "Michael was colorful in his report of your behavior, however."

"Should I give you my own report of his?" I asked.

His head moved as slowly as his hand amongst the animals that swam around his fingers. "It's being dealt with."

"Graceland was just defending me," I said, throat dry when he looked at me, through me. "That has to count for something."

It was his silence this time that crept between us, and I couldn't tell whether I'd done more harm than good.

"Did you appreciate my father's protocol?" I asked, trying to draw him into linear conversation.

"Of course, it's nice to know things will be done. Growth comes slowly or quickly or not at all. I also enjoy seeing if quicker is better."

"I don't understand."

His smile was an abrupt, happy thing. "That bothers you. It always bothers humans."

"It's what led to our downfall," I admitted and motioned to the beautiful garden behind me. "Knowledge taken before we earned it."

That only seemed to delight him further. "You think my children being expelled from Eden was a punishment?"

"What else would it be? You were angry that we took knowledge before you wanted us to have it.

"It wasn't a punishment, it was a consequence," he corrected gently. "When you know, there is so much more responsibility. Knowledge is a call to action. Knowledge forces one to choose, to be good, to be evil. My children—I wanted it easier for my children, but they couldn't help but be what they were made to be."

It was the wistfulness in his voice that forced me to my feet. "Have you decided?"

He sank on his heels to watch me with expressionless eyes. "I decided the day your father told me he was tired. Are you sure you don't wish to stay in Eden?" he asked. "You could, you know. I've offered it to all before you."

Glancing around at the never-ending sea before me and the world of green behind, I shook my head. "A cage is a cage regardless of beauty. You truly don't understand us, do you? You helped make us, and we still manage to surprise you?"

"No," he said as he pushed to his feet. "You don't have the capacity to stun me; you simply make me sad."

"My mother said something like that to me when I stole a snack cake from our bodega in Mexicantown. She told me she wasn't mad; she was disappointed."

His eyes were depthless, but soft, more like slipping into sleep than falling into a void. Silently, he passed by me, and I followed with question back up towards the tree line. His arms, strong, wiry muscle, reached up to pluck a lush apple from above him. Contemplating it for a second, he pressed it to his lips then held it out.

"Your mother sounds like a wise woman."

"But you wouldn't let her come here," I said, taking the apple. "My father prays to you every day. Do you listen?"

"Of course. I listen to them all. They are my children. Am I your god, Brigitte Fitzpatrick?"

I was so tired. Tired of balancing. Of placating. And I knew if I lied, he'd smell it in a second.

"There's a difference between acknowledging a king and serving him," I said and took a bite, tucking it into my cheek. "I know your power, your ability to create. I'm grateful, because being alive so far isn't the worst, and I will preserve peace, but I serve our people, the ones left behind, not the two of you."

He smiled, slightly twisted teeth against tan skin. "You will make a fine Divine Arbiter—if you manage to stay alive long enough."

Perhaps I couldn't surprise him, but I stared at him in confusion. "I thought you would be mad."

"I have patience," he said, turning away dismissively. "Safe travels, my Divine Arbiter."

Stunned, I went to leave, but like with Mother Eorthe, I felt compelled to turn back. "He's doing ok," I offered.

He stopped, not resembling the glory of his angels but a tired old man. Even though I could only see half his face, the smile was prevalent. "Good."

Was it possible for one word to be so soaked in pain? Had that been how I sounded as I wept over Margot's body? How was it that he could look at me with no tears, voice clear but words so encased in sorrow?

They were questions that stuck in my ribs as the apple tumbled from my hand, the bite of fruit sliding into my stomach. Magic, fierce and painful, rushed through me as my eyes rolled back and the ground came up to meet me.

CHAPTER 24

I woke up in an Uber and immediately kicked Graceland in the cheek. To the driver's credit, he didn't even glance back at us when my partner shrieked.

"For the love of all that's good and holy, watch your limbs, Fitzpatrick!"

Gasping, I stared at him with wide eyes, then grinned like an absolute fool.

"I passed."

"I would hope," he sniffed and touched his nose, "since I found you smoking like you were on fire up in the doorway of your apartment. Lucky you didn't get robbed."

I laughed at the thought, at the sheer relief, at the magic familiar and new tingling at my skin.

"Where are we going?"

"Haven," he said. "I figured Gaia would know what to do if your magic turned. Also, you owe me twenty bucks. That Mt. Elliot pothole claimed another victim."

Even though I was buzzing, I knew what was expected. Giving an exaggerated sigh, I pulled out my wallet.

"Dammit. Herbert promised me he would stop digging in that area."

"First rule of the fay: never trust a gnome geologist," Graceland said wisely, fingers plucking the money from my fingers. "Because I'm so generous I paid for the Uber."

I gave the driver a look, then squinted. He looked familiar.

As if hearing my thoughts, the driver gave a little wave, a dash of pink appearing across his cheeks in a narrow strip.

"Nice seeing you guys again."

"Again?" I asked.

Both men nodded, and Graceland patted my knee.

"She isn't bleeding out this time, but we'd still appreciate a speedy delivery," he told the driver. "You saved her life after she foolishly decided she could take on a vlkodlak."

"A vlkodlak?!"

"It's a joke," I reassured him and jammed my thumb into Graceland's side.

"If you do something stupid, public shaming works. You taught me that," he said as he swatted back.

"Lies."

Shrugging indifference, he pressed a foot behind mine in an attempt to get more room for his legs and flicked at my hair. "I'm assuming this is your new accessory?"

I touched the clay bead woven into my braid. Smiled. "Yes."

"I like it. It's nice seeing you wear something again. Used to be your hair held all kinds of mysticism."

It would again, but since we were already on our way to Haven, I'd grab my seer first.

"Was he ok?"

The words dampened my buzz, and I tried to catch Graceland's eye, but he was firmly invested in staring at the back of the headrest.

"He seemed tired," I said. "I can't say anymore."

Would it make him feel better or worse to know that his father asked the same question about him?

"You have that look," he said, brow raised, "the 'we're on the clock' look. I don't get paid for overtime."

"You don't get paid period," I pointed out.

"I'm calling the Bernsteins[39]. I don't have to take this abuse."

"Complaint noted. Until the court date, though, you still have responsibilities."

His theatrical sigh made me go for another swat when I noticed the Uber driver watching us.

"Are we almost there?" I asked.

"We've been here for about four minutes, ma'am," he said, tugging

39 The Bernstein family are accident lawyers in the Metro Detroit Area. Running joke in Michigan, when you feel slighted you hire them.

at his collar. "I—I didn't want to interrupt your argument, but it is peak time."

"Yeah, Brigitte, stop scaring the poor man," Graceland crowed. "How much do I owe you for the extra time, good sir?"

"Fifty."

"Dollars!" he said, scandalized. "If this was Jerusalem, I would only pay—"

Before he could date himself, I snatched his phone and sent more money to the kid's account. "He's a notorious cheapskate. Have a great night."

Shoving at Graceland, I clambered out. The usually busy street looked strange in the predawn hours, but as I inhaled, could smell the herbs coming from Haven.

"I could have flown us here for cheaper," Graceland complained.

"For free with those new wings," I agreed. "When we gonna test them out?"

"Don't get cocky. I'm doing the work, I'm getting paid for it."

Shaking my head, I moved to the door and peered in. It was dark, but when I touched the handle, it turned of its own accord. That enchantment was only for the few the Darkchilds trusted to be in their shop after dark.

"Come on," I whispered and ducked inside.

Like the street, the shop was still, the normal bell that would chime a movie soundtrack hanging silent. The chairs were all turned over on top of the tables and the counters gleamed.

"Wanna bet they're using the kid like Cinderella?" Graceland whispered.

"You've got to pick a better Disney Princess to idolize," I told him for the hundredth time. "Plus, look at that."

Hanging from a cactus magnet on Luna's minifridge of potions was a drawing. It was a rough sketch, but Martavious lying in a pile of wolves reading a book while they slept was clear enough.

"Ok, so maybe the kid is cute," he admitted.

"Freeze, criminals!" someone shouted from the darkness.

Ducking, I felt the air above my head being split, heard the whistle of a metal bat. Graceland's vivid cursing and the sounds of metal hitting flesh had me laughing despite myself, and when the bat came at me, I caught it smoothly. Martavious blinked at me with wide eyes.

"I changed my mind," Graceland wheezed from the floor. "I hate the kid."

Letting the bat go, I leaned across the counter and hit the lights. Soft florescence swept over the shop, and the young boy gave a yelp of joy and wrapped his arms around me. I realized he was wearing my leather jacket as I hugged him back.

"Oh, I'm so glad it was you guys," he declared and looked over his shoulder. "Sorry, Graceland."

Getting to his feet, he gave the kid a wave of his hand as he clutched his ribs. "With that swing, you should be a professional—but maybe use your eyes first."

"I need glasses," the boy admitted. "We're working on that though. Plus, I enchanted the bat!"

We looked to each other then back to him, and Martavious flushed, hands clutching the grip.

"Is that against the rules?" the boy asked. "I'm still learning."

"No, it's just impressive," I told him and held out my hand. "May I?"

Handing it over, he grinned when I immediately took a stance, elbow up, twisting my wrist a little.

"It's coated in silver. Beafore got me the wood underneath from some traitor tree or something."

The Judas tree, which accounted for why the bat was so light. Obviously, the boy didn't realize the level at which the Darkchilds already considered him pack. The tree loomed over the mouth of their sanctuary in the UP[40]. The jutting branches that resembled broken arms held the swinging skeletons of the hunters that destroyed Pack Darkchild. For months, they baked in the sun in front of their sanctuary, a reminder to all who came across their lands what the

---

40 UP refers to the upper peninsula of Michigan. It is pronounced as the letter U then the letter P, not like *Up* the movie.

price of betrayal would be. Each remaining member of the pack wore a piece of that tree, medallions and rings because they didn't need weapons.

"I enchanted it to give me extra weight behind my swing, because these arms aren't doing much," he said, pointing at his forearm. "We're working on that too."

Passing the bat back, I poked at his stomach. "Probably eating better than burgers and shakes, right?" I teased.

He gave a solemn nod. "Yep, did you know that you can stuff pasta with stuff? Luna made this thing with chicken and spinach. Thought it'd be gross."

"Are they upstairs?"

Bobbing his head, he took a step, then froze. "I messed up. I should have taken you up first."

"We're unusual cases, don't beat yourself up," I said gently. "They knew we were here the minute we stepped inside. I wanted to speak with you."

"About what?" he said, head cocked.

"It's complicated."

"I'm not going back," he blurted out, eyes skittering to the exit. "I signed a contract, so you can't legally take me back."

"Kid, she signed your paperwork," Graceland informed him firmly. "Don't be stupid; you're home."

I opened my mouth to chastise him, but the blunt words made the boy's shoulders ease.

"We need you to help us find someone," Graceland said, shrugging at me. "There's only so much this kid can do; it's not a far leap to make."

"Did you really get beat in a fiddle contest in Georgia?" Martavious asked him.

"Ditch him," Graceland advised. "We can find another seer."

"Go ask your Alpha for permission to come with us," I told him. "We'll have you back no later than tomorrow afternoon."

"I got school tomorrow," he said, chewing on his lip. "Will this count toward my sick days?"

"Graceland will buy you breakfast if it does."

The boy scuttled off, bat dropped to the floor in his haste, and we listened to his stumbling footsteps.

"I had to pay for the Uber. Now I get to buy breakfast," Graceland complained. "And I got bashed with a bat."

Lifting said bat, I leaned it against the counter. "Hard knock life."

"You really want to quote *Annie* at me? I've seen your senior photos," he warned.

"Fair enough," I murmured as footsteps came flying back down the stairs.

He'd tugged on jeans over his old basketball shorts and slung his backpack over his jacket.

"She says you have to make sure I'm fed and that I'm back in one piece," he recited and screwed up his face in Graceland's direction. "I also wasn't supposed to let it slip that they told me you were the devil."

"Just don't go spreading it around," he said.

Nodding his agreement, the boy glanced around for his bat, and I handed it over. Strapping it to his pack, he gave us both a grin.

"So where are we going first?"

"My office," I said. "I need to get some things."

"Cool, cool," he said, eyes casting over to Graceland.

"What?"

The floodgates opened at the simple question. "So if you had to choose who portrayed you better on screen, would you go with Harvey Keitel or Al Pacino?"

"What?" Graceland repeated.

"As Satan," Martavious clarified eagerly. "Which one did a better job?"

"When did Harvey Keitel play the devil?"

I shook my head at him. "*Little Nicky.*"

The horror that crossed his face was lightning fast. "Al Pacino, I guess."

"Ok, but what about Al Pacino or Ewan McGregor?" the boy demanded.

Graceland picked up his pace in a lazy escape. "How many of these do you have?"

"As many as Google does," he said, jogging as he held up a small cellphone. "Luna got me a cellphone; I have unlimited data."

"Congratulations," Graceland said flatly. "I'm not playing this game."

"Graceland," I teased.

Giving me a dark look, he said, "I'll get us a car and meet you at the Folly."

With that he disappeared, much to Martavious's delight. Spinning around, the boy looked in every direction, then laughed.

"What do you think that feels like?" he asked.

Even though I wondered the exact same thing, I was now alone with his insistent questioning. I motioned for him to follow. "Let's get to my office. Then, I'll tell you a story about how he once appeared inside my wall by accident because he bought a cursed totem. Deal?"

"Deal."

CHAPTER 25

It was supposed to be easy: a quick poke into my office, then out the door. Of course, being lucky is never a trait I've described myself having, so when I opened the door and found Thaddeus standing like a golem with his arms crossed, I took it as a sign of how the night was gonna go.

"Oooh, you're in trouble," Martavious muttered behind me.

The bearded man's eyes went wide as he tipped to one side to look behind me. "You were on fire like five hours ago. And now you bring a kid here?"

"We're getting weapons," Martavious offered.

Internally wincing, I gave a bright smile. "I'm getting tools for my case."

"That's a child, Brig."

"Excuse me, I have a bat," Martavious pointed out. "I could take out your knee with this thing."

Thaddeus leveled a firm look at him. "You want to beat on something, come on downstairs."

"Whatcha got?"

"Bread that needs to be slung," he said and gave me a hard look. "Where are his parents?"

"I don't have any," Martavious interjected, shoving his hands into his pockets to mimic the other man's pose. "Brigitte sold me to the Darkchilds."

"Martavious, he doesn't joke," I warned.

"Boring. Ok, I'm a seer, Scorpio, and now the emissary to pack Darkchild," he said, picking at his nail. "How do you sling bread?"

"Come downstairs and I'll show you," Thaddeus said, voice softer now. "Race you?"

That pulled a grin from Martavious, and he bent down like a sprinter. "You're on."

Without warning, Thaddeus dropped right through the floor, as if he had never been there at all. For the first time since I'd met him, Martavious seemed frozen, mouth agape and eyes wide in awe.

"He beat you," I said mildly.

His head swiveled to me then to the spot where Thaddeus had been. "What—I—but what?"

"Ghosts, kid. Try and keep up."

A blinding smile broke across his face, and he gave something akin to a war whoop. "A ghost. You've got to be shitting me. I just saw a ghost!"

"He's waiting for you," I said, nodding to the door. "I'll be down in a bit."

Bobbing his head, he took off, two steps of pure speed before he screeched to a halt. "Don't tell Gaia I swore, ok? I've reached my weekly quota already."

"Secret's safe with me."

With that, he was gone, a blur of limbs and pounding feet, and I returned my focus to the room. Tucked on the shelf below my safe was a steamer trunk. Rich leather the color of burnt caramel was smooth under my hands, and I felt the wild magic still humming even after centuries.

Popping the lid, I slipped to my knees. It was filled, bags and boxes, trinkets strewn about them. It had been Dad's, passed down from the original Patrick. When I was little, I'd climb inside and listen to the whispers of magic. No one believed when I said I heard the ocean, and the woman whose voice was like fog. Lightly, I lifted the small velvet pouch and tipped it into my palm. Rings tumbled out, silver and bronze. Most were simple, but next to Dad's signet on my middle finger, I slid on the only one with a stone. Blood red, it remained dull in the light, and I let myself weep.

He couldn't have known, but Thaddeus had done me a favor by giving me this moment alone.

I told myself it would be the same as before, weighed down by rings and cloth and sacrament, but now, as I stared blurrily at the dull, lifeless stone, I could admit my foolishness. Margot found the ring at a flea market near Eastern Market, and when she placed it on her pointer finger, it had glowed incessantly. It was a binding stone,

Margot explained happily. It would choose two people, and one wearer would be able to find the other, no matter what.

When Margot lay cold and blue in her casket, I tried to use it, watching in desperation as it flickered weakly and died too. I returned to our apartment that night and stared at everything as if it were from someone else's existence. In that moment, surrounded by the mausoleum of our life together, I pulled rings from my fingers, the strings and talismans from my hair, and let them drop to the floor. I left a wake of protection and whining magic behind and slept for two days straight.

When I woke, everything had been cleaned up, and it was weeks before I peeked into the trunk. There, in soft velvet, my items whispered apologies and love. It was too much softness to handle, an embrace when I wanted anger and harsh words. I'd failed, after all.

I stroked a thumb over the stone, giving myself one last long breath before sliding the rest onto my fingers. The serpent of bronze, a gift from Mama, went on my ring finger where it would rub against Dad's signet. Next was the silver feather, fit tight to my thumb. Staring at my hands—knuckles slightly swollen from the vicious joint popping, short, bitten nails—it felt a bit like coming home. Grabbing another bag, I moved quickly, the pain dissolving now as I dove straight in. By the time I fastened the last talisman around my neck, I smiled.

It was power, mellow and familiar, that thrummed. There wasn't, as I feared, a rush of pain that came from subverting magic, but the smooth slide of power that offered itself to me. At the sound of footsteps, I sniffled hard and wiped my eyes.

"Graceland, I'm almost ready, and—" The words died as I caught a whiff of decay, right before the sickening smell of saltwater taffy rolled over it.

Without thinking, I dove right, and my instincts were rewarded. The beast's clawed hand slashed through the air and hit the trunk. Protection magic punched back, a burst of black tar and seawater, and the creature was rocketed into the wall separating my office and the tiny kitchen. Rolling to my feet, I kicked the side of my desk, hand reaching down as the hidden drawer popped out. A dagger, jagged and rusted, lifted of its own accord into my palm, and I stalked to the beast.

The weapon turned out to be useless, because it was already dead, a certain fate for touching such a powerful object without permission. Slumped down, it resembled a vlkodlak, but the smell was wrong—there was corruption beyond the stench of rot, threads of bile and putrid kale. Gripping its head, I tilted it back, then let it go just as quickly to slap wetly against my wood floor.

"Brig, I got the—what is that smell?" Graceland complained as he came through the door. "I swear, if you left fish in the trash again—what the hell?"

I tapped the dagger against my thigh. "You ever hear of wendigos in Detroit?"

"In the city?" he scoffed. "What, strolling down Woodward, taking the q-line? We got our own version; it's called the meth addicts that live in Brightmoor."

"Well, it's not like it stumbled in here by mistake," I told him. "Get the kid."

With a heavy sigh, he disappeared and popped right back, holding Martavious by his backpack. The scrawny boy twisted in the air before he spotted the beast and went dead weight.

"Is that Bigfoot? He stinks."

Disgusted, Graceland dropped the boy back to his feet and flopped into his seat. "Bigfoot."

"Ignore him," I advised the boy. "He thinks because he hasn't seen one, it doesn't exist. This is a wendigo."

Martavious grabbed his phone, snapping photos in rapid succession. "Oh man! Luna and Gaia are going to lose it! They were just telling me about these. Can I have its head?"

"Are we sure he's not your child?" Graceland asked.

"I'll release the body to them, it's theirs by rite," I told the boy, "but first I need your help. I need you to tell me what you see."

When he hesitated, I tucked the dagger into my belt and offered a hand. He grasped it and let his eyes roll back.

"I need someone taught a lesson," he said, voice pitched high and haughty.

The gurgle that followed could only be the wendigo, which meant it had either been one for a long time or hadn't even attempted to curb its cannibalistic appetite. The Darkchilds had dedicated entire years to the study and capture of wendigos. Humans who ate the flesh of their family had no place in either fay or human society.

"There's a problem, lives in Corktown. If you choose to eat her, that's your business, but it can't be done in her apartment. Take her back to Zug Island if you have to, but she can't interfere anymore. We've been given a warning from the Pilgrim. You owe me this. Do that, and I'll have part of the next shipment brought to you."

"Woman's voice," Graceland commented from his seat. "Piss anyone off lately?"

The boy's fingers clenched hard, eyes rolling back down. He shuddered, narrow frame pulling inward. "It's like wading through syrup, trying to pull away from her."

My jaw locked, rage rising against it, so I clamped down harder. Knowing that look, Graceland hopped to his feet and shook his head.

"Brig—" he warned.

"She played me," I hissed through my teeth, "I really believed she didn't know. That bitch."

"You want my bat?" Martavious asked.

It was tempting, but I could do better. Snagging my bag, I slung it across my body and shot Graceland a look.

"No, I just got us a car," he replied. "Plus, if I take us there, it's going to drain you both a bit."

"I feel fine," Martavious said.

"That's because I took you upstairs, not all the way out to the West Riverend," he informed the boy blandly.

He was right; gods, I hated when he was right. Not willing to give him the time to gloat, I gave a sharp nod and started walking. Taking the steps two at a time, I nearly crashed into Thaddeus, but he went incorporeal. It was like being doused in ice water, and I sputtered despite being dry.

"What the hell?!"

"Sorry, sorry, I know you hate that," he apologized, then his eyes narrowed. "You're taking the kid with you? He staying in the car?"

"Bat Thaddeus," Martavious reminded him, "say it with me: magical bat."

"He's not staying in the car," I said and ignored the boy's smug look. "Oswald is going to watch him while I get some answers from the Angel of the West."

"A babysitter," Martavious said, disgusted.

"He's a troll bouncer," Graceland said as he swept by, patting a surprised Thaddeus on the cheek. "Don't worry."

"Yeah," Martavious said, rising up on his toes to pat the bartender on his chin, the highest point he could reach. "Don't worry."

Giving the ghost a nod, I made my way out to the street and the slick black car at the curb. Opening the passenger seat, I jerked my thumb at Martavious when he tried to scoot in.

"Worth a shot," he said and scrambled into the back.

I didn't bother with the seatbelt, instead opening my bag to grab a potion. Pulling off the cork, I drained it, throat closing as it punched into my stomach. Motioning for Graceland to drive, I leaned back against the headrest and closed my eyes.

"Are you meditating?" Martavious whispered from the back seat.

Instead of answering, I held out the empty bottle for him to sniff, then bit back a smile when he gagged.

"What is that?" he demanded. "Luna didn't make that."

Not even a week and the boy already knew his pack's potion signature. I'd made the right choice in placing him. Corking the bottle, I tossed it back into the bag.

"It's the Laveau signature. Nightshade rum, so don't taste any," I warned.

"You drink poison? That's crazy."

"I don't make a habit of it; it's triple distilled. There's just a thread so whoever uses it knows who crafted it. Like how the Darkchilds use orange peel."

"Big difference between orange and poison," Graceland reminded me.

"But what does it do?" Martavious asked.

"It's a guardian tincture: deer tongue, clove, and bay leaf. It's armor, mental and physical," I explained.

"So, you're going to fight?"

The car pulled up to the empty parking lot by the bedrock wall. There was ice among the water, and it loudly crashed against the stone. Behind us, the neon of the West Riverend flickered as closing time rushed to meet us. Soon the Rest would flood with workers eager to listen to a couple songs before dragging themselves home to scrub off glitter and grime. There'd been a time when I was among them.

"That's going to depend on her," I said and shoved my door open. "Let's go find out."

McGavin must have felt me coming, because the steps to Adam's Rest, down to the red velvet curtains, were a tribute to Maman. Transparent glass swirled with different colored smoke in each pane, and as my heels touched them, hands formed, grabbing for me. Continuing down, I shoved the curtain aside, coming face to face with Oswald. Instead of niceties, I whipped out my badge and pressed it into his hand.

"Watch the kid, I'll be back in five," I told him and placed a hand on his arm when he moved to follow. "For your own good, Ozzy, stay put."

Grateful that despite his apprehension he listened, I stalked across the floor, barely sparing a glance to the stage where Cyprus, a nymph, wailed out the impossible note of "Dream On." From the orchestra pit, Gillian watched as her fingers plucked notes. Gritting my teeth, I spared a sharp nod and ducked into the back.

Backstage was a maze of boxes, costumes, and props, but I felt the pull of the siren even before I got to Lenore's dressing room. Without knocking, I eased the door open and pulled it closed behind. There was music, which accounted for the fact that Lenore hadn't acknowledged me. Instead, she continued to cold cream her face, taking off the heavy stage makeup from the night.

"No rest for the wicked."

Watching the woman jerk and spin, her feather robe fluttering, I smiled. She was younger looking without the sharp glam McGavin demanded every night. She might have passed for twenty, if not for the scar that ran from her mouth to her ear on the right side of her face.

It was the same side she pressed a hand to as she looked at me. "Excuse me?"

I let my grin grow until it looked slightly predatory. "The music. 'Cage the Elephant,' right?"

Her shoulders relaxed, but she kept her hand pressed to her cheek as she pulled her hair down to cover that side of her face. "Yes, I'm researching new songs. It took me quite a few years to get McGavin to give me even a semblance of control. I won't take that for granted by making my pieces easy. So far, I haven't had a misstep."

Instead of answering, I hummed under my breath and walked the room, poking at costumes, pretending to examine props. There was tension snapping, but this time Lenore didn't try to overpower me, only moved with me like a turntable, watching as I ran a hand over the small bookshelf in the corner.

"Can I help you with something, Pilgrim? I haven't found any additional information yet."

"Divine Arbiter, actually," I commented idly. "Cyprus is doing quite well out there."

"To, what, three patrons?" she scoffed.

"The next shift is coming in," I pointed out, "yet you're cleaning up for the night. Hot date?"

"With the morgue," the siren snapped, eyes glittering. "They're finally releasing my sister's body so I can bury her, so if you'll excuse me, I need to get dressed."

"I don't mind, go ahead," I said, voice flat. "I'm sorry about your sister."

For a second, the siren hesitated before she ripped off the robe and stalked to the pile of clothes on her dresser. Now her power rolled off her, thick waves of suffocating perfume. Tucking the top into her slacks, she tilted her chin up, and I had to admire the lack of remorse.

"If you're so sorry, why won't you let her rest?" she demanded.

"You don't want justice for your sister?"

"Of course I do, but as I told you before, the West handles its own problems."

"Was your sister that problem?" I asked, watching her pale.

"There's your misstep, Lenore: thinking that anything in my town isn't my business."

"I think you should leave. I wasn't expecting visitors tonight, and I'm really not—"

"Visitors or me? The wendigo you sent—it's dead. You were a fool when you came to my office and tried to control me, but you're a monster for what you helped do to those girls, to your own sister."

It was as if the words chased her, the way she darted for the door, but I caught her wrist and twisted. A firm kick to the back of the siren's knee had her going down.

"Here's the thing: you can't lie to me, and you're going to tell me where the shipment of girls you're helping bring in tonight is dropping," I informed her. "Then you're going to tell me about Brood Vasile and Holloway. I want everything."

"How do you know about that?" the woman demanded.

Knowledge. In that single bite of the Allfather's apple, I tasted blood and pain and betrayal. Releasing her, I took a step back, watching dispassionately as the siren rubbed at her shoulder and stared up with watery eyes.

"If you let me go, I'll tell you everything," she agreed.

"I never said I would let you go," I corrected.

The siren popped to her feet, but she only made it a step when hands, followed by the scent of decayed flesh, shot out from thin air. They grabbed, nails splintering as they dug into her clothes to hold her in place.

Pulling up her sleeve, I showed the siren the small ward lightly scratched into my skin. "I'm not high up on the Laveau hierarchy of power, but if I snap my fingers, they will pull you apart."

"You wouldn't," she shot back, eyes wide. "Please."

"I thought you wouldn't ever beg the Conduit of Magic," I said and pressed my thumb to my middle finger, watching as nails began to dig into her skin. "What's it going to be?"

"I had no choice," Lenore spat, struggling against the hands. "We came from nothing, no prolific family's back to step on to get higher. I did everything for her, sang, fucked, conned till I was hoarse and bloody, so she could go to school, so she could get out, but what does she do? Falls in love. When have you ever heard of a siren falling in love, especially with something that was so clearly a fairytale?"

"What do you mean?"

Lenore laughed, "Please, the head of a brood comes looking for a cure for his curse and discovers the love of his life and they live happily ever after? I went to him to warn him off my sister—"

"But he changed your mind?"

The sound of disgust was as ugly as the spit at the corner of the woman's mouth. "He was as foolish as her, and she refused to listen to me. Dropped out of her courses, sold all her things, because Calvin would take care of her. Well, look how that turned out."

"And you just let her?"

"Of course I didn't, I'm her big sister. I made a deal with the brothers. They had to test the bite to see if worked. As many others as it took. The idiots stopped being discreet after the first dozen. Got on your radar."

I knew there were more, given the amount of blood and cages, but my bones ached at the thought. "And Holloway got them testers."

"Holloway was an idiot," she snarled, still trying to get loose. "Gregor and Roman played him like a fiddle. He thought we were just bringing girls in for partying, a little bit of sex until they earned their freedom. Humans have narrow imaginations."

"Then why is Annabel gone?"

For the first time, Lenore slumped. Like her naked face, she was stripped of artifice. "She knew the clock was ticking. Calvin would be heading back to Deep Europe as soon as they got what they needed from Tomes & Bones and Morphosis. She convinced him she could take it."

My blood went cold. "When was Morphosis?"

"Panic doesn't feel good, does it Pilgrim?"

Exhaling through my nose, I watched one dead hand press a thumb sharply into her collarbone. "Arbiter."

"Arbiter," she conceded. "Only Calvin could get in without bloodshed. He toured the facility, that's all they wanted. To know if you had the cure."

"There is *no* cure."

"Which I stated multiple times, but they had it on good authority from a Pilgrim that Pack Santee and the city of Detroit held answers."

At the mention of my cousin Bernard, my jaw tightened, "And what was the payment for that information?"

"They had to get him a shipment from Tomes & Bones."

A god killer. *The* god killer.

"By the time Annabel was dead, I was already in for penny, so Roman promised me a pound. I'd leave with him, out of this trap of a city," she said. "When I was told you wanted to meet, I figured it was the perfect way to assess how much of a pain in the ass you would be."

That made me grin. "You have no idea."

"Apparently," the siren said sarcastically. "I told Roman we could risk a couple more days, wait for his brood to get back from the Dakotas. He wanted to keep running tests, and I had already made sure we wouldn't be seen."

"The Fates," I said, stomach sinking. "How could you possibly fool the sisters?"

"I'm surprised you didn't recognize it, smell it; I guess you Pilgrims don't share everything with each other. I didn't believe it until I was sent to test them. They were blind, and even Atris was softened by my tears."

As my hands fisted again, the petrified fingers holding the siren dug deeper into her flesh.

"Where are the vlkodlak?" I demanded.

The siren hesitated, but the quick tightening of the hands on her shoulders had words flowing. "Brush Park, 261 Edmund Place. That's where Calvin's body is going to be found, confession and all."

"Doesn't that tell you who Roman is, that he would discard your sister and his own brother with ease?"

"Said from atop your own high horse," she shot back. "Your brother is the reason this even happened. My sister's blood, Calvin, all the girls, I'm surprised you aren't bathing in it, betrayer."

And I'd live with that. Because I had to. "And the last shipment of girls?"

"You can't save them all. Some have probably already gone, but those that are left will be somewhere in the mansions surrounding Edmund Place. Any house that has Three Brothers' Construction signs belongs to Brood Vasile. Holloway gave them contracts for restoration of the mansion district as a cover."

I could feel sickness rising in my throat. "That's an entire district. I want specifics."

"I don't have them," Lenore said, "but it's a lot of ground, so you might want to hurry."

I nodded. "You're absolutely right."

"I can't give you information on the Pilgrim if I'm dead," she said quickly, body shaking.

"I know plenty about Bernard Haas," I said, "and you'd be surprised what I can get from your dead body."

"Who the hell is B—"

"Put your hand down Pilgrim," a voice interrupted. "Release the girl."

I turned and held my palms up, giving Horace an annoyed look. "Graceland called you?"

The chief of police gave a nod as he moved past. "Funny, it almost seems like he's concerned for your soul. Let her go, will you?"

Clapping, the hands released the siren and disappeared. "She deserves it," I commented as he handcuffed her. "I could have called it Pilgrim's Justice."

"But you didn't," Horace pointed out as he slid a thin collar around the siren's neck, silencing her. "I was listening from the hall. Mansion district, huh?"

"Your crew up for smashing in some doors?"

"While conveniently leaving Edmund Place for last?" he commented mildly. "We'll start on Elliot."

"I'll give you 45 to get ready," I said and turned to leave. "If they attack me, I'm going to kill them."

Horace chuckled as he hauled Lenore up to her feet. "I'm pretending I didn't hear that, Senior Pilgrim."

"Divine Arbiter," I corrected.

His smile was bright, but I just moved out of the way to let him pass, lazily following as he diverted to the back exit. I would have paraded Lenore through the entirety of Adam's Rest.

"Which is why you aren't a cop," Graceland commented from behind me.

It was true, but I wasn't going to give him the satisfaction. "Shouldn't you be saving Ozzy from Martavious?"

"Oswald saved me from his incessant questioning. When I left, they were doing shots of cranberry juice. Martavious is up by one but he's slowing."

"You called Horace."

That had him coming around, I assumed to glare, but he moved so he was in line with the stage. From our spot, I could see the glitter of Cyprus's purple gown reflecting as the somber sounds of a Lana Del Ray cover flooded the room.

"I think Cyprus will do well as the new Angel of West Riverend."

"Graceland."

"That wasn't a question. You know I did," he pointed out, his face going still as stone. "I'm about to gut you, Brigitte, and I need you to keep it together. Can you do that?"

The tonal shift had me blinking, but he just stared back, waiting for a response. My throat felt tight for some reason, and for a second, I was back in Holloway's staring at the banshee. This time I didn't ask for ten seconds.

"Tell me."

"They found Bronson's body."

It was my turn to stare, ears full of cotton as I watched his mouth continue to move. Lifting a hand that felt like lead, I shook my head.

"Body?"

He reached out, but I shook my head again.

"I don't understand."

"He's dead, Brig. Bethel Ford called Moira about fifteen minutes ago. She said she tried calling you."

I reached into my pocket and pulled out my phone and the envelope Thaddeus had given me. I hit my phone, but the screen remained black.

"Dead," I whispered.

"He's got marks consistent with vlkodlak. Smelled of black incense. Bethel wants to run some more tests, but it sounds like—"

"Deep Europe," I said, nostrils flaring, "Somehow everything in my life is coming back to Deep Europe. I'm going to tear Haas in half."

I was a bullet of purpose, almost out from behind the stage when Graceland caught up, long fingers snagging me.

"Hey, stop and breathe."

I lifted my hand, still clutching my phone and the envelope, and for once I listened. Jerking away, I shoved the phone at him and tore into the envelope, desperate now in case it was from Bronson.

I suppose congratulations are in order. It seems despite your tainted blood, you managed to show yourself competent. It's too bad Bronson was too busy chasing smoke to celebrate his favorite cousin's victory. As for myself, I have no time for celebrations, not when Deep Europe continues to be the most difficult to manage, especially, it seems, after your meddling. Tread with caution, Arbiter. Once a shackle is broken, a slave cannot be forced back into submission.

B. Haas

"We got played," I said and shoved the note at him.

He handed off my phone and read, his jaw tightening.

"We need to warn Alexei," he said.

"That's it?" I snapped.

His eyes were cool as he leveled me with a look. "Bronson is dead. That's not changing. Alexei is alive—and no, that isn't it, but seconds matter right now."

He flicked my phone screen and it powered back on. I took it with raised brows.

"Yeah, things are—different since Phoebe."

"That's gonna be a talk," I muttered as I typed out one word, one I knew would send Alexei into hiding. I hit send.

"Give me the rest of it."

"Now we're gonna save our city," he said with a shrug. "Then we'll get your house in order."

The use of *we* and *our* isn't lost on me. Scoffing a laugh, I nodded.

"Ok," I said on a long exhale. "Bernard has the lance, Graceland."

For a split second, he was stricken, eyes bleak in a too pale face. Then he became stone, his eyes ice.

"Doesn't change what needs to be done right now. Let's go."

Sighing, I followed, rubbing a thumb over the now itching ward. Healing magic crept over it, aloe and mint that was instantly drowned out by cigar smoke.

I couldn't stop myself. "How can you just turn it off?"

He didn't turn, only kept walking, "This is gonna be your first time going to war, Arbiter," he said. "It isn't mine."

Adam's Rest was starting to fill, all matter of fay tucked into tables. Cyprus would be switching to something more upbeat after this to get them perked up. No one looked at us directly, but as I moved to the bar, I felt eyes. Slipping next to Martavious, I gave Oswald a nod and he got to his feet.

"Pilgrim," he said, passing back my badge. "Isadore will need another riddle the next time I see you."

"I'll bring two," I promised.

Rubbing a hand through Martavious's curls, Oswald gave the kid a nudge. "Nice meeting you, kid."

"Likewise," Martavious said, holding up his empty shot glass. "Maybe next time you'll beat me."

"You have juice on your face," Graceland told him.

Wiping viciously with his sleeve, he leaned into me. "Did you get what you were looking for?"

I had, but that didn't mean I wanted it. "Kind of. Think you can do me another favor before I have Graceland take you home?"

"I'm not coming with you to get the bad guys?" he said indignantly. "I thought I was your sidekick."

"Graceland is my sidekick," I said, ignoring his squawk. "I'm going to kill them, Martavious. You don't want to be there."

His eyes narrowed a little, like he was trying to see something beyond me, then he nodded. "You could have lied. It's nice you didn't."

Those words, the same ones he gave me when I first met him at Harvest Heart, made me smile. "I need you to tell me if the man you felt on Belle Isle—the upset one—is he alive? Can you feel him, his future?"

"I can try," he said, face scrunched in confusion. "Does it matter if you're just going to kill him?"

"It matters," I said simply.

With a small nod, he reached for my hand, fingers lacing them together as his eyes rolled back.

"It's fuzzy, wherever he's at, like I can't quite see or hear anything," he complained and tapped his finger to his tongue. "Numb, my tongue feels—"

Not letting him finish, both of us grabbed him, shaking his shoulders until his eyes came back and he shoved Graceland off.

"What gives?" he demanded.

"He's been poisoned. You wanna leach some of that from him?" Graceland asked bluntly, hands moving to slide on his coat. "Come on, I gotta get you home."

"We don't have time to wait the 45. I need you to do me a favor, too," I said. "Go to Beafore and tell her I asked you to bring me Iscariot."

His brows rose, but he tossed me the keys, grabbed the kid, and—despite the supposed inability to leave without physically exiting Adam's Rest—disappeared. The murmur of displeasure from around the room was cut short when I held up two coins of silver and slid them across to the bartender.

"Tell McGavin it was an emergency, but here's the fine regardless," I said and grabbed my bag.

The vampire's stiff nod of acknowledgement was enough, but I kept my hand tightly on my badge as I moved for the exit.

"You going hunting?" Oswald asked quietly.

"Vlkodlak. You tell everyone to stay out of Bush Park, you got me? If they got deals, tell them to move them elsewhere," I said, voice pitched low. I took the stairs at a jog.

CHAPTER 26

Brush Park, years ago, was one of the most beautiful places in Detroit. Tycoons built sprawling marvels of architecture, opulent mansions boasting that the city of Motown and automobiles had roots of gold. Then it went up in a smoke so thick and hot that it killed everything.

As I turned the corner of what used to be called "Little Paris" by the locals, I couldn't stop the pang of despair that hit every time I came here. Some of the mansions had been kept up or restored, but like many pockets of the city, it was dominated by desecration. Windows smashed and boarded haphazardly resembled gaping mouths and haunted eyes. It was a bit like the billboard in the Great Gatsby. Except it wasn't the eyes of God watching Brush Park, but ghosts of hatred and fire.

Parking half a block up from the house, I leaned the seat back, thankful that Graceland chose a car with tinted windows. Pulling up my hood, I settled back to watch the street. It was quiet, only the flutter of plastic coverings and the backfiring of an occasional car breaking the silence. Pressing my palms together, I channeled the tincture inside my blood, feeling it rise like the dead to coat bones and lick my spine with fire.

"I give respect to Ogou Feray[41], bringer of battle. I walk in your fire, but I will not be burned until my mission is complete," I recited and drew a small bag of cane sugar from my satchel.

Sprinkling it over my open palm, I held it out to the air. "May my body be a vessel of might. In return, loa Ogou, I will give you the glory of war. I am of iron; I am covered with iron."

My palm ignited, the sugar bubbling against skin, turning a furious brown as it caramelized. The faint pink of my palm beneath it didn't

---

41 There are variations of Ogou, but Ogou Feray is a Vodou god of war. He also tells the best campfire stories.

change at all, nor did pain come. Blowing gently, the fire went out, and across my palm was a clean pane of sugar glass.

"Impressive. Do you do parties?"

Giving Graceland an annoyed shake of my head, I punched my other fist into the pane, crumbling it to dust. The smell of sugar and iron filled the car.

"Took you long enough," I said mildly. "Though I suppose I should thank you for not just appearing while I was driving, or I probably would have crashed."

His nod was solemn as he pulled his own hood up. "I don't have a death wish, you're already a terrible driver. Do you really think that doing your whole berserker thing is the best route for this?" he asked.

"Do you have Iscariot?"

Sighing, he handed me the velvet-wrapped weapon. "Naming your dagger is incredibly disturbing. Why did you give it to Beafore anyway?"

"I killed Gregor with it—it had his blood on it. She got his brood's blood to protect Haven, and I got a free recoating of pure silver," I said, unrolling the weapon. "And I didn't name it."

"Who did then?"

I pushed open the door, leaving my bag but tucking the dagger into my belt. "You really don't know?"

"Would you rather I pull it from your mind?" he hissed as he followed down the block.

"Try it and I'll boot you in the dick. Judas Iscariot, betrayer of your father. There are two daggers that bear his seal," I said, turning the handle so he could see the hilt. "This is one of them."

"And they what, kill creatures?" he asked and rolled his eyes at my surprise. "During the whole Jesus thing, I was building a pantheon, Brigitte."

"You knew about the spear."

"Because it can kill my father. I didn't give a shit about humans."

I wondered if he realized he'd used past tense, but I shrugged. "People misuse his name. Judas doesn't mean deceiver. It means praise. Iscariot, his last name, that's what means traitor. Iscariot the dagger kills corrupted creatures, betrayers of the fay."

"What does praise do then?"

"Judas," I corrected. "And no one knows, because no one's ever seen it."

For a second, I thought he'd lapsed into contemplative silence as we approached the house. It was like that sometimes when I brought up lore connected to his people that he was ignorant to. I should have waited to—

"Ok, no, I'm calling bullshit," he blurted out.

It was my turn to be stunned. "What?"

"I hate those stories," he complained, putting up air quotes. "A friend of a friend told me that if you sleep with a goblin your dick turns green—that sort of thing."

"Are you comparing a holy relic to a sexually transmitted disease?" I sputtered.

"It's like how all 'paranormal investigators' find ghosts from the 1800s. Where are the white trash ghosts hollering about Tom Petty? Where are the 1950s ghosts haunting housewives telling them they iron like shit?"

"Graceland, I am not having this conversation right now."

"Because you have no defense," he said smugly. "It's like one long, hideous chain letter."

"No, because you're being—shit!" I said as something sprinted from the side yard.

"We got a runner," Graceland declared, wings bursting from his back. "I got him."

Knowing he'd catch whatever had attempted to make a break for it, I took the porch steps at a sprint. The building, a crumbling Victorian, looked wilted, but it took two full forced boots to get the door to crack open. Giving a silent prayer to Ogou, I stepped inside.

Like most of the mansions on this block, it was in a state of disrepair. Sawhorses with sheets of drywall, walls half fixed, timber exposed, but the floor spoke to me the most. Prints, too massive for a werewolf, smudged the loose dust on the floor. Bending down, I pressed fingers to the outline and tried to feel for magic. It was barely there, so either it was old, or whoever left them wasn't gifted.

A slow shuffle of feet, brought my hand to my waist. Holding the dagger out to the empty room, I kept my mouth pursed, pushing tiny breaths through my nose as I crept to the edge of one of the only finished walls. Shoving off, I spun around the corner, keeping the dagger close so it couldn't be knocked away. From across the room, thick, ratty plastic flapped against the vent, and I tucked the dagger back into my belt.

"Well, at least you'd survive a horror movie," I said out loud. "But this is why Horace won't approve you for a firearm. Too—"

There was splintering, like threads being ripped apart, as a hand burst from the wall and grabbed me by the waist. Ripping me through, I felt the force of the plaster and wood hit, but the tincture rippled around me. The hand released, and I found myself staring up at the ceiling as I flew.

When I was little, Dad always said the best way to land was on your knees and forearms, the strongest bones in the body. I didn't manage to do that, but I got my badge out, gripping it into my palm as I struggled off the floor.

"Brigitte Fitzpatrick, Senior Pilgrim of the North American Chapter," I said, then stopped. "Actually, Divine Arbiter as of like the last couple hours, so pretty big deal."

The troll—of course it was a damn troll—only watched me with narrowed, blood red eyes. He loomed over the room, crouched slightly to fit, and his sparsely haired head scraped against the ceiling.

"By law, you are required to submit to questioning, detainment, and trial," I said, swallowing hard as the beady eyes snapped up to mine. "Please?"

The creature's mouth opened, and rotted breath swept out with its laughter. Nodding my agreement, I backed up a step.

"Yeah, I figured as much," I said and slammed my boot into the sawhorse in front of me.

It rocketed across the floor, hitting the troll square in the gut. Immediately, the troll doubled over, hand coming to hold his stomach, but before I could move, he straightened and laughed harder.

I'd never considered myself someone with an ego problem, but having that display of strength—magically induced or not—laughed at was grating. Flicking my fingers to the pouch at my waist, I scooped out herbs and pressed them flat to my sweaty palm.

"Where is Roman?" I asked.

Lumbering forward, the troll inspected the sawhorse. Nodding to himself, he picked it up, snapping it easily so that the metal in the middle was sharp and pointed.

"I need to know," I said, eyeing the makeshift weapon.

"Nah, won't matter to you in a minute," he said.

The silence of the night filled the room, the flapping of the plastic in the kitchen the only noise. The troll took one step, like the heavy beat of a drum, then another. With gritted teeth, I tried to count the distance between them, and somewhere my high school math teacher, Mr. Polsgrove, was screaming, because as the troll swung his construction site sword, it was clear I'd misjudged. The metal bit at flesh, the tincture deflecting most of the pain, but the force sent me to the floor. Skidding, I dug my heels in and tucked my shoulder, rolling smoothly back to my feet.

Rushing from the side, I slid as he swung again, tossing the powder in my hand. I heard him shout, weapon dropping as he slapped at his skin. Howling, he tried to stomp me, but I dodged. Reaching for the dagger, I found myself clasped tightly in his hand, fingers tightened as he ignored the welts rising against his skin to pull me to his height.

"Little girl playing cop," he sneered, face already a swollen red as he squeezed harder.

"I'm not a cop," I wheezed and reared back.

The scent of burnt sugar split the air as my fist connected with the troll's throat. The soft flesh absorbed most of the blow, jowls jiggling, but he dropped me. As soon as my knees hit the floor, I struck, this time slamming my fist into his knee.

The force sang up my forearm, but he crashed forward, nearly taking me with him. His hiss of pain was sour breath that filled the space, and I gagged as I stumbled for the closest sawhorse. Picking up the plumbing pipe, a thick silver tube, I moved back to him.

"Where is Roman?" I demanded.

"I ain't telling you nothing," the troll spat, trying to get to his feet, but I slammed the pipe into his knee.

"Where is he?"

"You'll get nothing out of me."

"Good," I said. "Makes it easier to do this."

Like I had with Martavious's bat, I set my stance wide. Using all the tincture left inside, swung. The sound of bone against steel, the shatter and crunch, twisted my stomach, and the splash of green blood was going to put me off green tea frappuccinos for a while. Letting the pipe drop, I hobbled for the stairs, feeling the floor shake when his body hit the ground.

Gripping the rail, I took a deep breath as I managed the first step. The tincture was fading, and I would be spectacularly bruised in a couple hours. Sixteen steps, I counted as I reached the second floor. Reaching behind my neck, I gripped one of the gris-gris strung around it. It was the only glass one, with the beak of a bird inside it. I pulled it from my neck, snapping the thin thread. Tucking it into my pocket, I let out a shuddering breath and kept moving.

Unlike the first, the second floor was in complete disrepair, mostly studs that were dotted by pieces of pinned drywall. Stepping over wiring, I moved for the second set of stairs that would lead to the third floor, when the glint of something turned my head.

It was the Judas moon, full and spilling through the empty window. The light glowed around the vlkodlak that stared out the window into the garden. He was smaller than Gregor, fur russet and sleek, and his clawed hand was flat against the wall, the sharp tips cracking against the drywall with irritation.

"Excuse me?" I said.

The beast stiffened, and even before he turned around to snarl at me, I had my badge out.

"Here me out: I just killed a troll. If I can do that, then what chance do you have, buddy? So, unless you're Roman, just bail."

He raced toward me, long limbs tearing up the distance between us, and I ducked. His claws clacked above my head, catching only air, which should have made me feel better. The cheap shot I got to his ribs should've too. Unfortunately, it was my own hand that stung with pain, and his claw whipped me up by the shirt until my toes left the ground.

His eyes were nearly the same color as his fur, edging more toward red than brown. Swallowing hard, I gave him another cheeky smile, this one forced.

"So, I'm guessing that means you're Roman Vasile. Brigitte Laveau Fitzpatrick. Here to kill you," I offered.

In hindsight, it probably wasn't the best idea to bait him, because he tossed me through the air. Limply, I slammed through the flimsy drywall, trying to breathe, but the air was dust. My joints screamed, but instinctively I rolled, scrambling up as the plaster next to me exploded. The vlkodlak tilted his head, eyes narrow and toothy maw wide. White powder covered us both as we circled each other.

"You've cost my family everything, little bitch."

"Really? You're not going to take any responsibility for this?" I asked, waving around the room. "Because I was about to give you the option to surrender. Not now, asshole."

"You can't beat me."

"See, it's when you say things like that I just feel the need to prove you wrong," I complained, fingers touching the glass necklace in my pocket. "You ever heard of self-fulfilling prophecies?"

"What?"

"It's from like Psych 101—you know what? Forget it. We gonna do this or what?"

Letting his claws fall open, he flexed them. Keeping calm, I ignored the way my heart beat against my ribs as he raced forward. Crushing the talisman in my palm, I felt the glass rip into my skin. Blood, fresh and hot, rushed over the beak that turned to dust under the force of my fist.

It was old magic, only done with the sacrifice of blood and my mother's animals. Mama was beloved, but for one of her pets to willingly bind its spirit, its essence, to magic wasn't to be taken lightly. I'd held onto the talisman year after year, refusing to use it, out of the same respect.

There was a scream. At first; I could have sworn it came from my own lungs, but then a howl and the sound of claws eviscerating wood snapped me into action. Hands, much more feminine and fragile than the ones that had held Lenore, sprang up from the floor, dragging Roman down to his knees. His claws desperately tore at the floorboards, trying to find the bodies attached to the unnaturally strong fingers ripping at his fur.

Standing above him, I watched him panic as the smell of iron began to tinge the air. As the beast howled, the hands dug deeper, blood spattering across the floor. These spirits couldn't be controlled; they would continue until they were vindicated.

"This is what happens when you don't set a body to rest, Roman," I told him, pulling the dagger from my belt. "They wait for someone like me, like my mother. How many women—girls—have you disregarded, thought useless besides what they could give you?"

Kneeling in front of him, I raised the dagger above my head, ignoring the blood that splashed across my face as the hands continued to rip. "They mattered. They all mattered."

The blade slid smoothly in, like bone was sand, and his howl split the room. I knew the second the blade hit his heart; his howl cut short. Ripping the dagger from his chest, I stumbled back from the body and let the hands continue to tear at him. Dragging myself to the wall, I leaned heavily against it as I made my way to the second set of stairs. These were narrower, wood older than me creaking as I made my way up.

It wasn't a true third story, more like a turret or tower room, and at the center was Calvin Valise. He was transformed, impossible for him to remain in his human form when the Judas moon was full, but it was clear he was close to death. His silver fur was shedding around him, black veins running over his muzzle. He was manacled to the floor, but still I approached cautiously, going still when his eyes opened to stare at me. They were surprisingly human, a soft brown watching with distrust.

"Roman sent you to put me out of my misery?" he snapped, tapping a clipped claw against his throat. "Took my way of doing it myself from me so I could be further humiliated."

Shaking my head, I pulled my badge. "Divine Arbiter Fitzpatrick."

He stared for a second before he collapsed on himself in relief. His shoulders shook as he raised his head.

"My brother is dead then?"

"I killed both of them," I said carefully, "They—"

"Forced me to do the unforgivable," he interrupted bitterly. "They were bringing girls here,using them to—"

The words seized in his chest, disrupted as he coughed. Black, viscous liquid began to dribble from the corner of his mouth, but he ignored it to stare at me bleakly.

"You aren't surprised," he said. "You know everything then?"

"I was asked to investigate. For Annabel, for all of them."

At the mention of Annabel, his mouth tightened, shoulders shaking. "She was special. Everyone thought Lenore was the one to light up a room, but Annie, she had this smile, like she knew what you were thinking and was already two steps ahead. You know?"

I did. My first real date with Margot was like that, marveling at shy smiles.

"Why did you change her?"

It was as if the words were a blow to the chest; his shoulders crumpled in, and he stared at the floor. "We came here to find a cure—at least, that's what they told me. I've been searching for one since our father became mindless. That's what happens to us, you know? We lose our minds, become nothing but savages the older we get. Eventually the madness comes for us all. I was going to free our brood, make us like your wolves in the states. They told me they had found a lead, here in Detroit. I believed them."

The bitterness in his voice made my decision. Dropping to my knees, I pulled the finger bone from my hair and shoved it into the keyhole of his chains. Instantly the lock popped, but Calvin didn't move from his knees.

"Maybe we deserved our curse," he said, voice quiet. "After all, look at what horrors my brothers inflicted."

"You really believed there was a cure?"

He turned his head and stared. "We know there is. The Broken Shackle gave our father a taste, proved to us we have a chance to keep all our strengths and shed our weakness. I saw with my own eyes as the madness left my father for a night."

The last line of Bernard's note came back to me. *Tread with caution, Pilgrim. Once a shackle is broken, a slave cannot be forced back into submission.*

"The Broken Shackle?" I pressed.

His gaze sharpened even as he coughed up more blackened blood. "He said the world had forgotten. You have betrayer in you, Pilgrim. You of all people should know that not everyone who broke away from our Creators is keen to bend their knee like your gods."

"Do you—" My voice broke. "Do you have proof?"

"I sent our other members across your country to speak with elders of Pack Santee. We were brokering a deal. One of your Pilgrims offered to assist after your treaty. I sent men I trusted, but—" He stopped, scrubbing at his eyes. "I trusted my brothers, too. Two days after my men left, they stopped reporting in."

Bronson had been killed, laid bare to be easily found, just like the girls.

"And you didn't think to go out there?" I demanded, voice low but angry. "To check?"

"I planned to. I had my bags packed and my ticket ready when Lenore came to see my brothers to convince them that Annabel wasn't serious. I wanted to take Annie with me." he said, face slowly sinking into a frown. "No, no, NO!"

His anger rang out in sobbing howls as the realization sank in. Struggling to his feet, he hobbled a couple steps, broken claws striking out at the wall. Even though he was dying, the house still shook around us.

"Calvin."

The name seemed to ground him, had him swinging around to stare at me. Dropping his head into his hands, he sank to his knees.

"I killed her," he told me. "They knew. They knew it wouldn't work, didn't they?"

I was not paid enough for this job.

It was easy to chase perps down, to kick in doors, or do check-ins. It was another to see him crumble, reminding me painfully of when I'd realized Margot monitored for Holloway. Ice splintered in my stomach, carving its way into my bones, and my eyes held the same bleak horror as his.

"It was real, Calvin," I said firmly, trying to convince him as much as myself. "Lenore confirmed that she felt the same way about you that you did for her. Annie made the choice as much as you."

He stilled, hands falling to his side. Even in full transformation, his posture eerily resembled the paintings of men kneeling before their Creators.

"I'm dying," he told me, hands shaking as he motioned. "Can you end it? Will you end it?"

Instead of pulling Iscariot from my belt, I bent and drew a small knife from my boot. It had been Dad's. "If I kill you with this…it's meant for this sort of thing, giving peace to the dying. I have an in—below," I said coming forward. "Maybe you'll find her?"

"I loved her," he said, voice cracking. "She was everything. We were going to save our people. If there was a cure for me then there had to be one for her, right?"

There would be tears later. I would climb into my tub and sob under the hot spray of water and the garish mural Margot had painted, but for now, I nodded. There was a dichotomy, the white knuckled hand gripping the knife and the gentle one that tipped up his head.

"Yeah," I lied.

The motion was fluid, practiced, methodical, and when his body slumped against my feet, I flicked the blood from the blade. My boots weren't so lucky; blood already soaked through in thick patches.

The door blew off its hinges, slamming into the wall, but I only lazily looked to Graceland. He sucked in a breath, pale cheeks puffing out till he resembled a fish. I watched his eyes flick from the body to me before he shook a winded fist.

"I just ran up like three flights of stairs," he informed me. "And you left me to take care of like four vlkodlak by myself."

"Pssh, I killed a troll," I pointed out. "Besides, you have wings."

"The stairwell was too narrow," he spat. "Human designs are stupid. Want me to document the scene?"

"I'll help," I answered, sliding the knife back into my boot. "You could do the paperwork if you wanted."

"Pass."

It was a long shot, so I only shrugged as he tossed me a vial to collect the poisoned blood. We worked in silence, pictures and data, detailed so I could justify killing the three heads of a pack. Deep Europe would be told; there would be demands and questions, but for now it was mindless, muscle memory collection.

"You're shaking," he commented mildly.

Staring at my own hands, I nodded. "Wouldn't have happened if you hadn't taken your sweet time."

"Those bastards are fast, and on a Judas moon," he reminded, foot nudging Calvin's body. "This one give you any trouble?"

"No. Maybe too sick, but probably just too soft."

"Deep Europe isn't soft," Graceland scoffed.

"Gillian's husband carries around her picture in his wallet," I commented as I took a sample of Calvin's hair, fingers patting it gently. "I promised you'd help him find Annabel. Think you can put in a word with Penny?"

For a second it looked like he would give me the offended response I hoped for, but then his eyes narrowed. "Tell you what," he said, carefully watching, "you go downstairs and have Horace take you home. I'll finish here. You do that, Calvin can have his happyish ending."

"Promise?"

He raised a brow at my willingness, but nodded. "Promise."

I made it to the door before turning back. "Graceland, the girls?"

My throat wouldn't let me finish the sentence, but he gave me a smirk.

"I didn't mention that I saved them all before singlehandedly fighting four vlkodlak? I must be getting humble in my old age."

It was sick to be laughing in a house that held so many corpses inside it, but I leaned against the frame and held my stomach.

"Yes, yes, I'm hysterical," my partner dismissed. "Go home."

"I'm getting a drink first."

CHAPTER 27

It was five in the afternoon when I rejoined the land of the living. I'd spent most of the car ride home in the passenger seat listening to Feather on speaker phone cuss me out about not waiting for backup. After Horace finally hung up on his mother, it had been his quiet voice from the driver's seat that got me up to date.

Graceland played hero, bouncing like a manic pinball from house to house, dropping terrified girls practically on top of the cops. In the end, all the girls from the last shipment were accounted for and currently in secure housing until the police could figure out countries of origin.

Bittersweet, in my opinion, but Horace considered it a victory, so I kept my mouth shut. Instead, when he finished getting me up to the apartment and fending off a panicked Thaddeus, I kissed him on the cheek.

It turned him a blazing pink, and the laughter in my chest rattled my apparently broken ribs, but I still shoved him toward the door. "Go be a hero, Bukowski. Make the media your bitch."

He had, as he always managed to do, spun gold out of horseshit. The news story resembled a drug deal gone bad rather than a massive breach of Pilgrim immigration policy. Even dead, Holloway couldn't escape the blowback, turned into a Machiavellian with paid vlkodlak henchmen, which was probably less Horace and more city hall.

My own accounts were already drawn up and sent to the overseers. Madison and Malloy immediately directed all accounts to the council, indicated I should be ready to testify, and sent another disapproving letter about writing reports while drunk. I tried, really did, to take the hot bath and stupid green tea that Thaddeus always pushed at me, but staring up at the mural that was slowly beginning to peel away broke something in me. So, I stumbled to my desk, probably looking like one large bruise, and pulled out the emergency, emergency bottle of whiskey I'd stashed.

It was at that same desk that I woke up when Graceland burst through door, clipboard in hand, and I learned that my head and body could both throb like an infected thumb.

"Ok, I got your itinerary. Flight to New Orleans for the Last Supper, hellmouth style, leaves Friday at ten. Then—"

"I'm not waiting two days to go back," I interrupted, eyes closed as I patted the desk for my sunglasses. "I want a flight tonight."

"Yeah, well, I want to return to hell and watch *Brooklyn 99* with Penny," he informed me as he shifted his clipboard. "You leave Friday, mother's orders. You stay there for a single day, then right after, I got you a flight out to North Dakota to pick up Bronson. Bethel Ford will be meeting you; go easy on her. She was quite pleasant on the phone and—hey, you listening?"

I tilted the sunglasses so he could see I was awake. "Yeah, sorry."

Dropping into his chair, he gave me a raised brow, "Wanna try that again? This time try to Meryl Streep your lie, so I'll believe it."

"Any word on the Longinus Lance?" I said instead.

"You are interrupting my flow. Athena said she send word, so we wait," he said but didn't look convinced, "we are dealing with what we have in front of us, which is listening to your mother." He flipped a page on the clipboard and read, "I'm to make sure Brigitte sleeps, eats, and attempts to find a hobby that isn't drinking."

Tears welled up, sheer relief mixed with the guilt that Mama struck a deal with Maman to give me a minute to breathe. I rubbed at the phantom pain deep in my shoulder and pushed the sunglasses more firmly on my face.

"You wanna go grab a Coney dog?" I asked. "I could use some Lafayette's."

"We gotta rummage through Bronson's apartment today. Moira is gonna meet us to help," he reminded me. "But greasy food might fix you."

"So, Lafayette's?" I said again.

"American Coney," Graceland argued. "We did your swill shop last time."

Normally, those were fighting words, which was exactly how he meant them. The fact that he preferred me irate and snapping to demure and quiet like I would have to be when I went back to New Orleans flooded me with love. My smile had his eyes narrowing, and he jerked a little as I stood and slid my arm through his.

"How about we get one of each?" I asked.

"Ooooh-kay?"

We were nearly out the door when I flashed him a real smile. "That way I can see your face the minute you realize what a superior hot dog tastes like."

"That's my girl," he said, grin wide. "But you're buying."

ABOUT THE AUTHOR

V.L. Barycz became a writer when her elementary school convinced her that words were more constructive than fists. Since then, she's written for Foliate Oak Literary Magazine, Gravel Magazine, and Empty Sink Publishing. When not hoarding notebooks to write in, V.L. can be found somewhere in Detroit collecting the things people discard.